CHARLES DICKENS was born in 1812 at Landport near Portsmouth, where his father was a clerk in a navy pay office. The family removed to London in 1816, and in 1817 to Chatham. It was here that the happiest years of Dickens's childhood were spent. They returned to London in 1822, but their fortunes were severely impaired. Dickens was withdrawn from school, and in 1824, sent to work in a blacking warehouse managed by a relative when his father was imprisoned for debt. Both experiences deeply affected the future novelist. Once his father's financial position improved, however, Dickens returned to school, leaving at the age of 15 to become in turn a solicitor's clerk, a shorthand reporter in the law courts, and a parliamentary reporter. In 1833 he began contributing stories to newspapers and magazines, later reprinted as *Sketches by 'Boz'*, and in 1836 started the serial publication of *Pickwick Papers*. Before *Pickwick* had completed its run, Dickens, as editor of *Bentley's Miscellany*, had also begun the serialization of *Oliver Twist* (1837–8). In April 1836 he married Catherine Hogarth, who bore him ten children between 1837 and 1852. Finding serial publication both congenial and profitable, Dickens published *Nicholas Nickleby* (1838–9) in monthly parts, and *The Old Curiosity Shop* (1840–1) and *Barnaby Rudge* (1841) in weekly instalments. He visited America in 1842, publishing his observations as *American Notes* on his return and including an extensive American episode in *Martin Chuzzlewit* (1843–4). The first of the five 'Christmas Books', *A Christmas Carol*, appeared in 1843 and the travel-book, *Pictures from Italy*, in 1846. The carefully planned *Dombey and Son* was serialized in 1846–8, to be followed in 1849–50 by Dickens's 'favourite child', the semi-autobiographical *David Copperfield*. Then came *Bleak House* (1852–3), *Hard Times* (1854), and *Little Dorrit* (1855–7). Dickens edited and regularly contributed to the journals *Household Words* (1850–9) and *All the Year Round* (1859–70). A number of essays from the journals were later collected as *Reprinted Pieces* (1858) and *The Uncommercial Traveller* (1861). Dickens had acquired a country house, Gad's Hill near Rochester, in 1855 and he was separated from his wife in 1858. He returned to historical fiction in *A Tale of Two Cities* (1859) and to the use of a first-person narrator in *Great Expectations* (1860–1), both of which were serialized in *All the Year Round*. The last completed novel, *Our Mutual Friend*, was published in 1864–5. *Edwin Drood* was left unfinished at Dickens's death on 9 June 1870.

CLIVE HURST is Head of Rare Books and Printed Ephemera at the Bodleian Library, Oxford, and is currently preparing the Clarendon Edition of *Barnaby Rudge*.

IAIN MCCALMAN is the Director of the Humanities Research Centre at the Australian National University, and JON MEE is Margaret Candfield Fellow in English at University College, Oxford. They have published widely on eighteenth- and nineteenth-century history and literature and previously worked together editing *An Oxford Companion to the Romantic Age* (1999).

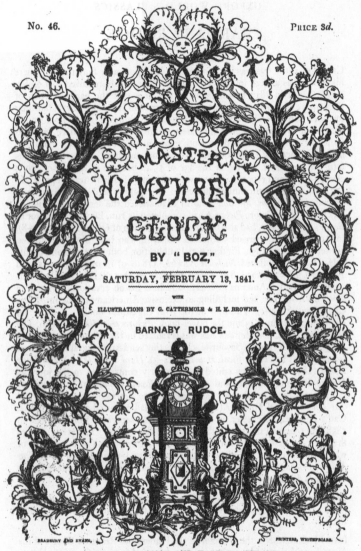

# MASTER HUMPHREY'S CLOCK

### BY "BOZ,"

### SATURDAY, FEBRUARY 13, 1841.

with

### ILLUSTRATIONS BY G. CATTERMOLE & H. K. BROWNE.

## BARNABY RUDGE.

BRADBURY AND EVANS.　　　　　　　　　　　PRINTERS, WHITEFRIARS.

LONDON: CHAPMAN AND HALL, 186, STRAND;

J. MENZIES, Edinburgh; J. FINLAY & Co., Glasgow · E. SMITH, Aberdeen; S. J. MACHEN & Co., Dublin; SIMMS & DINHAM, Manchester; WARING WEBB, Liverpool; WRIGHTSON & WEBB, Birmingham; S. SIMMS & SON, Bath; LIGHT & RIDLER, Bristol; T. N. MORTON, Boston; H. S. KING, Brighton; G. THOMPSON, Bury; R. JOHNSON, Cambridge; C. THURNAM, Carlisle; J. LEE, Cheltenham; EVANS & DUCKER, Chester; W. EDWARDS, Coventry; W. HOWBOTTOM, Derby; W. BYERS, Devonport; W. T. ROBERTS, Exeter; T. DAVIES, Gloucester; R. CUSSONS, Hull; HENRY SHALDERS, Ipswich; W. BRENS, Leamington; T. HARRISON, Leeds; J. R. SMITH, Lynn; J. SMITH, Maidstone; FINLAY & CHARLTON, Newcastle-on-Tyne; JARROLD & SON, Norwich; R. MERCER, Nottingham; H. SLATTER, Oxford; P. R. DRUMMOND, Perth; E. NETTLETON, Plymouth; BRODIE & Co., Salisbury; JOHN INNOCENT, Sheffield; W. SHARLAND, Southampton; F. MAY, Taunton; A. DEIGHTON, Worcester; W. ALEXANDER, Yarmouth; J. SHILLITO, York; J. B. BROWN, Windsor; and sold by all Booksellers and Newsmen.

OXFORD WORLD'S CLASSICS

CHARLES DICKENS

# *Barnaby Rudge*

## With the Original Illustrations

*Edited by*
CLIVE HURST

*With an Introduction and Notes by*
IAIN McCALMAN *and* JON MEE

OXFORD
UNIVERSITY PRESS

# OXFORD

UNIVERSITY PRESS

Great Clarendon Street, Oxford OX2 6DP

Oxford University Press is a department of the University of Oxford.
It furthers the University's objective of excellence in research, scholarship,
and education by publishing worldwide in

Oxford New York

Auckland Bangkok Buenos Aires Cape Town Chennai
Dar es Salaam Delhi Hong Kong Istanbul Karachi Kolkata
Kuala Lumpur Madrid Melbourne Mexico City Mumbai Nairobi
São Paulo Shanghai Taipei Tokyo Toronto

Oxford is a registered trade mark of Oxford University Press
in the UK and in certain other countries

Published in the United States
by Oxford University Press Inc., New York

British Library Cataloguing in Publication Data

Data available

Library of Congress Cataloging in Publication Data

Data available

ISBN 978-0-19-953820-1

10

Typeset in Ehrhardt
by RefineCatch Limited, Bungay, Suffolk

Printed and bound in Great Britain by Clays Ltd, Elcograf S.p.A.

# CONTENTS

# ACKNOWLEDGEMENTS

THIS edition of *Barnaby Rudge* could not have been completed without the tireless help of Georgina Fitzpatrick. The editors gratefully acknowledge her acumen, patience, and industry. Sara Lodge also gave invaluable assistance in the early stages. Iain McCalman and Jon Mee are grateful to Clive Hurst for permission to use the text of the forthcoming Clarendon edition, and also, above all, to Judith Luna at Oxford University Press for her sustaining encouragement and enthusiasm. The illustrations are reproduced by kind permission of the Bodleian Library, University of Oxford.

The volume is dedicated to the memory of Marion Screaton.

# INTRODUCTION

When in 1836 Dickens decided to mark his growing sense of himself as a serious novelist by writing a historical fiction, he chose for his subject an episode from English history that still resonated with horror for the Victorian reader. The Gordon Riots of 1780 were still widely remembered as an outpouring of religious hatred and popular violence unrivalled in the eighteenth century. They had originated in government measures to improve the rights of Catholics. The Protestant Association, led by the unstable Scottish aristocrat Lord George Gordon, had fiercely opposed the government's plans. Provoked by Gordon's campaign, but also expressing a diverse range of grievances against the authorities, the London mob rampaged through the capital between 2 and 10 June 1780, virtually taking over the city, and causing widespread apprehension that society as a whole was about to descend into chaos. Many lost their lives; the property of Catholics was attacked; and symbols of state authority, such as the recently rebuilt Newgate prison, were destroyed. The destruction of London's great prison provides the centrepiece of Dickens's novel. His treatment of the riots sees them—as modern historians still see them—not only as an expression of religious intolerance, but also as the articulation of a deep antagonism in the populace towards the political and social order of the day. The spectacle of the mob in full flow provides *Barnaby Rudge* with much of its ambivalent energy. Dickens condemns the effects of the riots, but wonders at and sometimes even applauds the violent fury against authority that fuelled them.

The novel, however, begins not with this larger historical canvas, but by detailing an altogether smaller domestic sphere, albeit one with dark spaces of its own. *Barnaby Rudge* opens in 1775, five years before the riots, and over several chapters slowly builds up the relations between a number of families implicated in a murder mystery. The story begins at the Maypole Inn, some miles outside London, where the keeper John Willet and his hangers-on are telling a mysterious stranger the story of the unsolved murder. This story centres on the Catholic Haredale family, Sir Geoffrey Haredale and his niece Emma, the local landowners, who live at the nearby Warren. Emma's father was murdered at the Warren over twenty years before the story opens. A body found at the time was believed to have been that of his steward Rudge, who it is assumed had provided the murderer with a second victim. The steward's son Barnaby—who flits between the Maypole and his mother's home in London—has the blight on his intelligence widely attributed to these dark events that preceded his birth. The cast at the Maypole is further supplemented by the stable-boy Hugh, as wild as Barnaby, but more threatening, and possessed of a dangerous animal cunning. Around this murder mystery, Dickens orchestrates a series of other family conflicts. Emma Haredale is in love with Edward Chester, son of Sir Geoffrey's enemy, the smooth hypocrite Sir John. Willet's son Joe chafes against his father's bovine authority, and longs for Dolly Varden. Dolly is the daughter of the other major figure introduced in the opening chapters, the benevolent locksmith Gabriel Varden. Gabriel keeps a shop under the sign of the Golden Key in the seething streets of London's East End. Even his benign authority, however, presides over a tense domestic scene. His wife is a bigoted Protestant, egged on in her zeal by her dyspeptic maidservant Miggs. Miggs is in love with Simon (Sim) Tappertit, the locksmith's apprentice, whose own sexual and social ambitions are centred on the unfortunate Dolly. Only in Chapter 35, after a break of five years, does Dickens paint in the larger historical backdrop against which these family histories subsequently develop towards tragedy. There, Lord George Gordon is introduced for the first time in the company of his villainous secretary, Gashford. When Barnaby and Hugh become involved in the machinations of the Protestant Association, throwing their lot in with the unhinged public hangman, Ned Dennis, their lives and those of their families are placed in danger. The vortex of violence created by the rioters threatens to destroy completely the familiar domestic world that Dickens has painstakingly constructed over the first half of the novel.

## Publishing History

Dickens first became famous as the writer of comic sketches for magazines between 1833 and 1836. These were collected together as *Sketches by 'Boz'* (1836) and were quickly followed by the series of illustrated comic sketches *Pickwick Papers*, first published in serial

form over 1836–7. *Pickwick* soon became hugely popular and
developed from a series of sketches into a novel as it was written (it
was eventually published as a single-volume novel in 1837). In May
1836, before the huge success of *Pickwick Papers* was fully apparent,
Dickens agreed with John Macrone, publisher of *Sketches by 'Boz'*,
to accept an advance for a work of fiction under the title 'Gabriel
Vardon, Locksmith of London'. Dickens initially put aside serial
publication in favour of the more respectable three-volume form.
Both the three-volume format and the historical subject matter suggest that Dickens was seeking to emulate the success and authority of
Sir Walter Scott (see Appendix C). Scott was widely believed by
Dickens and his contemporaries to have assured the place of the
novel as a serious literary medium by giving it a historical and
national purview previously unmatched. For all the delays and
wrangling with publishers over the novel that followed, study of his
work practices has shown that Dickens seems never to have lost his
'tenacity of purpose and the grip of an original idea'.[1] What he could
not have expected was the sensational success of *Pickwick* interrupting his plans for 'Gabriel Vardon'. That success opened up a world
of possibilities that led Dickens to pursue other projects, such as
*Oliver Twist* and *Nicholas Nickleby*, and seek to take advantage of his
new popularity by renegotiating the terms on which he would write
*Barnaby*. Only after five years of complicated negotiations, including
two changes of publisher (from Macrone to Richard Bentley, and
from Bentley to Chapman and Hall) and a false start on two chapters
in 1839, did anything of *Barnaby* appear. Abandoning the idea of
publishing directly in a three-volume format, Dickens chose to
return to the punishing schedule of writing for weekly instalments of
a magazine. *Barnaby Rudge* followed *The Old Curiosity Shop* as the
serial in Chapman and Hall's weekly miscellany *Master Humphrey's
Clock* between February and November 1841. Illustrations were
provided by Hablot Browne and George Cattermole in the form of
woodcuts 'dropped' into the text, reproduced in this edition. By this
stage, indeed as early as 1837, Gabriel Varden had been displaced
from the title by Barnaby Rudge. The novel was finally published in
a single volume at the end of 1841 with the subtitle 'A Tale of the
Riots of 'Eighty', along with the illustrations and Preface (included

[1] John Butt and Kathleen Tillotson, *Dickens at Work*, 2nd edn. (London: Methuen,
1968), 77.

in this edition) from *Master Humphrey's Clock*. A single-volume cheap edition—with a new Preface (also included here)—was published in 1849. The original Preface had promised his readers that the riots 'teach a good lesson' (p. 3). Exactly how to understand that lesson has increasingly exercised literary critics fascinated by Dickens's vision of the past and his understanding of its significance for his own time.

### *'Bitter discontent grown fierce and mad'*

Many critics have seen *Barnaby Rudge* as a displaced commentary on conflicts facing Dickens and his contemporaries in their own society (see Appendix B). Intolerance towards Catholics was a feature of the British political landscape in the 1830s, as in 1780, again partly because of further government moves to improve the lot of Catholics. The Catholic Relief Act of 1829 had for the first time allowed Catholics to take up seats in both houses of parliament. The result in England was that the Protestant Association was brought to life again amid a tide of anti-Catholic feeling.[2] Thomas Hood's early review of *Barnaby* remarked on the timeliness of Dickens's message of tolerance in this respect.[3] More often invoked now as a context for the novel are Victorian fears about political violence, associated mainly with the Chartist movement, which was pressing for widespread reform to the system of political representation.[4] Certainly Dickens had read Thomas Carlyle's *Chartism* (1839) by the time he started on the novel properly in 1841, although not, of course, before he decided to write a novel on the riots of 1780.[5] Carlyle defined Chartism as a manifestation of an inner fury latent in popular consciousness and capable of terrible destructive activity if roused. Chartism, he believed, was 'the bitter discontent grown fierce and mad, the wrong condition therefore or the wrong disposition, of the

[2] See Dennis Walder, *Dickens and Religion* (London: Allen and Unwin, 1981), ch. 4.

[3] Hood's review appeared in the *Athenaeum*, 743 (22 Jan. 1842), 77–9.

[4] See e.g. Humphry House, *The Dickens World* (London: Oxford University Press, 2nd edn., 1942), 180, and Steven Marcus, *Dickens: From Pickwick to Dombey* (London: Chatto and Windus, 1965), 173–5.

[5] For a full-length study of Carlyle's influence on Dickens, see William Oddie, *Dickens and Carlyle: The Question of Influence* (London: Centenary Press, 1972). Oddie points out (p. 2 n.) that Dickens had a copy of *Chartism* by 1840. For Dickens and *The French Revolution*, see John Forster, *The Life of Charles Dickens*, ed. J. W. T. Ley (London: Cecil Palmer, 1928), 505.

Working Classes of England. It is a new name for a thing which has had many names, which yet will have many names.'[6] Rather than inviting us to make some allegorical connection between the Gordon Riots and Chartism, however, *Barnaby Rudge* seems more interested in exploring Carlyle's idea of a transhistorical and universal conflict between unconscious forces of order and anarchy.[7] Dickens would have already come across such ideas in Carlyle's *The French Revolution* (1837), a book which eventually led to the direct treatment of the Revolution in *A Tale of Two Cities* (1859). Carlyle's book may have influenced the decision made by Dickens to replace Gabriel Varden with Barnaby Rudge in the title of the earlier novel. Barnaby's restless energy certainly has much more in common with Carlyle's idea of the unconscious power of the crowd than the locksmith's good nature, although Hugh's more menacing presence offers perhaps the more exact analogy with Carlyle's view of the instincts of the mob. Those instincts were represented by Carlyle as part of a perpetual struggle between authority and rebellion: 'The French Revolution means here the open violent Rebellion, and Victory, of disimprisoned Anarchy against corrupt worn-out Authority.'[8] From Carlyle, an idea of the mob as a manifestation of an elemental force figured in terms of volcanic flows or oceanic convulsions seems to have made its way into *Barnaby Rudge*:

A MOB is usually a creature of very mysterious existence, particularly in a large city. Where it comes from or whither it goes, few men can tell. Assembling and dispersing with equal suddenness, it is as difficult to follow to its various sources as the sea itself; nor does the parallel stop here, for the ocean is not more fickle and uncertain, more terrible when roused, more unreasonable, or more cruel. (pp. 413–14)

The writing of both Carlyle and Dickens often displays a relish for what they also revile elsewhere as mindless destruction. Most readers still find the descriptions of the mob in action the most compelling sections of Dickens's novel. Dickens himself wrote to his

[6] Carlyle, *Critical and Miscellaneous Essays*, Centenary Edition, 5 vols. (London: Chapman and Hall: 1899), iv. 119.

[7] For a contrary view that sees the novel as a very specific allegory of Dickens's historical situation, see Thomas J. Rice, 'The Politics of *Barnaby Rudge*', in Robert Giddings (ed.) *The Changing World of Barnaby Rudge* (London: Vision, 1983), 51–73.

[8] Carlyle, *The French Revolution*, Centenary Edition, 3 vols. (London: Chapman and Hall: 1896), i. 119.

close friend and biographer John Forster of his enthusiasm for these sections of the novel: 'I have let all the prisoners out of Newgate, burnt down Lord Mansfield's and played the very devil. Another number will finish the fires and help us on towards the end. I feel quite smoky when I am at work. I want elbow-room terribly.'[9] The relish in such passages seems to go beyond a sympathetic under-standing of the social causes of popular unrest and into a deeper desire to tap into the energy of the crowd itself. Carlyle conceived of the Revolution as a self-destructive force, but one that burnt itself out only to reveal a new order of things. In his descriptions of the riots, Dickens also returns again and again to the spectacle of the rioters 'sucked and drawn into the burning gulf' (p. 442): 'the wretched victims of a senseless outcry, became themselves the dust and ashes of the flames they had kindled, and strewed the public streets of London' (p. 548). Like Rudge senior, forced to revisit the scene of his crime, characters throughout the novel seem over-whelmed by forces within themselves that they may have roused but cannot control: 'I struggled against the impulse,' says Barnaby's father, 'but I was drawn back, through every difficult and adverse circumstance, as by a mighty engine' (p. 494). Where Dickens would seem to differ from Carlyle is by searching for a secure private and domestic space beyond these dramatic conflicts.[10] Nor does Dickens offer any clear sense of a new order emerging from his conflagration. 'Fear not Sansculottism,' Carlyle had enjoined his readers, 'recognise it for what it is, the portentous inevitable end of much, the miracu-lous beginning of much.'[11] Carlyle was attracted to the crowd's energy because of its role in this historical drama. For all his explicit admiration of Carlyle's writing, this overarching idea of history is not endorsed by Dickens in *Barnaby Rudge*.

[9] To John Forster, 18 September 1841, in *The Letters of Charles Dickens*, 12 vols. ed. Madeline House, Graham Storey, *et al.* (Oxford: Clarendon Press 1965–2002), ii: 385.

[10] See the discussion of this point in Andrew Sanders, *The Victorian Historical Novel 1840–1880* (London: Macmillan, 1978), 74. Dickens's investment in the domestic throughout his career as a novelist is discussed in Catherine Waters, 'Gender, Family, and Domestic Ideology', in John O. Jordan (ed.) *The Cambridge Companion to Charles Dickens* (Cambridge: Cambridge University Press, 2001), 120–35.

[11] Carlyle, *French Revolution*, i. 213.

## *'Dark history'*

Untangling the novel's attitude to social order and rebellion is complicated by the fact that *Barnaby Rudge* is a historical fiction looking back at a period sixty years since. Dickens seems at times to be urging his readers to learn the lessons of the past and apply them to their situation in the 1840s. One lesson proposed by the 1849 Preface seems to be that the oppressive nature of the eighteenth century's bloody legal code and unreformed political system were productive of an equal and opposite reaction of bloodthirstiness and violence. 'Bad criminal laws, bad prison regulations, and the worst conceivable police' (p. 393) are explicitly identified as the causes of the riots. Dickens was committed to and campaigned for reform on all three of these fronts during his own lifetime. Yet history in the novel does not always yield up a story of progress to encourage the reformer. Sim Tappertit's hostility 'to the innovating spirit of the times' (p. 76), like the bizarre notions of the ancient constitution he shares with Ned Dennis, may comically indicate their ignorance of real historical relations, but making sense of the past often seems more difficult than the novel's ostensible lesson would suggest. 'What dark history is this!' (p. 61), the reader might remark with Gabriel Varden when faced with understanding these relations. Dickens raises questions about the authority of historical narratives in the very first chapter of *Barnaby Rudge*. 'Matter-of-fact and doubtful folks' (p. 10) question the traditional story of Queen Elizabeth's visit to the Maypole. Should Dickens himself be numbered among these matter-of-fact, doubtful folks? Certainly the novel does not always provide its readers with a single, comfortable vantage point from which to view the past, even if sometimes it does affirm the superiority of Victorian England. A Carlylean idea of the sterility of the eighteenth century is affirmed in some respects by the description of the stolid presence of the inn in the first chapter: 'drowsy . . . nodding in its sleep . . . originally . . . a deep dark red, but . . . grown yellow and discoloured' (p. 11). Its obdurate resistance to progress is reflected in owner John Willet's 'profound obstinacy and slowness of apprehension' (p. 11). Willet refuses to have anything to do with newfangled stagecoaches (the eighteenth-century equivalent of the railways that were starting to define the age of Dickens) or to allow his son any independence. When Joe Willet runs away from his father and the inn, it seems an entirely natural development; a new generation is breaking with the complacency and intolerance of the old. Dickens sometimes represents the Gordon Riots, too, as the regrettable but inevitable outcome of the failings of a social order based on denial, repression, and corruption, but he does not offer obvious routes to a new order for society. On the personal level Joe may finally manage to attain domestic bliss, but it is less clear that progress is available for society as a whole. In *Barnaby Rudge*, phrases such as 'at that time', which suggest that the past has been left behind, jostle with sentiments that seem to fix human nature as a never-ending drama of conflicting passions that goes on 'at all times'. What lessons can the present learn from the errors of the past, if it is simply doomed to a cycle of repetition?

If Dickens is warning his readers that they may not have progressed as far from the intolerance of the Gordon rioters as they might like to think, he also opens up the possibility that progress is itself a phantasm. While far from abandoning the idea of reform, *Barnaby Rudge* does constantly think in terms of the return of the repressed and other kinds of repetition. 'Blood will have blood' is a principle announced early on in the novel. The circumstances of his birth seem to have marked Barnaby out with 'a smear of blood but half washed out' (p. 51). The sins of the fathers are also visited on the Chesters and even the Willets. These features cast dark Gothic shadows onto the novel's reformist attempt to make a lesson of the past. 'There are ghosts and dreams abroad' (p. 371), Barnaby's mother tells him. Barnaby himself may escape the scaffold, but Dickens has not released him from the 'breaking out of that one horror, in which, before his birth, his darkened intellect began' (p. 202). The reconciliation of Catholic and Protestant in the marriage of Emma Haredale and Edward Chester may suggest a message of national reconciliation of the kind often found in Scott, but the sense of lurking violence and inexplicable terror that permeates the novel is not completely absorbed by the wedding. Hugh's curse, for instance, leaves something hanging over the novel that Barnaby's redemption cannot entirely eclipse. If Hugh himself is cursed to repeat his mother's fate on the scaffold, so too does he pass a malediction on to the society that punishes him. Indeed, the novel seems ambivalent about whether Hugh is victim or villain. His animality is sometimes described as possessing the sublimity of a force of nature.

At other times the cruelty he rouses in the mob is described as against nature (witness the canaries thrown screaming into the flames). He has the mixed nature of a 'Centaur', but the human and the animal are not easy to tell apart. The idea of 'Nature' wherever it is invoked is one of those signs that offer little clear direction in the novel. Is it a Carlylean force of human liberation which seeks to burst out of the mannered society that keeps it imprisoned? Or is it a force for anarchy and chaos that needs to be controlled by the proper exercise of political and domestic authority? Dickens does not resolve the question into the apocalyptic vision of Carlyle, but keeps it open in a novel where the signs of the times are many but often inscrutable to the human eye.

## Reading the Signs

Although Gabriel Varden was displaced from the original title of the novel, his shop still provides one of the novel's central symbols: 'a great wooden emblem of a key, painted in vivid yellow to resemble gold, which dangled from the house-front, and swung to and fro with a mournful creaking noise, as if complaining that it had nothing to unlock' (p. 41). Even before we encounter Varden's 'emblem' itself, the very first chapter of the novel makes a distinction between signs and things with regard to the inn run by the Willets. Dickens tells his readers that by the Maypole 'from henceforth is meant the house, and not its sign' (pp. 9–10), but much of what follows belies such distinctions. How to understand signs in relation to the things that they signify is a thorny issue in the novel. 'The old practice of hanging out a sign' (p. 134), as it is described in a later chapter, does not seem to help anyone navigate their way through the city. When in Chapter 27 Haredale looks up at the Golden Key 'as in the hope that of its own accord it would unlock the mystery' (p. 215), the mute emblem offers him no guidance. The obscure significance of the Key takes us to the heart of the novel's fascination with the relationship between repression and liberation. Keys both lock and open doors: they offer the prospect of freedom but also of imprisonment. Despite the open good nature of its master, darker energies are simmering away under the sign of the Golden Key in the desires of Sim Tappertit. The apprentice even has a grotesque key of his own, in what seems a kind of parody of Varden's authority, which lets him in and out under cover of night. The novel both inveighs against incarceration and repression and yet sees them as the necessary props of domestic and social order. Newgate towers over the novel as much as the Golden Key illuminates it. Dickens sometimes treats it with all the visceral bitterness of the mob. Elsewhere he represents it as a necessary guarantee of the safety of the social order. Good-hearted Gabriel Varden himself, who fitted the lock to its gates in the first place, refuses to open the prison up to the crowd that finally tears Newgate down. Haredale hugs its walls with gratitude and relief when he finally has the murderer, Rudge senior, locked away inside. For them the prison offers an affirmation of civil and domestic harmony, but Dickens also points out to us among the mob two sons animated by the filial desire to release a father condemned by the Bloody Code. The prison is both a bastion of the natural order and as cruelly insensitive to the feelings of nature as Sir John Chester. Like many men of liberal opinions in his time, Dickens seems torn between the desperate cries of the crowd and a fear of a descent into social chaos.

One word that carries much of the burden of these ambiguities in the novel is 'enthusiasm'. Throughout the eighteenth century its meaning had been changing.[12] In 1780 it was still strongly identified with the religious passions of the mob, but it was also developing more benign associations. Both sets of associations jostle around the word in *Barnaby Rudge*. By the 1830s, 'enthusiasm' had come to something like its modern meaning of 'passionate eagerness in any pursuit, proceeding from an intense conviction of the worthiness of the object' (*OED*). In 1816, for instance, Samuel Taylor Coleridge had described enthusiasm as 'the oblivion and swallowing-up of self in an object dearer than self, or in an idea more vivid'.[13] This newer sense of the word is given a comic spin when used to describe Sim's admiration for his own legs, but darker associations soon emerge beneath the humour, as so often in Dickens. For much of the seventeenth and eighteenth centuries, enthusiasm had been associated with religious extremism, and sometimes mob action more generally. Carlyle had used the word in this sense to describe the violent con-

---

[12] See the excellent general account of these changes in Susie I. Tucker, *Enthusiasm: A Study in Semantic Change* (Cambridge: Cambridge University Press, 1972).

[13] Coleridge, *The Statesman's Manual*, in R. J. White (ed.), *Lay Sermons* (Princeton: Princeton University Press, 1972), 23.

geries of the French Revolution: 'Enthusiasm in general means simply excessive Congregating—*Schwärmerey*, or *Swarming*. At any rate, do we not see glimmering half-red embers, if laid together, get into the brightest white glow.'[14] This pejorative sense still spoke to Dickens's contemporaries of the way individual judgement could be lost in the fury of the crowd, especially in religious contexts such as the Gordon Riots. For many observers, even in the eighteenth century, the Protestant zeal of the Gordon Rioters was a late and anachronistic manifestation of the Puritan enthusiasm of the seventeenth century. The eighteenth century's own idea of itself as a time of enlightenment was usually predicated on the assumption that such phenomena had passed away. Thomas Holcroft's *Plain and Succinct Narrative of the Late Riots* (1780), one of Dickens's principal sources (see Appendix B), represented the riots as an anachronism in 'a philosophic age'.[15] Of course, Dickens was less concerned than Holcroft to defend the idea of the eighteenth century as an age of Enlightenment; like Carlyle, as we have seen, he often represents the century as one of stasis and hypocrisy. Irony and satire complicate the picture further. Attitudes to religious enthusiasm found in eighteenth-century novels such as Fielding's *Tom Jones* and Smollett's *Humphry Clinker* influence the comic representation of the religiosity of Miggs and her mistress, but Dickens's ideas on 'enthusiasm' are more ambivalent than theirs. Like Coleridge, he can see something potentially glorious in enthusiasm for an idea beyond the self, and perhaps even a necessity for such feelings in an age of cant and hypocrisy. The 'pure enthusiasm' (p. 618) exhibited by Barnaby in the face of the gallows, for instance, is presented as moving rather than foolish (a perception reinforced by Hugh's curse). The problem Dickens explores is the relation between enthusiasm as a form of popular fanaticism and the higher kind proposed by Coleridge's definition. Enthusiasm is a force that may lift us beyond self-interest, and potentially into heroic action, but also one that may lead to the loss of all rational control and even of proper subjectivity itself. Sim's enthusiasm for his legs points to a deeper and more troubling personality trait that helps explain his participation in the Protestant Association. His 'soul' continually threatens to get 'into

[14] Carlyle, *French Revolution*, ii. 30.
[15] Thomas Holcroft, *A Plain and Distinct Narrative of the Late Riots and Disturbances* (London: Fielding & Walker, 1780), 11.

his head' (p. 44) and overwhelm such power of rational judgement as Dickens grants him. Enthusiasm was always regarded as operating by a kind of sympathy—turning red embers into white heat—that required no rational articulation to transmit itself. Dickens himself, as we have seen, was capable of letting go his more considered attitude to the riots, when he smoked in sympathy with the rioters. These powerful forces of sympathy and liberation seem to have both fascinated and repelled Dickens when writing *Barnaby Rudge*.

## 'Gifts of Natur'

Describing Rudge senior's dash to London through a storm, Dickens comments that 'those who are bent on daring enterprises, or agitated by great thoughts whether of good or evil, feel a mysterious sympathy with the tumult of nature and are roused into corresponding violence' (p. 27). 'Whether of good', as in Coleridge's definition of enthusiasm, 'or evil', as in the older sense associated with religious fanaticism, Dickens suggests such sympathetic powers are attracted to whatever is most vivid. Dickens might almost be describing his own situation in writing of the riots in his description of the rider merging his identity with his environment. Sympathy has an important role in the novel's sense of what is 'natural'. The calculations of Stagg and the desperation of her husband threaten the domestic idyll based on 'natural' affections that Mary Rudge creates in the countryside. What is usually thought of as the sentimental side of Dickens operates in *Barnaby Rudge* to contrast this domestic haven with the animality of Hugh and the artificiality of Sir John Chester. The latter signals his inauthenticity with his constant hypocritical references to 'natural affections'. Yet distinctions between natural and unnatural sympathies are not very stable in the novel. Dickens writes of Gordon possessing 'something wild and ungovernable which broke through all restraint' (p. 287), but only a few pages later admits him to be 'sincere in his violence and in his wavering' (p. 292). When castigated by John Forster for being too sympathetic towards Gordon, Dickens countered that he 'must have been at heart a kind man, and a lover of the despised and rejected, after his own fashion'.[16] Sincerity and wild enthusiasm are not so far

---

[16] To John Forster, 3 June 1841, *Letters*, ii. 294.

apart in the novel, then, but part of a tangled skein of human affections. Edward Chester's virtuous desire to play the 'manly open part' (p. 128) looks naïve compared with his later recognition that there may be such things as 'monsters of affection' (p. 637). Sim comments to Miggs that 'there are strings . . . in the human heart that had better not be wibrated' (p. 184), but the novel goes on to suggest that judging which strings they are may be no easy matter. Volatility characterizes human affections even of the most familial sort in this novel. Certainly 'natural' relations often prove to be as destructive as the worst forms of enthusiasm. Hugh's own passions are represented as the product of a profound sympathy with the fate of his mother. The maternal bond in his case, like the 'strange promptings of nature' (p. 544) that unite Barnaby and his father, is ineluctable, moving, and, at the same time, dangerously destructive.

Ought the Golden Key to liberate such energies or lock them away? Varden tries to bring about a rapprochement between Hugh and his father, reiterating his faith in such 'natural' relations, but the novel rarely suggests things are as amenable to good nature as the locksmith wants to believe. The 'gift of Natur' (p. 18) to which John Willet lays claim turns out to be a troubling presence, easily misjudged (as Willet misjudges his own abilities). Like the 'preternatural sagacity' (p. 5) of the ravens described by Dickens in the 1849 Preface, echoed in Grip's tricks of mimicry throughout the novel, they represent powers of sympathetic identification whose consequences can work for good or ill. Judgements about such matters remain in suspension in *Barnaby Rudge*, despite the seeming preference for authentic or 'natural' sincerity over the superficialities of Sir John Chester's mannered code. Although the novel encourages its readers to believe in some more sincere mode of relation than the hypocrisies Chester has imbibed from Lord Chesterfield, what lies under the surface of things is often resistant to divination. The problem is that looking beneath the appearances, discerning the substance from the surface, continually proves to be a problem. Eyes do not always have the power to see into the heart of things to which they regularly pretend in the novel. Sim Tappertit has great faith in the magnetic 'power of his eye' (pp. 43–4) over those he wants to control, but the results are more laughable than dangerous. Hugh exercises an animal magnetism more successfully. Certainly his sexual power seems more threatening to Dolly than Sim's advances, while his vivid presence in the riots is a powerful catalyst for the crowd's enthusiasm. Haredale discerns in Hugh 'an evil eye' (p. 276). Earlier it has made even Sir John Chester bend to its power: 'There was a kind of fascination in meeting his steady gaze so suddenly, which took from the other the presence of mind to withdraw his eyes, and forced him, as it were, to meet his look' (p. 227). So the possibility of the kinds of powers Tappertit imagines himself to have is not discounted in the novel—far from it—but their operations are mysterious and unpredictable. Eyes are indeed everywhere, looking people over and trying to control them, but often unable to make sense of what they see. Once again this motif is set up in the opening chapter with the description of the 'raking fire of eyes' (p. 13) that searches the stranger in the Maypole. What the owners of these particular eyes fail to discern is that they are looking at the protagonist of the very story they presume to narrate. Like Barnaby's nightmarish dreams, the novel is haunted by many 'great faces coming and going' (p. 58), but seeing faces rarely leads to successful recognition or rational understanding. Varden calls on his own eyes as his witness, but quickly wishes himself 'half-blind, if I could but have the pleasure of mistrusting 'em' (p. 211). Stagg the blind man who feels faces to understand their owners is more successful than those who can see. Physiognomy may offer uncanny clues to character in the novel, but understanding those clues is another matter.[17] Those with eyes to see often find themselves in something more like the situation of Willet, surrounded by the ruins of his inn: 'John saw this desolation, and yet saw it not' (p. 437). Not only Barnaby suffers from 'blindness of the intellect' (p. 363). Throughout the novel, as Stagg himself tells Barnaby's mother, there 'are various degrees and kinds of blindness' (p. 363). For all the power of Hugh's eyes to draw others in enthusiasm after him, *Barnaby Rudge* offers its readers no art really sufficient to find the mind's construction in the face.

## 'Unutterable horror'

As a historical novelist Dickens follows Scott in attempting to explain the relevance of the past to the present, but his interest in horror and the uncanny give *Barnaby Rudge* strong tinges of Gothic

[17] See Michael Hollington, 'Monstrous Faces: Physiognomy in *Barnaby Rudge*', *Dickens Quarterly*, 8/1 (1991), 6–14, on the thematics of reading faces in the novel.

colouring that dwell on areas of experience beyond rational understanding. The tradition of the Gothic novel has always been concerned with what Virginia Woolf called 'the ghosts within us'.[18]
*Barnaby Rudge* too is not so much concerned with the supernatural
aspect of the Gothic tradition as the idea that the human psyche is
governed by powerful unconscious drives that escape rational control and even explanation. There are always energies beneath the
surface working away at confident rational judgements about the
truth in *Barnaby Rudge*. The civil authorities cannot see through Sir
John Chester's smiling knavery. He is knighted and becomes an MP
basically on the grounds of his ability to ape politeness, but if his case
seems a clear-cut one of villainy lurking beneath a smooth exterior,
other cases are more troubling. Not only the public but also the
private sphere is plagued by haunting duplicities. Behind the face of
Mary Rudge, which Varden thinks he knows so well, there lies 'the
faintest, palest shadow of some look, to which an instant of intense
and most unutterable horror only could have given birth' (p. 51). For
Varden this look is 'the very one he seemed to know so well and yet
had never seen before' (p. 53). The account calls to mind Freud's
idea of the uncanny or *unheimlich*. The terrors provoked by the
*unheimlich* for Freud were to do with 'nothing new or alien, but
something which is familiar and old-established in the mind and
which has become alienated through the process of repression'.[19]
Varden recognizes in Mary Rudge's face the horror of a past event
and its consequences that he has repressed and told himself to forget. Certainly, as if anticipating Freud's German phrase, in Dickens
such fears seem to disrupt even the safe haven of home. That which
is *heimlich* or homely is haunted by the *unheimlich* that it has
repressed from the past. The return of Barnaby's father ironically
spells the destruction of the fragile home his mother has built in
their rural retreat. What was once known and familiar—the father of
the family himself—returns in strange and disruptive forms to
haunt the present. *Barnaby Rudge*'s Victorian readers, thinking
about the crowds around them in the modern metropolis, may not
have found the past depicted in the novel a comfortably different

[18] See Woolf's essay 'Gothic Romance', in *The Essays of Virginia Woolf*, ed. Leonard
Woolf, 4 vols. (London: The Hogarth Press, 1966–7), i. 133.

[19] Sigmund Freud, 'The "Uncanny"', in *Art and Literature*, ed. Albert Dickson
(Harmondsworth: Penguin, 1985), 363–4.

place. Its tentacles reached out uncannily into the present. The character upon whom Dickens probably based Gashford, Gordon's sometime secretary Robert Watson (see Appendix B), lived on into Victorian times, if only to commit suicide. Discovered after Dickens had decided to write on the riots of 1780, but during his novel's long gestation, Watson's body was found to be covered with nineteen wounds at the inquest reported in *The Times*. These wounds may have suggested the name Gashford to Dickens once he got to work, but they may also have provided him with a sign of the uncanny ways in which the past could scar the present.

*Barnaby Rudge* is a historical novel, but one that defies neat lessons about the relationship between past and future. Similarly, its concern with human sympathy and toleration is not made into the stuff of easy didacticism. Hugh is a Centaur: his affections shift between animal fury and humane fellow feeling. His violent enthusiasm translates into an almost heroic sympathy for Barnaby as he waits to be taken to the scaffold:

'If this was not faith, and strong belief!' cried Hugh, raising his right arm aloft, and looking upward like a savage prophet whom the near approach of Death had filled with inspiration, 'where are they! What else should teach me—me, born as I was born, and reared as I have been—to hope for any mercy in this hardened, cruel, unrelenting place!'   (p. 622)

The rough enthusiasm of the crowd seems to be sublimated in an altogether higher kind of energy here: like a biblical prophet, Hugh is granted a vision of a deeper sense of justice unknown to the legal codes of his society. The fact that Barnaby is reprieved may seem a potential vindication of the possibility of public authorities co-ordinating the interests of both order and mercy, but even here we are made aware of other possibilities haunting the novel's happy resolution. 'The general enthusiasm' of the crowd in its joy at Barnaby's homecoming puts Varden 'in a fair way to be torn to pieces' (p. 635). These phrases may be appearing in a comic context here, but they remind the reader of other sorts of enthusiasm that sustained the violent crowd scenes earlier in the novel. Later still, in another scene that marks the novel's resistance to neat closure, Edward Chester stands by Hugh's grave and makes his comment about 'monsters of affection'. Dickens may differ from Carlyle in proposing 'the bright household world' (p. 638) as a redemptive space beyond the patterns of historical conflict, but this space is not without shadows of its own. Dickens may not approve Sir John's view that we must 'be content to take froth for substance, the surface for the depth, the counterfeit for the real coin' (p. 103), but telling them apart in the novel proves no easy matter. 'So do the shadows of our own desires', as the narrator tells us at one point, 'stand between us and our better angels, and thus their brightness is eclipsed' (p. 231).

## Barnaby *and the Critics*

Perhaps because it confronted its first readers with a complex sense of themselves and their history, *Barnaby* was not well received on first publication. Thomas Rice, its modern bibliographer, has called it among Dickens's novels 'the least loved and the least read'.[20] Weekly sales of *Master Humphrey's Clock* dropped by more than 50 per cent over the course of its serialization. John Forster thought there were serious structural problems with the book: 'The interest with which the tale begins, has ceased to be its interest before the close.' Edgar Allan Poe thought the murder mystery did not make a proper fit with the riots.[21] More recently it is the interlacing of these two aspects that has been seen as the great achievement of the novel. Among the most important and influential statements of this view has been Steven Marcus's account of the way conflicts over authority in both spheres provide the novel with its underlying unity.[22] Literary criticism is perhaps less obsessed with the question of narrative closure than it was even when Marcus wrote his groundbreaking study. Perhaps now we can see that the excitement of reading *Barnaby Rudge* lies in the way Dickens keeps questions about the relation between repression and liberation in play for the reader. If Scott's novels encouraged their readers to see their situation as the natural and necessary outcome of historical forces of reconciliation, however painful they might be, the Gothic aspects of *Barnaby Rudge* refuse

---

[20] See Thomas J. Rice, *Barnaby Rudge: An Annotated Bibliography* (New York: Garland, 1987), p. xv.

[21] See Forster, *Life of Dickens*, 170, and Poe's review from *Graham's Magazine* 19 (Feb. 1842), 124–9, reprinted in Philip Collins, *The Critical Heritage* (London: Routledge and Kegan Paul, 1971), 105–11.

[22] See Marcus, *Dickens: From Pickwick to Dombey*, ch. 5.

its readers such an affirming vantage point. If there is a kind of resolution in the marriages of the coming generation, it is private and domestic rather than historical. Outside these fragile domestic spaces others are left facing a less comfortable future. For the past has not simply created the present, it continues to haunt it in dangerous ways. 'By-gone bugbears which had lain quietly in their graves for centuries' may have been raised again by Gordon 'to haunt the ignorant and credulous' (p. 294), but few characters be they ever so wise or good-natured seem to be able to escape this fate entirely in the novel. 'I have no peace or quiet,' Haredale tells Varden, 'I am haunted' (p. 338). Surface and depth, past and present, sympathy and violence remain entangled in each other in profoundly disturbing ways throughout *Barnaby Rudge*. The condemned men in Newgate torture themselves until their deaths by 'the vague restless craving for something undefined, which nothing could satisfy' (p. 611). The pattern was to remain a recurrent one in the later, even darker fiction of Dickens. Betsy Trotwood tells David Copperfield that 'It's in vain . . . to recall the past, unless it works some influence upon the present'.[23] Yet like so many characters in *Barnaby Rudge*, David finds himself constantly besieged by vague memories and inarticulate sympathies. No less than Barnaby's father riding through the storm, David finds that 'something within me, faintly answering to the storm without, tossed up the depths of my memory, and made a tumult in them'.[24] *Barnaby Rudge* represents a compelling staging post in Dickens's understanding of the disruptive persistence of the past in the life of the individual and of society.

J.M.

[23] *David Copperfield*, ed. Nina Burgis (Oxford: Oxford University Press, 1997), 339.
[24] Ibid. 770.

# NOTE ON THE TEXT

*Barnaby Rudge* was first published in *Master Humphrey's Clock* in 42 weekly portions or numbers between February and November 1841. It had the longest gestation period of any of Dickens's novels: the first contract for it was made with John Macrone in May 1836, and it was to be published as 'Gabriel Vardon' 'in Three Volumes of the usual size' by the end of that year. It would have been Dickens's first completed novel. Many contracts later, it followed *The Old Curiosity Shop* as the weekly contents of *Master Humphrey's Clock*. The weekly numbers were collected into monthly parts, and the monthly parts into volumes (*Barnaby* was contained in parts XI–XX, February–November 1841, and volumes two and three, published in April and December 1841). It was published separately in one volume in that same December from the same setting of type as *Master Humphrey's Clock*. An authorized edition was published more or less simultaneously in serial form in Philadelphia from proofs of the London edition. The novel subsequently appeared in the three collected editions published in Dickens's lifetime: the Cheap, 1849; the Library, 1858; and the Charles Dickens edition, 1868. None of these was systematically revised by the author and they show a progressive corruption of the 1841 text, with the very occasional correction of an error. The present text, which will appear with full apparatus in the forthcoming Clarendon edition, is based on that of 1841, carefully collated against the manuscript (in the Forster Collection in the National Art Library at the Victoria and Albert Museum), the only extant proofs (for Chapters 17 and 18, also in the Forster Collection), the Philadelphia edition, and the three later London editions. It has been emended from the manuscript where necessary owing to the failure of Dickens to correct a printer's error, or to make clear the sense where excisions demanded by lack of space in the weekly serial left it muddied. However, inconsistencies of spelling and punctuation have not been regularized.

C.H.

# NOTE ON THE ILLUSTRATIONS

THE original illustrations in *Master Humphrey's Clock* are untitled. The following list is based on Thomas Hatton's 'A Bibliographical List of the Original Illustrations to the Works of Charles Dickens Being Those Made under his Supervision', *Nonesuch Dickensiana* (1937), 55–78. Where Hatton is imprecise or mistaken, titles have been supplied by the editor (mistakes being noted). Where the illustration was published in the Charles Dickens Edition its caption there has been used in preference to Hatton's as it possibly derives from Dickens himself; these captions are asterisked. Nine illustrations are unsigned: one of Browne's (no. 4) and eight of Cattermole's (nos. 1, 17, 22, 26, 28, 40, 41, and 76).[1] The engravers of the blocks were Charles Gray (thirty-seven illustrations) and Ebenezer Landells (whose name appears on the other thirty-nine illustrations, though ten of these were in fact engraved by the brothers Dalziel).[2]

1 The Maypole.* Cattermole; Landells.
2 The stranger. Browne; Landells.
3 The stranger's departure. Browne; Gray.
4 The wounded man. Browne; Landells.
5 Breakfast at Mr. Varden's. Browne; Gray.
6 Simon Tappertit dangerous.* Browne; Landells.
7 The locksmith questions Mr. Edward.[3] Browne; Gray.
8 Phantom-haunted dreams. Browne; Landells (really Dalziels).
9 Meeting of the 'prentices. Browne; Landells.
10 Miss Miggs waiting. Browne; Gray.
11 The best appartment. Cattermole; Gray.
12 Hugh asleep. Browne; Landells.
13 Barnaby and Grip. Browne; Gray.
14 The Warren. Cattermole; Gray.
15 Mr. Haredale thrusting Edward away. Browne; Landells.

---

[1] See *Letters*, ii. 8, 9 and nn.
[2] Identified from a scrap-book in the British Museum; see J. R. Harvey, *Victorian Novelists and their Illustrators* (London: Sidgwick and Jackson, 1970), 194–5.
[3] Mistakenly entitled by Hatton as 'Mr. Varden and the widow'.

---

[4] Hatton mistakenly attributes to Cattermole.

51 Liberties are taken with John Willet's bar.* Cattermole; Landells.

52 The stranger and John Willet. Browne; Gray.

53 Mr. Haredale arrests Rudge on the turret. Cattermole; Landells.

54 Barnaby taken prisoner. Browne; Landells.

55 Barnaby in jail. Browne; Gray.

56 The carriage. Cattermole; Landells.

57 Hugh carrying Dolly. Browne; Gray.

58 Stagg visits Rudge in prison. Browne; Gray.

59 Barnaby meets his father. Browne; Landells.

60 Mr. Varden refuses to pick the lock. Browne; Gray.

61 Dennis the rum dog. Browne; Gray.

62 The rioters at Moorfields. Browne; Landells.

63 Mr. Haredale sees Edward Chester and Joe Willet. Browne; Landells.

64 The rioters drink from the gutters. Browne; Gray.

65 Hugh taken.* Cattermole; Landells.

66 Dennis looking soothingly on Miggs. Browne; Gray.

67 Rescue of Dolly and Emma. Browne; Landells (really Dalziels).

68 Lord George in his cell.* Cattermole; Gray.

69 Dennis and Hugh in the condemned cell. Browne; Landells (really Dalziels).

70 Varden's pressing business with Sir John. Browne; Landells.

71 Barnaby and his mother in the condemned cell. Browne; Gray.

72 Hugh's curse. Browne; Landells (really Dalziels).

73 Dolly clings to Joe.[5] Browne; Gray.

73 Mr. Haredale giving Emma to Edward. Browne; Landells.

75 Miggs's ecstacy. Browne; Gray.

76 Death of Sir John. Cattermole; Gray.

The woodcut initials, which open the novel, and subsequently each monthly part (i.e. Chapters 1, 6, 13, 23, 31, 39, 49, 57, 65, and 75) and Chapter 33, the first after the lapse of five years, were not listed by Hatton. They are the work of Browne;[6] the engravers are not identified.

---

[5] Hatton mistakenly places this scene in the Maypole instead of the Black Lion.

[6] See T. Hatton and A. H. Cleaver, *A Bibliography of the Periodical Works of Dickens, Bibliographical, Analytical and Statistical* (London: Chapman and Hall, 1933), 165.

1  I   A maypole.
2  B   A couple dancing.
3  I   John Willet.
4  T   A corkscrew, &c.
5  P   (Reversed) A Chinese junk.
6  O   A rotund man.
7  T   At the Boot.
8  T   A gallows' tree and Dennis.
9  B   A soldier.
10 D   Barnaby and his father(?) in jail.
11 A   A cauldron over a fire.

In addition this volume reproduces the cover of the wrapper for the first part of *Barnaby Rudge* in *Master Humphrey's Clock* (p. ii), the frontispiece to volume three in *Master Humphrey's Clock* (p. l), and the title-page of the first separate issue of *Barnaby Rudge*.

C.H.

# SELECT BIBLIOGRAPHY

For a detailed account of the textual history of *Barnaby Rudge*, see the forthcoming Clarendon edition ed. Clive Hurst. For Dickens's working methods, see Sylvère Monod, *Dickens the Novelist* (1953; repr. Norman, Okla.: University of Oklahoma Press, 1968), and John Butt and Kathleen Tillotson, *Dickens at Work* (1957; 2nd edn., London: Methuen, 1968). For details of the sales and earnings, see Robert L. Patten, *Dickens and His Publishers* (Oxford: Clarendon Press, 1978).

## General Background

Peter Ackroyd, *Dickens' London: An Imaginative Vision* (London: Headline, 1987).

J. Paul de Castro, *The Gordon Riots* (London: Oxford University Press, 1926).

Philip Collins, *Dickens and Crime* (Basingstoke and London: Macmillan, 3rd edn., 1994).

Robert Kent Donovan, *No Popery and Radicalism: Opposition to Roman Catholic Relief in Scotland, 1778–1782* (New York: Garland, 1987).

Ian Duncan, *Modern Romance and Transformations of the Novel: The Gothic, Scott, Dickens* (Cambridge: Cambridge University Press 1992).

James Epstein and Dorothy Thompson (eds.), *The Chartist Experience: Studies in Working-Class Radicalism and Culture, 1830–1860* (London: Macmillan, 1982).

V. A. C. Gatrell, *The Hanging Tree: Execution and the English People 1770–1868* (Oxford: Oxford University Press, 1994).

Ian Gilmour, *Riot, Risings and Revolution: Governance and Violence in Eighteenth-Century England* (London: Hutchinson, 1992).

Colin Haydon, *Anti-Catholicism in Eighteenth-Century England, c. 1710–1780: A Political and Social Study* (Manchester: Manchester University Press, 1993).

Tony Hayter, *The Army and the Crowd in Mid-Georgian England* (London: Macmillan, 1978).

Christopher Hibbert, *King Mob: The Story of Lord George Gordon and the London Riots of 1780* (New York: World Publishing, 1958).

Humphrey House, *The Dickens World* (1941; 2nd edn., London: Oxford University Press, 1942).

Peter Linebaugh, *The London Hanged: Crime and Civil Society in the Eighteenth Century* (Cambridge: Cambridge University Press, 1992).

Georg Lukács, *The Historical Novel*, translated from the German by Hannah and Stanley Mitchell (Harmondsworth: Penguin, 1981).

Nicholas Rogers, *Crowds, Culture and Politics in Georgian Britain* (Oxford: Clarendon Press, 1998).

George Rudé, *Paris and London in the Eighteenth Century: Studies in Popular Protest.* (New York: Viking Press, 1971).

Andrew Sanders, *The Victorian Historical Novel 1840–1880* (London: Macmillan, 1978).

Kathleen Wilson, *The Sense of the People: Politics, Culture and Imperialism in England, 1715–1785* (Cambridge: Cambridge University Press, 1995).

## Bibliography

Thomas J. Rice, *Barnaby Rudge: An Annotated Bibliography* (New York: Garland, 1987).

Paul Schlicke, 'Charles Dickens 1912–70', in Joanne Shattock *et al.* (eds.) *The Cambridge Bibliography of English Literature* (Cambridge: Cambridge University Press, 3rd edn., 1999).

## Biography

Peter Ackroyd, *Dickens* (London: Sinclair-Stevenson, 1990).

John Forster, *The Life of Charles Dickens*, ed. J. W. T. Ley (London: Cecil Palmer, 1928).

*The Letters of Charles Dickens*, Pilgrim Edition, ed. Madeline House, Graham Storey, Kathleen Tillotson, *et al.*, 12 vols. (Oxford: Clarendon Press, 1965–2002).

## Criticism

### Books

*Barnaby Rudge* is not always given substantial treatment in general books on Dickens; below is a selection of those that do provide relevant accounts of the novel.

Peter Ackroyd, *Introduction to Dickens* (London: Sinclair-Stevenson, 1991).

John Bowen, *Other Dickens: Pickwick to Chuzzlewit* (Oxford: Oxford University Press, 2000).

Kathryn Chittick, *Dickens and the 1830s* (Cambridge: Cambridge University Press, 1990).

Michael Hollington, *Dickens and the Grotesque* (London: Croom Helm, 1984).

Myron Magnet, *Dickens and the Social Order* (Philadelphia: University of Pennsylvania Press, 1985).

Steven Marcus, *Dickens: From Pickwick to Dombey* (London: Chatto and Windus, 1965).

William Oddie, *Dickens and Carlyle: The Question of Influence* (London: Centenary Press, 1972).

William J. Palmer, *Dickens and the New Historicism* (New York: Columbia University Press, 1997).

Andrew Sanders, *Dickens and the Spirit of the Age* (Oxford: Clarendon Press, 1999).

Paul Schlicke (ed.), *Oxford Reader's Companion to Dickens* (Oxford: Oxford University Press, 1999).

F. S. Schwarzbach, *Dickens and the City* (London: Athlone Press 1979).

Jeremy Tambling, *Dickens, Violence and the Modern State: Dreams of the Scaffold* (Basingstoke: Macmillan, 1995).

Dennis Walder, *Dickens and Religion* (London: Allen and Unwin, 1981).

*Articles and Essays*

Patrick Brantlinger, 'Did Dickens Have a Philosophy of History? The Case of *Barnaby Rudge*', *Dickens Studies Annual*, 30 (2001), 59–74.

Joel J. Bratten, '"Secrets Inside ... To Strike To Your Heart": New Readings From Dickens' Manuscript of *Barnaby Rudge*', *Dickens Quarterly*, 8/1 (1991), 15–28.

Jerome H. Buckley, '"Quoth the Raven": The Role of Grip in *Barnaby Rudge*', *Dickens Studies Annual*, 21 (1992), 27–35.

Alison Case, 'Against Scott: The Antihistory of Dickens's *Barnaby Rudge*', *Clio*, 19/2 (1990), 127–45.

Steven Connor, 'Space, Place and the Body of Riot in *Barnaby Rudge*', in Steven Connor (ed.), *Charles Dickens* (London: Longman, 1996), 211–29.

David Craig, 'The Crowd in Dickens', in Robert Giddings (ed.) *The Changing World of Dickens* (London: Vision, 1983), 75–90.

Iain Crawford, '"Drenched in Blood": *Barnaby Rudge* and Wordsworth's "Idiot Boy"', *Dickens Quarterly*, 8/1 (1991), 38–47.

—— 'Dickens, Classical Myth and the Representation of Social Order in *Barnaby Rudge*', *Dickensian*, 93/3 (1997), 185–97.

S. Dransfield, 'Reading the Gordon Riots in 1841: Social Violence and Moral Management in *Barnaby Rudge*', *Dickens Studies Annual*, 27 (1998), 69–96.

John Glavin, 'Politics and *Barnaby Rudge*: Surrogation, Restoration and Revival', *Dickens Studies Annual*, 30 (2001), 95–112.

T. W. Hill, 'Notes on *Barnaby Rudge*', *Dickensian*, 50 (1954), 91–4; 51 (1951), 93–6, 137–41; 52 (1956), 136–40, 185–8; 53 (1957), 52–7.

Michael Hollington, 'Monstrous Faces: Physiognomy in *Barnaby Rudge*', *Dickens Quarterly*, 8/1 (1991), 6–14.

Jack Lindsay, 'Barnaby Rudge', in John Gross and Gabriel Pearson (eds.), *Dickens and the Twentieth Century* (London: Routledge and Kegan Paul, 1962), 91–106.

Iain McCalman, 'Controlling the Riots: Dickens, *Barnaby Rudge* and Romantic Revolution', *History*, 84 (1999), 458–76.

John McGowan, 'Mystery and History in *Barnaby Rudge*', *Dickens Studies Annual*, 9 (1981), 33–52.

Tom Middlebro', 'Burke, Dickens and the Gordon Riots', *Humanities Association Review*, 31 (Winter/Spring 1980), 87–95.

Goldie Morgentaler, 'Executing Beauty: Dickens and the Aesthetics of Death', *Dickens Studies Annual*, 30 (2001), 45–57.

S. J. Newman, '*Barnaby Rudge*: Dickens and Scott', in R. T. Davies and B. G. Beatty (eds.) *Literature of the Romantic Period, 1750–1850* (Liverpool: Liverpool University Press, 1976), 171–88.

Anthony O'Brien, 'Benevolence and Insurrection: The Conflicts of Form and Purpose in *Barnaby Rudge*', *Dickens Studies Annual*, 5 (1969), 26–44.

William J. Palmer, 'Dickens and the Eighteenth Century', *Dickens Studies Annual*, 6 (1977), 15–39.

—— 'New Historicizing Dickens', *Dickens Studies Annual*, 28 (1999), 173–96.

Thomas J. Rice, 'The Politics of *Barnaby Rudge*', in Robert Giddings (ed.), *The Changing World of Charles Dickens* (London: Vision, 1983), 51–73.

Peter Scheckner, 'Chartism, Class and Social Struggle: A Study of Charles Dickens', *Midwest Quarterly*, 29/1 (1987), 93–112.

Paul Stignant and Peter Widdowson, '*Barnaby Rudge* – a Historical Novel?', *Literature and History*, 2 (1975), 2–42.

Barbara L. Stuart, 'The Centaur in *Barnaby Rudge*', *Dickens Quarterly*, 8/1 (1991), 29–37.

Robert Tracy, 'Clock Work: *The Old Curiosity Shop* and *Barnaby Rudge*', *Dickens Studies Annual*, 30 (2001), 23–43.

Judith Wilt, 'Masques of the English in *Barnaby Rudge*', *Dickens Studies Annual*, 30 (2001), 75–94.

## Websites

*http://lang.nagoya-u.ac.jp/~matsuoka/Dickens.html* A wide-ranging and accessible general information page on Dickens with many useful links.

*http://lang.nagoya-u.ac.jp/~matsuoka/CD-Forster.html* Online edition of John Forster's biography of Dickens, *The Life of Charles Dickens*.

*file://A:\webrudgebibliog.htm* List of websites devoted specifically to *Barnaby Rudge*.

*http://www.fidnet.com/~dap1955/dickens/rudge.html* List of websites devoted specifically to *Barnaby Rudge*.

## Further Reading in Oxford World's Classics

Dickens, Charles, *Bleak House*, ed. Stephen Gill.

—— *Christmas Books*, ed. Ruth Glancy.

—— *David Copperfield*, ed. Andrew Sanders.

—— *Dombey and Son*, ed. Alan Horsman and Dennis Walder.

—— *Great Expectations*, ed. Margaret Caldwell and Kate Flint.

—— *Hard Times*, ed. Paul Schlicke.

—— *Little Dorrit*, ed. Harvey Peter Sucksmith.

—— *Martin Chuzzlewit*, ed. Margaret Caldwell.

—— *The Mystery of Edwin Drood*, ed. Margaret Caldwell.

—— *Nicholas Nickleby*, ed. Paul Schlicke.

—— *The Old Curiosity Shop*, ed. Elizabeth M. Brennan.

—— *Oliver Twist*, ed. Stephen Gill.

—— *Our Mutual Friend*, ed. Michael Cotsell.

—— *The Pickwick Papers*, ed. James Kinsley.

—— *A Tale of Two Cities*, ed. Andrew Sanders.

# A CHRONOLOGY OF CHARLES DICKENS

Dickens's major fictions are indicated by bold type.

| Life | Historical and Cultural Background |
| --- | --- |
| 1809 (13 June) John Dickens, a clerk in the Navy Pay Office, marries Elizabeth Barrow. | |
| 1810 (28 Oct.) Frances Dickens ('Fanny') born. | |
| 1811 | Prince of Wales becomes Prince Regent. W. M. Thackeray born. Jane Austen, *Sense and Sensibility* |
| 1812 (7 Feb.) Charles Dickens born at Mile End Terrace, Landport, Portsea (now 393 Old Commercial Road, Portsmouth). | Luddite riots. War between Britain and the United States. Napoleon's retreat from Moscow. Robert Browning and Edward Lear born. Lord Byron, *Childe Harold's Pilgrimage*, i and ii (completed 1818) |
| 1813 | Robert Southey becomes Poet Laureate. Napoleon defeated at Leipzig. Austen, *Pride and Prejudice*; Byron, *The Bride of Abydos*, *The Giaour*; P. B. Shelley, *Queen Mab* |
| 1814 Birth (Mar.) and death (Sept.) of Alfred Allen Dickens. | Napoleon exiled to Elba. Austen, *Mansfield Park*; Sir Walter Scott, *Waverley*; William Wordsworth, *The Excursion* |
| 1815 (1 Jan.) Dickens family moves to London. | Escape of Napoleon; Battle of Waterloo. Anthony Trollope born. Thomas Robert Malthus, *An Inquiry into Rent*; Scott, *Guy Mannering* |
| 1816 (Apr.) Letitia Dickens born. | Charlotte Brontë born. Austen, *Emma*; S. T. Coleridge, *Christabel and Other Poems*; Thomas Love Peacock, *Headlong Hall*; Scott, *The Antiquary*, *Old Mortality* |
| 1817 (Apr.) Dickens family settles in Chatham. | Jane Austen dies. Byron, *Manfred*; Coleridge, *Biographia Literaria*; John Keats, *Poems*; Robert Owen, *Report to the Committee on the Poor Law*; Scott, *Rob Roy* |

| *Life* | *Historical and Cultural Background* |
|---|---|
| 1818 | Emily Brontë born. Austen, *Northanger Abbey*, *Persuasion* (posth.); Keats, *Endymion*; Peacock, *Nightmare Abbey*; Scott, *The Heart of Midlothian*; Mary Shelley, *Frankenstein* |
| 1819 (Sept.) Harriet Dickens born. | Princess Victoria born. Peterloo 'Massacre' (11 deaths). A. H. Clough, Mary Anne Evans (George Eliot), Charles Kingsley, John Ruskin born. Byron, *Don Juan*, i–ii (continued till 1824); Scott, *The Bride of Lammermoor*; Wordsworth, *Peter Bell*, *The Waggoner* |
| 1820 Frederick Dickens ('Fred') born. | Death of George III; accession of Prince Regent as George IV. Trial of Queen Caroline. Anne Brontë born. John Clare, *Poems, Descriptive of Rural Life*; Keats, *Lamia, Isabella, The Eve of St Agnes and Other Poems*; Malthus, *Principles of Political Economy*; Charles Robert Maturin, *Melmoth the Wanderer*; P. B. Shelley, *The Cenci*, *Prometheus Unbound*; Scott, *Ivanhoe* |
| 1821 CD goes to school run by William Giles. | Greek War of Independence starts. Napoleon dies. Keats dies. Clare, *The Village Minstrel and Other Poems*; Thomas De Quincey, *Confessions of an English Opium Eater*; Pierce Egan, *Life in London*; Thomas Moore, *Irish Melodies*; Scott, *Kenilworth*; P. B. Shelley, *Adonais*; Southey, *A Vision of Judgement* |
| 1822 (Mar.) Alfred Lamert Dickens born; Harriet Dickens dies. CD stays in Chatham when family moves to Camden Town, London; rejoins them later, but his education is discontinued. | Shelley dies. Matthew Arnold born. Byron, *The Vision of Judgement* |
| 1823 (Dec.) Family moves to 4 Gower Street North, where Mrs Dickens fails in her attempt to run a school. | Building of present British Museum begins. Coventry Patmore born. Charles Lamb, *Essays of Elia*; Scott, *Quentin Durward* |

| Life | Historical and Cultural Background |
|---|---|
| 1824 (late Jan. or early Feb.) CD sent to work at Jonathan Warren's blacking-warehouse, Hungerford Stairs; (20 Feb.) John Dickens arrested and imprisoned for debt in the Marshalsea till 28 May; CD in lodgings; family moves to Somers Town. | National Gallery founded in London. Repeal of acts forbidding formation of trades unions. Byron dies. Wilkie Collins born. James Hogg, *The Private Memoirs and Confessions of a Justified Sinner*; Walter Savage Landor, *Imaginary Conversations* (completed 1829); Scott, *Redgauntlet* |
| 1825 (9 Mar.) John Dickens retires from Navy Pay Office with a pension; (Mar./Apr.) CD leaves Warren's and recommences his schooling at Wellington House Academy. | Stockton–Darlington railway opens. Hazlitt, *Table-Talk*, *The Spirit of the Age*; Alessandro Manzoni, *I promessi sposi* |
| 1826 John Dickens works as Parliamentary correspondent for *The British Press*. | University College London and Royal Zoological Society founded. J. Fenimore Cooper, *The Last of the Mohicans*; Benjamin Disraeli, *Vivian Grey* (completed 1827); Mary Shelley, *The Last Man* |
| 1827 (Mar.) Family evicted for non-payment of rates; CD becomes a solicitor's clerk; (Nov.) Augustus Dickens born. | Battle of Navarino. William Blake dies. Clare, *The Shepherd's Calendar*; De Quincey, 'On Murder Considered as One of the Fine Arts' |
| 1828 John Dickens works as reporter for *The Morning Herald*. | Duke of Wellington PM. George Meredith, D. G. Rossetti, Leo Tolstoy born. Pierce Egan, *Finish to the Adventures of Tom, Jerry and Logic* |
| 1829 CD works at Doctors' Commons as a shorthand reporter. | Catholic Emancipation Act; Robert Peel establishes Metropolitan Police. |
| 1830 (8 Feb.) Admitted as reader to British Museum; (May) falls in love with Maria Beadnell. | George IV dies; William IV succeeds. Opening of Manchester–Liverpool Railway. July revolution in France; accession of Louis-Philippe as emperor. Greece independent. Hazlitt dies. Christina Rossetti born. William Cobbett, *Rural Rides*; Sir Charles Lyell, *Principles of Geology* (completed 1832); Alfred Tennyson, *Poems, Chiefly Lyrical* |

| *Life* | *Historical and Cultural Background* |
|---|---|
| 1831 Composes poem 'The Bill of Fare'; starts work as reporter for *The Mirror of Parliament*. | Reform Bill. Major cholera epidemic. Michael Faraday's electro-magnetic current.<br>Peacock, *Crotchet Castle*; Edgar Allan Poe, *Poems*; Stendhal, *Le Rouge et le noir* |
| 1832 Becomes Parliamentary reporter on the *True Sun*. | Lord Grey PM. First Reform Act. Jeremy Bentham, Crabbe, Goethe, and Scott die. Charles Lutwidge Dodgson (Lewis Carroll) born.<br>Goethe, *Faust*, ii; Mary Russell Mitford, *Our Village*; Tennyson, *Poems*; Frances Trollope, *Domestic Manners of the Americans* |
| 1833 Concludes relationship with Maria Beadnell; first story, 'A Dinner at Poplar Walk' (later called 'Mr Minns and his Cousin') published in *Monthly Magazine*. | First steamship crosses the Atlantic. Abolition of slavery in all British colonies (from Aug. 1834). Factory Act forbids employment of children under 9. First government grant for schools. Oxford Movement starts.<br>Robert Browning, *Pauline*; John Henry Newman, 'Lead, Kindly Light' and (with others) the first *Tracts for the Times* |
| 1834 (Jan.–Feb.) Six more stories appear in *Monthly Magazine*; (Aug.) meets Catherine Hogarth; becomes reporter on *The Morning Chronicle*, which publishes (Sept.–Dec.) first five 'Street Sketches'; (Dec.) moves to Furnival's Inn, Holborn. | Robert Owen's Grand National Trades Union. 'Tolpuddle Martyrs' transported to Australia. Lord Melbourne PM; then Peel. Workhouses set up under Poor Law Amendment Act. Coleridge, Lamb, and Malthus die. William Morris born.<br>Balzac, *Eugénie Grandet*; Thomas Carlyle, *Sartor Resartus*; Harriet Martineau, *Illustrations of Political Economy* |
| 1835 (?May) Engaged to Catherine Hogarth ('Kate'); publishes stories, sketches, and scenes in *Monthly Magazine*, *Evening Chronicle*, and *Bell's Life in London*. | Lord Melbourne PM. Municipal Corporations Act reforms local government. Cobbett and James Hogg die.<br>Browning, *Paracelsus*; Alexis de Tocqueville, *La Démocratie en Amérique* |

|  | *Life* | *Historical and Cultural Background* |
|---|---|---|
| 1836 | (Feb.) Takes larger chambers in Furnival's Inn; (8 Feb.) *Sketches by Boz, First Series* published; (31 Mar.) first monthly number of *Pickwick Papers* issued; (2 Apr.) marries Catherine Hogarth; (June) publishes *Sunday Under Three Heads*; leaves the *Morning Chronicle* (Nov.); (17 Dec.) *Sketches by Boz, Second Series*; (?Dec.) meets John Forster. | Beginning of Chartism. First London train (to Greenwich). Forms of telegraph used in England and America. Augustus Pugin's *Contrasts* advocates Gothic style of architecture. Browning, 'Porphyria's Lover'; Nicolai Gogol, *The Government Inspector*; Frederick Marryat, *Mr Midshipman Easy* |
| 1837 | (1 Jan.) First monthly number of *Bentley's Miscellany*, edited by CD, published; (6 Jan.) birth of first child, Charles ('Charley'); (31 Jan.) serialization of *Oliver Twist* begins in *Bentley's*; (3 Mar.) *Is She His Wife?* produced at the St James's; (Apr.) family moves to 48 Doughty Street; (7 May) sudden death of his sister-in-law, Mary Hogarth, at 17; CD suspends publication of *Pickwick Papers* and *Oliver Twist* for a month; (Aug.– Sept.) first family holiday in Broadstairs; (17 Nov.) *Pickwick Papers* published in one volume. | William IV dies; Queen Victoria succeeds. Carlyle, *The French Revolution*; Isaac Pitman, *Stenographic Short-Hand*; J. G. Lockhart, *Memoirs of the Life of Sir Walter Scott* |
| 1838 | (Jan.–Feb.) Visits Yorkshire schools with Hablot Browne ('Phiz'); (6 Mar.) second child, Mary ('Mamie'), born; (31 Mar.) monthly serialization of *Nicholas Nickleby* begins; (9 Nov.) *Oliver Twist* published in three volumes. | Isambard Kingdom Brunel's *Great Western* inaugurates regular steamship service between England and USA. London– Birmingham railway completed. Irish Poor Law. Anti-Corn Law League founded by Richard Cobden. People's Charter advocates universal suffrage. Carlyle, *Sartor Resartus*; John Ruskin, *The Poetry of Architecture*; R. S. Surtees, *Jorrocks's Jaunts and Jollities*; Wordsworth, *Sonnets* |

*Life*

*Historical and Cultural Background*

1839  (31 Jan.) Resigns editorship of *Bentley's*; (23 Oct.) *Nicholas Nickleby* published in one volume; (29 Oct.) third child, Kate ('Katey'), born; (Dec.) family moves to 1 Devonshire Terrace, Regent's Park.

Opium War between Britain and China. Chartist riots. Louis Daguerre and W. H. Fox Talbot independently develop photography.
Carlyle, *Chartism*; Darwin, *Journal of Researches into the Geology and Natural History of . . . Countries Visited by HMS Beagle*; Harriet Martineau, *Deerbrook*

1840  (4 Apr.) First weekly issue of *Master Humphrey's Clock* (also published monthly) in which *The Old Curiosity Shop* is serialized from 25 Apr.; (1 June) moves family to Broadstairs; (11 Oct.) returns to London; (15 Oct.) *Master Humphrey's Clock*, Vol. I published.

Queen Victoria marries Prince Albert. Maoris yield sovereignty of New Zealand to Queen Victoria by Treaty of Waitangi. Rowland Hill introduces penny postage. Fanny Burney dies.

1841  (8 Feb.) Fourth child, Walter, born; *The Old Curiosity Shop* concluded and *Barnaby Rudge* commenced in *Master Humphrey's Clock* (6 and 13 Feb.); operated on for fistula (without anaesthetic). *Master Humphrey's Clock*, Vols. II and III published (Apr. and Dec.); one-volume editions of *The Old Curiosity Shop* and *Barnaby Rudge* published (15 Dec.).

Peel PM. Hong Kong and New Zealand proclaimed British. *Punch* founded. W. H. Ainsworth, *Old St Paul's*; Browning, *Pippa Passes*; Carlyle, *On Heroes, Hero-Worship, and the Heroic in History*; R. W. Emerson, *Essays*. Dion Boucicault's *London Assurance* acted

1842  (Jan.–June) CD and Catherine visit North America; (Aug.–Sept.) with family in Broadstairs; (Oct.–Nov.) visits Cornwall with Forster and others; (19 Oct.) *American Notes* published; (31 Dec.) first monthly number of *Martin Chuzzlewit* published.

End of wars with China and Afghanistan. Mines Act: no underground work by women or by children under 10. Chadwick report on sanitary condition of the working classes. Chartist riots. Copyright Act. Stendhal dies.
Browning, *Dramatic Lyrics*; Gogol, *Dead Souls*; Thomas Babington Macaulay, *Lays of Ancient Rome*; Tennyson, *Poems*

| *Life* | *Historical and Cultural Background* |
|---|---|
| 1843 (19 Dec.) *A Christmas Carol* published. | British annexation of Sind and Natal. I. K. Brunel's *Great Britain*, the first ocean screw-steamer, launched. Southey dies; Wordsworth becomes Poet Laureate. Carlyle, *Past and Present*; Thomas Hood, 'Song of the Shirt'; Macaulay, *Essays*; J. S. Mill, *System of Logic*; Ruskin, *Modern Painters*, i (completed 1860) |
| 1844 (15 Jan.) Fifth child, Francis, born; (16 July) takes family to Genoa; one-volume edition of *Martin Chuzzlewit* published; (30 Nov.–8 Dec.) returns to London to read *The Chimes* (published 16 Dec.) to his friends. | Factory Act restricts working hours of women and children. 'Rochdale Pioneers' found first co-operative society. Ragged School Union. William Barnes, *Poems of Rural Life in the Dorset Dialect*; E. B. Barrett, *Poems*; Disraeli, *Coningsby*; Dumas, *Les Trois Mousquetaires*; A. W. Kinglake, *Eōthen* |
| 1845 Travels in Italy with Catherine before returning to London from Genoa; (20 Sept.) directs and acts in first performance of the Amateur Players, Ben Jonson's *Every Man In His Humour*; (28 Oct.) sixth child, Alfred, born; (20 Dec.) *The Cricket on the Hearth* published. | Disappearance of Sir John Franklin's expedition to find a North-West Passage from the Atlantic to the Pacific. War with Sikhs. 1845–9: potato famine in Ireland: 1 million die; 8 million emigrate. Thomas Hood and Sydney Smith die. Browning, *Dramatic Romances and Lyrics*; Disraeli, *Sybil*; Engels, *Condition of the Working Class in England*; Poe, *The Raven and other Poems*, *Tales of Mystery and Imagination* |
| 1846 (21 Jan.–9 Feb.) Edits *The Daily News*; (May) *Pictures from Italy* published; (31 May) leaves with family for Switzerland via the Rhine; (11 June) settles in Lausanne; (30 Sept.) monthly serialization of *Dombey and Son* commences; (16 Nov.) family moves to Paris; (Dec.) *The Battle of Life* published. | Corn Laws repealed; Peel resigns; Lord John Russell PM. Ether first used as a general anaesthetic. Robert Browning and Elizabeth Barrett marry secretly and leave for Italy. Balzac, *La Cousine Bette*; *Poems by Currer, Ellis and Acton Bell* (i.e. Charlotte, Emily, and Anne Brontë); Edward Lear, *Book of Nonsense* |

| *Life* | *Historical and Cultural Background* |
|---|---|
| 1847 (28 Feb.) Returns from Paris; (18 Apr.) seventh child, Sydney, is born; (June–Sept.) with family at Broadstairs; (27–8 July) performs in Manchester and Liverpool with the Amateurs; (Nov.) Urania Cottage, Miss Coutts's 'Home for Homeless Women', in whose administration CD is involved, opened in Shepherd's Bush. | Factory Act limits working day for women and young persons to 10 hours. James Simpson discovers anaesthetic properties of chloroform. Louis Napoleon escapes to England from prison.<br>A. Brontë, *Agnes Grey*; C. Brontë, *Jane Eyre*; E. Brontë, *Wuthering Heights*; Tennyson, *The Princess*. J. M. Morton's *Box and Cox* acted |
| 1848 (12 Apr.) One-volume edition of *Dombey and Son* published; (May–July) the Amateurs perform in London, Manchester, Liverpool, Birmingham, Edinburgh, and Glasgow; (2 Sept.) sister Fanny dies; (19 Dec.) *The Haunted Man* published. | Outbreak of cholera in London. Public Health Act. End of Chartist Movement. Pre-Raphaelite Brotherhood founded. 'The Year of Revolutions' in Europe. Louis Napoleon becomes President of France. Emily Brontë, Branwell Brontë die.<br>A. Brontë, *The Tenant of Wildfell Hall*; Elizabeth Gaskell, *Mary Barton*; Marx and Engels, *Communist Manifesto*; J. S. Mill, *Principles of Political Economy*; Thackeray, *Vanity Fair* |
| 1849 (16 Jan.) Eighth child, Henry ('Harry'), born; (30 Apr.) monthly serialization of *David Copperfield* begins; (July–Oct.) with family at Bonchurch, Isle of Wight. | Revolt against the British in Montreal. Punjab annexed. Rome proclaimed a republic; later taken by the French. Suppression of Communist riots in Paris. Californian gold rush. Anne Brontë, E. A. Poe die.<br>C. Brontë, *Shirley*; Sir John Herschel, *Outlines of Astronomy*; Macaulay, *History of England*, i–ii (unfinished at his death, in 1859); Ruskin, *The Seven Lamps of Architecture* |
| 1850 (30 Mar.) First issue of *Household Words*, a weekly journal edited and contributed to by CD; (16 Aug.) ninth child, Dora, born; (Aug.–Oct.) at Broadstairs; (15 Nov.) one-volume edition of *David Copperfield* published. | Restoration of Roman Catholic hierarchy in England. Factory Act: 60-hour week for women and young persons. Public Libraries Act. Dover–Calais telegraph cable laid. Balzac and Wordsworth die. Tennyson becomes Poet Laureate.<br>E. B. Browning, 'Sonnets from the Portuguese', in *Poems*; Nathaniel Hawthorne, *The Scarlet Letter*; Tennyson, *In Memoriam A.H.H.*; Thackeray, *The History of Pendennis*; Wordsworth, *The Prelude* (posth.) |

| Life | Historical and Cultural Background |
|---|---|
| 1851 (25 Jan.) *A Child's History of England* starts serialization in *Household Words*; (31 Mar.) John Dickens dies; (14 Apr.) Dora dies suddenly, aged 8 months; (May) directs and acts in Bulwer-Lytton's *Not So Bad As We Seem* before the Queen, in aid of the Guild of Literature and Art; (May–Oct.) last family holiday at Broadstairs; (Nov.) moves to Tavistock House. | Great Exhibition in the Crystal Palace, Hyde Park. Fall of French Second Republic. Gold found in Australia. George Borrow, *Lavengro*; Henry Mayhew, *London Labour and the London Poor*; Herman Melville, *Moby Dick*; George Meredith, *Poems*; Ruskin, *The King of the Golden River*, *The Stones of Venice*, i (completed 1853) |
| 1852 (28 Feb.) Monthly serialization of *Bleak House* begins; (14 Apr.) birth of tenth child, Edward ('Plorn'); (Feb.–Sept.) provincial performances of *Not So Bad As We Seem*; (July–Oct.) family stays in Dover. | Lord Derby becomes PM; then Lord Aberdeen. Louis Napoleon proclaimed Emperor Napoleon III. 1852–6: David Livingstone crosses Africa. Tom Moore and the Duke of Wellington die. M. P. Roget, *Roget's Thesaurus of English Words and Phrases*; Harriet Beecher Stowe, *Uncle Tom's Cabin*; Thackeray, *Henry Esmond* |
| 1853 (June–Oct.) Family stays in Boulogne; (12 Sept.) one-volume edition of *Bleak House* published; (Oct.–Dec.) in Switzerland and Italy with Wilkie Collins and Augustus Egg; (10 Dec.) *A Child's History of England* concluded in *Household Words*; (27–30 Dec.) gives public readings of *A Christmas Carol* and *The Cricket on the Hearth* in Birmingham. | Arnold, *Poems*; C. Brontë, *Villette*; Gaskell, *Ruth*, *Cranford*; Surtees, *Mr Sponge's Sporting Career* |
| 1854 (28–30 Jan.) Visits Preston; (1 Apr.–12 Aug.) weekly serialization of *Hard Times* in *Household Words*; (June–Oct.) family stays in Boulogne; (7 Aug.) *Hard Times* published in one volume; (Dec.) reads *A Christmas Carol* in Reading, Sherborne, and Bradford. | Reform of the Civil Service. France and Britain join Turkey against Russia in the Crimean War; battles of Alma, Balaclava, Inkerman and siege of Sebastopol; Florence Nightingale goes to Scutari. Patmore, *The Angel in the House*, i (completed 1862); Tennyson, 'The Charge of the Light Brigade'; H. D. Thoreau, *Walden* |

| *Life* | *Historical and Cultural Background* |
|---|---|
| 1855 (Feb.) Meets Maria Winter (neé Beadnell) again; (27 Mar.) reads *A Christmas Carol* in Ashford, Kent; (June) directs and acts in Collins's *The Lighthouse* at Tavistock House; family stays in Folkestone, where CD reads *A Christmas Carol* on 5 Oct.; (15 Oct.) settles family in Paris; (1 Dec.) monthly serialization of *Little Dorrit* begins; (Dec.) reads *A Christmas Carol* at Peterborough and Sheffield. | Lord Palmerston PM. Newspaper tax abolished. *Daily Telegraph*, first London penny newspaper, founded. Fall of Sebastopol. 1855–6: G. J. Mendel discovers laws of heredity. Charlotte Brontë and Mary Russell Mitford die. R. Browning, *Men and Women*; Gaskell, *North and South*; Longfellow, *Hiawatha*; Tennyson, *Maud and other Poems*; Thackeray, *The Newcomes*, *The Rose and the Ring*; A. Trollope, *The Warden*; Walt Whitman, *Leaves of Grass* |
| 1856 (Mar.) Buys Gad's Hill Place, Kent; (29 Apr.) family returns from Paris; (June–Sept.) family stays in Boulogne. | End of Crimean War. Britain annexes Oudh; Sir Henry Bessemer patents his steel-making process. Synthetic colours invented. Henry Irving's first stage appearance. National Gallery founded in London. Mrs Craik (Dinah Maria Mulock), *John Halifax, Gentleman*; Flaubert, *Madame Bovary* |
| 1857 (Jan.) Directs and acts in Collins's *The Frozen Deep* at Tavistock House; (13 Feb.) moves to Gad's Hill Place; (30 May) *Little Dorrit* published in one volume; Walter leaves for service with the East India Company; (June–July) visited by Hans Andersen; gives three public readings of *A Christmas Carol* (July–Aug.) performances of *The Frozen Deep* in London and, with Ellen Ternan, her sister and mother in the cast, in Manchester. | Divorce courts established in England. Arnold becomes Professor of Poetry at Oxford. Museum—later, the Victoria and Albert Museum—opened in South Kensington. Beginning of Indian mutiny; siege and relief of Lucknow. Baudelaire, *Les Fleurs du mal*; C. Brontë, *The Professor* (posth.); E. B. Browning, *Aurora Leigh*; Gaskell, *The Life of Charlotte Brontë*; Hughes, *Tom Brown's Schooldays*; Livingstone, *Missionary Travels and Researches in South Africa*; A. Trollope, *Barchester Towers* |

| Life | Historical and Cultural Background |
|---|---|
| 1858 (19 Jan.; 26 Mar; 15 Apr.) Reads *A Christmas Carol* for charity; (29 Apr.–22 July) series of 17 public readings; (May) separation from Catherine; (7 and 12 June) publishes 'personal' statement about it in *The Times* and *Household Words*; (Aug.) *Reprinted Pieces* published; (Aug.–Nov.) first provincial reading tour, extending to Ireland and Scotland (85 readings); (24 Dec.) first series of London Christmas readings begins. | Derby PM. Indian Mutiny suppressed; powers of East India Company transferred to the Crown. Queen Victoria proclaimed Empress of India. Launch of I. K. Brunel's *Great Eastern*. Darwin and A. R. Wallace give joint paper on evolution. R. M. Ballantyne, *The Coral Island*; Clough, *Amours de Voyage*; Eliot, *Scenes of Clerical Life*; A. Trollope, *Doctor Thorne* |
| 1859 (30 Apr.) Begins to edit *All the Year Round* in which *A Tale of Two Cities* appears weekly till 26 November; (28 May) final number of *Household Words*; (Oct.) gives 14 readings on second provincial tour; (21 Nov.) *A Tale of Two Cities* published in one volume; (24 Dec.) begins series of three London Christmas readings. | Palmerston PM. Franco–Austrian War: Austrians defeated at Solferino. War of Italian Liberation. The abolitionist John Brown hanged for treason at Charlestown, Virginia. Thomas de Quincey, Leigh Hunt, and Lord Macaulay die. Darwin, *On the Origin of Species by Means of Natural Selection*; Eliot, *Adam Bede*; Edward Fitzgerald, *The Rubáiyát of Omar Khayyám*; J. S. Mill, *On Liberty*; Samuel Smiles, *Self-Help*; Tennyson, *Idylls of the King* |
| 1860 (17 July) Katey marries Charles Collins; (27 July) CD's brother Alfred dies, at 38; (21 Aug.) sells Tavistock House; (Oct.) settles permanently at Gad's Hill; (1 Dec.) weekly serialization of *Great Expectations* begins in *All the Year Round*, continuing till 3 Aug. 1861. | Abraham Lincoln elected US president; Carolina secedes from the Union. Collins, *The Woman in White*; Eliot, *The Mill on the Floss*; Faraday, *Various Forces of Matter*. Boucicault's *The Colleen Bawn* acted |
| 1861 (Mar.–Apr.) Series of 6 London readings; (6 July) *Great Expectations* published in three volumes; (Oct.–Jan. 1862) gives 46 readings on third provincial tour; (19 Nov.) Charley marries Elizabeth ('Bessie') Evans: CD refuses to be present. | Abolition of Paper Tax. Prince Albert dies. Victor Emmanuel becomes King of Italy. Serfdom abolished in Russia. Outbreak of American Civil War. E. B. Browning and A. H. Clough die. Mrs Isabella Mary Beeton, *Book of Household Management*; Eliot, *Silas Marner*; J. S. Mill, *Utilitarianism*; F. T. Palgrave, *The Golden Treasury*; Reade, *The Cloister and the Hearth*; A. Trollope, *Framley Parsonage*; Mrs Henry Wood, *East Lynne* |

|  | *Life* | *Historical and Cultural Background* |
|---|---|---|
| 1862 | (Feb.–May) Exchanges Gad's Hill Place for a house in London but also uses rooms at the office of *All the Year Round*; (Mar.–June) London readings; (June–Oct.) makes several visits to France; (Oct.) settles Mamie and her aunt, Georgina Hogarth, in Paris; (Dec.) returns to Gad's Hill for Christmas. | Famine among Lancashire cotton workers. Bismarck becomes Chancellor of Prussia. Thoreau dies. Mary Elizabeth Braddon, *Lady Audley's Secret*; Hugo, *Les Misérables*; Meredith, *Modern Love*; Christina Rossetti, *Goblin Market and Other Poems*; Herbert Spencer, *First Principles*; Turgenev, *Fathers and Sons* |
| 1863 | (Jan.) Gives 3 readings for charity at British Embassy in Paris; (Feb. and Aug.) makes further visits to France; (Mar.–May) London readings; (13 Sept.) Elizabeth Dickens dies; (31 Dec.) Walter dies in Calcutta, India, aged 22. | Beginning of work on London underground railway. Lincoln's Gettysburg Address; emancipation of US slaves. Thackeray and Frances Trollope die. Eliot, *Romola*; Margaret Oliphant, *Salem Chapel* |
| 1864 | (1 May) Monthly serialization of *Our Mutual Friend* begins; (27 June–6 July) probably in France; (Nov.) in France. | Karl Marx organizes first Socialist International in London. Louis Pasteur publishes his theory of germs as the cause of disease. International Red Cross founded. John Clare, W. S. Landor, R. S. Surtees, and Hawthorne die. Sheridan Le Fanu, *Uncle Silas*; Newman, *Apologia pro Vita Sua*; Tennyson, *Enoch Arden and Other Poems*; Trollope, *The Small House at Allington, Can You Forgive Her?* |
| 1865 | (Feb.–June) Three trips to France; (Feb.–Apr.) first attack of lameness from swollen left foot; (29 May) sees Alfred off to Australia; (9 June) returning from France with Ellen Ternan and her mother, is in fatal railway accident at Staplehurst, Kent; (Sept.) visit to France; (20 Oct.) *Our Mutual Friend* published in two volumes. | Russell PM. William Booth founds Christian Mission in Whitechapel, known from 1878 as the Salvation Army. Completion of transatlantic cable. End of American Civil War. Abraham Lincoln assassinated. Elizabeth Gaskell dies. Arnold, *Essays in Criticism, First Series*; Lewis Carroll, *Alice's Adventures in Wonderland* |

| *Life* | *Historical and Cultural Background* |
|---|---|
| 1866 (Apr.–June) Readings in London and the provinces; (June) CD's brother Augustus Dickens dies in Chicago, aged 38. | Derby PM. Second Reform Bill. Fenians active in Ireland: Habeas Corpus suspended. Elizabeth Garrett opens dispensary for women. Dr T. J. Barnardo opens home for destitute children in London's East End. Peacock and John Keble die.<br><br>Fyodor Dostoevsky, *Crime and Punishment*; Eliot, *Felix Holt, the Radical*; Gaskell, *Wives and Daughters* (posth., unfinished); Swinburne, *Poems and Ballads*, First Series |
| 1867 (Jan.–May) Readings in England and Ireland; (Nov.) begins American reading tour in Boston; (Dec.) *No Thoroughfare*, written jointly with Collins, published in *All the Year Round*. | Fenian outrages in England. Second Reform Act. Factory Act. Joseph Lister practises antiseptic surgery. Building of Royal Albert Hall commenced.<br><br>Arnold, 'Dover Beach', 'Thyrsis', in *New Poems*; Walter Bagehot, *The English Constitution*; Henrik Ibsen, *Peer Gynt*; Karl Marx, *Das Kapital*, i; A. Trollope, *The Last Chronicle of Barset*; Emile Zola, *Thérèse Raquin* |
| 1868 (22 Apr.) Sails home from New York, having cancelled planned readings in the USA and Canada; (26 Sept.) Plorn sails to Australia to join Alfred; (Oct.) Harry enters Trinity College, Cambridge; CD begins Farewell Reading Tour; CD's brother Fred dies, aged 48. | Disraeli PM; Gladstone PM. Trades' Union Congress founded. Basutoland annexed.<br><br>Louisa May Alcott, *Little Women*; Collins, *The Moonstone*; Queen Victoria, *Leaves from a Journal of Our Life in the Highlands* |
| 1869 (5 Jan.) Introduces 'Sikes and Nancy' into his repertoire; (22 Apr.) serious illness forces CD to break off reading tour after 74 readings. | Girton College for Women founded. Suez Canal opened.<br><br>Arnold, *Culture and Anarchy*; R. D. Blackmore, *Lorna Doone*; R. Browning, *The Ring and the Book*; J. S. Mill, *On the Subjection of Women*; Leo Tolstoy, *War and Peace*; A. Trollope, *Phineas Finn, He Knew He Was Right*; Paul Verlaine, *Fêtes galantes* |
| 1870 (Jan.– Mar.) Farewell readings in London; (9 Mar.) received by Queen Victoria; (1 Apr.) first of six completed numbers of *The Mystery of Edwin Drood* issued; (9 June) dies, aged 58, following a cerebral haemorrhage, at Gad's Hill; (14 June) buried in Westminster Abbey. | Gladstone's Irish Land Act. Married Women's Property Act gives wives the right to their own earnings. Elementary Education Act for England and Wales. Outbreak of Franco-Prussian War: Napoleon III defeated and exiled; siege of Paris (till 1871).<br><br>E. C. Brewer, *Dictionary of Phrase and Fable*; D. G. Rossetti, *Poems* |

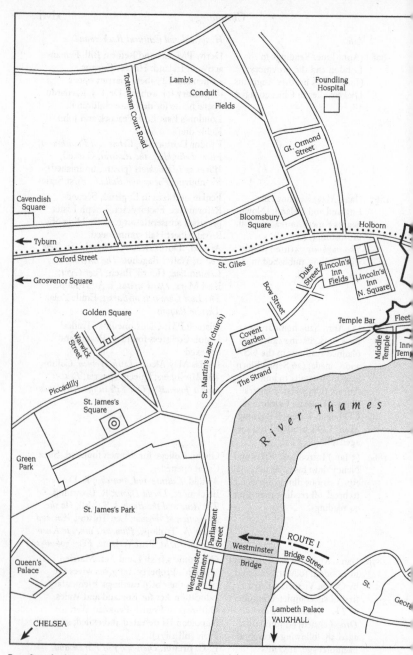

London during the Gordon Riots, 1780

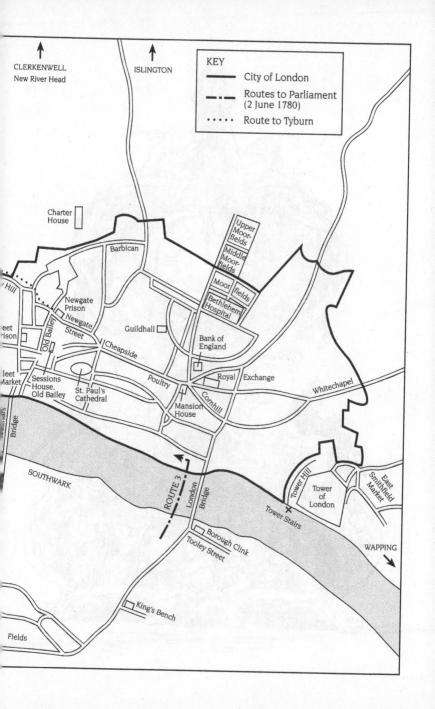

KEY

CLERKENWELL
New River Head

ISLINGTON

KEY

—— City of London

—·—·— Routes to Parliament
(2 June 1780)

· · · · · Route to Tyburn

Charter
House

Barbican

Upper
Moor-
fields

Middle
Moor-
fields

Moor fields

Bethlehem
Hospital

Newgate
Prison

Newgate
Street

Guildhall

Bank of
England

Cheapside

Poultry

Royal Exchange

Whitechapel

Sessions
House,
Old Bailey

St. Paul's
Cathedral

Cornhill

Mansion
House

ROUTE 3

London Bridge

Tower Hill

Tower
of
London

East
Smithfield
Market

SOUTHWARK

Tower Stairs

WAPPING

Borough Clink

Tooley Street

King's Bench

Fields

Fleet
Prison

Fleet
Market

Old Bailey

Hill

Bridge

# BARNABY RUDGE;

A TALE OF THE RIOTS OF 'EIGHTY.

———◆———

## BY CHARLES DICKENS.

———◆———

WITH ILLUSTRATIONS

BY

GEORGE CATTERMOLE AND HABLOT K. BROWNE.

———

COMPLETE IN ONE VOLUME.

———

LONDON:
CHAPMAN AND HALL, STRAND.
MDCCCXLI.

# PREFACE TO BARNABY RUDGE.

IF the object an author has had, in writing a book, cannot be discovered from its perusal, the probability is that it is either very deep, or very shallow. Hoping that mine may lie somewhere between these two extremes, I shall say very little about it, and that, only in reference to one point.

No account of the Gordon Riots, having been to my knowledge introduced into any Work of Fiction, and the subject presenting very extraordinary and remarkable features, I was led to project this Tale.

It is unnecessary to say, that those shameful tumults, while they reflect indelible disgrace upon the time in which they occurred, and all who had act or part in them, teach a good lesson. That what we falsely call a religious cry is easily raised by men who have no religion, and who in their daily practice set at nought the commonest principles of right and wrong; that it is begotten of intolerance and persecution; that it is senseless, besotted, inveterate, and unmerciful; all History teaches us. But perhaps we do not know it in our hearts too well, to profit by even so humble and familiar an example as the "No Popery" riots of Seventeen Hundred and Eighty.

However imperfectly those disturbances are set forth in the following pages, they are impartially painted by one who has no sympathy with the Romish Church, although he acknowledges, as most men do, some esteemed friends among the followers of its creed.

It may be observed that, in the description of the principal outrages, reference has been had to the best authorities of that time, such as they are; and that the account given in this Tale, of all the main features of the Riots, is substantially correct.

It may be further remarked, that Mr. Dennis's allusions to the flourishing condition of his trade* in those days, have their foundation in Truth, not in the Author's fancy. Any file of old Newspapers, or odd volume of the Annual Register, will prove this with terrible ease.

Even the case of Mary Jones,* dwelt upon with so much pleasure by the same character, is no effort of invention. The facts were stated exactly as they are stated here, in the House of Commons. Whether

4

Preface

they afforded as much entertainment to the merry gentlemen
assembled there, as some other most affecting circumstances of a
similar nature mentioned by Sir Samuel Romilly,* is not recorded.

It is a great pleasure to me to add in this place—for which I have
reserved the acknowledgment—that for a beautiful thought, in the
last chapter but one of "The Old Curiosity Shop," I am indebted to
Mr. Rogers. It is taken from his charming Tale, "Ginevra:"

> "And long might'st thou have seen
> An old man wandering *as in quest of something*,
> Something he could not find—he knew not what."

DEVONSHIRE TERRACE, YORK GATE,
*November* 1841.

# PREFACE.

As it is Mr. Waterton's opinion* that ravens are gradually becoming extinct in England, I offer a few words here about mine.

The raven in this story is a compound of two great originals, of whom I have been, at different times, the proud possessor. The first was in the bloom of his youth, when he was discovered in a modest retirement in London, by a friend of mine, and given to me. He had from the first, as Sir Hugh Evans says of Anne Page,* "good gifts," which he improved by study and attention in a most exemplary manner. He slept in a stable—generally on horseback—and so terrified a Newfoundland dog by his preternatural sagacity, that he has been known, by the mere superiority of his genius, to walk off unmolested with the dog's dinner, from before his face. He was rapidly rising in acquirements and virtues, when, in an evil hour, his stable was newly painted. He observed the workmen closely, saw that they were careful of the paint, and immediately burned to possess it. On their going to dinner, he ate up all they had left behind, consisting of a pound or two of white lead; and this youthful indiscretion terminated in death.

While I was yet inconsolable for his loss, another friend of mine in Yorkshire discovered an older and more gifted raven at a village public-house, which he prevailed upon the landlord to part with for a consideration, and sent up to me. The first act of this Sage, was, to administer to the effects of his predecessor, by disinterring all the cheese and halfpence he had buried in the garden—a work of immense labour and research, to which he devoted all the energies of his mind. When he had achieved this task, he applied himself to the acquisition of stable language, in which he soon became such an adept, that he would perch outside my window and drive imaginary horses with great skill, all day. Perhaps even I never saw him at his best, for his former master sent his duty with him, "and if I wished the bird to come out very strong, would I be so good as show him a drunken man"—which I never did, having (unfortunately) none but sober people at hand. But I could hardly have respected him more, whatever the stimulating influences of this sight might have been. He had not the least respect, I am sorry to say, for me in return, or for anybody but the cook; to whom he was attached—but only, I fear, as a Policeman might have been. Once, I met him unexpectedly, about half-a-mile off, walking down the middle of the public street, attended by a pretty large crowd, and spontaneously exhibiting the whole of his accomplishments. His gravity under those trying circumstances, I never can forget, nor the extraordinary gallantry with which, refusing to be brought home, he defended himself behind a pump, until overpowered by numbers. It may have been that he was too bright a genius to live long, or it may have been that he took some pernicious substance into his bill, and thence into his maw—which is not improbable, seeing that he new-pointed the greater part of the garden-wall by digging out the mortar, broke countless squares of glass by scraping away the putty all round the frames, and tore up and swallowed, in splinters, the greater part of a wooden staircase of six steps and a landing—but after some three years he too was taken ill, and died before the kitchen fire. He kept his eye to the last upon the meat as it roasted, and suddenly turned over on his back with a sepulchral cry of "Cuckoo!" Since then I have been ravenless.

Of the story of BARNABY RUDGE itself, I do not think I can say anything here, more to the purpose than the following passages from the original Preface.

"No account of the Gordon Riots having been to my knowledge introduced into any Work of Fiction, and the subject presenting very extraordinary and remarkable features, I was led to project this Tale.

"It is unnecessary to say, that those shameful tumults, while they reflect indelible disgrace upon the time in which they occurred, and all who had act or part in them, teach a good lesson. That what we falsely call a religious cry is easily raised by men who have no religion, and who in their daily practice set at nought the commonest principles of right and wrong; that it is begotten of intolerance and persecution; that it is senseless, besotted, inveterate, and unmerciful; all History teaches us. But perhaps we do not know it in our hearts too well, to profit by even so humble an example as the 'No Popery' riots of Seventeen Hundred and Eighty.

"However imperfectly those disturbances are set forth in the following pages, they are impartially painted by one who has no sympathy with the Romish Church, although he acknowledges, as most men do, some esteemed friends among the followers of its creed.

"It may be observed that, in the description of the principal out-rages, reference has been had to the best authorities of that time, such as they are; and that the account given in this Tale, of all the main features of the Riots, is substantially correct.

"It may be further remarked, that Mr. Dennis's allusions to the flourishing condition of his trade in those days, have their foundation in Truth, and not in the Author's fancy. Any file of old Newspapers, or odd volume of the Annual Register, will prove this, with terrible ease.

"Even the case of Mary Jones, dwelt upon with so much pleasure by the same character, is no effort of invention. The facts were stated, exactly as they are stated here, in the House of Commons. Whether they afforded as much entertainment to the merry gentlemen assembled there, as some other most affecting circum-stances of a similar nature mentioned by Sir Samuel Romilly, is not recorded."

That the case of Mary Jones may speak the more emphatically for itself, I now subjoin it, as related by SIR WILLIAM MEREDITH* in a speech in Parliament, "on Frequent Executions," made in 1777.

"Under this act," the Shop-lifting Act,* "one Mary Jones was executed, whose case I shall just mention; it was at the time when press-warrants were issued, on the alarm about Falkland Islands.* The woman's husband was pressed,* their goods seized for some debts of his, and she, with two small children, turned into the streets a-begging. It is a circumstance not to be forgotten, that she was very young (under nineteen), and most remarkably handsome. She went to a linen-draper's shop, took some coarse linen off the counter, and slipped it under her cloak; the shopman saw her, and she laid it down: for this she was hanged. Her defence was (I have the trial in my pocket), 'that she had lived in credit, and wanted for nothing, till a press-gang came and stole her husband from her; but, since then, she had no bed to lie on; nothing to give her children to eat; and they were almost naked; and perhaps she might have done something wrong, for she hardly knew what she did.' The parish officers testi-fied the truth of this story; but it seems, there had been a good deal of shop-lifting about Ludgate; an example was thought necessary; and this woman was hanged for the comfort and satisfaction of shop-keepers in Ludgate Street. When brought to receive sentence, she

behaved in such a frantic manner, as proved her mind to be in a
distracted and desponding state; and the child was sucking at her
breast when she set out for Tyburn.*"

LONDON,
    *March*, 1849.

# BARNABY RUDGE.

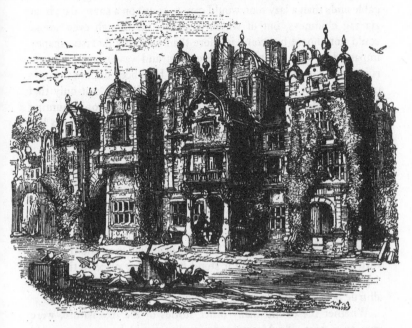

## CHAPTER THE FIRST.

N the year 1775, there stood upon the borders of Epping Forest, at a distance of about twelve miles from London—measuring from the Standard in Cornhill* or rather from the spot on or near to which the Standard used to be in days of yore—a house of public entertainment called the Maypole; which fact was demonstrated to all such travellers as could neither read nor write (and sixty-six years ago a vast number both of travellers and stay-at-homes were in this condition) by the emblem reared on the roadside over against the house, which, if not of those goodly proportions that Maypoles were wont to present in olden times, was a fair young ash, thirty feet in height, and straight as any arrow that ever English yeoman drew.

The Maypole—by which term from henceforth is meant the

house, and not its sign—the Maypole was an old building, with more
gable ends than a lazy man would care to count on a sunny day; huge
zig-zag chimneys, out of which it seemed as though even smoke
could not choose but come in more than naturally fantastic shapes,
imparted to it in its tortuous progress; and vast stables, gloomy,
ruinous and empty. The place was said to have been built in the days
of King Henry the Eighth; and there was a legend, not only that
Queen Elizabeth had slept there one night while upon a hunting
excursion, to wit in a certain oak-panneled room with a deep bay
window, but that next morning, while standing on a mounting block
before the door with one foot in the stirrup, the virgin monarch had
then and there boxed and cuffed an unlucky page for some neglect of
duty. The matter-of-fact and doubtful folks, of whom there were a
few among the Maypole customers, as unluckily there always are in
every little community, were inclined to look upon this tradition as
rather apocryphal; but whenever the landlord of that ancient hostelry appealed to the mounting block itself as evidence, and triumphantly pointed out that there it stood in the same place to that very
day, the doubters never failed to be put down by a large majority, and
all true believers exulted as in a victory.

Whether these, and many other stories of the like nature, were
true or untrue, the Maypole was really an old house, a very old
house, perhaps as old as it claimed to be, and perhaps older, which
will sometimes happen with houses of an uncertain, as with ladies of
a certain age. Its windows were old diamond pane lattices, its floors
were sunken and uneven, its ceilings blackened by the hand of time
and heavy with massive beams. Over the doorway was an ancient
porch, quaintly and grotesquely carved; and here on summer evenings the more favoured customers smoked and drank—ay, and sang
many a good song too, sometimes—reposing on two grim-looking
high backed settles, which, like the twin dragons of some fairy tale,
guarded the entrance to the mansion.

In the chimneys of the disused rooms, swallows had built their
nests for many a long year, and from earliest spring to latest autumn
whole colonies of sparrows chirped and twittered in the eaves. There
were more pigeons about the dreary stable yard and outbuildings
than anybody but the landlord could reckon up. The wheeling and
circling flights of runts, fantails, tumblers, and pouters, were perhaps
not quite consistent with the grave and sober character of the

building, but the monotonous cooing, which never ceased to be raised by some among them all day long, suited it exactly, and seemed to lull it to rest. With its overhanging stories, drowsy little panes of glass, and front bulging out and projecting over the pathway, the old house looked as if it were nodding in its sleep. Indeed it needed no very great stretch of fancy to detect in it other resemblances to humanity. The bricks of which it was built had originally been a deep dark red, but had grown yellow and discoloured like an old man's skin; the sturdy timbers had decayed like teeth; and here and there the ivy, like a warm garment to comfort it in its age, wrapt its green leaves closely round the time-worn walls.

It was a hale and hearty age though, still: and in the summer or autumn evenings, when the glow of the setting sun fell upon the oak and chestnut trees of the adjacent forest, the old house, partaking of its lustre, seemed their fit companion, and to have many good years of life in him yet.

The evening with which we have to do, was neither a summer nor an autumn one, but the twilight of a day in March, when the wind howled dismally among the bare branches of the trees, and rumbling in the wide chimneys and driving the rain against the windows of the Maypole Inn, gave such of its frequenters as chanced to be there at the moment, an undeniable reason for prolonging their stay, and caused the landlord to prophesy that the night would certainly clear at eleven o'clock precisely,—which by a remarkable coincidence was the hour at which he always closed his house.

The name of him upon whom the spirit of prophecy thus descended was John Willet, a burly, large-headed man with a fat face, which betokened profound obstinacy and slowness of apprehension, combined with a very strong reliance upon his own merits. It was John Willet's ordinary boast in his more placid moods that if he was slow he was sure; which assertion could in one sense at least be by no means gainsaid, seeing that he was in everything unquestionably the reverse of fast, and withal one of the most dogged and positive fellows in existence—always sure that what he thought or said or did was right, and holding it as a thing quite settled and ordained by the laws of nature and Providence, that anybody who said or did or thought otherwise must be inevitably and of necessity wrong.

Mr. Willet walked slowly up to the window, flattened his fat nose against the cold glass, and shading his eyes that his sight might not be affected by the ruddy glow of the fire, looked abroad. Then he walked slowly back to his old seat in the chimney-corner, and, composing himself in it with a slight shiver, such as a man might give way to and so acquire an additional relish for the warm blaze, said, looking round upon his guests:

"It'll clear at eleven o'clock. No sooner and no later. Not before and not arterwards."

"How do you make out that?" said a little man in the opposite corner. "The moon is past the full, and she rises at nine."

John looked sedately and solemnly at his questioner until he had brought his mind to bear upon the whole of his observation, and then made answer, in a tone which seemed to imply that the moon was peculiarly his business and nobody else's:

"Never you mind about the moon. Don't you trouble yourself about her. You let the moon alone, and I'll let you alone."

"No offence I hope?" said the little man.

Again John waited leisurely until the observation had thoroughly penetrated to his brain, and then replying, "No offence *as yet*," applied a light to his pipe and smoked in placid silence; now and then casting a sidelong look at a man wrapped in a loose riding-coat with huge cuffs ornamented with tarnished silver lace and large metal buttons, who sat apart from the regular frequenters of the house, and wearing a hat flapped over his face, which was still further shaded by the hand on which his forehead rested, looked unsociable enough.

There was another guest, who sat, booted and spurred, at some distance from the fire also, and whose thoughts—to judge from his folded arms and knitted brows, and from the untasted liquor before him—were occupied with other matters than the topics under discussion or the persons who discussed them. This was a young man of about eight-and-twenty, rather above the middle height, and though of a somewhat slight figure, gracefully and strongly made. He wore his own dark hair, and was accoutred in a riding-dress, which, together with his large boots (resembling in shape and fashion those worn by our Life Guardsmen* at the present day), showed indisputable traces of the bad condition of the roads. But travel-stained though he was, he was well and even richly attired, and without being over-dressed looked a gallant gentleman.

Lying upon the table beside him, as he had carelessly thrown them down, were a heavy riding-whip and a slouched hat, the latter worn no doubt as being best suited to the inclemency of the weather. There, too, were a pair of pistols in a holster-case, and a short riding-cloak. Little of his face was visible, except the long dark lashes which concealed his downcast eyes, but an air of careless ease and natural gracefulness of demeanour pervaded the figure, and seemed to comprehend even these slight accessories, which were all handsome, and in good keeping.

Towards this young gentleman the eyes of Mr. Willet wandered but once, and then as if in mute inquiry whether he had observed his silent neighbour. It was plain that John and the young gentleman had often met before. Finding that his look was not returned, or indeed observed by the person to whom it was addressed, John gradually concentrated the whole power of his eyes into one focus, and brought it to bear upon the man in the flapped hat, at whom he came to stare in course of time with an intensity so remarkable, that it affected his fireside cronies, who all, as with one accord, took their pipes from their lips, and stared with open mouths at the stranger likewise.

The sturdy landlord had a large pair of dull fish-like eyes, and the little man who had hazarded the remark about the moon (and who was the parish clerk and bell-ringer of Chigwell;* a village hard by,) had little round black shiny eyes like beads; moreover this little man wore at the knees of his rusty black breeches, and on his rusty black coat, and all down his long flapped waistcoat, little queer buttons like nothing except his eyes; but so like them, that as they twinkled and glistened in the light of the fire, which shone too in his bright shoe-buckles, he seemed all eyes from head to foot, and to be gazing with every one of them at the unknown customer. No wonder that a man should grow restless under such an inspection as this, to say nothing of the eyes belonging to short Tom Cobb the general chandler and post-office keeper, and long Phil Parkes the ranger, both of whom, infected by the example of their companions, regarded him of the flapped hat no less attentively.

The stranger became restless; perhaps from being exposed to this raking fire of eyes, perhaps from the nature of his previous meditations—most probably from the latter cause, for as he changed his position and looked hastily round, he started to find himself the object of such keen regard, and darted an angry and suspicious glance at the fireside group. It had the effect of immediately diverting all eyes to the chimney, except those of John Willet, who finding himself, as it were, caught in the fact, and not being (as has been already observed) of a very ready nature, remained staring at his guest in a particularly awkward and disconcerted manner.

"Well?" said the stranger.

Well. There was not much in well. It was not a long speech. "I thought you gave an order," said the landlord, after a pause of two or three minutes for consideration.

The stranger took off his hat, and disclosed the hard features of a man of sixty or thereabouts, much weather-beaten and worn by time, and the naturally harsh expression of which was not improved by a dark handkerchief which was bound tightly round his head, and, while it served the purpose of a wig, shaded his forehead, and almost hid his eyebrows. If it were intended to conceal or divert attention from a deep gash, now healed into an ugly seam, which when it was first inflicted must have laid bare his cheekbone, the object was but indifferently attained, for it could scarcely fail to be noted at a glance. His complexion was of a cadaverous hue, and he had a grizzly jagged beard of some three weeks' date. Such was the figure (very meanly and poorly clad) that now rose from the seat, and stalking across the room sat down in a corner of the chimney, which the politeness or fears of the little clerk very readily assigned to him.

"A highwayman!" whispered Tom Cobb to Parkes the ranger.

"Do you suppose highwaymen don't dress handsomer than that?" replied Parkes. "It's a better business than you think for, Tom, and highwaymen don't need or use to be shabby, take my word for it."

Meanwhile, the subject of their speculations had done due honour to the house by calling for some drink, which was promptly supplied by the landlord's son Joe, a broad-shouldered strapping young fellow of twenty, whom it pleased his father still to consider a little boy, and to treat accordingly. Stretching out his hands to warm them by the blazing fire, the man turned his head towards the company, and after running his eye sharply over them, said in a voice well suited to his appearance:

"What house is that which stands a mile or so from here?"

"Public-house?" said the landlord, with his usual deliberation.

"Public-house, father!" exclaimed Joe, "where's the public-house within a mile or so of the Maypole? He means the great house—the Warren*—naturally and of course. The old red brick house, sir, that stands in its own grounds—?"

"Ay," said the stranger.

"And that fifteen or twenty years ago stood in a park five times as broad, which with other and richer property has bit by bit changed hands and dwindled away—more's the pity!" pursued the young man.

"Maybe," was the reply. "But my question related to the owner. What it has been I don't care to know, and what it is I can see for myself."

The heir-apparent to the Maypole pressed his finger on his lips, and glancing at the young gentleman already noticed, who had changed his attitude when the house was first mentioned, replied in a lower tone,

"The owner's name is Haredale, Mr. Geoffrey Haredale, and"— again he glanced in the same direction as before—"and a worthy gentleman too—hem!"

Paying as little regard to this admonitory cough, as to the

significant gesture that had preceded it, the stranger pursued his questioning.

"I turned out of my way coming here, and took the footpath that crosses the grounds. Who was the young lady that I saw entering a carriage? His daughter?"

"Why, how should I know, honest man?" replied Joe, contriving in the course of some arrangements about the hearth, to advance close to his questioner and pluck him by the sleeve, "*I* didn't see the young lady you know. Whew! There's the wind again—*and* rain—well it *is* a night!"

"Rough weather indeed!" observed the strange man.

"You're used to it?" said Joe, catching at anything which seemed to promise a diversion of the subject.

"Pretty well," returned the other. "About the young lady—has Mr. Haredale a daughter?"

"No, no," said the young fellow fretfully, "he's a single gentleman—he's—be quiet, can't you, man? Don't you see this talk is not relished yonder?"

Regardless of this whispered remonstrance and affecting not to hear it, his tormentor provokingly continued:

"Single men have had daughters before now. Perhaps she may be his daughter, though he is not married."

"What do you mean?" said Joe, adding in an under tone as he approached him again, "You'll come in for it presently, I know you will!"

"I mean no harm"—returned the traveller boldly, "and have said none that I know of. I ask a few questions—as any stranger may, and not unnaturally—about the inmates of a remarkable house in a neighbourhood which is new to me, and you are as aghast and disturbed as if I were talking treason against King George. Perhaps you can tell me why, sir, for (as I say) I am a stranger, and this is Greek to me?"

The latter observation was addressed to the obvious cause of Joe Willet's discomposure, who had risen and was adjusting his riding-cloak preparatory to sallying abroad. Briefly replying that he could give him no information, the young man beckoned to Joe, and handing him a piece of money in payment of his reckoning, hurried out attended by young Willet himself, who taking up a candle followed to light him to the house door.

While Joe was absent on this errand, the elder Willet and his three companions continued to smoke with profound gravity, and in a deep silence, each having his eyes fixed on a huge copper boiler that was suspended over the fire. After some time John Willet slowly shook his head, and thereupon his friends slowly shook theirs; but no man withdrew his eyes from the boiler, or altered the solemn expression of his countenance in the slightest degree.

At length Joe returned—very talkative and conciliatory, as though with a strong presentiment that he was going to be found fault with.

"Such a thing as love is!" he said, drawing a chair near the fire, and looking round for sympathy. "He has set off to walk to London,—all the way to London. His nag gone lame in riding out here this blessed afternoon, and comfortably littered down in our stable at this minute; and he giving up a good hot supper and our best bed, because Miss Haredale has gone to a masquerade up in town, and he has set his heart upon seeing her! I don't think I could persuade myself to do that, beautiful as she is,—but then I'm not in love, (at least I don't think I am,) and that's the whole difference."

"He is in love then?" said the stranger.

"Rather," replied Joe. "He'll never be more in love, and may very easily be less."

"Silence sir!" cried his father.

"What a chap you are Joe!" said Long Parkes.

"Such a inconsiderate lad!" murmured Tom Cobb.

"Putting himself forward and wringing the very nose off his own father's face!" exclaimed the parish clerk, metaphorically.

"What *have* I done?" reasoned poor Joe.

"Silence sir!" returned his father, "what do you mean by talking, when you see people that are more than two or three times your age, sitting still and silent and not dreaming of saying a word?"

"Why that's the proper time for me to talk, isn't it?" said Joe rebelliously.

"The proper time sir!" retorted his father, "the proper time's no time."

"Ah to be sure!" muttered Parkes, nodding gravely to the other two who nodded likewise, observing under their breaths that that was the point.

"The proper time's no time sir," repeated John Willet; "when I was your age I never talked, I never wanted to talk, I listened and improved myself, that's what *I* did."

"And you'd find your father rather a tough customer in argeyment, Joe, if anybody was to try and tackle him"—said Parkes.

"For the matter o' that Phil!" observed Mr. Willet, blowing a long, thin, spiral cloud of smoke out of the corner of his mouth, and staring at it abstractedly as it floated away; "For the matter o' that, Phil, argeyment is a gift of Natur. If Natur has gifted a man with powers of argeyment, a man has a right to make the best of 'em, and has not a right to stand on false delicacy, and deny that he is so gifted; for that is a turning of his back on Natur, a flouting of her, a slighting of her precious caskets, and a proving of one's self to be a swine that isn't worth her scattering pearls before."

The landlord pausing here for a very long time, Mr. Parkes naturally concluded that he had brought his discourse to an end; and therefore, turning to the young man with some austerity, exclaimed:

"You hear what your father says, Joe? You wouldn't much like to tackle him in argeyment, I'm thinking sir."

"—If," said John Willet, turning his eyes from the ceiling to the face of his interrupter, and uttering the monosyllable in capitals, to apprise him that he had put in his oar, as the vulgar say, with unbecoming and irreverent haste; "If, sir, Natur has fixed upon me the gift of argeyment, why should I not own to it, and rather glory in the same? Yes sir, I *am* a tough customer that way. You are right sir. My toughness has been proved, sir, in this room many and many a time, as I think you know; and if you don't know," added John, putting his pipe in his mouth again, "so much the better, for I an't proud and am not a going to tell you."

A general murmur from his three cronies, and a general shaking of heads at the copper boiler, assured John Willet that they had had good experience of his powers and needed no further evidence to assure them of his superiority. John smoked with a little more dignity and surveyed them in silence.

"It's all very fine talking," muttered Joe, who had been fidgeting in his chair with divers uneasy gestures. "But if you mean to tell me that I'm never to open my lips—"

"Silence sir!" roared his father. "No, you never are. When your opinion's wanted, you give it. When you're spoke to, you speak. When your opinion's not wanted and you're not spoke to, don't you give an opinion and don't you speak. The world's undergone a nice alteration since my time, certainly. My belief is that there an't any boys left—that there isn't such a thing as a boy—that there's nothing now between a male baby and a man—and that all the boys went out with his blessed Majesty King George the Second."

"That's a very true observation, always excepting the young princes," said the parish-clerk, who, as the representative of church and state in that company, held himself bound to the nicest loyalty. "If it's godly and righteous for boys, being of the ages of boys, to behave themselves like boys, then the young princes must be boys and cannot be otherwise."

"Did you ever hear tell of mermaids, sir?" said Mr. Willet.

"Certainly I have," replied the clerk.

"Very good," said Mr. Willet. "According to the constitution of mermaids, so much of a mermaid as is not a woman must be a fish. According to the constitution of young princes, so much of a young prince (if anything) as is not actually an angel, must be godly and righteous. Therefore if it's becoming and godly and righteous in the young princes (as it is at their ages) that they should be boys, they are and must be boys, and cannot by possibility be anything else."

This elucidation of a knotty point being received with such marks of approval as to put John Willet into a good humour, he contented himself with repeating to his son his command of silence, and addressing the stranger, said:

"If you had asked your questions of a grown-up person—of me or any of these gentlemen—you'd have had some satisfaction, and wouldn't have wasted breath. Miss Haredale is Mr. Geoffrey Haredale's niece."

"Is her father alive?" said the man carelessly.

"No," rejoined the landlord, "he is not alive, and he is not dead—"

"Not dead!" cried the other.

"Not dead in a common sort of way," said the landlord.

The cronies nodded to each other, and Mr. Parkes remarked in an under tone, shaking his head meanwhile as who should say, "let no man contradict me, for I won't believe him," that John Willet was in amazing force to-night, and fit to tackle a Chief Justice.

The stranger suffered a short pause to elapse, and then asked abruptly, "What do you mean?"

"More than you think for, friend," returned John Willet. "Perhaps there's more meaning in them words than you suspect."

"Perhaps there is," said the strange man, gruffly; "but what the devil do you speak in such mysteries for? You tell me first that a man is not alive, nor yet dead—then that he's not dead in a common sort of way—then, that you mean a great deal more than I think for. To tell you the truth, you may do that easily; for so far as I can make out, you mean nothing. What *do* you mean, I ask again?"

"That," returned the landlord, a little brought down from his dignity by the stranger's surliness, "is a Maypole story, and has been any time these four-and-twenty years. That story is Solomon Daisy's story. It belongs to the house; and nobody but Solomon Daisy has ever told it under this roof, or ever shall—that's more."

The man glanced at the parish-clerk, whose air of consciousness and importance plainly betokened him to be the person referred to, and, observing that he had taken his pipe from his lips, after a very long whiff to keep it alight, and was evidently about to tell his story without further solicitation, gathered his large coat about him, and shrinking further back was almost lost in the gloom of the spacious chimney corner, except when the flame, struggling from under a great faggot whose weight almost crushed it for the time, shot upward with a strong and sudden glare, and illumining his figure for a moment, seemed afterwards to cast it into deeper obscurity than before.

By this flickering light, which made the old room, with its heavy timbers and panneled walls, look as if it were built of polished ebony—the wind roaring and howling without, now rattling the latch and creaking the hinges of the stout oaken door, and now driving at the casement as though it would beat it in—by this light, and under circumstances so auspicious, Solomon Daisy began his tale:

"It was Mr. Reuben Haredale, Mr. Geoffrey's elder brother—"

Here he came to a dead stop, and made so long a pause that even John Willet grew impatient and asked why he did not proceed.

"Cobb," said Solomon Daisy, dropping his voice and appealing to the post-office keeper; "what day of the month is this?"

"The nineteenth."

"Of March," said the clerk, bending forward, "the nineteenth of March; that's very strange."

In a low voice they all acquiesced, and Solomon went on:

"It was Mr. Reuben Haredale, Mr. Geoffrey's elder brother, that twenty-two years ago was the owner of the Warren, which, as Joe has said—not that you remember it, Joe, for a boy like you can't do that, but because you have often heard me say so—was then a much larger and better place, and a much more valuable property than it is now. His lady was lately dead, and he was left with one child—the Miss Haredale you have been inquiring about—who was then scarcely a year old."

Although the speaker addressed himself to the man who had shown so much curiosity about this same family, and made a pause here as if expecting some exclamation of surprise or encouragement, the latter made no remark, nor gave any indication that he heard or was interested in what was said. Solomon therefore turned to his old companions, whose noses were brightly illuminated by the deep red glow from the bowls of their pipes; assured, by long experience, of their attention, and resolved to show his sense of such indecent behaviour.

"Mr. Haredale," said Solomon, turning his back upon the strange man, "left this place when his lady died, feeling it lonely like, and went up to London, where he stopped some months; but finding that place as lonely as this—as I suppose and have always heard say—he suddenly came back again with his little girl to the Warren, bringing with him besides, that day, only two women servants, and his steward, and a gardener."

Mr. Daisy stopped to take a whiff at his pipe, which was going out, and then proceeded—at first in a snuffling tone, occasioned by keen enjoyment of the tobacco and strong pulling at the pipe, and afterwards with increasing distinctness:

"—Bringing with him two women servants, and his steward and a gardener. The rest stopped behind up in London, and were to follow next day. It happened that that night, an old gentleman who lived at Chigwell-row, and had long been poorly, deceased, and an order came to me at half after twelve o'clock at night to go and toll the passing-bell."

There was a movement in the little group of listeners, sufficiently indicative of the strong repugnance any one of them would have felt to have turned out at such a time upon such an errand. The clerk felt and understood it, and pursued his theme accordingly.

"It *was* a dreary thing, especially as the grave-digger was laid up in his bed, from long working in a damp soil and sitting down to take his dinner on cold tombstones, and I was consequently under obligation to go alone, for it was too late to hope to get any other companion. However, I wasn't unprepared for it; as the old gentleman had often made it a request that the bell should be tolled as soon as possible after the breath was out of his body, and he had been expected to go for some days. I put as good a face upon it as I could, and muffling myself up (for it was mortal cold), started out with a lighted lantern in one hand and the key of the church in the other."

At this point of the narrative, the dress of the strange man rustled as if he had turned himself to hear more distinctly. Slightly pointing over his shoulder, Solomon elevated his eyebrows and nodded a silent inquiry to Joe whether this was the case. Joe shaded his eyes with his hand and peered into the corner, but could make out nothing, and so shook his head.

"It was just such a night as this; blowing a hurricane, raining heavily, and very dark—I often think now, darker than I ever saw it before or since; that may be my fancy, but the houses were all close shut and the folks in-doors, and perhaps there is only one other man who knows how dark it really was. I got into the church, chained the door back so that it should keep ajar—for to tell the truth, I didn't like to be shut in there alone—and putting my lantern on the stone seat in the little corner where the bell-rope is, sat down beside it to trim the candle.

"I sat down to trim the candle, and when I had done so, I could not persuade myself to get up again and go about my work. I don't know how it was, but I thought of all the ghost stories I had ever heard, even those that I had heard when I was a boy at school, and had forgotten long ago; and they didn't come into my mind one after another, but all crowding at once, like. I recollected one story there was in the village, how that on a certain night in the year (it might be that very night for anything I knew), all the dead people came out of the ground and sat at the heads of their own graves till morning. This made me think how many people I had known were buried between the church door and the churchyard gate, and what a dreadful thing it would be to have to pass among them and know them again, so earthy and unlike themselves. I had known all the niches and arches in the church from a child; still I couldn't persuade myself that those were their natural shadows which I saw on the pavement, but felt sure there were some ugly figures hiding among 'em and peeping out. Thinking on in this way, I began to think of the old gentleman who was just dead, and I could have sworn, as I looked up the dark chancel, that I saw him in his usual place, wrapping his shroud about him and shivering as if he felt it cold. All this time I sat listening and listening, and hardly dared to breathe. At length I started up and took the bell-rope in my hands. At that minute there rang—not that bell, for I had hardly touched the rope—but another!

"I heard the ringing of another bell, and a deep bell too, plainly. It was only for an instant, and even then the wind carried the sound away, but I heard it. I listened for a long time, but it rang no more. I had heard of corpse candles,* and at last I persuaded myself that this must be a corpse bell tolling of itself at midnight for the dead. I tolled my bell—how, or how long, I don't know—and ran home to bed as fast as I could touch the ground.

"I was up early next morning after a restless night, and told the story to my neighbours. Some were serious and some made light of it: I don't think anybody believed it real. But that morning, Mr. Reuben Haredale was found murdered in his bedchamber, and in his hand was a piece of the cord attached to an alarm-bell outside the roof, which hung in his room and had been cut asunder, no doubt by the murderer when he seized it.

That was the bell I heard.

"A bureau was found opened, and a cash-box, which Mr. Haredale had brought down that day, and was supposed to contain a large sum of money, was gone. The steward and gardener were both missing and both suspected for a long time, but they were never found, though hunted far and wide. And far enough they might have looked for poor Mr. Rudge the steward, whose body—scarcely to be recognized but by his clothes and the watch and ring he wore—was found, months afterwards, at the bottom of a piece of water in the grounds, with a deep gash in the breast where he had been stabbed with a knife. He was only partly dressed; and people all agreed that he had been sitting up reading in his own room, where there were many traces of blood, and was suddenly fallen upon and killed before his master.

"Everybody now knew that the gardener must be the murderer, and though he has never been heard of from that time to this, he will be, mark my words. The crime was committed this day two-and-twenty years—on the nineteenth of March, one thousand seven hundred and fifty-three. On the nineteenth of March in some year, no matter when—I know it, I am sure of it, for we have always, in some strange way or other, been brought back to the subject on that day ever since—on the nineteenth of March in some year, sooner or later, that man will be discovered."

## CHAPTER THE SECOND.

"A STRANGE story!" said the man who had been the cause of the narration.—"Stranger still if it comes about as you predict. Is that all?"

A question so unexpected nettled Solomon Daisy not a little. By dint of relating the story very often, and ornamenting it (according to village report) with a few flourishes suggested by the various hearers from time to time, he had come by degrees to tell it with great effect; and "is that all?" after the climax, was not what he was accustomed to.

"Is that all!" he repeated, "yes, that's all sir. And enough too, I think."

"I think so too. My horse, young man. He is but a hack hired from a road-side posting house, but he must carry me to London to-night."

"To-night!" said Joe.

"To-night," returned the other. "What do you stare at? This tavern would seem to be a house of call for all the gaping idlers of the neighbourhood!"

At this remark, which evidently had reference to the scrutiny he had undergone, as mentioned in the foregoing chapter, the eyes of John Willet and his friends were diverted with marvellous rapidity to the copper boiler again. Not so with Joe, who, being a mettlesome fellow, returned the stranger's angry glance with a steady look, and rejoined:

"It's not a very bold thing to wonder at your going on to-night. Surely you have been asked such a harmless question in an inn before, and in better weather than this. I thought you mightn't know the way, as you seem strange to this part."

"The way—" repeated the other, irritably.

"Yes. *Do* you know it?"

"I'll—humph!—I'll find it," replied the man, waving his hand and turning on his heel. "Landlord, take the reckoning here."

John Willet did as he was desired; for on that point he was seldom slow, except in the particulars of giving change, and testing the goodness of any piece of coin that was proffered to him, by the application of his teeth or his tongue, or some other test, or, in doubtful cases, by a long series of tests terminating in its rejection. The guest then wrapt his garments about him so as to shelter himself as effectually as he could from the rough weather, and without any word or sign of farewell betook himself to the stable-yard. Here Joe (who had left the room on the conclusion of their short dialogue) was protecting himself and the horse from the rain under the shelter of an old pent-house roof.

"He's pretty much of my opinion," said Joe, patting the horse upon the neck; "I'll wager that your stopping here to-night would please him better than it would please me."

"He and I are of different opinions, as we have been more than once on our way here," was the short reply.

"So I was thinking before you came out, for he has felt your spurs, poor beast."

The stranger adjusted his coat-collar about his face, and made no answer.

"You'll know me again, I see," he said, marking the young fellow's earnest gaze, when he had sprung into the saddle.

"The man's worth knowing, master, who travels a road he don't know, mounted on a jaded horse, and leaves good quarters to do it on such a night as this."

"You have sharp eyes and a sharp tongue I find."

"Both I hope by nature, but the last grows rusty sometimes for want of using."

"Use the first less too, and keep their sharpness for your sweet-hearts, boy," said the man.

So saying he shook his hand from the bridle, struck him roughly on the head with the butt end of his whip, and galloped away; dashing through the mud and darkness with a headlong speed, which few badly mounted horsemen would have cared to venture, even had they been thoroughly acquainted with the country; and which, to

one who knew nothing of the way he rode, was attended at every step with great hazard and danger.

The roads even within twelve miles of London were at that time ill paved, seldom repaired, and very badly made. The way this rider traversed had been ploughed up by the wheels of heavy wagons, and rendered rotten by the frosts and thaws of the preceding winter, or possibly of many winters. Great holes and gaps had worn into the soil, which, being now filled with water from the late rains, were not easily distinguishable even by day; and a plunge into any one of them might have brought down a surer-footed horse than the poor beast now urged forward to the utmost extent of his powers. Sharp flints and stones rolled from under his hoofs continually; the rider could scarcely see beyond the animal's head, or further on either side than his own arm would have extended. At that time, too, all the roads in the neighbourhood of the metropolis were infested by footpads or highwaymen, and it was a night, of all others, in which any evil-disposed person of this class might have pursued his unlawful calling with little fear of detection.

Still, the traveller dashed forward at the same reckless pace, regardless alike of the dirt and wet which flew about his head, the profound darkness of the night, and the probability of encountering some desperate characters abroad. At every turn and angle, even where a deviation from the direct course might have been least expected, and could not possibly be seen until he was close upon it, he guided the bridle with an unerring hand and kept the middle of the road. Thus he sped onward, raising himself in the stirrups, leaning his body forward until it almost touched the horse's neck, and flourishing his heavy whip above his head with the fervour of a madman.

There are times when, the elements being in unusual commotion, those who are bent on daring enterprises, or agitated by great thoughts whether of good or evil, feel a mysterious sympathy with the tumult of nature and are roused into corresponding violence. In the midst of thunder, lightning, and storm, many tremendous deeds have been committed; men self-possessed before, have given a sudden loose to passions they could no longer control. The demons of wrath and despair have striven to emulate those who ride the whirlwind and direct the storm;* and man, lashed into madness with the roaring winds and boiling waters, has become for the time as wild and merciless as the elements themselves.

Whether the traveller was possessed by thoughts which the fury of the night had heated and stimulated into a quicker current, or was merely impelled by some strong motive to reach his journey's end, on he swept more like a hunted phantom than a man, nor checked his pace until, arriving at some cross roads one of which led by a longer route to the place whence he had lately started, he bore down so suddenly upon a vehicle which was coming towards him, that in the effort to avoid it he well nigh pulled his horse upon his haunches, and narrowly escaped being thrown.

"Yoho!" cried the voice of a man. "What's that? who goes there?"

"A friend!" replied the traveller.

"A friend!" repeated the voice. "Who calls himself a friend and rides like that, abusing Heaven's gifts in the shape of horseflesh, and endangering, not only his own neck, which might be no great matter, but the necks of other people?"

"You have a lantern there, I see," said the traveller dismounting, "lend it me for a moment. You have wounded my horse, I think, with your shaft or wheel."

"Wounded him!" cried the other, "if I haven't killed him, it's no fault of yours. What do you mean by galloping along the king's highway like that, eh?"

"Give me the light," returned the traveller, snatching it from his hand, "and don't ask idle questions of a man who is in no mood for talking."

"If you had said you were in no mood for talking before, I should perhaps have been in no mood for lighting," said the voice. "Hows'ever as it's the poor horse that's damaged and not you, one of you is welcome to the light at all events—but it's not the crusty one."

The traveller returned no answer to this speech, but holding the light near to his panting and reeking beast, examined him in limb and carcase. Meanwhile the other man sat very composedly in his vehicle, which was a kind of chaise with a depository for a large bag of tools, and watched his proceedings with a careful eye.

The looker-on was a round, red-faced, sturdy yeoman, with a double chin, and a voice husky with good living, good sleeping, good humour, and good health. He was past the prime of life, but Father Time is not always a hard parent, and, though he tarries for none of his children, often lays his hand lightly upon those who have used him well; making them old men and women inexorably enough, but leaving their hearts and spirits young and in full vigour. With such people the grey head is but the impression of the old fellow's hand in giving them his blessing, and every wrinkle but a notch in the quiet calendar of a well-spent life.

The person whom the traveller had so abruptly encountered was of this kind, bluff, hale, hearty, and in a green old age: at peace with himself, and evidently disposed to be so with all the world. Although muffled up in divers coats and handkerchiefs—one of which, passed over his crown and tied in a convenient crease of his double chin, secured his three-cornered hat and bob-wig* from blowing off his head—there was no disguising his plump and comfortable figure; neither did certain dirty finger-marks upon his face give it any other than an odd and comical expression, through which its natural good humour shone with undiminished lustre.

"He is not hurt,"—said the traveller at length, raising his head and the lantern together.

"You have found that out at last, have you?" rejoined the old man.

"My eyes have seen more light than yours, but I wouldn't change with you."

"What do you mean?"

"Mean! I could have told you he wasn't hurt, five minutes ago. Give me the light, friend; ride forward at a gentler pace; and good night."

In handing up the lantern, the man necessarily cast its rays full on the speaker's face. Their eyes met at the instant. He suddenly dropped it and crushed it with his foot.

"Saw you never a locksmith before, that you start as if you had come upon a ghost?" cried the old man in the chaise, "or is this," he added hastily, thrusting his hand into the tool basket and drawing out a hammer, "a scheme for robbing me? I know these roads, friend. When I travel them, I carry nothing but a few shillings, and not a crown's worth of them. I tell you plainly, to save us both trouble, that there's nothing to be got from me but a pretty stout arm considering my years, and this tool, which mayhap from long acquaintance with I can use pretty briskly. You shall not have it all your own way, I promise you, if you play at that game." With these words he stood upon the defensive.

"I am not what you take me for, Gabriel Varden," replied the other.

"Then what and who are you?" returned the locksmith. "You know my name it seems. Let me know yours."

"I have not gained the information from any confidence of yours, but from the inscription on your cart which tells it to all the town," replied the traveller.

"You have better eyes for that than you had for your horse then," said Varden, descending nimbly from his chaise; "who are you? Let me see your face."

While the locksmith alighted, the traveller had regained his saddle, from which he now confronted the old man, who, moving as the horse moved in chafing under the tightened rein, kept close beside him.

"Let me see your face, I say."

"Stand off!"

"No masquerading tricks," said the locksmith, "and tales at the club to-morrow how Gabriel Varden was frightened by a surly voice and a dark night. Stand—let me see your face."

Finding that further resistance would only involve him in a personal struggle with an antagonist by no means to be despised, the traveller threw back his coat, and stooping down looked steadily at the locksmith.

Perhaps two men more powerfully contrasted, never opposed each other face to face. The ruddy features of the locksmith so set off and heightened the excessive paleness of the man on horseback, that he looked like a bloodless ghost, while the moisture, which hard riding had brought out upon his skin, hung there in dark and heavy drops, like dews of agony and death. The countenance of the old locksmith was lighted up with the smile of one expecting to detect in this unpromising stranger some latent roguery of eye or lip, which should reveal a familiar person in that arch disguise, and spoil his jest. The face of the other, sullen and fierce, but shrinking too, was that of a man who stood at bay; while his firmly closed jaws, his puckered mouth, and more than all a certain stealthy motion of the hand within his breast, seemed to announce a desperate purpose very foreign to acting, or child's play.

Thus they regarded each other for some time, in silence.

"Humph!" he said when he had scanned his features; "I don't know you."

"Don't desire to!"—returned the other, muffling himself as before.

"I don't," said Gabriel; "to be plain with you, friend, you don't carry in your countenance a letter of recommendation."

"It's not my wish," said the traveller. "My humour is to be avoided."

"Well," said the locksmith bluntly, "I think you'll have your humour."

"I will, at any cost," rejoined the traveller. "In proof of it, lay this to heart—that you were never in such peril of your life as you have been within these few moments; when you are within five minutes of breathing your last, you will not be nearer death than you have been to-night!"

"Aye!" said the sturdy locksmith.

"Aye! and a violent death."

"From whose hand?"

"From mine," replied the traveller.

With that he put spurs to his horse, and rode away; at first plashing heavily through the mire at a smart trot, but gradually increasing in speed until the last sound of his horse's hoofs died away upon the wind; when he was again hurrying on at the same furious gallop, which had been his pace when the locksmith first encountered him.

Gabriel Varden remained standing in the road with the broken lantern in his hand, listening in stupified silence until no sound reached his ear but the moaning of the wind, and the fast-falling rain; when he struck himself one or two smart blows in the breast by way of rousing himself, and broke into an exclamation of surprise.

"What in the name of wonder can this fellow be! a madman? a highwayman? a cut-throat? If he had not scoured off so fast, we'd have seen who was in most danger, he or I. I never nearer death than I have been to-night! I hope I may be no nearer to it for a score of years to come—if so, I'll be content to be no further from it. My stars!—a pretty brag this to a stout man—pooh, pooh!"

Gabriel resumed his seat, and looked wistfully up the road by which the traveller had come; murmuring in a half whisper:

"The Maypole—two miles to the Maypole. I came the other road from the Warren after a long day's work at locks and bells, on purpose that I should not come by the Maypole and break my promise to Martha by looking in—there's resolution! It would be dangerous to go on to London without a light; and it's four miles, and a good half-mile besides, to the Halfway-House; and between this and that is the very place where one needs a light most. Two miles to the Maypole! I told Martha I wouldn't; I said I wouldn't, and I didn't—there's resolution!"

Repeating these two last words very often, as if to compensate for the little resolution he was going to show by piquing himself on the great resolution he had shown, Gabriel Varden quietly turned back, determining to get a light at the Maypole, and to take nothing but a light.

When he got to the Maypole, however, and Joe, responding to his well-known hail, came running out to the horse's head, leaving the door open behind him, and disclosing a delicious perspective of warmth and brightness—when the ruddy gleam of the fire, streaming through the old red curtains of the common room, seemed to bring with it, as part of itself, a pleasant hum of voices, and a fragrant odour of steaming grog and rare tobacco, all steeped as it were in the cheerful glow—when the shadows, flitting across the curtain, showed that those inside had risen from their snug seats, and were making room in the snuggest corner (how well he knew that corner!) for the honest locksmith, and a broad glare, suddenly streaming up, bespoke the goodness of the crackling log from which a brilliant train of sparks was doubtless at that moment whirling up the chimney in honour of his coming—when, superadded to these enticements, there stole upon him from the distant kitchen a gentle sound of frying, with a musical clatter of plates and dishes, and a savoury smell that made even the boisterous wind a perfume—Gabriel felt his firmness oozing rapidly away. He tried to look stoically at the tavern, but his features would relax into a look of fondness. He turned his head the other way, and the cold black country seemed to frown him off, and to drive him for a refuge into its hospitable arms.

"The merciful man, Joe," said the locksmith, "is merciful to his beast. I'll get out for a little while."

And how natural it was to get out. And how unnatural it seemed for a sober man to be plodding wearily along through miry roads, encountering the rude buffets of the wind and pelting of the rain, when there was a clean floor covered with crisp white sand, a well swept hearth, a blazing fire, a table decorated with white cloth, bright pewter flagons, and other tempting preparations for a well-cooked meal—when there were these things, and company disposed to make the most of them, all ready to his hand, and entreating him to enjoyment!

## CHAPTER THE THIRD.

SUCH were the locksmith's thoughts when first seated in the snug corner, and slowly recovering from a pleasant defect of vision—pleasant, because occasioned by the wind blowing in his eyes; which made it a matter of sound policy and duty to himself, that he should take refuge from the weather, and tempted him, for the same reason, to aggravate a slight cough, and declare he felt but poorly. Such were still his thoughts more than a full hour afterwards, when supper over, he still sat with shining jovial face in the same warm nook, listening to the cricket-like chirrup of little Solomon Daisy, and bearing no unimportant or slightly respected part in the social gossip round the Maypole fire.

"I wish he may be an honest man, that's all," said Solomon, winding up a variety of speculations relative to the stranger, concerning whom Gabriel had compared notes with the company, and so raised a grave discussion; "*I* wish he may be an honest man."

"So we all do, I suppose, don't we?" observed the locksmith.

"I don't," said Joe.

"No!" cried Gabriel.

"No. He struck me with his whip, the coward, when he was mounted and I afoot, and I should be better pleased that he turned out what I think him."

"And what may that be, Joe?"

"No good, Mr. Varden. You may shake your head father, but I say no good, and will say no good, and I would say no good a hundred times over, if that would bring him back to have the drubbing he deserves."

"Hold your tongue sir," said John Willet.

"I won't, father. It's all along of you that he dared to do what he did. Seeing me treated like a child, and put down like a fool, *he* plucks up a heart and has a fling at a fellow that he thinks—and may well think too—hasn't a grain of spirit. But he's mistaken, as I'll show him, and as I'll show all of you before long."

"Does the boy know what he's a saying of!" cried the astonished John Willet.

"Father," returned Joe, "I know what I say and mean, well— better than you do when you hear me. I can bear with you, but I cannot bear the contempt that your treating me in the way you do, brings upon me from others every day. Look at other young men of my age. Have they no liberty, no will, no right to speak? Are they obliged to sit mumchance,* and to be ordered about till they are the laughing-stock of young and old? I am a bye-word all over Chigwell, and I say—and it's fairer my saying so now, than waiting till you are dead, and I have got your money—I say that before long I shall be driven to break such bounds, and that when I do, it won't be me that you'll have to blame, but your own self, and no other."

John Willet was so amazed by the exasperation and boldness of his hopeful son, that he sat as one bewildered, staring in a ludicrous manner at the boiler, and endeavouring, but quite ineffectually, to collect his tardy thoughts, and invent an answer. The guests, scarcely less disturbed, were equally at a loss; and at length, with a variety of muttered, half-expressed condolences, and pieces of advice, rose to depart; being at the same time slightly muddled with liquor.

The honest locksmith alone addressed a few words of coherent and sensible advice to both parties, urging John Willet to remember that Joe was nearly arrived at man's estate, and should not be ruled with too tight a hand, and exhorting Joe himself to bear with his father's caprices, and rather endeavour to turn them aside by temperate remonstrance than by ill-timed rebellion. This advice was received as such advice usually is. On John Willet it made almost as much impression as on the sign outside the door, while Joe, who took it in the best part, avowed himself more obliged than he could well express, but politely intimated his intention nevertheless of taking his own course uninfluenced by anybody.

"You have always been a very good friend to me, Mr. Varden," he said, as they stood without the porch, and the locksmith was equipping himself for his journey home; "I take it very kind of you to say all this, but the time's nearly come when the Maypole and I must part company."

"Roving stones gather no moss, Joe," said Gabriel.

"Nor mile-stones much," replied Joe. "I'm little better than one here, and see as much of the world."

"Then what would you do, Joe," pursued the locksmith, stroking his chin reflectively. "What could you be? where could you go, you see?"

"I must trust to chance, Mr. Varden."

"A bad thing to trust to, Joe. I don't like it. I always tell my girl when we talk about a husband for her, never to trust to chance, but to make sure beforehand that she has a good man and true, and then chance will neither make her nor break her. What are you fidgeting about there, Joe? Nothing gone in the harness I hope?"

"No no," said Joe—finding, however, something very engrossing to do in the way of strapping and buckling—"Miss Dolly quite well?"

"Hearty, thankye. She looks pretty enough to be well, and good too."

"She's always both sir"—

"So she is, thank God!"

"I hope,"—said Joe after some hesitation, "that you won't tell this story against me—this of my having been beat like the boy they'd make of me—at all events, till I have met this man again and settled the account. It'll be a better story then."

"Why who should I tell it to?" returned Gabriel. "They know it here, and I'm not likely to come across anybody else who would care about it."

"That's true enough"—said the young fellow with a sigh. "I quite forgot that. Yes, that's true!"

So saying, he raised his face, which was very red,—no doubt from the exertion of strapping and buckling as aforesaid,—and giving the reins to the old man, who had by this time taken his seat, sighed again and bade him good night.

"Good night!" cried Gabriel. "Now think better of what we have just been speaking of, and don't be rash, there's a good fellow; I have an interest in you, and wouldn't have you cast yourself away. Good night!"

Returning his cheery farewell with cordial good will, Joe Willet lingered until the sound of wheels ceased to vibrate in his ears, and then, shaking his head mournfully, re-entered the house.

Gabriel Varden wended his way towards London, thinking of a great many things, and most of all of flaming terms in which to relate his adventure, and so account satisfactorily to Mrs. Varden for visiting the Maypole, despite certain solemn covenants between himself and that lady. Thinking begets, not only thought, but drowsiness occasionally, and the more the locksmith thought, the more sleepy he became.

A man may be very sober—or at least firmly set upon his legs on that neutral ground which lies between the confines of perfect sobriety and slight tipsiness—and yet feel a strong tendency to mingle up present circumstances with others which have no manner of connexion with them; to confound all consideration of persons, things, times, and places; and to jumble his disjointed thoughts together in a kind of mental kaleidoscope, producing combinations as unexpected as they are transitory. This was Gabriel Varden's state, as, nodding in his dog sleep, and leaving his horse to pursue a road with which he was well acquainted, he got over the ground unconsciously, and drew nearer and nearer home. He had roused himself once, when the horse stopped until the turnpike gate was opened, and had cried a lusty "good night" to the toll-keeper, but then he woke out of a dream about picking a lock in the stomach of the Great Mogul,* and even when he did wake, mixed up the turn-pike man with his mother-in-law who had been dead twenty years. It is not surprising, therefore, that he soon relapsed, and jogged heavily along, quite insensible to his progress.

And now he approached the great city, which lay outstretched before him like a dark shadow on the ground, reddening the sluggish air with a deep dull light, that told of labyrinths of public ways and shops, and swarms of busy people. Approaching nearer and nearer yet, this halo began to fade, and the causes which produced it slowly to develop themselves. Long lines of poorly lighted streets might be faintly traced, with here and there a brighter spot, where lamps were clustered about a square or market, or round some great building; after a time these grew more distinct, and the lamps themselves were visible; slight yellow specks, that seemed to be rapidly snuffed out one by one as intervening obstacles hid them from the sight. Then sounds arose—the striking of church clocks, the distant bark of dogs, the hum of traffic in the streets; then outlines might be traced—tall steeples looming in the air, and piles of unequal roofs oppressed by chimneys: then the noise swelled into a louder sound, and forms grew more distinct and numerous still, and London—visible in the darkness by its own faint light, and not by that of Heaven—was at hand.

The locksmith, however, all unconscious of its near vicinity, still jogged on, half sleeping and half waking, when a loud cry at no great distance ahead, roused him with a start.

For a moment or two he looked about him like a man who had been transported to some strange country in his sleep, but soon recognizing familiar objects, rubbed his eyes lazily and might have relapsed again, but that the cry was repeated—not once or twice or thrice, but many times, and each time, if possible, with increased vehemence. Thoroughly aroused, Gabriel, who was a bold man and not easily daunted, made straight to the spot, urging on his stout little horse as if for life or death.

The matter indeed looked sufficiently serious, for, coming to the place whence the cries had proceeded, he descried the figure of a man extended in an apparently lifeless state upon the pathway, and hovering round him another person with a torch in his hand, which he waved in the air with a wild impatience, redoubling meanwhile those cries for help which had brought the locksmith to the spot.

"What's here to do?" said the old man, alighting. "How's this—what—Barnaby?"

The bearer of the torch shook his long loose hair back from his eyes, and thrusting his face eagerly into that of the locksmith, fixed upon him a look which told his history at once.

"You know me, Barnaby?" said Varden.

He nodded—not once or twice, but a score of times, and that with a fantastic exaggeration which would have kept his head in motion for an hour, but that the locksmith held up his finger, and fixing his eye sternly upon him caused him to desist; then pointed to the body with an inquiring look.

"There's blood upon him," said Barnaby with a shudder. "It makes me sick."

"How came it there?" demanded Varden.

"Steel, steel, steel!" he replied fiercely, imitating with his hand the thrust of a sword.

"Is he robbed?" said the locksmith.

Barnaby caught him by the arm, and nodded "Yes;" then pointed towards the city.

"Oh!" said the old man, bending over the body and looking round as he spoke into Barnaby's pale face, strangely lighted up by something which was *not* intellect. "The robber made off that way, did he? Well well, never mind that just now. Hold your torch this way—a little further off—so. Now stand quiet while I try to see what harm is done."

With these words, he applied himself to a closer examination of the prostrate form, while Barnaby, holding the torch as he had been directed, looked on in silence, fascinated by interest or curiosity, but repelled nevertheless by some strong and secret horror which convulsed him in every nerve.

As he stood at that moment, half shrinking back and half bending forward, both his face and figure were full in the strong glare of the link, and as distinctly revealed as though it had been broad day. He was about three-and-twenty years old, and though rather spare, of a fair height and strong make. His hair, of which he had a great profusion, was red, and hanging in disorder about his face and shoulders, gave to his restless looks an expression quite unearthly—enhanced by the paleness of his complexion, and the glassy lustre of his large protruding eyes. Startling as his aspect was, the features were good, and there was something even plaintive in his wan and haggard aspect. But the absence of the soul is far more terrible in a living man than in a dead one; and in this unfortunate being its noblest powers were wanting.

His dress was of green, clumsily trimmed here and there—apparently by his own hands—with gaudy lace; brightest where the cloth was most worn and soiled, and poorest where it was at the best. A pair of tawdry ruffles dangled at his wrists, while his throat was nearly bare. He had ornamented his hat with a cluster of peacock's feathers, but they were limp and broken, and now trailed negligently down his back. Girded to his side was the steel hilt of an old sword without blade or scabbard; and some parti-coloured ends of ribands and poor glass toys completed the ornamental portion of his attire. The fluttered and confused disposition of all the motley scraps that formed his dress, bespoke, in a scarcely less degree than his eager and unsettled manner, the disorder of his mind, and by a grotesque contrast set off and heightened the more impressive wildness of his face.

"Barnaby," said the locksmith, after a hasty but careful inspection, "this man is not dead, but he has a wound in his side, and is in a fainting-fit."

"I know him, I know him!" cried Barnaby, clapping his hands.

"Know him?" repeated the locksmith.

"Hush!" said Barnaby, laying his fingers on his lips. "He went out to-day a wooing. I wouldn't for a light guinea* that he should never go a wooing again, for if he did some eyes would grow dim that are now as bright as—see, when I talk of eyes, the stars come out. Whose eyes are they? If they are angels' eyes, why do they look down here and see good men hurt, and only wink and sparkle all the night?"

"Now Heaven help this silly fellow," murmured the perplexed locksmith, "can he know this gentleman? His mother's house is not far off; I had better see if she can tell me who he is. Barnaby my man, help me to put him in the chaise, and we'll ride home together."

"I can't touch him!" cried the idiot falling back, and shuddering as with a strong spasm; "he's bloody."

"It's in his nature I know," muttered the locksmith, "it's cruel to ask him, but I must have help. Barnaby—good Barnaby—dear Barnaby—if you know this gentleman, for the sake of his life and everybody's life that loves him, help me to raise him and lay him down."

"Cover him then, wrap him close—don't let me see it—smell it—hear the word. Don't speak the word—don't!"

"No, no, I'll not. There, you see he's covered now. Gently. Well done, well done!"

They placed him in the carriage with great ease, for Barnaby was strong and active, but all the time they were so occupied he shivered from head to foot, and evidently experienced such an ecstacy of terror that the locksmith could scarcely endure to witness his suffering.

This accomplished, and the wounded man being covered with Varden's own great-coat which he took off for the purpose, they proceeded onwards at a brisk pace: Barnaby gaily counting the stars upon his fingers, and Gabriel inwardly congratulating himself upon having an adventure now, which would silence Mrs. Varden on the subject of the Maypole for that night, or there was no faith in woman.

## CHAPTER THE FOURTH.

In the venerable suburb—it was a suburb once—of Clerkenwell,* towards that part of its confines which is nearest to the Charter House,* and in one of those cool, shady streets, of which a few, widely scattered and dispersed, yet remain in such old parts of the metropolis,—each tenement quietly vegetating like an ancient citizen who long ago retired from business, and dozing on in its infirmity until in course of time it tumbles down, and is replaced by some extravagant young heir, flaunting in stucco and ornamental work, and all the vanities of modern days,—in this quarter, and in a street of this description, the business of the present chapter lies.

At the time of which it treats, though only six-and-sixty years ago,* a very large part of what is London now had no existence. Even in the brains of the wildest speculators, there had sprung up no long rows of streets connecting Highgate with Whitechapel,* no assemblages of palaces in the swampy levels, nor little cities in the open fields. Although this part of town was then, as now, parcelled out in streets and plentifully peopled, it wore a different aspect. There were gardens to many of the houses, and trees by the pavement side; with an air of freshness breathing up and down, which in these days would be sought in vain. Fields were nigh at hand, through which the New River* took its winding course, and where there was merry hay-making in the summer time. Nature was not so far removed or hard to get at, as in these days; and although there were busy trades in Clerkenwell, and working jewellers by scores, it was a purer place, with farm-houses nearer to it than many modern Londoners would readily believe; and lovers' walks at no great distance, which turned into squalid courts, long before the lovers of this age were born, or, as the phrase goes, thought of.

In one of these streets, the cleanest of them all, and on the shady side of the way—for good housewives know that sunlight damages their cherished furniture, and so choose the shade rather than its intrusive glare—there stood the house with which we have to deal. It was a modest building, not over-newly fashioned, not very straight, not large, not tall; not bold-faced, with great staring windows, but a shy, blinking house, with a conical roof going up into a peak over its garret window of four small panes of glass, like a cocked hat on the head of an elderly gentleman with one eye. It was not built of brick or lofty stone, but of wood and plaster; it was not planned with a dull and wearisome regard to regularity, for no one window matched the other, or seemed to have the slightest reference to anything besides itself.

The shop—for it had a shop—was, with reference to the first floor, where shops usually are; and there all resemblance between it and any other shop stopped short and ceased. People who went in and out didn't go up a flight of steps to it, or walk easily in upon a level with the street, but dived down three steep stairs, as into a cellar. Its floor was paved with stone and brick, as that of any other cellar might be; and in lieu of window framed and glazed it had a great black wooden flap or shutter, nearly breast high from the ground, which turned back in the day-time, admitting as much cold air as light, and very often more. Behind this shop was a wainscoted parlour, looking first into a paved yard, and beyond that again into a little terrace garden, raised some few feet above it. Any stranger would have supposed that this wainscoted parlour, saving for the door of communication by which he had entered, was cut off and detached from all the world; and indeed most strangers on their first entrance were observed to grow extremely thoughtful, as weighing and pondering in their minds whether the upper rooms were only approachable by ladders from without; never suspecting that two of the most unassuming and unlikely doors in existence, which the most ingenious mechanician on earth must of necessity have supposed to be the doors of closets, opened out of this room—each without the smallest preparation, or so much as a quarter of an inch of passage—upon two dark winding flights of stairs, the one upward, the other downward; which were the sole means of communication between that chamber and the other portions of the house.

With all these oddities, there was not a neater, more scrupulously tidy, or more punctiliously ordered house, in Clerkenwell, in London, in all England. There were not cleaner windows, or whiter floors, or brighter stoves, or more highly shining articles of furniture in old mahogany; there was not more rubbing, scrubbing, burnishing and polishing, in the whole street put together. Nor was this excellence attained without some cost and trouble and great expenditure of voice, as the neighbours were frequently reminded when the good lady of the house overlooked and assisted in its being put to rights on cleaning days; which were usually from Monday morning till Saturday night, both days inclusive.

Leaning against the door-post of this, his dwelling, the locksmith stood early on the morning after he had met with the wounded man, gazing disconsolately at a great wooden emblem of a key, painted in vivid yellow to resemble gold, which dangled from the house-front, and swung to and fro with a mournful creaking noise, as if complaining that it had nothing to unlock. Sometimes he looked over his shoulder into the shop, which was so dark and dingy with numerous tokens of his trade, and so blackened by the smoke of a little forge, near which his 'prentice was at work, that it would have been difficult for one unused to such espials to have distinguished anything but various tools of uncouth make and shape, great bunches of rusty keys, fragments of iron, half-finished locks, and such-like things, which garnished the walls and hung in clusters from the ceiling.

After a long and patient contemplation of the golden key, and many such backward glances, Gabriel stepped into the road, and stole a look at the upper windows. One of them chanced to be thrown open at the moment, and a roguish face met his; a face lighted up by the loveliest pair of sparkling eyes that ever locksmith looked upon; the face of a pretty, laughing, girl; dimpled and fresh, and healthful—the very impersonation of good-humour and blooming beauty.

"It's like the morning looking out of window," said Gabriel; his honest features lighting up directly, "upon my word it is. She's the prettiest wench alive. I say it, though I *am* her father."

"Hush!" whispered the girl, bending forward, and pointing archly to the window underneath. "Mother is still asleep."

"Still, my dear," returned the locksmith in the same tone. "You talk as if she had been asleep all night, instead of little more than half an hour. But I'm very thankful. Sleep's a blessing—no doubt about it." The last few words he muttered to himself.

"How cruel of you to keep us up so late this morning, and never tell us where you were, or send us word!" said the girl.

"Ah Dolly, Dolly!" returned the locksmith, shaking his head, and smiling, "how cruel of you to run up stairs to bed! Come down to breakfast, madcap, and come down lightly, or you'll wake your mother. She must be tired, I am sure—*I* am!"

Keeping these latter words to himself, and returning his daughter's nod, he was passing into the workshop, with the smile she had awakened still beaming on his face, when he just caught sight of his 'prentice's brown paper cap ducking down to avoid observation, and shrinking from the window back to its former place, which the wearer no sooner reached than he began to hammer lustily.

"Listening again, Simon!" said Gabriel to himself. "That's bad. What in the name of wonder does he expect the girl to say, that I always catch him listening when *she* speaks, and never at any other time! A bad habit, Sim, a sneaking, underhanded way. Ah! you may hammer, but you won't beat that out of me, if you work at it till your time's up!"

So saying, and shaking his head gravely, he re-entered the work-shop, and confronted the subject of these remarks.

"There's enough of that just now," said the locksmith. "You needn't make any more of that confounded clatter. Breakfast's ready."

"Sir," said Sim, looking up with amazing politeness, and a peculiar little bow cut short off at the neck, "I shall attend you immediately."

"I suppose," muttered Gabriel, "that's out of the 'Prentice's Garland, or the 'Prentice's Delight, or the 'Prentice's Warbler, or the 'Prentice's Guide to the Gallows, or some such improving text-book. Now he's going to beautify himself—here's a precious locksmith!"

Quite unconscious that his master was looking on from the dark corner by the parlour door, Sim threw off the paper cap, sprang from his seat, and in two extraordinary steps, something between skating and minuet dancing, bounded to a washing place at the other end of the shop, and there removed from his face and hands all traces of his previous work—practising the same step all the time with the utmost gravity. This done, he drew from some concealed place a little scrap of looking-glass, and with its assistance arranged his hair, and ascertained the exact state of a little carbuncle on his nose. Having now completed his toilet, he placed the fragment of mirror on a low bench, and looked over his shoulder at so much of his legs as could be reflected in that small compass, with the greatest possible complacency and satisfaction.

Sim, as he was called in the locksmith's family, or Mr. Simon Tappertit, as he called himself, and required all men to style him out of doors, on holidays, and Sundays out,—was an old-fashioned, thin-faced, sleek-haired, sharp-nosed, small-eyed little fellow, very little more than five feet high, and thoroughly convinced in his own mind that he was above the middle size; rather tall, in fact, than otherwise. Of his figure, which was well enough formed, though somewhat of the leanest, he entertained the highest admiration; and with his legs, which, in knee-breeches, were perfect curiosities of littleness, he was enraptured to a degree amounting to enthusiasm. He also had some majestic, shadowy ideas, which had never been quite fathomed by his most intimate friends, concerning the power of his eye. Indeed he had been known to go so far as to boast that he could utterly quell and subdue the haughtiest beauty by a simple process, which he termed "eyeing her over;" but it must be added, that neither of this faculty, nor of the power he claimed to have, through the same gift, of vanquishing and heaving down dumb animals, even in a rabid state, had he ever furnished evidence which could be deemed quite satisfactory and conclusive.

It may be inferred from these premises, that in the small body of Mr. Tappertit there was locked up an ambitious and aspiring soul. As certain liquors, confined in casks too cramped in their dimensions, will ferment, and fret, and chafe in their imprisonment, so the spiritual essence or soul of Mr. Tappertit would sometimes fume within that precious cask, his body, until, with great foam and froth and splutter, it would force a vent, and carry all before it. It was his custom to remark, in reference to any one of these occasions, that his soul had got into his head; and in this novel kind of intoxication many scrapes and mishaps befel him, which he had frequently concealed with no small difficulty from his worthy master.

Sim Tappertit, among the other fancies upon which his before-mentioned soul was for ever feasting and regaling itself (and which fancies, like the liver of Prometheus,* grew as they were fed upon), had a mighty notion of his order; and had been heard by the servant-maid openly expressing his regret that the 'prentices no longer carried clubs wherewith to mace the citizens: that was his strong expression. He was likewise reported to have said that in former times a stigma had been cast upon the body by the execution of George Barnwell,* to which they should not have basely submitted, but should have demanded him of the legislature—temperately at first; then by an appeal to arms, if necessary—to be dealt with as they in their wisdom might think fit. These thoughts always led him to consider what a glorious engine the 'prentices might yet become if they had but a master spirit at their head; and then he would darkly, and to the terror of his hearers, hint at certain reckless fellows that he knew of, and at a certain Lion Heart* ready to become their captain, who, once afoot, would make the Lord Mayor tremble on his throne.

In respect of dress and personal decoration, Sim Tappertit was no less of an adventurous and enterprising character. He had been seen, beyond dispute, to pull off ruffles of the finest quality at the corner of the street on Sunday nights, and to put them carefully in his pocket before returning home; and it was quite notorious that on all great holiday occasions it was his habit to exchange his plain steel knee-buckles for a pair of glittering paste, under cover of a friendly post, planted most conveniently in that same spot. Add to this that he was in years just twenty, in his looks much older, and in conceit at least two hundred; that he had no objection to be jested with touching his admiration of his master's daughter; and had even, when called upon at a certain obscure tavern to pledge the lady whom he honoured with his love, toasted, with many winks and leers, a fair creature whose Christian name, he said, began with a D—; — and as much is known of Sim Tappertit, who has by this time followed the locksmith in to breakfast, as is necessary to be known in making his acquaintance.

It was a substantial meal; for over and above the ordinary tea equipage, the board creaked beneath the weight of a jolly round of beef, a ham of the first magnitude, and sundry towers of buttered Yorkshire cake, piled slice upon slice in most alluring order. There was also a goodly jug of well-browned clay, fashioned into the form of an old gentleman, not by any means unlike the locksmith, atop of whose bald head was a fine white froth answering to his wig, indicative, beyond dispute, of sparkling home-brewed ale. But better far than fair home-brewed, or Yorkshire cake, or ham, or beef, or anything to eat or drink that earth or air or water can supply, there sat, presiding over all, the locksmith's rosy daughter, before whose dark eyes even beef grew insignificant, and malt became as nothing.

Fathers should never kiss their daughters when young men are by. It's too much. There are bounds to human endurance. So thought Sim Tappertit when Gabriel drew those rosy lips to his—those lips within Sim's reach from day to day, and yet so far off. He had a respect for his master, but he wished the Yorkshire cake might choke him.

"Father," said the locksmith's daughter, when this salute was over, and they took their seats at table, "what is this I hear about last night?"

"All true, my dear; true as the Gospel, Doll."

"Young Mr. Chester robbed, and lying wounded in the road, when you came up?"

"Ay—Mr. Edward. And beside him, Barnaby, calling for help with all his might. It was well it happened as it did; for the road's a lonely one, the hour was late, and, the night being cold, and poor Barnaby even less sensible than usual from surprise and fright, the young gentleman might have met his death in a very short time."

"I dread to think of it!" cried his daughter with a shudder. "How did you know him?"

"Know him!" returned the locksmith. "I didn't know him—how could I? I had never seen him, often as I had heard and spoken of him. I took him to Mrs. Rudge's; and she no sooner saw him than the truth came out."

"Miss Emma, father—If this news should reach her, enlarged upon as it is sure to be, she will go distracted."

"Why, lookye there again, how a man suffers for being good-natured," said the locksmith. "Miss Emma was with her uncle at the masquerade at Carlisle House,* where she had gone, as the people at the Warren told me, sorely against her will. What does your block-head father when he and Mrs. Rudge have laid their heads together, but goes there when he ought to be abed, makes interest with his friend the doorkeeper, slips him on a mask and domino,* and mixes with the masquers."

"And like himself to do so!" cried the girl, putting her fair arm round his neck, and giving him a most enthusiastic kiss.

"Like himself!" repeated Gabriel, affecting to grumble, but evidently delighted with the part he had taken, and with her praise. "Very like himself—so your mother said. However, he mingled with the crowd, and prettily worried and badgered he was, I warrant you, with people squeaking, 'Don't you know me?' and 'I've found you out,' and all that kind of nonsense in his ears. He might have wandered on till now, but in a little room there was a young lady who had taken off her mask, on account of the place being very warm, and was sitting there alone."

"And that was she?" said his daughter hastily.

"And that was she," replied the locksmith; "and I no sooner whispered to her what the matter was—as softly, Doll, and with nearly as much art as you could have used yourself—than she gives a kind of scream and faints away."

"What did you do—what happened next?" asked his daughter.

"Why, the masks came flocking round, with a general noise and hubbub, and I thought myself in luck to get clear off, that's all," rejoined the locksmith. "What happened when I reached home you may guess, if you didn't hear it. Ah! Well, it's a poor heart that never rejoices.—Put Toby* this way, my dear."

This Toby was the brown jug of which previous mention has been made. Applying his lips to the worthy old gentleman's benevolent forehead, the locksmith, who had all this time been ravaging among the eatables, kept them there so long, at the same time raising the vessel slowly in the air, that at length Toby stood on his head upon his nose, when he smacked his lips, and set him on the table again with fond reluctance.

Although Sim Tappertit had taken no share in this conversation, no part of it being addressed to him, he had not been wanting in such silent manifestations of astonishment, as he deemed most compatible with the favourable display of his eyes. Regarding the pause which now ensued, as a particularly advantageous opportunity for doing great execution with them upon the locksmith's daughter (who he had no doubt was looking at him in mute admiration), he began to screw and twist his face, and especially those features, into such extraordinary, hideous, and unparalleled contortions, that Gabriel, who happened to look towards him, was stricken with amazement.

"Why, what the devil's the matter with the lad!" cried the locksmith. "Is he choking?"

"Who?" demanded Sim, with some disdain.

"Who? why, you," returned his master. "What do you mean by making those horrible faces over your breakfast?"

"Faces are matters of taste, sir," said Mr. Tappertit, rather discomfited; not the less so because he saw the locksmith's daughter smiling.

"Sim," rejoined Gabriel, laughing heartily. "Don't be a fool, for I'd rather see you in your senses. These young fellows," he added, turning to his daughter, "are always committing some folly or another. There was a quarrel between Joe Willet and old John last night—though I can't say Joe was much in fault either. He'll be missing one of these mornings, and will have gone away upon some wild-goose errand, seeking his fortune.—Why, what's the matter, Doll? *You* are making faces now. The girls are as bad as the boys every bit!"

"It's the tea," said Dolly, turning alternately very red and very white, which is no doubt the effect of a slight scald—"so very hot."

Mr. Tappertit looked immensely big at a quartern loaf on the table and breathed hard.

"Is that all?" returned the locksmith. "Put some more milk in it. Yes, I am sorry for Joe, because he is a likely young fellow, and gains upon one every time one sees him. But he'll start off you'll find. Indeed he told me as much himself!"

"Indeed!" cried Dolly in a faint voice. "In—deed!"

"Is the tea tickling your throat still, my dear?" said the locksmith.

But before his daughter could make him any answer, she was taken with a troublesome cough, and it was such a very unpleasant cough, that when she left off the tears were starting in her bright eyes. The good-natured locksmith was still patting her on the back and applying such gentle restoratives, when a message arrived from Mrs. Varden, making known to all whom it might concern, that she felt too much indisposed to rise after her great agitation and anxiety of the previous night; and therefore desired to be immediately accommodated with the little black tea-pot of strong mixed tea, a couple of rounds of buttered toast, a middling-sized dish of beef and ham cut thin, and the Protestant Manual in two volumes post octavo.* Like some other ladies who in remote ages flourished upon this globe, Mrs. Varden was most devout when most ill-tempered. Whenever she and her husband were at unusual variance, then the Protestant Manual was in high feather.

Knowing from experience what these requests portended, the triumvirate broke up: Dolly to see the orders executed with all despatch; Gabriel to some out-of-door work in his little chaise; and Sim to his daily duty in the workshop, to which retreat he carried the big look, although the loaf remained behind.

Indeed the big look increased immensely, and when he had tied his apron on was quite gigantic. It was not until he had several times walked up and down with folded arms, and the longest strides he could take, and had kicked a great many small articles out of his way, that his lip began to curl. At length a gloomy derision came upon his features, and he smiled; uttering meanwhile with supreme contempt the monosyllable "Joe!"

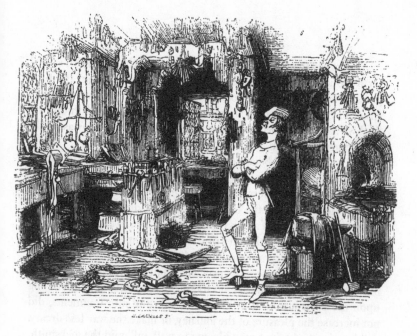

"I eyed her over while he talked about the fellow," he said, "and that was of course the reason of her being confused. Joe!"

He walked up and down again much quicker than before, and if possible with longer strides; sometimes stopping to take a glance at his legs, and sometimes to jerk out as it were, and cast from him, another "Joe!" In the course of quarter an hour or so he again assumed the paper cap and tried to work. No. It could not be done.

"I'll do nothing to-day" said Mr. Tappertit, dashing it down again, "but grind. I'll grind up all the tools. Grinding will suit my present humour well. Joe!"

Whirr-r-r-r. The grindstone was soon in motion; the sparks were flying off in showers. This was the occupation for his heated spirit.

Whirr-r-r-r-r-r.

"Something will come of this!" said Mr. Tappertit, pausing as if in triumph, and wiping his heated face upon his sleeve. "Something will come of this. I hope it mayn't be human gore."

Whirr-r-r-r-r-r-r.

CHAPTER THE FIFTH.

As soon as the business of the day was over, the locksmith sallied forth alone to visit the wounded gentleman and ascertain the progress of his recovery. The house where he had left him was in a by-street in Southwark, not far from London Bridge;* and thither he hied with all speed, bent upon returning with as little delay as might be, and getting to bed betimes.

The evening was boisterous—scarcely better than the previous night had been. It was not easy for a stout man like Gabriel to keep his legs at the street corners, or to make head against the busy wind; which often fairly got the better of him, and drove him back some paces, or, in defiance of all his energy, forced him to take shelter in an arch or doorway until the fury of the gust was spent. Occasionally a hat or wig, or both, came spinning and trundling past him, like a mad thing; while the more serious spectacle of falling tiles and slates, or of masses of brick and mortar or fragments of stone-coping rattling upon the pavement near at hand, and splitting into fragments, did not increase the pleasure of the journey, or make the way less dreary.

"A trying night for a man like me to walk in!" said the locksmith, as he knocked softly at the widow's door. "I'd rather be in old John's chimney-corner, faith!"

"Who's there?" demanded a woman's voice from within. Being answered, it added a hasty word of welcome, and the door was quickly opened.

She was about forty—perhaps two or three years older—with a cheerful aspect, and a face that had once been pretty. It bore traces of affliction and care, but they were of an old date, and Time had smoothed them. Any one who had bestowed but a casual glance on Barnaby might have known that this was his mother, from the strong resemblance between them; but where in his face there was wildness and vacancy, in hers there was the patient composure of long effort and quiet resignation.

One thing about this face was very strange and startling. You could not look upon it in its most cheerful mood without feeling that it had some extraordinary capacity of expressing terror. It was not on the surface. It was in no one feature that it lingered. You could not take the eyes, or mouth, or lines upon the cheek, and say, if this or that were otherwise, it would not be so. Yet there it always lurked— something for ever dimly seen, but ever there, and never absent for a moment. It was the faintest, palest shadow of some look, to which an instant of intense and most unutterable horror only could have given birth; but indistinct and feeble as it was, it did suggest what that look must have been, and fixed it in the mind as if it had had existence in a dream.

More faintly imaged, and wanting force and purpose, as it were, because of his darkened intellect, there was this same stamp upon the son. Seen in a picture, it must have had some legend with it, and would have haunted those who looked upon the canvas. They who knew the Maypole story, and could remember what the widow was, before her husband's and his master's murder, understood it well. They recollected how the change had come, and could call to mind that when her son was born, upon the very day the deed was known, he bore upon his wrist what seemed a smear of blood but half washed out.

"God save you, neighbour!" said the locksmith, as he followed her with the air of an old friend into a little parlour where a cheerful fire was burning.

"And you," she answered, smiling. "Your kind heart has brought you here again. Nothing will keep you at home, I know of old, if there are friends to serve or comfort, out of doors."

"Tut, tut," returned the locksmith, rubbing his hands and warming them. "You women are such talkers. What of the patient, neighbour?"

"He is sleeping now. He was very restless towards daylight, and for some hours tossed and tumbled sadly. But the fever has left him, and the doctor says he will soon mend. He must not be removed until to-morrow."

"He has had visitors to-day—humph?" said Gabriel, slyly.

"Yes. Old Mr. Chester has been here ever since we sent for him, and had not been gone many minutes when you knocked."

"No ladies?" said Gabriel, elevating his eyebrows and looking disappointed.

"A letter," replied the widow.

"Come. That's better than nothing!" cried the locksmith. "Who was the bearer?"

"Barnaby, of course."

"Barnaby's a jewel!" said Varden; "and comes and goes with ease where we who think ourselves much wiser would make but a poor hand of it. He is not out wandering, again, I hope?"

"Thank Heaven he is in his bed; having been up all night, as you know, and on his feet all day. He was quite tired out. Ah, neighbour, if I could but see him oftener so—if I could but tame down that terrible restlessness—"

"In good time," said the locksmith kindly, "in good time—don't be down-hearted. To my mind he grows wiser every day."

The widow shook her head. And yet, though she knew the locksmith sought to cheer her, and spoke from no conviction of his own, she was glad to hear even this praise of her poor benighted son.

"He will be a 'cute man yet," resumed the locksmith. "Take care, when we are growing old and foolish, Barnaby doesn't put us to the blush, that's all. But our other friend," he added, looking under the table and about the floor—"sharpest and cunningest of all the sharp and cunning ones—where's he?"

"In Barnaby's room," rejoined the widow, with a faint smile.

"Ah! He's a knowing blade!" said Varden, shaking his head. "I should be sorry to talk secrets before him. Oh! He's a deep customer. I've no doubt he can read and write and cast accounts if he chooses. What was that—him tapping at the door?"

"No," returned the widow. "It was in the street, I think. Hark! Yes. There again! 'Tis some one knocking softly at the shutter. Who can it be!"

They had been speaking in a low tone, for the invalid lay overhead, and the walls and ceilings being thin and poorly built, the sound of their voices might otherwise have disturbed his slumber. The party without, whoever it was, could have stood close to the shutter without hearing anything spoken; and, seeing the light through the chinks and finding all so quiet, might have been persuaded that only one person was there.

"Some thief or ruffian, maybe," said the locksmith. "Give me the light."

"No, no," she returned hastily. "Such visitors have never come to this poor dwelling. Do you stay here. You're within call, at the worst. I would rather go myself—alone."

"Why?" said the locksmith, unwillingly relinquishing the candle he had caught up from the table.

"Because—I don't know why—because the wish is strong upon me," she rejoined. "There again—do not detain me, I beg of you!"

Gabriel looked at her, in great surprise to see one who was usually so mild and quiet thus agitated, and with so little cause. She left the room and closed the door behind her. She stood for a moment as if hesitating, with her hand upon the lock. In this short interval the knocking came again, and a voice close to the window—a voice the locksmith seemed to recollect, and to have some disagreeable association with—whispered "Make haste."

The words were uttered in that low distinct voice which finds its way so readily to sleepers' ears, and wakes them in a fright. For a moment it startled even the locksmith; who involuntarily drew back from the window, and listened.

The wind rumbling in the chimney made it difficult to hear what passed, but he could tell that the door was opened, that there was the tread of a man upon the creaking boards, and then a moment's silence—broken by a suppressed something which was not a shriek, or groan, or cry for help, and yet might have been either or all three; and the words "My God!" uttered in a voice it chilled him to hear.

He rushed out upon the instant. There, at last, was that dreadful look—the very one he seemed to know so well and yet had never seen before—upon her face. There she stood, frozen to the ground, gazing with starting eyes, and livid cheeks, and every feature fixed and ghastly, upon the man he had encountered in the dark last night. His eyes met those of the locksmith. It was but a flash, an instant, a breath upon a polished glass, and he was gone.

The locksmith was upon him—had the skirts of his streaming garment almost in his grasp—when his arms were tightly clutched, and the widow flung herself upon the ground before him.

"The other way—the other way," she cried. "He went the other way. Turn—turn."

"The other way! I see him now," rejoined the locksmith, pointing—"yonder—there—there is his shadow passing by that light. What—who is this? Let me go."

"Come back, come back!" exclaimed the woman, wrestling with and clasping him; "Do not touch him on your life. I charge you, come back. He carries other lives besides his own. Come back!"

"What does this mean?" cried the locksmith.

"No matter what it means, don't ask, don't speak, don't think about it. He is not to be followed, checked, or stopped. Come back!"

The old man looked at her in wonder, as she writhed and clung about him; and, borne down by her passion, suffered her to drag him into the house. It was not until she had chained and double-locked the door, fastened every bolt and bar with the heat and fury of a maniac, and drawn him back into the room, that she turned upon him once again that stony look of horror, and, sinking down into a chair, covered her face, and shuddered, as though the hand of death were on her.

## CHAPTER THE SIXTH.

EYOND all measure astonished by the strange occurrences which had passed with so much violence and rapidity, the locksmith gazed upon the shuddering figure in the chair like one half stupified, and would have gazed much longer, had not his tongue been loosened by compassion and humanity.

"You are ill," said Gabriel. "Let me call some neighbour in."

"Not for the world," she rejoined, motioning to him with her trembling hand, and still holding her face averted. "It is enough that you have been by, to see this."

"Nay, more than enough—or less," said Gabriel.

"Be it so," she returned. "As you like. Ask me no questions, I entreat you."

"Neighbour," said the locksmith, after a pause. "Is this fair, or reasonable, or just to yourself? Is it like you, who have known me so long and sought my advice in all matters—like you, who from a girl have had a strong mind and a staunch heart?"

"I have had need of them," she replied. "I am growing old, both in years and care. Perhaps that, and too much trial, have made them weaker than they used to be. Do not speak to me."

"How can I see what I have seen, and hold my peace!" returned the locksmith. "Who was that man, and why has his coming made this change in you?"

She was silent, but clung to the chair as though to save herself from falling on the ground.

"I take the license of an old acquaintance, Mary," said the locksmith, "who has ever had a warm regard for you, and maybe has tried to prove it when he could. Who is this ill-favoured man, and what has he to do with you? Who is this ghost, that is only seen in the black nights and bad weather? How does he know you and why does he haunt this house, whispering through chinks and crevices, as if there was that between him and you, which neither durst so much as speak aloud of? Who is he?"

"You do well to say he haunts this house," returned the widow, faintly. "His shadow has been upon it and me, in light and darkness, at noonday and midnight. And now, at last, he has come in the body!"

"But he wouldn't have gone in the body," returned the locksmith with some irritation, "if you had left my arms and legs at liberty. What riddle is this?"

"It is one," she answered, rising as she spoke, "that must remain for ever as it is. I dare not say more than that."

"Dare not!" repeated the wondering locksmith.

"Do not press me," she replied. "I am sick and faint, and every faculty of life seems dead within me.—No!—Do not touch me, either."

Gabriel, who had stepped forward to render her assistance, fell back as she made this hasty exclamation, and regarded her in silent wonder.

"Let me go my way alone," she said in a low voice, "and let the hands of no honest man touch mine to-night." When she had tottered to the door, she turned, and added with a stronger effort. "This is a secret, which, of necessity, I trust to you. You are a true man. As you have ever been good and kind to me,—keep it. If any noise was heard above, make some excuse—say anything but what you really saw, and never let a word or look between us, recal this circumstance.

I trust to you. Mind, I trust to you. How much I trust, you never can conceive."

Fixing her eyes upon him for an instant, she withdrew, and left him there alone.

Gabriel, not knowing what to think, stood staring at the door with a countenance full of surprise and dismay. The more he pondered on what had passed, the less able he was to give it any favourable interpretation. To find this widow woman, whose life for so many years had been supposed to be one of solitude and retirement, and who, in her quiet suffering character, had gained the good opinion and respect of all who knew her—to find her linked mysteriously with an ill-omened man, alarmed at his appearance, and yet favouring his escape, was a discovery that pained as much as it startled him. Her reliance on his secrecy, and his tacit acquiescence, increased his distress of mind. If he had spoken boldly, persisted in questioning her, detained her when she rose to leave the room, made any kind of protest, instead of silently compromising himself, as he felt he had done, he would have been more at ease.

"Why did I let her say it was a secret, and she trusted it to me!" said Gabriel, tilting his wig on one side to scratch his head with greater ease, and looking ruefully at the fire. "I have no more readiness than old John himself. Why didn't I say firmly, 'You have no right to such secrets, and I demand of you to tell me what this means,' instead of standing gaping at her, like an old mooncalf as I am! But there's my weakness. I can be obstinate enough with men if need be, but women may twist me round their fingers at their pleasure."

He took his wig off outright as he made this reflection, and warming his handkerchief at the fire began to rub and polish his bald head with it, until it glistened again.

"And yet," said the locksmith, softening under this soothing process, and stopping to smile, "it *may* be nothing. Any drunken brawler trying to make his way into the house, would have alarmed a quiet soul like her. But then"—and here was the vexation—"how came it to be that man; how comes he to have this influence over her; how came she to favour his getting away from me; and more than all, how came she not to say it was a sudden fright, and nothing more? It's a sad thing to have, in one minute, reason to mistrust a person I have known so long, and an old sweetheart into the bargain; but what else can I do, with all this upon my mind!—Is that Barnaby outside there?"

"Ay!" he cried, looking in and nodding. "Sure enough it's Barnaby—how did you guess?"

"By your shadow," said the locksmith.

"Oho!" cried Barnaby, glancing over his shoulder, "He's a merry fellow, that shadow, and keeps close to me, though I *am* silly. We have such pranks, such walks, such runs, such gambols on the grass. Sometimes he'll be half as tall as a church steeple, and sometimes no bigger than a dwarf. Now he goes on before, and now behind, and anon he'll be stealing slyly on, on this side, or on that, stopping whenever I stop, and thinking I can't see him, though I have my eye on him sharp enough. Oh! he's a merry fellow. Tell me—is he silly too? I think he is."

"Why?" asked Gabriel.

"Because he never tires of mocking me, but does it all day long.— Why don't you come?"

"Where?"

"Up stairs. He wants you. Stay—where's his shadow? Come. You're a wise man; tell me that."

"Beside him, Barnaby; beside him, I suppose," returned the locksmith.

"No!" he replied, shaking his head. "Guess again."

"Gone out a walking, maybe?"

"He has changed shadows with a woman," the idiot whispered in his ear, and then fell back with a look of triumph. "Her shadow's always with him, and his with her. That's sport I think, eh?"

"Barnaby," said the locksmith, with a grave look; "come hither, lad."

"I know what you want to say. I know!" he replied, keeping away from him. "But I'm cunning, I'm silent. I only say so much to you— are you ready?" As he spoke, he caught up the light, and waved it with a wild laugh above his head.

"Softly—gently," said the locksmith, exerting all his influence to keep him calm and quiet. "I thought you had been asleep."

"So I *have* been asleep," he rejoined, with widely-opened eyes. "There have been great faces coming and going—close to my face, and then a mile away—low places to creep through, whether I would or no—high churches to fall down from—strange creatures crowded up together neck and heels, to sit upon the bed—that's sleep, eh?"

"Dreams, Barnaby, dreams," said the locksmith.

"Dreams!" he echoed softly, drawing closer to him. "Those are not dreams."

"What are," replied the locksmith, "if they are not?"

"I dreamed," said Barnaby, passing his arm through Varden's, and peering close into his face as he answered in a whisper, "I dreamed just now that something—it was in the shape of a man—followed me—came softly after me—wouldn't let me be—but was always hiding and crouching, like a cat in dark corners, waiting till I should pass; when it crept out and came softly after me.—Did you ever see me run?"

"Many a time, you know."

"You never saw me run as I did in this dream. Still it came creeping on to worry me. Nearer, nearer, nearer—I ran faster—leaped—sprung out of bed, and to the window—and there, in the street below—but he is waiting for us. Are you coming?"

"What in the street below, dear Barnaby?" said Varden, imagining that he traced some connexion between this vision and what had actually occurred.

Barnaby looked into his face, muttered incoherently, waved the light above his head again, laughed, and drawing the locksmith's arm more tightly through his own, led him up the stairs in silence.

They entered a homely bedchamber, garnished in a scanty way with chairs whose spindle-shanks bespoke their age, and other furniture of very little worth; but clean and neatly kept. Reclining in an easy chair before the fire, pale and weak from waste of blood, was Edward Chester, the young gentleman who had been the first to quit the Maypole on the previous night, and who, extending his hand to the locksmith, welcomed him as his preserver and friend.

"Say no more, sir, say no more," said Gabriel. "I hope I would have done at least as much for any man in such a strait, and most of all for you, sir. A certain young lady," he added, with some hesitation, "has done us many a kind turn, and we naturally feel—I hope I give you no offence in saying this, sir?"

The young man smiled and shook his head; at the same time moving in his chair as if in pain.

"It's no great matter," he said, in answer to the locksmith's sympathising look, "a mere uneasiness arising at least as much from being cooped up here, as from the slight wound I have, or from the loss of blood. Be seated, Mr. Varden."

"If I may make so bold, Mr. Edward, as to lean upon your chair," returned the locksmith, accommodating his action to his speech, and bending over him, "I'll stand here, for the convenience of speaking low. Barnaby is not in his quietest humour to-night, and at such times talking never does him good."

They both glanced at the subject of this remark, who had taken a seat on the other side of the fire, and, smiling vacantly, was making puzzles on his fingers with a skein of string.

"Pray, tell me, sir," said Varden, dropping his voice still lower, "exactly what happened last night. I have my reason for inquiring. You left the Maypole, alone?"

"And walked homeward alone until I had nearly reached the place where you found me, when I heard the gallop of a horse."

"—Behind you?" said the locksmith.

"Indeed, yes—behind me. It was a single rider, who soon overtook me, and checking his horse, inquired the way to London."

"You were on the alert, sir, knowing how many highwaymen there are, scouring the roads in all directions?" said Varden.

"I was, but I had only a stick, having imprudently left my pistols in their holster-case with the landlord's son. I directed him as he desired. Before the words had passed my lips, he rode upon me furiously, as if bent on trampling me down beneath his horse's hoofs. In starting aside I slipped and fell. You found me with this stab and an ugly bruise or two, and without my purse—in which he found little enough for his pains. And now, Mr. Varden," he added, shaking the locksmith by the hand, "saving the extent of my gratitude to you, you know as much as I."

"Except," said Gabriel, bending down yet more, and looking cautiously towards their silent neighbour, "except in respect of the robber himself. What like was he, sir? Speak low, if you please. Barnaby means no harm, but I have watched him oftener than you, and I know, little as you would think it, that he's listening now."

It required a strong confidence in the locksmith's veracity to lead any one to this belief, for every sense and faculty that Barnaby possessed, seemed to be fixed upon his game, to the exclusion of all other things. Something in the young man's face expressed this opinion, for Gabriel repeated what he had just said, more earnestly

than before, and with another glance towards Barnaby, again asked
what like the man was.

"The night was so dark," said Edward, "the attack so sudden, and
he so wrapped and muffled up, that I can hardly say. It seems that—"

"Don't mention his name, sir," returned the locksmith, following
his look towards Barnaby; "I know *he* saw him. I want to know what
*you* saw."

"All I remember is," said Edward, "that as he checked his horse
his hat was blown off. He caught it and replaced it on his head, which
I observed was bound with a dark handkerchief. A stranger entered
the Maypole while I was there, whom I had not seen, for I sat apart
for reasons of my own, and when I rose to leave the room and
glanced round, he was in the shadow of the chimney and hidden
from my sight. But if he and the robber were two different persons,
their voices were strangely and most remarkably alike; for directly
the man addressed me in the road, I recognised his speech again."

"It is as I feared. The very man was here to-night," thought the
locksmith, changing colour. "What dark history is this!"

"Halloa!" cried a hoarse voice in his ear. "Halloa, halloa, halloa!
Bow wow wow. What's the matter here! Hal-loa!"

The speaker—who made the locksmith start, as if he had been
some supernatural agent—was a large raven; who had perched upon
the top of the easy-chair, unseen by him and Edward, and listened
with a polite attention and a most extraordinary appearance of com-
prehending every word, to all they had said up to this point; turning
his head from one to the other, as if his office were to judge between
them, and it were of the very last importance that he should not lose
a word.

"Look at him!" said Varden, divided between admiration of the
bird and a kind of fear of him. "Was there ever such a knowing imp
as that! Oh he's a dreadful fellow!"

The raven, with his head very much on one side, and his bright eye
shining like a diamond, preserved a thoughtful silence for a few seconds, and then replied in a voice so hoarse and distant, that it seemed
to come through his thick feathers rather than out of his mouth.

"Halloa, halloa, halloa! What's the matter here! Keep up your
spirits. Never say die. Bow wow wow. I'm a devil, I'm a devil, I'm a
devil. Hurrah!"—And then, as if exulting in his infernal character,
he began to whistle.

"I more than half believe he speaks the truth. Upon my word I do," said Varden. "Do you see how he looks at me, as if he knew what I was saying?"

To which the bird, balancing himself on tiptoe, as it were, and moving his body up and down in a sort of grave dance, rejoined, "I'm a devil, I'm a devil, I'm a devil," and flapped his wings against his sides as if he were bursting with laughter. Barnaby clapped his hands, and fairly rolled upon the ground in an ecstacy of delight.

"Strange companions, sir," said the locksmith, shaking his head and looking from one to the other. "The bird has all the wit."

"Strange indeed!" said Edward, holding out his forefinger to the raven, who, in acknowledgement of the attention, made a dive at it immediately with his iron bill. "Is he old?"

"A mere boy, sir," replied the locksmith. "A hundred and twenty, or thereabouts. Call him down, Barnaby my man."

"Call him!" echoed Barnaby, sitting upright upon the floor, and staring vacantly at Gabriel, as he thrust his hair back from his face. "But who can make him come! He calls me, and makes me go where he will. He goes on before, and I follow. He's the master, and I'm the man. Is that the truth, Grip?"

The raven gave a short, comfortable, confidential kind of croak;— a most expressive croak, which seemed to say, "You needn't let these fellows into our secrets. We understand each other. It's all right."

"I make *him* come!" cried Barnaby, pointing to the bird. "Him, who never goes to sleep, or so much as winks!—Why, any time of night, you may see his eyes in my dark room, shining like two sparks. And every night, and all night too, he's broad awake, talking to himself, thinking what he shall do to-morrow, where we shall go, and what he shall steal, and hide, and bury. I make *him* come! Ha, ha, ha!"

On second thoughts, the bird appeared disposed to come of himself. After a short survey of the ground, and a few sidelong looks at the ceiling and at everybody present in turn, he fluttered to the floor, and went to Barnaby—not in a hop, or walk, or run, but in a pace like that of a very particular gentleman with exceedingly tight boots on, trying to walk fast over loose pebbles. Then, stepping into his extended hand, and condescending to be held out at arm's length, he gave vent to a succession of sounds, not unlike the drawing of some eight or ten dozen of long corks, and again asserted his brimstone birth and parentage with great distinctness.

The locksmith shook his head—perhaps in some doubt of the creature's being really nothing but a bird—perhaps in pity for Barnaby, who by this time had him in his arms, and was rolling about with him on the ground. As he raised his eyes from the poor fellow he encountered those of his mother, who had entered the room, and was looking on in silence.

She was quite white in the face, even to her lips, but had wholly subdued her emotion, and wore her usual quiet look. Varden fancied as he glanced at her that she shrunk from his eye; and that she busied herself about the wounded gentleman to avoid him the better.

It was time he went to bed, she said. He was to be removed to his own home on the morrow, and he had already exceeded his time for sitting up, by a full hour. Acting on this hint, the locksmith prepared to take his leave.

"By the bye," said Edward, as he shook him by the hand, and looked from him to Mrs. Rudge and back again, "what noise was that below? I heard your voice in the midst of it, and should have inquired before, but our other conversation drove it from my memory. What was it?"

The locksmith looked towards her, and bit his lip. She leant against the chair, and bent her eyes upon the ground. Barnaby too— he was listening.

—"Some mad or drunken fellow, sir," Varden at length made answer, looking steadily at the widow as he spoke. "He mistook the house, and tried to force an entrance."

She breathed more freely, but stood quite motionless. As the locksmith said "Good night," and Barnaby caught up the candle to light him down the stairs, she took it from him, and charged him—with more haste and earnestness than so slight an occasion appeared to warrant—not to stir. The raven followed them to satisfy himself that all was right below, and when they reached the street-door, stood on the bottom stair, drawing corks out of number.

With a trembling hand she unfastened the chain and bolts, and turned the key. As she had her hand upon the latch, the locksmith said in a low voice,

"I have told a lie to-night, for your sake, Mary, and for the sake of bygone times and old acquaintances, when I would scorn to do so for my own. I hope I may have done no harm, or led to none. I can't help the suspicions you have forced upon me, and I am loath, I tell you plainly, to leave Mr. Edward here. Take care he comes to no hurt. I doubt the safety of this roof, and am glad he leaves it so soon. Now, let me go."

For a moment she hid her face in her hands and wept; but resisting the strong impulse which evidently moved her to reply, opened the door—no wider than was sufficient for the passage of his body—and motioned him away. As the locksmith stood upon the step, it was chained and locked behind him, and the raven, in furtherance of these precautions, barked like a lusty house-dog.

"In league with that ill-looking figure that might have fallen from a gibbet—he listening and hiding here—Barnaby first upon the spot last night—can she who has always borne so fair a name be guilty of such crimes in secret!" said the locksmith, musing. "Heaven forgive me if I am wrong, and send me just thoughts; but she is poor, the temptation may be great, and we daily hear of things as strange.—Ay, bark away, my friend. If there's any wickedness going on, that raven's in it, I'll be sworn."

### CHAPTER THE SEVENTH.

MRS. VARDEN was a lady of what is commonly called an uncertain temper—a phrase which being interpreted signifies a temper tolerably certain to make every body more or less uncomfortable. Thus it generally happened, that when other people were merry, Mrs. Varden was dull; and that when other people were dull, Mrs. Varden was disposed to be amazingly cheerful. Indeed the worthy housewife was of such a capricious nature, that she not only attained a higher pitch of genius than Macbeth,* in respect of her ability to be wise, amazed, temperate and furious, loyal and neutral in an instant, but would sometimes ring the changes backwards and forwards on all possible moods and flights in one short quarter of an hour; performing, as it were, a kind of triple bob major* on the peal of instruments in the female belfry, with a skilfulness and rapidity of execution that astonished all who heard her.

It had been observed in this good lady (who did not want for personal attractions, being plump and buxom to look at, though like her fair daughter, somewhat short in stature) that this uncertainty of disposition strengthened and increased with her temporal prosperity; and divers wise men and matrons, on friendly terms with the locksmith and his family, even went so far as to assert, that a tumble down some half-dozen rounds in the world's ladder—such as the breaking of the bank in which her husband kept his money, or some little fall of that kind—would be the making of her, and could hardly fail to render her one of the most agreeable companions in existence. Whether they were right or wrong in this conjecture, certain it is that minds, like bodies, will often fall into a pimpled ill-conditioned state from mere excess of comfort, and like them, are often successfully cured by remedies in themselves very nauseous and unpalatable.

Mrs. Varden's chief aider and abettor, and at the same time her principal victim and object of wrath, was her single domestic servant, one Miss Miggs; or as she was called, in conformity with those prejudices of society which lop and top from poor handmaidens all such genteel excrescences—Miggs. This Miggs was a tall young lady, very much addicted to pattens* in private life; slender and shrewish, of a rather uncomfortable figure, and though not absolutely ill-looking, of a sharp and acid visage. As a general principle and abstract proposition, Miggs held the male sex to be utterly contemptible and unworthy of notice; to be fickle, false, base, sottish, inclined to perjury, and wholly undeserving. When particularly exasperated against them (which, scandal said, was when Sim Tappertit slighted her most) she was accustomed to wish with great emphasis that the whole race of women could but die off, in order that the men might be brought to know the real value of the blessings by which they set so little store; nay, her feeling for her order ran so high, that she sometimes declared, if she could only have good security for a fair, round number—say ten thousand—of young virgins following her example, she would, to spite mankind, hang, drown, stab, or poison herself, with a joy past all expression.

It was the voice of Miggs that greeted the locksmith, when he knocked at his own house, with a shrill cry of "Who's there?"

"Me, girl, me," returned Gabriel.

"What, already, sir!" said Miggs, opening the door with a look of surprise. "We was just getting on our nightcaps to sit up,—me and mistress. Oh, she has been *so* bad!"

Miggs said this with an air of uncommon candour and concern; but the parlour-door was standing open, and as Gabriel very well knew for whose ears it was designed, he regarded her with anything but an approving look as he passed in.

"Master's come home, mim," cried Miggs, running before him into the parlour. "You was wrong, mim, and I was right. I thought he wouldn't keep us up so late, two nights running, mim. Master's always considerate so far. I'm so glad, mim, on your account. I'm a little"—here Miggs simpered—"a little sleepy myself; I'll own it now, mim, though I said I wasn't when you asked me. It an't of no consequence, mim, of course."

"You had better," said the locksmith, who most devoutly wished that Barnaby's raven was at Miggs' ancles, "you had better get to bed at once then."

"Thanking you kindly, sir," returned Miggs, "I couldn't take my rest in peace, nor fix my thoughts upon my prayers, otherways than that I knew mistress was comfortable in her bed this night; by rights she should have been there, hours ago."

"You're talkative, mistress," said Varden, pulling off his great-coat, and looking at her askew.

"Taking the hint, sir," cried Miggs, with a flushed face, "and thanking you for it most kindly, I will make bold to say, that if I give offence by having consideration for my mistress, I do not ask your pardon, but am content to get myself into trouble and to be in suffering."

Here Mrs. Varden, who, with her countenance shrouded in a large nightcap, had been all this time intent upon the Protestant Manual, looked round, and acknowledged Miggs' championship by commanding her to hold her tongue.

Every little bone in Miggs' throat and neck developed itself with a spitefulness quite alarming, as she replied, "Yes, mim, I will."

"How do you find yourself now, my dear?" said the locksmith, taking a chair near his wife (who had resumed her book), and rubbing his knees hard, as he made the inquiry.

"You're very anxious to know, an't you?" returned Mrs. Varden, with her eyes upon the print. "You, that have not been near me all day, and wouldn't have been if I was dying!"

"My dear Martha—" said Gabriel.

Mrs. Varden turned over to the next page; then went back again to the bottom line over leaf to be quite sure of the last words; and then went on reading with an appearance of the deepest interest and study.

"My dear Martha," said the locksmith, "how can you say such things, when you know you don't mean them? If you were dying!

Why, if there was anything serious the matter with you, Martha, shouldn't I be in constant attendance upon you?"

"Yes!" cried Mrs. Varden, bursting into tears, "yes, you would. I don't doubt it, Varden. Certainly you would. That's as much as to tell me that you would be hovering round me like a vulture, waiting till the breath was out of my body, that you might go and marry somebody else."

Miggs groaned in sympathy—a little short groan, checked in its birth, and changed into a cough. It seemed to say, "I can't help it. It's wrung from me by the dreadful brutality of that monster master."

"But you'll break my heart one of these days," added Mrs. Varden, with more resignation, "and then we shall both be happy. My only desire is to see Dolly comfortably settled, and when she is, you may settle *me* as soon as you like."

"Ah!" cried Miggs—and coughed again.

Poor Gabriel twisted his wig about in silence for a long time, and then said mildly, "Has Dolly gone to bed?"

"Your master speaks to you," said Mrs. Varden, looking sternly over her shoulder at Miss Miggs in waiting.

"No, my dear, I spoke to you," suggested the locksmith.

"Did you hear me, Miggs?" cried the obdurate lady, stamping her foot upon the ground. "*You* are beginning to despise me now, are you? But this is example!"

At this cruel rebuke, Miggs, whose tears were always ready, for large or small parties, on the shortest notice and the most reasonable terms, fell a crying violently; holding both her hands tight upon her heart meanwhile, as if nothing less would prevent its splitting into small fragments. Mrs. Varden, who likewise possessed that faculty in high perfection, wept too, against Miggs; and with such effect that Miggs gave in after a time, and, except for an occasional sob, which seemed to threaten some remote intention of breaking out again, left her mistress in possession of the field. Her superiority being thoroughly asserted, that lady soon desisted likewise, and fell into a quiet melancholy.

The relief was so great, and the fatiguing occurrences of last night so completely overpowered the locksmith, that he nodded in his chair, and would doubtless have slept there all night, but for the voice of Mrs. Varden, which, after a pause of some five minutes, awoke him with a start.

"If I am ever," said Mrs V.—not scolding, but in a sort of monotonous remonstrance—"in spirits, if I am ever cheerful, if I am ever more than usually disposed to be talkative and comfortable, this is the way I am treated."

"Such spirits as you was in too, mim, but half an hour ago!" cried Miggs. "I never see such company!"

"Because," said Mrs. Varden, "because I never interfere or interrupt; because I never question where anybody comes or goes; because my whole mind and soul is bent on saving where I can save, and labouring in this house;—therefore, they try me as they do."

"Martha," urged the locksmith, endeavouring to look as wakeful as possible, "what is it you complain of? I really came home with every wish and desire to be happy. I did, indeed."

"What do I complain of!" retorted his wife. "Is it a chilling thing to have one's husband sulking and falling asleep directly he comes home—to have him freezing all one's warm-heartedness, and throwing cold water over the fireside? Is it natural, when I know he went out upon a matter in which I am as much interested as anybody can be, that I should wish to know all that has happened, or that he should tell me without my begging and praying him to do it? Is that natural, or is it not?"

"I am very sorry, Martha," said the good-natured locksmith. "I was really afraid you were not disposed to talk pleasantly; I'll tell you everything; I shall only be too glad, my dear."

"No, Varden," returned his wife, rising with dignity. "I dare say— thank you. I'm not a child to be corrected one minute and petted the next—I'm a little too old for that, Varden. Miggs, carry the light. *You* can be cheerful, Miggs, at least."

Miggs, who, to this moment, had been in the very depths of compassionate despondency, passed instantly into the liveliest state conceivable, and tossing her head as she glanced towards the locksmith, bore off her mistress and the light together.

"Now, who would think," thought Varden, shrugging his shoulders and drawing his chair nearer to the fire, "that that woman could ever be pleasant and agreeable? And yet she can be. Well, well, all of us have our faults. I'll not be hard upon hers. We have been man and wife too long for that."

He dozed again—not the less pleasantly, perhaps, for his hearty temper. While his eyes were closed, the door leading to the upper stairs was partially opened; and a head appeared, which, at sight of him, hastily drew back again.

"I wish," murmured Gabriel, waking at the noise, and looking round the room, "I wish somebody would marry Miggs. But that's impossible! I wonder whether there's any madman alive, who would marry Miggs!"

This was such a vast speculation that he fell into a doze again, and slept until the fire was quite burnt out. At last he roused himself; and having double-locked the street-door according to custom, and put the key in his pocket, went off to bed.

He had not left the room in darkness many minutes, when the head again appeared, and Sim Tappertit entered, bearing in his hand a little lamp.

"What the devil business has he to stop up so late!" muttered Sim, passing into the workshop, and setting it down upon the forge. "Here's half the night gone already. There's only one good that has ever come to me, out of this cursed old rusty mechanical trade, and that's this piece of ironmongery, upon my soul!"

As he spoke, he drew from the right hand, or rather right leg pocket of his smalls,* a clumsy large-sized key, which he inserted cautiously in the lock his master had secured, and softly opened the door. That done, he replaced his piece of secret workmanship in his pocket; and leaving the lamp burning, and closing the door carefully and without noise, stole out into the street—as little suspected by the locksmith in his sound deep sleep, as by Barnaby himself in his phantom-haunted dreams.

## CHAPTER THE EIGHTH.

CLEAR of the locksmith's house, Sim Tappertit laid aside his cautious manner, and assuming in its stead that of a ruffling, swaggering, roving blade, who would rather kill a man than otherwise, and eat him too if needful, made the best of his way along the darkened streets.

Half pausing for an instant now and then to smite his pocket and assure himself of the safety of his master key, he hurried on to Barbican,* and turning into one of the narrowest of the narrow streets which diverged from that centre, slackened his pace and wiped his heated brow, as if the termination of his walk were near at hand.

It was not a very choice spot for midnight expeditions, being in truth one of more than questionable character, and of an appearance by no means inviting. From the main street he had entered, itself little better than an alley, a low-browed doorway led into a blind court, or yard, profoundly dark, unpaved, and reeking with stagnant odours. Into this ill-favoured pit, the locksmith's vagrant 'prentice groped his way; and stopping at a house from whose defaced and rotten front the rude effigy of a bottle swung to and fro like some gibbeted malefactor, struck thrice upon an iron grating with his foot. After listening in vain for some response to his signal, Mr. Tappertit became impatient, and struck the grating thrice again.

A further delay ensued, but it was not of long duration. The ground seemed to open at his feet, and a ragged head appeared.

"Is that the captain?" said a voice as ragged as the head.

"Yes," replied Mr. Tappertit haughtily, descending as he spoke, "who should it be?"

"It's so late, we gave you up," returned the voice, as its owner stopped to shut and fasten the grating. "You're late, sir."

"Lead on," said Mr. Tappertit, with a gloomy majesty, "and make remarks when I require you. Forward!"

This latter word of command was perhaps somewhat theatrical and unnecessary, inasmuch as the descent was by a very narrow, steep, and slippery flight of steps, and any rashness or departure from the beaten track must have ended in a yawning water-butt. But Mr. Tappertit being, like some other great commanders, favourable to strong effects, and personal display, cried "Forward!" again, in the hoarsest voice he could assume; and led the way, with folded arms and knitted brows, to the cellar down below, where there was a small copper fixed in one corner, a chair or two, a form and table, a glimmering fire, and a truckle-bed, covered with a ragged patchwork rug.

"Welcome, noble captain!" cried a lanky figure, rising as from a nap.

The captain nodded. Then, throwing off his outer coat, he stood composed in all his dignity, and eyed his follower over.

"What news to-night?" he asked, when he had looked into his very soul.

"Nothing particular," replied the other, stretching himself—and he was so long already that it was quite alarming to see him do it— "how come you to be so late?"

"No matter," was all the captain deigned to say in answer. "Is the room prepared?"

"It is," replied his follower.

"The comrade—is he here?"

"Yes. And a sprinkling of the others—you hear 'em?"

"Playing skittles!" said the captain moodily. "Light-hearted revellers!"

There was no doubt respecting the particular amusement in which these heedless spirits were indulging, for even in the close and stifling atmosphere of the vault, the noise sounded like distant thunder. It certainly appeared, at first sight, a singular spot to choose, for that or any other purpose of relaxation, if the other cellars answered to the one in which this brief colloquy took place; for the floors were of sodden earth, the walls and roof of damp bare brick tapestried with the tracks of snails and slugs; the air was sickening, tainted, and offensive. It seemed, from one strong flavour which was uppermost among the various odours of the place, that it had, at no very distant period, been used as a storehouse for cheeses; a circumstance which, while it accounted for the greasy moisture that hung about it, was agreeably suggestive of rats. It was naturally damp besides, and little trees of fungus sprung from every mouldering corner.

The proprietor of this charming retreat, and owner of the ragged head before mentioned—for he wore an old tie-wig as bare and frouzy as a stunted hearth-broom—had by this time joined them; and stood a little apart, rubbing his hands, wagging his hoary bristled chin, and smiling in silence. His eyes were closed; but had they been wide open, it would have been easy to tell, from the attentive expression of the face he turned towards them—pale and unwholesome as might be expected in one of his underground exist- ence—and from a certain anxious raising and quivering of the lids, that he was blind.

"Even Stagg hath been asleep," said the long comrade, nodding towards this person.

"Sound, captain, sound!" cried the blind man; "what does my noble captain drink—is it brandy, rum, usquebaugh?* Is it soaked gunpowder, or blazing oil? Give it a name, heart of oak, and we'd get it for you, if it was wine from a bishop's cellar, or melted gold from King George's mint."

"See," said Mr. Tappertit haughtily, "that it's something strong, and comes quick; and so long as you take care of that, you may bring it from the devil's cellar, if you like."

"Boldly said, noble captain!" rejoined the blind man. "Spoken like the 'Prentices' Glory. Ha, ha! From the devil's cellar! A brave joke! The captain joketh. Ha, ha, ha!"

"I'll tell you what, my fine feller," said Mr. Tappertit, eyeing the host over as he walked to a closet, and took out a bottle and glass as carelessly as if he had been in full possession of his sight, "if you make that row, you'll find that the captain's very far from joking, and so I tell you."

"He's got his eyes on me!" cried Stagg, stopping short on his way back, and affecting to screen his face with the bottle. "I feel 'em though I can't see 'em. Take 'em off, noble captain. Remove 'em, for they pierce like gimlets."

Mr. Tappertit smiled grimly at his comrade; and twisting out one more look—a kind of ocular screw—under the influence of which the blind man feigned to undergo great anguish and torture, bade him, in a softened tone, approach, and hold his peace.

"I obey you, captain," cried Stagg, drawing close to him and filling out a bumper without spilling a drop, by reason that he held his little finger at the brim of the glass, and stopped at the instant the liquor touched it, "drink, noble governor. Death to all masters, life to all 'prentices, and love to all fair damsels. Drink, brave general, and warm your gallant heart!"

Mr. Tappertit condescended to take the glass from his out- stretched hand. Stagg then dropped on one knee, and gently smoothed the calves of his legs, with an air of humble admiration.

"That I had but eyes!" he cried, "to behold my captain's sym-metrical proportions! That I had but eyes, to look upon these twin invaders of domestic peace!"

"Get out!" said Mr. Tappertit, glancing downward at his favourite limbs. "Go along, will you, Stagg!"

"When I touch my own afterwards," cried the host, smiting them reproachfully, "I hate 'em. Comparatively speaking, they've no more shape than wooden legs, beside these models of my noble captain's."

"Yours!" exclaimed Mr. Tappertit. "No, I should think not. Don't talk about those precious old toothpicks in the same breath with mine; that's rather too much. Here. Take the glass. Benjamin. Lead on. To business!"

With these words, he folded his arms again; and frowning with a sullen majesty, passed with his companion through a little door at the upper end of the cellar, and disappeared; leaving Stagg to his private meditations.

The vault they entered, strewn with sawdust and dimly lighted, was between the outer one from which they had just come, and that in which the skittle-players were diverting themselves; as was mani-fested by the increased noise and clamour of tongues, which was suddenly stopped, however, and replaced by a dead silence, at a signal from the long comrade. Then, this young gentleman, going to a little cupboard, returned with a thigh-bone, which in former times must have been part and parcel of some individual at least as long as himself, and placed the same in the hands of Mr. Tappertit; who, receiving it as a sceptre and staff of authority, cocked his three-cornered hat fiercely on the top of his head, and mounted a large table, whereon a chair of state, cheerfully ornamented with a couple of skulls, was placed ready for his reception.

He had no sooner assumed this position, than another young gentleman appeared, bearing in his arms a huge clasped book, who made him a profound obeisance, and delivering it to the long com-rade, advanced to the table, and turning his back upon it, stood there Atlas-wise.* Then, the long comrade got upon the table too; and seating himself in a lower chair than Mr. Tappertit's, with much state and ceremony, placed the large book on the shoulders of their mute companion as deliberately as if he had been a wooden desk, and prepared to make entries therein with a pen of corresponding size.

When the long comrade had made these preparations, he looked towards Mr. Tappertit; and Mr. Tappertit, flourishing the bone, knocked nine times therewith upon one of the skulls. At the ninth stroke, a third young gentleman emerged from the door leading to the skittle ground, and bowing low, awaited his commands.

"'Prentice!" said the mighty captain, "who waits without?"

The 'prentice made answer that a stranger was in attendance, who claimed admission into that secret society of 'Prentice Knights, and a free participation in their rights, privileges, and immunities. Thereupon Mr. Tappertit flourished the bone again, and giving the other skull a prodigious rap on the nose, exclaimed "Admit him!" At these dread words the 'prentice bowed once more, and so withdrew as he had come.

There soon appeared at the same door, two other 'prentices, having between them a third, whose eyes were bandaged, and who was attired in a bag-wig,* and a broad-skirted coat, trimmed with tarnished lace; and who was girded with a sword, in compliance with the laws of the Institution regulating the introduction of candidates, which required them to assume this courtly dress, and kept it

constantly in lavender, for their convenience. One of the conductors of this novice held a rusty blunderbuss pointed towards his ear, and the other a very ancient sabre, with which he carved imaginary offenders as he came along in a sanguinary and anatomical manner.

As this silent group advanced, Mr. Tappertit fixed his hat upon his head. The novice then laid his hand upon his breast and bent before him. When he had humbled himself sufficiently, the captain ordered the bandage to be removed, and proceeded to eye him over.

"Ha!" said the captain, thoughtfully, when he had concluded this ordeal. "Proceed."

The long comrade read aloud as follows:—"Mark Gilbert. Age, nineteen. Bound to Thomas Curzon, hosier, Golden Fleece, Aldgate. Loves Curzon's daughter. Cannot say that Curzon's daughter loves him. Should think it probable. Curzon pulled his ears last Tuesday week."

"How!" cried the captain, starting.

"For looking at his daughter, please you," said the novice.

"Write Curzon down, Denounced," said the captain. "Put a black cross against the name of Curzon."

"So please you," said the novice, "that's not the worst—he calls his 'prentice idle dog, and stops his beer unless he works to his liking. He gives Dutch cheese, too, eating Cheshire sir, himself; and Sundays out, are only once a month."

"This," said Mr. Tappertit gravely, "is a flagrant case. Put two black crosses to the name of Curzon."

"If the society," said the novice, who was an ill-looking, one-sided, shambling lad, with sunken eyes set close together in his head—"if the society would burn his house down—for he's not insured—or beat him as he comes home from his club at night, or help me to carry off his daughter, and marry her at the Fleet,* whether she gave consent or no—"

Mr. Tappertit waved his grizzly truncheon as an admonition to him not to interrupt, and ordered three black crosses to the name of Curzon.

"Which means," he said in gracious explanation, "vengeance, complete and terrible. 'Prentice, do you love the Constitution?"

To which the novice (being to that end instructed by his attendant sponsors) replied "I do!"

"The Church, the State, and everything established—but the masters?" quoth the captain.

Again the novice said "I do."

Having said it, he listened meekly to the captain, who, in an address prepared for such occasions, told him how that under that same Constitution (which was kept in a strong-box somewhere, but where exactly he could not find out, or he would have endeavoured to procure a copy of it), the 'prentices had, in times gone by, had frequent holidays of right, broken people's heads by scores, defied their masters, nay, even achieved some glorious murders in the streets, which privileges had gradually been wrested from them, and in all which noble aspirations they were now restrained; how the degrading checks imposed upon them were unquestionably attributable to the innovating spirit of the times, and how they united therefore to resist all change, except such change as would restore those good old English customs, by which they would stand or fall. After illustrating the wisdom of going backward, by reference to that sagacious fish, the crab, and the not unfrequent practice of the mule and donkey, he described their general objects; which were briefly vengeance on their Tyrant Masters (of whose grievous and insupportable oppression no 'prentice could entertain a moment's doubt) and the restoration, as aforesaid, of their ancient rights and holidays; for neither of which objects were they now quite ripe, being barely twenty strong, but which they pledged themselves to pursue with fire and sword when needful. Then he described the oath which every member of that small remnant of a noble body took, and which was of a dreadful and impressive kind; binding him, at the bidding of his chief, to resist and obstruct the Lord Mayor, sword-bearer, and chaplain; to despise the authority of the sheriffs; and to hold the court of aldermen* as nought; but not on any account, in case the fullness of time should bring a general rising of 'prentices, to damage or in any way disfigure Temple Bar,* which was strictly constitutional and always to be approached with reverence. Having gone over these several heads with great eloquence and force, and having further informed the novice that this society had had its origin in his own teeming brain, stimulated by a swelling sense of wrong and outrage, Mr. Tappertit demanded whether he had strength of heart to take the mighty pledge required, or whether he would withdraw while retreat was yet within his power.

To this, the novice made rejoinder that he would take the vow, though it should choke him; and it was accordingly administered with many impressive circumstances, among which the lighting up of the two skulls with a candle-end inside of each, and a great many flourishes with the bone, were chiefly conspicuous; not to mention a variety of grave exercises with the blunderbuss and sabre, and some dismal groaning by unseen 'prentices without. All these dark and direful ceremonies being at length completed, the table was put aside, the chair of state removed, the sceptre locked up in its usual cupboard, the doors of communication between the three cellars thrown freely open, and the 'Prentice Knights resigned themselves to merriment.

But Mr. Tappertit, who had a soul above the vulgar herd, and who, on account of his greatness, could only afford to be merry now and then, threw himself on a bench with the air of a man who was faint with dignity. He looked with an indifferent eye, alike on skittles, cards, and dice, thinking only of the locksmith's daughter, and the base degenerate days on which he had fallen.

"My noble captain neither games, nor sings, nor dances," said his host, taking a seat beside him. "Drink, gallant general!"

Mr. Tappertit drained the proffered goblet to the dregs; then thrust his hands into his pockets, and with a lowering visage walked among the skittles, while his followers (such is the influence of superior genius) restrained the ardent ball, and held his little shins in dumb respect.

"If I had been born a corsair or a pirate, a brigand, gen-teel highwayman or patriot—and they're the same thing," thought Mr. Tappertit, musing among the nine-pins, "I should have been all right. But to drag out a ignoble existence unbeknown to mankind in general—patience! I will be famous yet. A voice within me keeps on whispering Greatness. I shall burst out one of these days, and when I do, what power can keep me down? I feel my soul getting into my head at the idea. More drink there!"

"The novice," pursued Mr. Tappertit, not exactly in a voice of thunder, for his tones, to say the truth, were rather cracked and shrill,—but very impressively, notwithstanding—"where is he?"

"Here, noble captain!" cried Stagg. "One stands beside me who I feel is a stranger."

"Have you," said Mr. Tappertit, letting his gaze fall on the party indicated, who was indeed the new knight, by this time restored to his own apparel; "Have you the impression of your street-door key in wax?"

The long comrade anticipated the reply, by producing it from the shelf on which it had been deposited.

"Good," said Mr. Tappertit, scrutinising it attentively, while a breathless silence reigned around; for he had constructed secret door-keys for the whole society, and perhaps owed something of his influence to that mean and trivial circumstance—on such slight accidents do even men of mind depend!—"This is easily made. Come hither, friend."

With that, he beckoned the new knight apart, and putting the pattern in his pocket, motioned to him to walk by his side.

"And so," he said, when they had taken a few turns up and down, "you—you love your master's daughter?"

"I do," said the 'prentice. "Honour bright. No chaff, you know."

"Have you," rejoined Mr. Tappertit, catching him by the wrist, and giving him a look which would have been expressive of the most deadly malevolence, but for an accidental hiccup that rather interfered with it; "have you a—a rival?"

"Not as I know on," replied the 'prentice.

"If you had now—" said Mr. Tappertit—"what would you—eh—?"

The 'prentice looked fierce and clenched his fists.

"It is enough," cried Mr. Tappertit hastily, "we understand each other. We are observed. I thank you."

So saying, he cast him off again; and calling the long comrade aside after taking a few hasty turns by himself, bade him immediately write and post against the wall, a notice, proscribing one Joseph Willet (commonly known as Joe) of Chigwell; forbidding all 'Prentice Knights to succour, comfort, or hold communion with him; and requiring them, on pain of excommunication, to molest, hurt, wrong, annoy, and pick quarrels with the said Joseph, whensoever and wheresoever they, or any of them, should happen to encounter him.

Having relieved his mind by this energetic proceeding, he condescended to approach the festive board, and warming by degrees, at length deigned to preside, and even to enchant the company with a song. After this, he rose to such a pitch as to consent to regale the society with a hornpipe, which he actually performed to the music of a fiddle (played by an ingenious member) with such surpassing agility and brilliancy of execution, that the spectators could not be sufficiently enthusiastic in their admiration; and their host protested, with tears in his eyes, that he had never truly felt his blindness until that moment.

But the host withdrawing—probably to weep in secret—soon returned with the information that it wanted little more than an hour of day, and that all the cocks in Barbican had already begun to crow, as if their lives depended on it. At this intelligence, the 'Prentice Knights arose in haste, and marshalling into a line, filed off one by one and dispersed with all speed to their several homes, leaving their leader to pass the grating last.

"Good night, noble captain," whispered the blind man as he held it open for his passage out; "Farewell brave general. Bye, bye, illustrious commander. Good luck go with you for a—conceited, bragging, empty-headed, duck-legged idiot."

With which parting words, coolly added as he listened to his receding footsteps and locked the grate upon himself, he descended the steps, and lighting the fire below the little copper, prepared, without any assistance, for his daily occupation; which was to retail at the area-head above pennyworths of broth and soup, and savoury puddings, compounded of such scraps as were to be bought in the heap for the least money at Fleet Market* in the evening time; and for the sale of which he had need to have depended chiefly on his private connexion, for the court had no thoroughfare, and was not that kind of place in which many people were likely to take the air, or to frequent as an agreeable promenade.

## CHAPTER THE NINTH.

CHRONICLERS are privileged to enter where they list, to come and go through keyholes, to ride upon the wind, to overcome, in their soarings up and down, all obstacles of distance, time, and place. Thrice blessed be this last consideration, since it enables us to follow the disdainful Miggs even into the sanctity of her chamber, and to hold her in sweet companionship through the dreary watches of the night!

Miss Miggs, having undone her mistress, as she phrased it (which means, assisted to undress her), and having seen her comfortably to bed in the back room on the first floor, withdrew to her own apartment, in the attic story. Notwithstanding her declaration in the locksmith's presence, she was in no mood for sleep; so, putting her light upon the table and withdrawing the little window curtain, she gazed out pensively at the wild night sky.

Perhaps she wondered what star was destined for her habitation when she had run her little course below; perhaps speculated which of those glimmering spheres might be the natal orb of Mr. Tappertit; perhaps marvelled how they could gaze down on that perfidious creature, man, and not sicken and turn green as chemists' lamps; perhaps thought of nothing in particular. Whatever she thought about, there she sat, until her attention, alive to anything connected with the insinuating 'prentice, was attracted by a noise in the next room to her own—his room; the room in which he slept, and dreamed—it might be, sometimes dreamed of her.

That he was not dreaming now, unless he was taking a walk in his sleep, was clear, for every now and then there came a shuffling noise, as though he were engaged in polishing the whitewashed wall; then a gentle creaking of his door; then the faintest indication of his stealthy footsteps on the landing-place outside. Noting this latter circumstance, Miss Miggs turned pale and shuddered, as mistrusting his intentions; and more than once exclaimed, below her breath, "Oh! what a Providence it is as I am bolted in!"—which, owing doubtless to her alarm, was a confusion of ideas on her part between a bolt and its use; for though there was one on the door, it was not fastened.

Miss Miggs' sense of hearing, however, having as sharp an edge as her temper, and being of the same snappish and suspicious kind, very soon informed her that the footsteps passed her door, and appeared to have some object quite separate and disconnected from herself. At this discovery she became more alarmed than ever, and was about to give utterance to those cries of "Thieves!" and "Murder!" which she had hitherto restrained, when it occurred to her to look softly out, and see that her fears had some good palpable foundation.

Looking out accordingly, and stretching her neck over the handrail, she descried, to her great amazement, Mr. Tappertit completely dressed, stealing down stairs, one step at a time, with his shoes in one hand and a lamp in the other. Following him with her eyes, and going down a little way herself to get the better of an intervening angle, she beheld him thrust his head in at the parlour door, draw it back again with great swiftness, and immediately begin a retreat up stairs with all possible expedition.

"Here's mysteries!" said the damsel, when she was safe in her own room again, quite out of breath. "Oh gracious, here's mysteries!"

The prospect of finding anybody out in anything, would have kept Miss Miggs awake under the influence of henbane.* Presently she heard the step again, as she would have done if it had been that of a feather endowed with motion and walking down on tiptoe. Then gliding out as before, she again beheld the retreating figure of the 'prentice; again he looked cautiously in at the parlour door, but this time, instead of retreating, he passed in and disappeared.

Miggs was back in her room, and had her head out of the window, before an elderly gentleman could have winked and recovered from it. Out he came at the street door, shut it carefully behind him, tried it with his knee, and swaggered off, putting something in his pocket as he went along. At this spectacle Miggs cried "Gracious!" again, and then "Goodness gracious!" and then, "Goodness gracious me!" and then, candle in hand, went down stairs as he had done. Coming to the workshop, she saw the lamp burning on the forge, and everything as Sim had left it.

"Why I wish I may only have a walking funeral, and never be buried decent with a mourning-coach and feathers, if the boy hasn't been and made a key for his own self!" cried Miggs. "Oh the little villain!"

This conclusion was not arrived at without consideration, and much peeping and peering about; nor was it unassisted by the recollection that she had on several occasions come upon the 'prentice suddenly, and found him busy at some mysterious occupation. Lest the fact of Miss Miggs calling him, on whom she stooped to cast a favourable eye, a boy, should create surprise in any breast, it may be observed that she invariably affected to regard all male bipeds under thirty as mere chits and infants; which phenomenon is not unusual in ladies of Miss Miggs's temper, and is indeed generally found to be the associate of such indomitable and savage virtue.

Miss Miggs deliberated within herself for some little time, looking hard at the shop door while she did so, as though her eyes and thoughts were both upon it; and then, taking a sheet of paper from a drawer, twisted it into a long thin spiral tube. Having filled this instrument with a quantity of small coal dust from the forge, she approached the door, and dropping on one knee before it, dexterously blew into the keyhole as much of these fine ashes as the lock would hold. When she had filled it to the brim in a very workmanlike and skilful manner, she crept up stairs again, and chuckled as she went.

"There!" cried Miggs, rubbing her hands, "now let's see whether you won't be glad to take some notice of me, mister. He, he, he! You'll have eyes for somebody besides Miss Dolly now, I think. A fat-faced puss she is, as ever *I* come across!"

As she uttered this criticism, she glanced approvingly at her small mirror, as who should say, I thank my stars that can't be said of me!—as it certainly could not; for Miss Miggs' style of beauty was of that kind which Mr. Tappertit himself had not inaptly termed, in private, "scraggy."

"I don't go to bed this night!" said Miggs, wrapping herself in a shawl, drawing a couple of chairs near the window, flouncing down upon one, and putting her feet upon the other, "till you come home, my lad. I wouldn't," said Miggs viciously, "no, not for five-and-forty pound!"

With that, and with an expression of face in which a great number of opposite ingredients, such as mischief, cunning, malice, triumph, and patient expectation, were all mixed up together in a kind of physiognomical punch, Miss Miggs composed herself to wait and listen, like some fair ogress who had set a trap and was watching for a nibble from a plump young traveller.

She sat there, with perfect composure, all night. At length, just upon break of day, there was a footstep in the street, and presently she could hear Mr. Tappertit stop at the door. Then she could make out that he tried his key—that he was blowing into it—that he knocked it on the nearest post to beat the dust out—that he took it under a lamp to look at it—that he poked bits of stick into the lock to clear it—that he peeped into the keyhole, first with one eye, and then with the other—that he tried the key again—that he couldn't turn it, and what was worse, couldn't get it out—that he bent it—that then it was much less disposed to come out than before—that he gave it a

mighty twist and a great pull, and then it came out so suddenly that
he staggered backwards—that he kicked the door—that he shook
it—finally, that he smote his forehead, and sat down on the step in
despair.

When this crisis had arrived, Miss Miggs, affecting to be
exhausted with terror, and to cling to the window-sill for support,
put out her nightcap, and demanded in a faint voice who was there.

Mr. Tappertit cried "Hush!" and, backing into the road, exhorted
her in frenzied pantomime to secrecy and silence.

"Tell me one thing," said Miggs. "Is it thieves?"

"No—no—no!" cried Mr. Tappertit.

"Then," said Miggs, more faintly than before, "it's fire. Where
is it, sir? It's near this room, I know. I've a good conscience, sir,
and would much rather die than go down a ladder. All I wish

is, respecting my love to my married sister, Golden Lion Court, number twenty-sivin, second bell-handle on the right hand door-post."

"Miggs!" cried Mr. Tappertit, "don't you know me? Sim, you know—Sim—"

"Oh! what about him!" cried Miggs, clasping her hands. "Is he in any danger? Is he in the midst of flames and blazes? Oh gracious, gracious!"

"Why I'm here, an't I?" rejoined Mr. Tappertit, knocking himself on the breast. "Don't you see me? What a fool you are, Miggs!"

"There!" cried Miggs, unmindful of this compliment. "Why—so it—Goodness, what is the meaning of—If you please mim here's—"

"No, no!" cried Mr. Tappertit, standing on tiptoe, as if by that means he, in the street, were any nearer being able to stop the mouth of Miggs in the garret. "Don't!—I've been out without leave, and something or another's the matter with the lock. Come down, and undo the shop window, that I may get in that way."

"I durstn't do it, Simmun," cried Miggs—for that was her pronunciation of his christian name. "I durstn't do it, indeed. You know as well as anybody, how particular I am. And to come down in the dead of night, when the house is wrapped in slumbers and weiled in obscurity." And there she stopped and shivered, for her modesty caught cold at the very thought.

"But Miggs," cried Mr. Tappertit, getting under the lamp, that she might see his eyes. "My darling Miggs—"

Miggs screamed slightly.

"—That I love so much, and never can help thinking of,"—and it is impossible to describe the use he made of his eyes when he said this—"do—for my sake, do."

"Oh Simmun," cried Miggs, "this is worse than all. I know if I come down, you'll go, and—"

"And what, my precious?" said Mr. Tappertit.

"And try," said Miggs, hysterically, "to kiss me, or some such dreadfulness; I know you will!"

"I swear I won't," said Mr. Tappertit, with remarkable earnestness. "Upon my soul I won't. It's getting broad day and the watchman's waking up. Angelic Miggs! If you'll only come and let me in, I promise you faithfully and truly I won't."

Miss Miggs, whose gentle heart was touched, did not wait for the oath (knowing how strong the temptation was, and fearing he might forswear himself), but tripped lightly down the stairs, and with her own fair hands drew back the rough fastenings of the workshop window. Having helped the wayward 'prentice in, she faintly articulated the words "Simmun is safe!" and yielding to her woman's nature, immediately became insensible.

"I knew I should quench her," said Sim, rather embarrassed by this circumstance. "Of course I was certain it would come to this, but there was nothing else to be done—if I hadn't eyed her over, she wouldn't have come down. Here. Keep up a minute, Miggs. What a slippery figure she is! There's no holding her, comfortably. Do keep up a minute, Miggs, will you?"

As Miggs, however, was deaf to all entreaties, Mr. Tappertit leant her against the wall as one might dispose of a walking-stick or umbrella, until he had secured the window, when he took her in his arms again, and, in short stages and with great difficulty—arising mainly from her being tall and his being short, and perhaps in some degree from that peculiar physical conformation on which he had already remarked—carried her up stairs, and planting her, in the same umbrella or walking-stick fashion, just inside her own door, left her to her repose.

"He may be as cool as he likes," said Miss Miggs, recovering as soon as she was left alone; "but I'm in his confidence and he can't help himself, nor couldn't if he was twenty Simmunses!"

## CHAPTER THE TENTH.

IT was on one of those mornings, common in early spring, when the year, fickle and changeable in its youth like all other created things, is undecided whether to step backward into winter or forward into summer, and in its uncertainty inclines now to the one and now to the other, and now to both at once—wooing summer in the sunshine, and lingering still with winter in the shade—it was, in short, on one of those mornings, when it is hot and cold, wet and dry, bright and lowering, sad and cheerful, withering and genial, in the compass of one short hour, that old John Willet, who was dropping asleep over the copper boiler, was roused by the sound of a horse's feet, and glancing out at window, beheld a traveller of goodly promise checking his bridle at the Maypole door.

He was none of your flippant young fellows, who would call for a tankard of mulled ale, and make themselves as much at home as if they had ordered a hogshead of wine; none of your audacious young swaggerers, who would even penetrate into the bar—that solemn sanctuary—and, smiting old John upon the back, inquire if there was never a pretty girl in the house, and where he hid his little chambermaids, with a hundred other impertinencies of that nature; none of your free-and-easy companions, who would scrape their boots upon the fire-dogs* in the common room, and be not at all particular on the subject of spittoons; none of your unconscionable blades, requiring impossible chops, and taking unheard-of pickles for granted. He was a staid, grave, placid gentleman, something past the prime of life, yet upright in his carriage, for all that, and slim as a greyhound. He was well-mounted upon a sturdy chesnut cob, and had the graceful seat of an experienced horseman; while his riding gear, though free from such fopperies as were then in vogue, was handsome and well chosen. He wore a riding-coat of a somewhat brighter green than might have been expected to suit the taste of a gentleman of his years, with a short black velvet cape, laced pocket-holes and cuffs, all of a jaunty fashion; his linen, too, was of the finest kind, worked in a rich pattern at the wrists and throat, and scrupulously white. Although he seemed, judging from the mud he had picked up on the way, to have come from London, his horse was as smooth and cool as his own iron-grey periwig and pig-tail. Neither man nor beast had turned a single hair; and, saving for his soiled skirts and spatter-dashes,* this gentleman, with his blooming face, white teeth, exactly-ordered dress, and perfect calmness, might have come from making an elaborate and leisurely toilet, to sit for an equestrian portrait at old John Willet's gate.

It must not be supposed that John observed these several characteristics by other than very slow degrees, or that he took in more than half a one at a time, or that he even made up his mind upon that, without a great deal of very serious consideration. Indeed, if he had been distracted in the first instance by questionings and orders, it would have taken him at the least a fortnight to have noted what is here set down; but it happened that the gentleman, being struck with the old house, or with the plump pigeons which were skimming and curtseying about it, or with the tall maypole, on the top of which a weathercock, which had been out of order for fifteen years, performed a perpetual waltz to the music of its own creaking, sat for some little time looking round in silence. Hence John, standing with his hand upon the horse's bridle, and his great eyes on the rider, and with nothing passing to divert his thoughts, had really got some of these little circumstances into his brain, by the time he was called upon to speak.

"A quaint place this," said the gentleman—and his voice was as rich as his dress. "Are you the landlord?"

"At your service, sir," replied John Willet.

"You can give my horse good stabling, can you, and me an early dinner (I am not particular what, so that it be cleanly served), and a decent room—of which there seems to be no lack in this great mansion," said the stranger, again running his eyes over the exterior.

"You can have, sir," returned John, with a readiness quite surprising, "anything you please."

"It's well I am easily satisfied," returned the other with a smile, "or that might prove a hardy pledge, my friend." And saying so, he dismounted, with the aid of the block before the door, in a twinkling.

"Halloa there! Hugh!" roared John. "I ask your pardon, sir, for keeping you standing in the porch; but my son has gone to town on business, and the boy being, as I may say, of a kind of use to me, I'm rather put out when he's away. Hugh!—a dreadful idle vagrant fellow, sir—half a gipsy as I think—always sleeping in the sun in summer, and in the straw in winter time sir—Hugh! Dear Lord, to keep a gentleman a waiting here, through him!—Hugh! I wish that chap was dead, I do indeed."

"Possibly he is," returned the other. "I should think if he were living he would have heard you by this time."

"In his fits of laziness, he sleeps so desperate hard," said the distracted host, "if you were to fire off cannon-balls into his ears, it wouldn't wake him, sir."

The guest made no remark upon this novel cure for drowsiness, and recipe for making people lively, but with his hands clasped behind him stood in the porch, apparently very much amused to see old John, with the bridle in his hand, wavering between a strong impulse to abandon the animal to his fate, and a half disposition to lead him into the house, and shut him up in the parlour, while he waited on his master.

"Pillory the fellow, here he is at last," cried John, in the very height and zenith of his distress. "Did you hear me a calling, villain?"

The figure he addressed made no answer, but putting his hand upon the saddle, sprung into it at a bound, turned the horse's head towards the stable, and was gone in an instant.

"Brisk enough when he is awake," said the guest.

"Brisk enough, sir!" replied John, looking at the place where the horse had been, as if not yet understanding quite, what had become of him. "He melts, I think. He goes like a drop of froth. You look at him, and there he is. You look at him again, and—there he isn't."

Having, in the absence of any more words, put this sudden climax to what he had faintly intended should be a long explanation of the whole life and character of his man, the oracular John Willet led the gentleman up his wide dismantled staircase into the Maypole's best apartment.

It was spacious enough in all conscience, occupying the whole depth of the house, and having at either end a great bay window, as large as many modern rooms; in which some few panes of stained glass, emblazoned with fragments of armorial bearings, though cracked, and patched, and shattered, yet remained; attesting, by their presence, that the former owner had made the very light subservient to his state, and pressed the sun itself into his list of flatterers; bidding it, when it shone into his chamber, reflect the badges of his ancient family, and take new hues and colours from their pride.

But those were old days, and now every little ray came and went as it would; telling the plain, bare, searching truth. Although the best room of the inn, it had the melancholy aspect of grandeur in decay, and was much too vast for comfort. Rich rustling hangings, waving on the walls; and, better far, the rustling of youth and beauty's dress; the light of women's eyes, outshining the tapers and their own rich jewels; the sound of gentle tongues, and music, and the tread of maiden feet, had once been there, and filled it with delight. But they were gone, and with them all its gladness. It was no longer a home; children were never born and bred there; the fireside had become mercenary—a something to be bought and sold—a very courtezan: let who would die, or sit beside, or leave it, it was still the same—it

missed nobody, cared for nobody, had equal warmth and smiles for all. God help the man whose heart ever changes with the world, as an old mansion when it becomes an inn!

No effort had been made to furnish this chilly waste, but before the broad chimney a colony of chairs and tables had been planted on a square of carpet, flanked by a ghostly screen, enriched with figures, grinning and grotesque. After lighting with his own hands the faggots which were heaped upon the hearth, old John withdrew to hold grave council with his cook, touching the stranger's entertainment; while the guest himself, seeing small comfort in the yet unkindled wood, opened a lattice in the distant window, and basked in a sickly gleam of cold March sun.

Leaving the window now and then, to rake the crackling logs together, or pace the echoing room from end to end, he closed it when the fire was quite burnt up, and having wheeled the easiest chair into the warmest corner, summoned John Willet.

"Sir," said John.

He wanted pen, ink, and paper. There was an old standish* on the high mantel-shelf containing a dusty apology for all three. Having set this before him, the landlord was retiring, when he motioned him to stay.

"There's a house not far from here," said the guest when he had written a few lines, "which you call the Warren, I believe?"

As this was said in the tone of one who knew the fact, and asked the question as a thing of course, John contented himself with nodding his head in the affirmative; at the same time taking one hand out of his pockets to cough behind, and then putting it in again.

"I want this note"—said the guest, glancing on what he had written, and folding it, "conveyed there without loss of time, and an answer brought back here. Have you a messenger at hand?"

John was thoughtful for a minute or thereabouts, and then said Yes.

"Let me see him," said the guest.

This was disconcerting; for Joe being out, and Hugh engaged in rubbing down the chesnut cob, he designed sending on the errand, Barnaby, who had just then arrived in one of his rambles, and who, so that he thought himself employed on grave and serious business, would go anywhere.

"Why, the truth is," said John after a long pause, "that the person who'd go quickest, is a sort of natural, as one may say, sir; and though quick of foot, and as much to be trusted as the post itself, he's not good at talking, being touched and flighty, sir."

"You don't" said the guest, raising his eyes to John's fat face, "you don't mean—what's the fellow's name—you don't mean Barnaby?"

"Yes I do," returned the landlord, his features turning quite expressive with surprise.

"How comes he to be here?" inquired the guest, leaning back in his chair; speaking in the bland, even tone, from which he never varied; and with the same soft, courteous, never-changing smile upon his face. "I saw him in London last night."

"He's for ever here one hour, and there the next," returned old John, after the usual pause to get the question in his mind. "Sometimes he walks, and sometimes runs. He's known along the road by everybody, and sometimes comes here in a cart or chaise, and sometimes riding double. He comes and goes, through wind, rain, snow, and hail, and on the darkest nights. Nothing hurts *him*."

"He goes often to this Warren, does he not?" said the guest carelessly. "I seem to remember his mother telling me something to that effect yesterday. But I was not attending to the good woman much."

"You're right sir," John made answer, "he does. His father, sir, was murdered in that house."

"So I have heard," returned the guest, taking a gold toothpick from his pocket with the same sweet smile. "A very disagreeable circumstance for the family."

"Very," said John with a puzzled look, as if it occurred to him, dimly and afar off, that this might by possibility be a cool way of treating the subject.

"All the circumstances after a murder," said the guest soliloquising, "must be dreadfully unpleasant—so much bustle and disturbance—no repose—a constant dwelling upon one subject—and the running in and out, and up and down stairs, intolerable. I wouldn't have such a thing happen to anybody I was nearly interested in, on any account. 'T would be enough to wear one's life out.—You were going to say, friend—" he added, turning to John again.

"Only that Mrs. Rudge lives on a little pension from the family, and that Barnaby's as free of the house as any cat or dog about it," answered John. "Shall he do your errand sir?"

"Oh yes," replied the guest. "Oh certainly. Let him do it by all means. Please to bring him here that I may charge him to be quick. If he objects to come you may tell him it's Mr. Chester. He will remember my name, I dare say."

John was so very much astonished to find who his visitor was, that he could express no astonishment at all, by looks or otherwise, but left the room as if he were in the most placid and imperturbable of all possible conditions. It has been reported that when he got down stairs, he looked steadily at the boiler for ten minutes by the clock, and all that time never once left off shaking his head; for which statement there would seem to be some ground of truth and feasibility, inasmuch as that interval of time did certainly elapse, before he returned with Barnaby to the guest's apartment.

"Come hither, lad," said Mr. Chester. "You know Mr. Geoffrey Haredale?"

Barnaby laughed, and looked at the landlord as though he would say, "You hear him?" John, who was greatly shocked at this breach of decorum, clapped his finger to his nose, and shook his head, in mute remonstrance.

"He knows him sir," said John, frowning aside at Barnaby, "as well as you or I do."

"I haven't the pleasure of much acquaintance with the gentleman," returned his guest. "*You* may have. Limit the comparison to yourself, my friend."

Although this was said with the same easy affability, and the same smile, John felt himself put down, and laying the indignity at Barnaby's door, determined to kick his raven, on the very first opportunity.

"Give that," said the guest, who had by this time sealed the note, and who beckoned his messenger towards him as he spoke, "into Mr. Haredale's own hands. Wait for an answer, and bring it back to me—here. If you should find that Mr. Haredale is engaged just now, tell him—can he remember a message, landlord?"

"When he chooses sir," replied John. "He won't forget this one."

"How are you sure of that?"

John merely pointed to him as he stood with his head bent forward, and his earnest gaze fixed closely on his questioner's face; and nodded sagely.

"Tell him then, Barnaby, should he be engaged," said Mr. Chester, "that I shall be glad to wait his convenience here, and to see him (if he will call) at any time this evening.—At the worst I can have a bed here, Willet, I suppose?"

Old John, immensely flattered by the personal notoriety implied in this familiar form of address, answered, with something like a knowing look, "I should believe you could sir," and was turning over in his mind various forms of eulogium, with the view of selecting one appropriate to the qualities of his best bed, when his ideas were put to flight by Mr. Chester giving Barnaby the letter, and bidding him make all speed away.

"Speed!" said Barnaby, folding the little packet in his breast, "Speed! If you want to see hurry and mystery, come here. Here!"

With that, he put his hand, very much to John Willet's horror, on the guest's fine broadcloth sleeve, and led him stealthily to the back window.

"Look down there," he said softly; "do you mark how they whisper in each other's ears; then dance and leap, to make believe they are in sport? Do you see how they stop for a moment, when they think there is no one looking, and mutter among themselves again; and then how they roll and gambol, delighted with the mischief they've been plotting? Look at 'em now. See how they whirl and plunge. And now they stop again, and whisper, cautiously together—little thinking, mind, how often I have lain upon the grass and watched them. I say—what is it that they plot and hatch? Do you know?"

"They are only clothes," returned the guest, "such as we wear; hanging on those lines to dry, and fluttering in the wind."

"Clothes!" echoed Barnaby, looking close into his face, and falling quickly back. "Ha ha! Why, how much better to be silly, than as wise as you! You don't see shadowy people there, like those that live in sleep—not you. Nor eyes in the knotted panes of glass, nor swift ghosts when it blows hard, nor do you hear voices in the air, nor see men stalking in the sky—not you! I lead a merrier life than you, with all your cleverness. You're the dull men. We're the bright ones. Ha! ha! I'll not change with you, clever as you are,—not I!"

With that, he waved his hat above his head, and darted off.

"A strange creature, upon my word!" said the guest, pulling out a handsome box, and taking a pinch of snuff.

"He wants imagination," said Mr. Willet, very slowly, and after a long silence; "that's what he wants. I've tried to instil it into him, many and many's the time; but"—John added this, in confidence—"he an't made for it; that's the fact."

To record that Mr. Chester smiled at John's remark would be little to the purpose, for he preserved the same conciliatory and pleasant look at all times. He drew his chair nearer to the fire though, as a kind of hint that he would prefer to be alone, and John, having no reasonable excuse for remaining, left him to himself.

Very thoughtful old John Willet was, while the dinner was preparing; and if his brain were ever less clear at one time than another, it is but reasonable to suppose that he addled it in no slight degree by shaking his head so much that day. That Mr. Chester, between whom and Mr. Haredale, it was notorious to all the neighbourhood, a deep and bitter animosity existed, should come down there for the sole purpose, as it seemed, of seeing him, and should choose the Maypole for their place of meeting, and should send to him express, were stumbling blocks John could not overcome. The only resource he had, was to consult the boiler, and wait impatiently for Barnaby's return.

But Barnaby delayed beyond all precedent. The visitor's dinner was served, removed, his wine was set, the fire replenished, the hearth clean swept; the light waned without, it grew dusk, became quite dark, and still no Barnaby appeared. Yet, though John Willet was full of wonder and misgiving, his guest sat cross-legged in the easy chair, to all appearance as little ruffled in his thoughts as in his dress—the same calm, easy, cool gentleman, without a care or thought beyond his golden toothpick.

"Barnaby's late," John ventured to observe, as he placed a pair of tarnished candlesticks, some three feet high, upon the table, and snuffed the lights they held.

"He is rather so," replied the guest, sipping his wine. "He will not be much longer, I dare say."

John coughed and raked the fire together.

"As your roads bear no very good character, if I may judge from my son's mishap, though," said Mr. Chester, "and as I have no fancy to be knocked on the head—which is not only disconcerting at the moment, but places one, besides, in a ridiculous position with respect to the people who chance to pick one up—I shall stop here to-night. I think you said you had a bed to spare?"

"Such a bed, sir," returned John Willet; "ay, such a bed as few, even of the gentry's houses, own. A fixter here, sir. I've heard say that bedstead is nigh two hundred years of age. Your noble son—a fine young gentleman—slept in it last, sir, half a year ago."

"Upon my life, a recommendation!" said the guest, shrugging his shoulders and wheeling his chair nearer to the fire. "See that it be well aired, Mr. Willet, and let a blazing fire be lighted there at once. This house is something damp and chilly."

John raked the faggots up again, more from habit than presence of mind, or any reference to this remark, and was about to withdraw, when a bounding step was heard upon the stair, and Barnaby came panting in.

"He'll have his foot in the stirrup in an hour's time," he cried, advancing. "He has been riding hard all day—has just come home—but will be in the saddle again as soon as he has eat and drank, to meet his loving friend."

"Was that his message?" asked the visitor, looking up, but without the smallest discomposure—or at least without the smallest show of any.

"All but the last words," Barnaby rejoined. "He meant those. I saw that, in his face."

"This for your pains," said the other, putting money in his hand, and glancing at him stedfastly. "This for your pains, sharp Barnaby."

"For Grip, and me, and Hugh, to share among us," he rejoined, putting it up, and nodding, as he counted it on his fingers. "Grip one, me two, Hugh three; the dog, the goat, the cats—well, we shall spend it pretty soon, I warn you. Stay.—Look. Do you wise men see nothing there, now?"

He bent eagerly down on one knee, and gazed intently at the smoke, which was rolling up the chimney in a thick black cloud. John Willet, who appeared to consider himself particularly and chiefly referred to under the term wise men, looked that way likewise, and with great solidity of feature.

"Now, where do they go to, when they spring so fast up there," asked Barnaby; "eh? Why do they tread so closely on each other's heels, and why are they always in a hurry—which is what you blame me for, when I only take pattern by these busy folk about me. More of 'em! catching to each other's skirts; and as fast as they go, others come! What a merry dance it is! I would that Grip and I could frisk like that!"

"What has he in that basket at his back?" asked the guest after a few moments, during which Barnaby was still bending down to look higher up the chimney, and earnestly watching the smoke.

"In this?" he answered, jumping up, before John Willet could reply—shaking it as he spoke, and stooping his head to listen. "In this? What is there here? Tell him!"

"A devil, a devil, a devil," cried a hoarse voice.

"Here's money!" said Barnaby, chinking it in his hand, "money for a treat, Grip!"

"Hurrah! Hurrah! Hurrah!" replied the raven, "keep up your spirits. Never say die. Bow, wow, wow!"

Mr. Willet, who appeared to entertain strong doubts whether a customer in a laced coat and fine linen could be supposed to have any acquaintance even with the existence of such unpolite gentry as the bird claimed to belong to, took Barnaby off at this juncture, with the view of preventing any other improper declarations, and quitted the room with his very best bow.

## CHAPTER THE ELEVENTH.

THERE was great news that night for the regular Maypole customers, to each of whom, as he straggled in to occupy his allotted
seat in the chimney corner, John, with a most impressive slowness of
delivery, and in an apoplectic whisper, communicated the fact that
Mr. Chester was alone in the large room up-stairs, and was waiting
the arrival of Mr. Geoffrey Haredale, to whom he had sent a letter
(doubtless of a threatening nature) by the hands of Barnaby, then
and there present.

For a little knot of smokers and solemn gossips, who had seldom
any new topics of discussion, this was a perfect Godsend. Here was a
good, dark-looking, mystery progressing under that very roof—
brought home to the fireside as it were, and enjoyable without the
smallest pains or trouble. It is extraordinary what a zest and relish it
gave to the drink, and how it heightened the flavour of the tobacco.
Every man smoked his pipe with a face of grave and serious delight,
and looked at his neighbour with a sort of quiet congratulation. Nay,
it was felt to be such a holiday and special night, that, on the motion
of little Solomon Daisy, every man (including John himself) put
down his sixpence for a can of flip,* which grateful beverage was
brewed with all despatch, and set down in the midst of them on the
brick floor; both that it might simmer and stew before the fire, and
that its fragrant steam, rising up among them and mixing with the
wreaths of vapour from their pipes, might shroud them in a delicious
atmosphere of their own, and shut out all the world. The very furniture of the room seemed to mellow and deepen in its tone; the ceiling
and walls looked blacker and more highly polished, the curtains of a
ruddier red; the fire burnt clear and high, and the crickets in the
hearth-stone chirped with a more than wonted satisfaction.

There were present, two, however, who showed but little interest
in the general contentment. Of these, one was Barnaby himself, who
slept, or, to avoid being beset with questions, feigned to sleep, in the
chimney-corner; the other, Hugh, who, sleeping too, lay stretched
upon the bench on the opposite side, in the full glare of the blazing
fire.

The light that fell upon this slumbering form, showed it in all its
muscular and handsome proportions. It was that of a young man, of

a hale athletic figure, and a giant's strength, whose sunburnt face and
swarthy throat, overgrown with jet black hair, might have served a
painter for a model. Loosely attired, in the coarsest and roughest
garb, with scraps of straw and hay—his usual bed—clinging here
and there, and mingling with his uncombed locks, he had fallen
asleep in a posture as careless as his dress. The negligence and disorder of the whole man, with something fierce and sullen in his
features, gave him a picturesque appearance, that attracted the
regards even of the Maypole customers who knew him well, and
caused Long Parkes to say that Hugh looked more like a poaching
rascal to-night than ever he had seen him yet.

"He's waiting here, I suppose," said Solomon, "to take Mr.
Haredale's horse."

"That's it, sir," replied John Willet. "He's not often in the house, you know. He's more at his ease among horses than men. I look upon him as a animal himself."

Following up this opinion with a shrug that seemed meant to say, "we can't expect everybody to be like us," John put his pipe into his mouth again, and smoked like one who felt his superiority over the general run of mankind.

"That chap, sir," said John, taking it out again after a time, and pointing at him with the stem, "though he's got all his faculties about him—bottled up and corked down, if I may say so, somewheres or another—"

"Very good!" said Parkes, nodding his head. "A very good expression, Johnny. You'll be a tackling somebody presently. You're in twig to-night, I see."

"Take care," said Mr. Willet, not at all grateful for the compliment, "that I don't tackle you, sir, which I shall certainly endeavour to do, if you interrupt me when I'm making observations.—That chap, I was a saying, though he has all his faculties about him, somewheres or another, bottled up and corked down, has no more imagination than Barnaby has. And why hasn't he?"

The three friends shook their heads at each other; saying by that action, without the trouble of opening their lips, "Do you observe what a philosophical mind our friend has?"

"Why hasn't he?" said John, gently striking the table with his open hand. "Because they was never drawed out of him when he was a boy. That's why. What would any of us have been, if our fathers hadn't drawed our faculties out of us? What would my boy Joe have been, if I hadn't drawed his faculties out of him?—Do you mind what I'm a saying of, gentlemen?"

"Ah! we mind you," cried Parkes. "Go on improving of us, Johnny."

"Consequently, then," said Mr. Willet, "that chap, whose mother was hung when he was a little boy, along with six others, for passing bad Notes*—and it's a blessed thing to think how many people are hung in batches every six weeks for that, and such like offences, as showing how wide awake our government is—that chap that was then turned loose, and had to mind cows, and frighten birds away, and what not, for a few pence to live on, and so got on by degrees to mind horses, and to sleep in course of time in lofts and litter, instead of under haystacks and hedges, till at last he come to be hostler at the

Maypole for his board and lodging and a annual trifle—that chap that can't read nor write, and has never had much to do with anything but animals, and has never lived in any way but like the animals he has lived among, *is* a animal. And," said Mr. Willet, arriving at his logical conclusion, "is to be treated accordingly."

"Willet," said Solomon Daisy, who had exhibited some impatience at the intrusion of so unworthy a subject on their more interesting theme, "when Mr. Chester come this morning, did he order the large room?"

"He signified, sir," said John, "that he wanted a large apartment. Yes. Certainly."

"Why then, I'll tell you what," said Solomon, speaking softly and with an earnest look. "He and Mr. Haredale are going to fight a duel in it."

Everybody looked at Mr. Willet, after this alarming suggestion. Mr. Willet looked at the fire, weighing in his own mind the effect which such an occurrence would be likely to have, on the establishment.

"Well," said John, "I don't know—I am sure—I remember that when I went up last, he *had* put the lights upon the mantel-shelf."

"It's as plain," returned Solomon, "as the nose on Parkes's face"—Mr. Parkes, who had a large nose, rubbed it, and looked as if he considered this a personal allusion—"they'll fight in that room. You know by the newspapers what a common thing it is for gentlemen to fight in coffee-houses without seconds. One of 'em will be wounded or perhaps killed in this house."

"That was a challenge that Barnaby took then, eh?" said John.

"—Inclosing a slip of paper with the measure of his sword upon it, I'll bet a guinea," answered the little man. "We know what sort of gentleman Mr. Haredale is. You have told us what Barnaby said about his looks, when he came back. Depend upon it, I'm right. Now, mind."

The flip had had no flavour till now. The tobacco had been of mere English growth, compared with its present taste. A duel in that great old rambling room up stairs, and the best bed ordered already for the wounded man!

"Would it be swords or pistols now?" said John.

"Heaven knows. Perhaps both," returned Solomon. "The gentlemen wear swords, and may easily have pistols in their pockets—most likely have, indeed. If they fire at each other without effect, then they'll draw, and go to work in earnest."

A shade passed over Mr. Willet's face as he thought of broken windows and disabled furniture, but bethinking himself that one of the parties would probably be left alive to pay the damage, he brightened up again.

"And then," said Solomon, looking from face to face, "then we shall have one of those stains upon the floor that never come out. If Mr. Haredale wins, depend upon it, it'll be a deep one; or if he loses, it will perhaps be deeper still, for he'll never give in unless he's beaten down. We know him better, eh?"

"Better indeed!" they whispered all together.

"As to its ever being got out again," said Solomon, "I tell you it never will, or can be. Why, do you know that it has been tried, at a certain house we are acquainted with?"

"The Warren!" cried John. "No, sure!"

"Yes, sure—yes. It's only known by very few. It has been whispered about though, for all that. They planed the board away, but there it was. They went deep, but it went deeper. They put new boards down, but there was one great spot that came through still, and showed itself in the old place. And—harkye—draw nearer—Mr. Geoffrey made that room his study, and sits there, always, with his foot (as I have heard) upon it; and he believes, through thinking of it long and very much, that it will never fade until he finds the man who did the deed."

As this recital ended, and they all drew closer round the fire, the tramp of a horse was heard without.

"The very man!" cried John, starting up. "Hugh! Hugh!"

The sleeper staggered to his feet, and hurried after him. John quickly returned, ushering in with great attention and deference (for Mr. Haredale was his landlord) the long expected visitor, who strode into the room clanking his heavy boots upon the floor; and looking keenly round upon the bowing group, raised his hat in acknowledgement of their profound respect.

"You have a stranger here, Willet, who sent to me," he said, in a voice which sounded naturally stern and deep. "Where is he?"

"In the great room up-stairs, sir," answered John.

"Show the way. Your staircase is dark, I know. Gentlemen, good night."

With that, he signed to the landlord to go on before; and went clanking out, and up the stairs; old John, in his agitation, ingeniously lighting everything but the way, and making a stumble at every second step.

"Stop!" he said, when they reached the landing. "I can announce myself. Don't wait."

He laid his hand upon the door, entered, and shut it heavily. Mr. Willet was by no means disposed to stand there listening by himself, especially as the walls were very thick; so descended, with much greater alacrity than he had come up, and joined his friends below.

### CHAPTER THE TWELFTH.

THERE was a brief pause in the state-room of the Maypole, as Mr. Haredale tried the lock to satisfy himself that he had shut the door securely, and, striding up the dark chamber to where the screen inclosed a little patch of light and warmth, presented himself, abruptly and in silence, before the smiling guest.

If the two had no greater sympathy in their inward thoughts than in their outward bearing and appearance, the meeting did not seem likely to prove a very calm or pleasant one. With no great disparity between them in point of years, they were, in every other respect, as unlike and far removed from each other as two men could well be. The one was soft-spoken, delicately made, precise, and elegant; the other, a burly square-built man, negligently dressed, rough and abrupt in manner, stern, and, in his present mood, forbidding both in look and speech. The one preserved a calm and placid smile; the other, a distrustful frown. The new-comer, indeed, appeared bent on showing by his every tone and gesture his determined opposition and hostility to the man he had come to meet. The guest who received him, on the other hand, seemed to feel that the contrast between them was all in his favour, and to derive a quiet exultation from it which put him more at his ease than ever.

"Haredale," said this gentleman, without the least appearance of embarrassment or reserve, "I am very glad to see you."

"Let us dispense with compliments. They are misplaced between us," returned the other, waving his hand, "and say plainly what we have to say. You have asked me to meet you. I am here. Why do we stand face to face again?"

"Still the same frank and sturdy character I see!"

"Good or bad, sir, I am" returned the other, leaning his arm upon the chimney-piece, and turning a haughty look upon the occupant of the easy-chair, "the man I used to be. I have lost no old likings or dislikings; my memory has not failed me by a hair's-breadth. You ask me to give you a meeting. I say, I am here."

"Our meeting, Haredale," said Mr. Chester, tapping his snuff-box, and following with a smile the impatient gesture he had made—perhaps unconsciously—towards his sword, "is one of conference and peace, I hope?"

"I have come here," returned the other, "at your desire, holding myself bound to meet you, when and where you would. I have not come to bandy pleasant speeches, or hollow professions. You are a smooth man of the world, sir, and at such play have me at a disadvantage. The very last man on this earth with whom I would enter the lists to combat with gentle compliments and masked faces, is Mr. Chester, I do assure you. I am not his match at such weapons, and have reason to believe that few men are."

"You do me a great deal of honour, Haredale," returned the other, most composedly, "and I thank you. I will be frank with you—"

"I beg your pardon—will be what?"

"Frank—open—perfectly candid."

"Hah!" cried Mr. Haredale, drawing in his breath with a sarcastic smile. "But don't let me interrupt you."

"So resolved am I to hold this course," returned the other, tasting his wine with great deliberation, "that I have determined not to quarrel with you, and not to be betrayed into a warm expression or a hasty word."

"There again," said Mr. Haredale, "you will have me at a great advantage. Your self-command—"

"Is not to be disturbed, when it will serve my purpose, you would say"—rejoined the other, interrupting him with the same complacency. "Granted. I allow it. And I have a purpose to serve now. So have you. I am sure our object is the same. Let us attain it like sensible men, who have ceased to be boys some time.—Do you drink?"

"With my friends," returned the other.

"At least," said Mr. Chester, "you will be seated?"

"I will stand," returned Mr. Haredale impatiently, "on this dismantled, beggared hearth, and not pollute it, fallen as it is, with
mockeries. Go on!"

"You are wrong, Haredale" said the other, crossing his legs, and
smiling as he held his glass up in the bright glow of the fire. "You are
really very wrong. The world is a lively place enough, in which we
must accommodate ourselves to circumstances, sail with the stream
as glibly as we can, be content to take froth for substance, the surface
for the depth, the counterfeit for the real coin. I wonder no phil-
osopher has ever established that our globe itself is hollow. It should
be, if Nature is consistent in her works."

"*You* think it is, perhaps?"

"I should say," he returned, sipping his wine, "there could be no
doubt about it. Well; we, in our trifling with this jingling toy, have
had the ill luck to jostle and fall out. We are not what the world calls
friends; but we are as good and true and loving friends for all that, as
nine out of every ten of those on whom it bestows the title. You have
a niece, and I a son—a fine lad, Haredale, but foolish. They fall in
love with each other, and form what this same world calls an attachment; meaning a something fanciful and false like all the rest, which,
if it took its own free time, would break like any other bubble. But it
may not have its own free time—will not, if they are left alone—and
the question is, shall we two, because society calls us enemies, stand
aloof, and let them rush into each other's arms, when, by approaching each other sensibly, as we do now, we can prevent it, and part
them?"

"I love my niece," said Mr. Haredale, after a short silence. "It may
sound strangely in your ears; but I love her."

"Strangely, my good fellow!" cried Mr. Chester, lazily filling his
glass again, and pulling out his toothpick. "Not at all. I like Ned
too—or, as you say, love him—that's the word among such near
relations. I'm very fond of Ned. He's an amazingly good fellow, and a
handsome fellow—foolish and weak as yet; that's all. But the thing
is, Haredale—for I'll be very frank, as I told you I would at first—
independently of any dislike that you and I might have to being
related to each other, and independently of the religious differences
between us—and damn it, that's important—I couldn't afford a
match of this description. Ned and I couldn't do it. It's impossible."

"Curb your tongue, in God's name, if this conversation is to last," retorted Mr. Haredale fiercely. "I have said I love my niece. Do you think that, loving her, I would have her fling her heart away on any man who had your blood in his veins?"

"You see," said the other, not at all disturbed, "the advantage of being so frank and open. Just what I was about to add, upon my honour! I am amazingly attached to Ned—quite doat upon him, indeed—and even if we could afford to throw ourselves away, that very objection would be quite insuperable.—I wish you'd take some wine."

"Mark me," said Mr. Haredale, striding to the table, and laying his hand upon it heavily. "If any man believes—presumes to think—that I, in word, or deed, or in the wildest dream, ever entertained remotely the idea of Emma Haredale's favouring the suit of one who was akin to you—in any way—I care not what—he lies. He lies, and does me grievous wrong, in the mere thought."

"Haredale," returned the other, rocking himself to and fro as in assent, and nodding at the fire, "it's extremely manly, and really very generous in you, to meet me in this unreserved and handsome way. Upon my word, those are exactly my sentiments, only expressed with much more force and power than I could use—you know my sluggish nature, and will forgive me, I am sure."

"While I would restrain her from all correspondence with your son, and sever their intercourse here, though it should cause her death," said Mr. Haredale, who had been pacing to and fro, "I would do it kindly and tenderly if I can. I have a trust to discharge which my nature is not formed to understand, and, for this reason, the bare fact of there being any love between them comes upon me to-night, almost for the first time."

"I am more delighted than I can possibly tell you," rejoined Mr. Chester with the utmost blandness, "to find my own impression so confirmed. You see the advantage of our having met. We understand each other. We quite agree. We have a most complete and thorough explanation, and we know what course to take.—Why don't you taste your tenant's wine? It's really very good."

"Pray who," said Mr. Haredale, "have aided Emma, or your son? Who are their go-betweens, and agents—do you know?"

"All the good people hereabouts—the neighbourhood in general, I think," returned the other, with his most affable smile. "The messenger I sent to you to-day, foremost among them all."

"The idiot? Barnaby?"

"You are surprised? I am glad of that, for I was rather so myself. Yes. I wrung that from his mother—a very decent sort of woman—from whom, indeed, I chiefly learnt how serious the matter had become, and so determined to ride out here to-day, and hold a parley with you on this neutral ground.—You're stouter than you used to be, Haredale, but you look extremely well."

"Our business, I presume, is nearly at an end," said Mr. Haredale, with an expression of impatience he was at no pains to conceal. "Trust me, Mr. Chester, my niece shall change from this time. I will appeal," he added in a lower tone, "to her woman's heart, her dignity, her pride, her duty"—

"I shall do the same by Ned," said Mr. Chester, restoring some errant faggots to their places in the grate with the toe of his boot. "If there is anything real in the world, it is those amazingly fine feelings and those natural obligations which must subsist between father and son. I shall put it to him on every ground of moral and religious feeling. I shall represent to him that we cannot possibly afford it—that I have always looked forward to his marrying well, for a genteel provision for myself in the autumn of life—that there are a great many clamorous dogs to pay, whose claims are perfectly just and right, and who must be paid out of his wife's fortune. In short, that the very highest and most honourable feelings of our nature, with every consideration of filial duty and affection, and all that sort of thing, imperatively demand that he should run away with an heiress."

"And break her heart as speedily as possible?" said Mr. Haredale, drawing on his glove.

"There Ned will act exactly as he pleases," returned the other, sipping his wine; "that's entirely his affair. I wouldn't for the world interfere with my son, Haredale, beyond a certain point. The relationship between father and son, you know, is positively quite a holy kind of bond.—*Won't* you let me persuade you to take one glass of wine? Well! as you please, as you please," he added, helping himself again.

"Chester," said Mr. Haredale, after a short silence, during which he had eyed his smiling face from time to time intently, "you have the head and heart of an evil spirit in all matters of deception."

"Your health!" said the other, with a nod. "But I have interrupted you—"

"If now," pursued Mr. Haredale, "we should find it difficult to separate these young people, and break off their intercourse—if, for instance, you find it difficult on your side, what course do you intend to take?"

"Nothing plainer, my good fellow, nothing easier," returned the other, shrugging his shoulders and stretching himself more comfortably before the fire. "I shall then exert those powers on which you flatter me so highly—though, upon my word, I don't deserve your compliments to their full extent—and resort to a few little trivial subterfuges for rousing jealousy and resentment. You see?"

"In short, justifying the means by the end, we are, as a last resource for tearing them asunder, to resort to treachery and—and lying," said Mr. Haredale.

"Oh dear no. Fie, fie!" returned the other, relishing a pinch of snuff extremely. "Not lying. Only a little management, a little diplomacy, a little—intriguing, that's the word."

"I wish," said Mr. Haredale, moving to and fro, and stopping, and moving on again, like one who was ill at ease, "that this could have been foreseen or prevented. But as it has gone so far, and it is necessary for us to act, it is of no use shrinking or regretting. Well! I shall second your endeavours to the utmost of my power. There is one topic in the whole wide range of human thoughts on which we both agree. We shall act in concert, but apart. There will be no need, I hope, for us to meet again."

"Are you going?" said Mr. Chester, rising with a graceful indolence. "Let me light you down the stairs."

"Pray keep your seat," returned the other dryly, "I know the way." So, waving his hand slightly, and putting on his hat as he turned upon his heel, he went clanking out as he had come, shut the door behind him, and tramped down the echoing stairs.

"Pah! A very coarse animal, indeed!" said Mr. Chester, composing himself in the easy chair again. "A rough brute. Quite a human badger!"

John Willet and his friends, who had been listening intently for the clash of swords, or firing of pistols in the great room, and had indeed settled the order in which they should rush in when summoned—in which procession old John had carefully arranged that he should bring up the rear—were very much astonished to see Mr. Haredale come down without a scratch, call for his horse, and ride away thoughtfully at a footpace. After some consideration, it was decided that he had left the gentleman above, for dead, and had adopted this stratagem to divert suspicion or pursuit.

As this conclusion involved the necessity of their going up stairs forthwith, they were about to ascend in the order they had agreed upon, when a smart ringing of the guest's bell, as if he had pulled it vigorously, overthrew all their speculations, and involved them in great uncertainty and doubt. At length Mr. Willet agreed to go up stairs himself, escorted by Hugh and Barnaby, as the strongest and stoutest fellows on the premises, who were to make their appearance under pretence of clearing away the glasses.

Under this protection, the brave and broad-faced John boldly entered the room, half a foot in advance, and received an order for a boot-jack without trembling. But when it was brought, and he leant his sturdy shoulder to the guest, Mr. Willet was observed to look very hard into his boots as he pulled them off, and, by opening his eyes much wider than usual, to appear to express some surprise and disappointment at not finding them full of blood. He took occasion too, to examine the gentleman as closely as he could, expecting to discover sundry loop-holes in his person, pierced by his adversary's sword. Finding none, however, and observing in course of time that his guest was as cool and unruffled, both in his dress and temper, as he had been all day, old John at last heaved a deep sigh, and began to think no duel had been fought that night.

"And now, Willet," said Mr. Chester, "if the room's well aired, I'll try the merits of that famous bed."

"The room, sir," returned John, taking up a candle, and nudging Barnaby and Hugh to accompany them, in case the gentleman should unexpectedly drop down faint or dead, from some internal wound, "the room's as warm as any toast in a tankard. Barnaby, take you that other candle, and go on before. Hugh! Follow up, sir, with the easy-chair."

In this order—and still, in his earnest inspection, holding his candle very close to the guest; now making him feel extremely warm about the legs, now threatening to set his wig on fire, and constantly begging his pardon with great awkwardness and embarrassment— John led the party to the best bed-room, which was nearly as large as the chamber from which they had come, and held, drawn out near the fire for warmth, a great old spectral bedstead, hung with faded brocade, and ornamented, at the top of each carved post, with a plume of feathers that had once been white, but with dust and age had now grown hearse-like and funereal.

"Good night, my friends," said Mr. Chester with a sweet smile, seating himself, when he had surveyed the room from end to end, in the easy-chair which his attendants wheeled before the fire. "Good night! Barnaby, my good fellow, you say some prayers before you go to bed, I hope?"

Barnaby nodded. "He has some nonsense that he calls his prayers, sir," returned old John, officiously. "I'm afraid there an't much good in 'em."

"And Hugh?" said Mr. Chester, turning to him.

"Not I," he answered. "I know his"—pointing to Barnaby— "they're well enough. He sings 'em sometimes in the straw. I listen."

"He's quite a animal, sir," John whispered in his ear with dignity. "You'll excuse him, I'm sure. If he has any soul at all, sir, it must be such a very small one, that it don't signify what he does or doesn't in that way. Good night, sir!"

The guest rejoined "God bless you!" with a fervour that was quite affecting; and John, beckoning his guards to go before, bowed himself out of the room, and left him to his rest in the Maypole's ancient bed.

## CHAPTER THE THIRTEENTH.

 F Joseph Willet, the denounced and proscribed of 'prentices, had happened to be at home when his father's courtly guest presented himself before the Maypole door—that is, if it had not perversely chanced to be one of the half-dozen days in the whole year on which he was at liberty to absent himself for as many hours without question or reproach—he would have contrived, by hook or crook, to dive to the very bottom of Mr. Chester's mystery, and to come at his purpose with as much certainty as though he had been his confidential adviser. In that fortunate case, the lovers would have had quick warning of the ills that threatened them, and the aid of various timely and wise suggestions to boot; for all Joe's readiness of thought and action, and all his sympathies and good wishes, were enlisted in favour of the young people, and were staunch in devotion to their cause. Whether this disposition arose out of his old prepossessions in

favour of the young lady, whose history had surrounded her in his mind, almost from his cradle, with circumstances of unusual interest; or from his attachment towards the young gentleman, into whose confidence he had, through his shrewdness and alacrity, and the rendering of sundry important services as a spy and messenger, almost imperceptibly glided; whether they had their origin in either of these sources, or in the habit natural to youth, or in the constant badgering and worrying of his venerable parent, or in any hidden little love affair of his own which gave him something of a fellow-feeling in the matter; it is needless to inquire—especially as Joe was out of the way, and had no opportunity on that particular occasion of testifying to his sentiments either on one side or the other.

It was, in fact, the twenty-fifth of March, which, as most people know to their cost, is, and has been time out of mind, one of those unpleasant epochs termed quarter-days.* On this twenty-fifth of March, it was John Willet's pride annually to settle, in hard cash, his account with a certain vintner and distiller in the city of London; to give into whose hands a canvas bag containing its exact amount, and not a penny more or less, was the end and object of a journey for Joe, so surely as the year and day came round.

This journey was performed upon an old grey mare, concerning whom John had an indistinct set of ideas hovering about him, to the effect that she could win a plate or cup if she tried. She never had tried, and probably never would now, being some fourteen or fifteen years of age, short in wind, long in body, and rather the worse for wear in respect of her mane and tail. Notwithstanding these slight defects, John perfectly gloried in the animal; and when she was brought round to the door by Hugh, actually retired into the bar, and there, in a secret grove of lemons, laughed with pride.

"There's a bit of horseflesh, Hugh!" said John, when he had recovered enough self-command to appear at the door again. "There's a comely creatur! There's high mettle! There's bone!"

There was bone enough beyond all doubt; and so Hugh seemed to think, as he sat sideways in the saddle, lazily doubled up with his chin nearly touching his knees; and heedless of the dangling stirrups and loose bridle-rein, sauntered up and down on the little green before the door.

"Mind you take good care of her, sir," said John, appealing from this insensible person to his son and heir, who now appeared, fully equipped and ready. "Don't you ride hard."

"I should be puzzled to do that, I think, father," Joe replied, casting a disconsolate look at the animal.

"None of your impudence, sir, if you please," retorted old John. "What would you ride, sir? A wild ass or zebra would be too tame for you, wouldn't he, eh sir? You'd like to ride a roaring lion, wouldn't you sir, eh sir? Hold your tongue, sir." When Mr. Willet, in his differences with his son, had exhausted all the questions that occurred to him, and Joe had said nothing at all in answer, he generally wound up by bidding him hold his tongue.

"And what does the boy mean," added Mr. Willet, after he had stared at him for a little time, in a species of stupefaction, "by cocking his hat, to such an extent! Are you a going to kill the wintner, sir?"

"No," said Joe, tartly; "I'm not. Now your mind's at ease, father."

"With a militnary air, too!" said Mr. Willet, surveying him from top to toe; "with a swaggering, fire-eating, biling-water drinking sort of way with him! And what do you mean by pulling up the crocuses and snowdrops, eh sir?"

"It's only a little nosegay," said Joe, reddening. "There's no harm in that, I hope?"

"You're a boy of business, you are, sir!" said Mr. Willet, disdainfully, "to go supposing that wintners care for nosegays."

"I don't suppose anything of the kind," returned Joe. "Let them keep their red noses for bottles and tankards. These are going to Mr. Varden's house."

"And do you suppose *he* minds such things as crocuses?" demanded John.

"I don't know, and to say the truth, I don't care," said Joe. "Come father, give me the money, and in the name of patience let me go."

"There it is, sir," replied John; "and take care of it; and mind you don't make too much haste back, but give the mare a long rest.—Do you mind?"

"Ay, I mind," returned Joe. "She'll need it, Heaven knows."

"And don't you score up too much at the Black Lion," said John. "Mind that too."

"Then why don't you let me have some money of my own?" retorted Joe, sorrowfully; "why don't you, father? What do you send me into London for, giving me only the right to call for my dinner at the Black Lion, which you're to pay for next time you go, as if I was not to be trusted with a few shillings? Why do you use me like this? It's not right of you. You can't expect me to be quiet under it."

"Let him have money!" cried John, in a drowsy reverie. "What does he call money—guineas? Hasn't he got money? Over and above the tolls, hasn't he one and sixpence?"

"One and sixpence!" repeated his son contemptuously.

"Yes, sir," returned John, "one and sixpence. When I was your age, I had never seen so much money, in a heap. A shilling of it is in case of accidents—the mare casting a shoe, or the like of that. The other sixpence is to spend in the diversions of London; and the diversion I recommend is going to the top of the Monument, and sitting there. There's no temptation there, sir—no drink—no young women—no bad characters of any sort—nothing but imagination. That's the way I enjoyed myself when I was your age, sir."

To this, Joe made no answer, but beckoning Hugh, leaped into the saddle and rode away; and a very stalwart manly horseman he looked, deserving a better charger than it was his fortune to bestride. John stood staring after him, or rather after the grey mare, (for he had no eyes for her rider) until man and beast had been out of sight some twenty minutes, when he began to think they were gone, and slowly re-entering the house, fell into a gentle doze.

The unfortunate grey mare, who was the agony of Joe's life, floundered along at her own will and pleasure until the Maypole was no longer visible, and then, contracting her legs into what in a puppet would have been looked upon as a clumsy and awkward imitation of a canter, mended her pace all at once, and did it of her own accord. The acquaintance with her rider's usual mode of proceeding, which suggested this improvement in hers, impelled her likewise to turn up a bye-way, leading—not to London, but through lanes running parallel with the road they had come, and passing within a few hundred yards of the Maypole, which led finally to an inclosure surrounding a large, old, red-brick mansion—the same of which mention was made as the Warren in the first chapter of this history. Coming to a dead stop in a little copse thereabout, she suffered her rider to dismount with right good-will, and to tie her to the trunk of a tree.

"Stay there, old girl," said Joe, "and let us see whether there's any little commission for me to-day." So saying, he left her to browze upon such stunted grass and weeds as happened to grow within the length of her tether, and passing through a wicket gate, entered the grounds on foot.

The pathway, after a very few minutes' walking, brought him close to the house, towards which, and especially towards one particular window, he directed many covert glances. It was a dreary, silent building, with echoing courtyards, deserted turret-chambers, and whole suites of rooms shut up and mouldering to ruin.

The terrace-garden, dark with the shade of overhanging trees, had an air of melancholy that was quite oppressive. Great iron gates, disused for many years, and red with rust, drooping on their hinges and overgrown with long rank grass, seemed as though they tried to sink into the ground, and hide their fallen state among the friendly weeds. The fantastic monsters on the walls, green with age and damp, and covered here and there with moss, looked grim and desolate. There was a sombre aspect even on that part of the mansion which was inhabited and kept in good repair, that struck the beholder with a sense of sadness; of something forlorn and failing, whence cheerfulness was banished. It would have been difficult to imagine a bright fire blazing in the dull and darkened rooms, or to picture any gaiety of heart or revelry that the frowning walls shut in. It seemed a place where such things had been, but could be no more—the very ghost of a house, haunting the old spot in its old outward form, and that was all.

Much of this decayed and sombre look was attributable, no doubt, to the death of its former master, and the temper of its present occupant; but remembering the tale connected with the mansion, it seemed the very place for such a deed, and one that might have been its predestined theatre years upon years ago. Viewed with reference to this legend, the sheet of water where the steward's body had been found appeared to wear a black and sullen character, such as no other pool might own; the bell upon the roof that had told the tale of murder to the midnight wind, became a very phantom whose voice would raise the listener's hair on end; and every leafless bough that nodded to another, had its stealthy whispering of the crime.

Joe paced up and down the path, sometimes stopping in affected contemplation of the building or the prospect, sometimes leaning against a tree with an assumed air of idleness and indifference, but always keeping an eye upon the window he had singled out at first.

After some quarter of an hour's delay, a small white hand was waved to him for an instant from this casement, and the young man, with a respectful bow, departed; saying under his breath as he crossed his horse again, "No errand for me to-day!"

But the air of smartness, the cock of the hat to which John Willet had objected, and the spring nosegay, all betokened some little errand of his own, having a more interesting object than a vintner or even a locksmith. So, indeed, it turned out; for when he had settled with the vintner—whose place of business was down in some deep cellars hard by Thames-street, and who was as purple-faced an old gentleman as if he had all his life supported their arched roof on his head—when he had settled the account, and taken the receipt, and declined tasting more than three glasses of old sherry, to the unbounded astonishment of the purple-faced vintner, who, gimlet in hand, had projected an attack upon at least a score of dusty casks, and who stood transfixed, or morally gimleted as it were, to his own wall—when he had done all this, and disposed besides of a frugal dinner at the Black Lion in Whitechapel; spurning the Monument and John's advice, he turned his steps towards the locksmith's house, attracted by the eyes of blooming Dolly Varden.

Joe was by no means a sheepish fellow, but, for all that, when he got to the corner of the street in which the locksmith lived, he could by no means make up his mind to walk straight to the house. First, he resolved to stroll up another street for five minutes, then up another street for five minutes more, and so on until he had lost full half an hour, when he made a bold plunge and found himself with a red face and a beating heart in the smoky workshop.

"Joe Willet, or his ghost!" said Varden, rising from the desk at which he was busy with his books, and looking at him under his spectacles. "Which is it? Joe in the flesh, eh? That's hearty. And how are all the Chigwell company, Joe?"

"Much as usual, sir—they and I agree as well as ever."

"Well, well!" said the locksmith. "We must be patient, Joe, and bear with old folks' foibles. How's the mare, Joe? Does she do the four miles an hour as easily as ever? Ha, ha, ha! Does she, Joe? Eh?—What have we there, Joe—a nosegay?"

"A very poor one, sir—I thought Miss Dolly—"

"No, no," said Gabriel, dropping his voice and shaking his head, "not Dolly. Give 'em to her mother, Joe. A great deal better give 'em to her mother. Would you mind giving 'em to Mrs. Varden, Joe?"

"Oh no, sir," Joe replied, and endeavouring, but not with the greatest possible success, to hide his disappointment. "I shall be very glad, I'm sure."

"That's right," said the locksmith, patting him on the back. "It don't matter who has 'em, Joe?"

"Not a bit, sir."—Dear heart, how the words stuck in his throat!

"Come in," said Gabriel. "I have just been called to tea. She's in the parlour."

"She," thought Joe. "Which of 'em I wonder—Mrs. or Miss?" The locksmith settled the doubt as neatly as if it had been expressed aloud, by leading him to the door, and saying, "Martha, my dear, here's young Mr. Willet."

Now, Mrs. Varden, regarding the Maypole as a sort of humane man-trap, or decoy for husbands; viewing its proprietor, and all who aided and abetted him, in the light of so many poachers among Christian men; and believing, moreover, that the publicans coupled with sinners in Holy Writ were veritable licensed victuallers; was far from being favourably disposed towards her visitor. Wherefore she was taken faint directly; and being duly presented with the crocuses and snowdrops, divined on further consideration that they were the occasion of the languor which had seized upon her spirits. "I'm afraid I couldn't bear the room another minute," said the good lady, "if they remained here. *Would* you excuse my putting them out of window?"

Joe begged she wouldn't mention it on any account, and smiled feebly as he saw them deposited on the sill outside. If anybody could have known the pains he had taken to make up that despised and misused bunch of flowers!—

"I feel it quite a relief to get rid of them, I assure you," said Mrs. Varden. "I'm better already." And indeed she did appear to have plucked up her spirits.

Joe expressed his gratitude to Providence for this favourable dispensation, and tried to look as if he didn't wonder where Dolly was.

"You're sad people at Chigwell, Mr. Joseph," said Mrs. V.

"I hope not, ma'am," returned Joe.

"You're the cruellest and most inconsiderate people in the world," said Mrs. Varden, bridling. "I wonder old Mr. Willet, having been a married man himself, doesn't know better than to conduct himself as he does. His doing it for profit is no excuse. I would rather pay the money twenty times over, and have Varden come home like a respectable and sober tradesman. If there is one character," said Mrs. Varden with great emphasis, "that offends and disgusts me more than another, it is a sot."

"Come, Martha, my dear," said the locksmith cheerily, "let us have tea, and don't let us talk about sots. There are none here, and Joe don't want to hear about them, I dare say."

At this crisis, Miggs appeared with toast.

"I dare say he does not," said Mrs. Varden; "and I dare say you do not, Varden. It's a very unpleasant subject I have no doubt, though I won't say it's personal"—Miggs coughed—"whatever I may be forced to think"—Miggs sneezed expressively. "You never will know, Varden, and nobody at young Mr. Willet's age—you'll excuse me, sir—can be expected to know, what a woman suffers when she is waiting at home under such circumstances. If you don't believe me, as I know you don't, here's Miggs, who is only too often a witness of it—ask her."

"Oh! she were very bad the other night, sir, indeed she were," said Miggs. "If you hadn't the sweetness of an angel in you, mim, I don't think you could abear it, I raly don't."

"Miggs," said Mrs. Varden, "you're profane."

"Begging your pardon, mim," returned Miggs, with shrill rapidity, "such was not my intentions, and such I hope is not my character, though I am but a servant."

"Answering me, Miggs, and providing yourself," retorted her mistress, looking round with dignity, "is one and the same thing. How dare you speak of angels in connection with your sinful fellow-beings—mere"—said Mrs. Varden, glancing at herself in a neighbouring mirror, and arranging the ribbon of her cap in a more becoming fashion—"mere worms and grovellers as we are!"

"I did not intend, mim, if you please, to give offence," said Miggs, confident in the strength of her compliment, and developing strongly in the throat as usual, "and I did not expect it would be took as such. I hope I know my own unworthiness, and that I hate and despise myself and all my fellow-creeturs as every practicable Christian should."

"You'll have the goodness, if you please," said Mrs. Varden loftily, "to step up stairs and see if Dolly has finished dressing, and to tell her that the chair that was ordered for her* will be here in a minute, and that if she keeps it waiting, I shall send it away that instant.— I'm sorry to see that you don't take your tea, Varden, and that you don't take yours, Mr. Joseph; though of course it would be foolish of me to expect that anything that can be had at home, and in the company of females, would please *you*."

This pronoun was understood in the plural sense, and included both gentlemen, upon both of whom it was rather hard and undeserved, for Gabriel had applied himself to the meal with a very promising appetite, until it was spoilt by Mrs. Varden herself, and Joe had as great a liking for the female society of the locksmith's house—or for a part of it at all events—as man could well entertain.

But he had no opportunity to say anything in his own defence, for at that moment Dolly herself appeared, and struck him quite dumb with her beauty. Never had Dolly looked so handsome as she did then, in all the glow and grace of youth, with all her charms increased a hundred fold by a most becoming dress, by a thousand little coquettish ways which nobody could assume with a better grace, and all the sparkling expectation of that accursed party. It is impossible to tell how Joe hated that party wherever it was, and all the other people who were going to it, whoever they were.

And she hardly looked at him—no, hardly looked at him. And when the chair was seen through the open door coming blundering into the workshop, she actually clapped her hands and seemed glad to go. But Joe gave her his arm—there was some comfort in that— and handed her into it. To see her seat herself inside, with her laughing eyes brighter than diamonds, and her hand—surely she had the prettiest hand in the world—on the ledge of the open window, and her little finger provokingly and pertly tilted up, as if it wondered why Joe didn't squeeze or kiss it! To think how well one or two of the modest snowdrops would have become that delicate boddice, and how they were lying neglected outside the parlour window! To see how Miggs looked on, with a face expressive of knowing how all this loveliness was got up, and of being in the secret of every string and pin and hook and eye, and of saying it ain't half as real as you think, and I could look quite as well myself if I took the pains! To hear that provoking precious little scream when the chair was hoisted on its poles, and to catch that transient but not-to-be-forgotten vision of the happy face within—what torments and aggravations, and yet what delights were these! The very chairmen seemed favoured rivals as they bore her down the street.

There never was such an alteration in a small room in a small time as in that parlour when they went back to finish tea. So dark, so deserted, so perfectly disenchanted. It seemed such sheer nonsense to be sitting tamely there, when she was at a dance with more lovers than man could calculate fluttering about her—with the whole party doting on and adoring her, and wanting to marry her. Miggs was hovering about too; and the fact of her existence, the mere circumstance of her ever having been born, appeared, after Dolly, such an unaccountable practical joke. It was impossible to talk. It couldn't be done. He had nothing left for it but to stir his tea round, and round, and round, and ruminate on all the fascinations of the locksmith's lovely daughter.

Gabriel was dull too. It was a part of the certain uncertainty of Mrs. Varden's temper, that when they were in this condition, she should be gay and sprightly.

"I need have a cheerful disposition, I am sure," said the smiling housewife, "to preserve any spirits at all; and how I do it I can scarcely tell."

"Ah, mim," sighed Miggs, "begging your pardon for the interruption, there an't a many like you."

"Take away, Miggs," said Mrs. Varden, rising, "take away, pray. I know I'm a restraint here, and as I wish everybody to enjoy themselves as they best can, I feel I had better go."

"No, no, Martha," cried the locksmith. "Stop here. I'm sure we shall be very sorry to lose you, eh Joe?" Joe started, and said "Certainly."

"Thank you, Varden, my dear," returned his wife; "but I know your wishes better. Tobacco, and beer, or spirits, have much greater attractions than any *I* can boast of, and therefore I shall go and sit up stairs and look out of window, my love. Good night, Mr. Joseph. I'm very glad to have seen you, and only wish I could have provided something more suitable to your taste. Remember me very kindly if you please to old Mr. Willet, and tell him that whenever he comes here I have a crow to pluck with him. Good night!"

Having uttered these words with great sweetness of manner, the good lady dropped a curtsey remarkable for its condescension, and serenely withdrew.

And it was for this Joe had looked forward to the twenty-fifth of March for weeks and weeks, and had gathered the flowers with so much care, and had cocked his hat, and made himself so smart! This was the end of all his bold determination, resolved upon for the hundredth time, to speak out to Dolly and tell her how he loved her! To see her for a minute—for but a minute—to find her going out to a party and glad to go; to be looked upon as a common pipe-smoker, beer-bibber, spirit-guzzler, and tosspot! He bade farewell to his friend the locksmith, and hastened to take horse at the Black Lion, thinking as he turned towards home, as many another Joe has thought before and since, that here was an end to all his hopes—that the thing was impossible and never could be—that she didn't care for him—that he was wretched for life—and that the only congenial prospect left him, was to go for a soldier or a sailor, and get some obliging enemy to knock his brains out as soon as possible.

## CHAPTER THE FOURTEENTH.

JOE WILLET rode leisurely along in his desponding mood, picturing the locksmith's daughter going down long country-dances, and poussetting* dreadfully with bold strangers—which was almost too much to bear—when he heard the tramp of a horse's feet behind him, and looking back, saw a well-mounted gentleman advancing at a smart canter. As this rider passed, he checked his steed, and called him of the Maypole by his name. Joe set spurs to the grey mare, and was at his side directly.

"I thought it was you, sir," he said, touching his hat. "A fair evening, sir. Glad to see you out of doors again."

The gentleman smiled and nodded. "What gay doings have been going on to-day, Joe? Is she as pretty as ever? Nay, don't blush, man."

"If I coloured at all, Mr. Edward," said Joe, "which I didn't know I did, it was to think I should have been such a fool as ever to have any hope of her. She's as far out of my reach as—as Heaven is."

"Well, Joe, I hope that's not altogether beyond it," said Edward good-humouredly. "Eh?"

"I have no chance of her, sir, whether or no. How can I expect to have? I that haven't a will of my own, or a sixpence of my own, or anything of my own—except my father." And really Joe added this saving clause as if he could have very well dispensed with that piece of property.

"Obstacles certainly, but I should be sorry to admit they were utter disqualifications," said Edward, "or my own affairs would be almost as unpromising as yours. Cheer up, Joe. Remember the proverb about faint hearts and fair ladies."

"Ah!" sighed Joe. "It's all very fine talking, sir. Proverbs are easily made in cold blood. But it can't be helped. Are you bound for our house, sir?"

"Yes. As I am not quite strong yet, I shall stay there to-night, and ride home coolly in the morning."

"If you're in no particular hurry," said Joe after a short silence, "and will bear with the pace of this poor jade, I shall be glad to ride on with you to the Warren, sir, and hold your horse when you dismount. It'll save you having to walk from the Maypole, there and back again. I can spare the time well, sir, for I am too soon."

"And so am I," returned Edward, "though I was unconsciously riding fast just now, in compliment I suppose to the pace of my thoughts, which were travelling post.* We will keep together, Joe, willingly, and be as good company as may be. So I say again, cheer up, think of the locksmith's daughter with a stout heart, and you shall win her yet."

Joe shook his head; but there was something so cheery in the buoyant hopeful manner of this speech, that his spirits rose under its influence, and communicated as it would seem some new impulse even to the grey mare, who, breaking from her sober amble into a gentle trot, emulated the pace of Edward Chester's horse, and appeared to flatter herself that he was doing his very best.

It was a fine dry night, and the light of a young moon, which was then just rising, shed around that peace and tranquillity which gives to evening time its most delicious charm. The lengthened shadows of the trees, softened as if reflected in still water, threw their carpet on the path the travellers pursued, and the light wind stirred yet more softly than before, as though it were soothing Nature in her sleep. By little and little they ceased talking, and rode on side by side in a pleasant silence.

"The Maypole lights are brilliant to-night," said Edward, as they rode along the lane from which, while the intervening trees were bare of leaves, that hostelry was visible.

"Brilliant indeed, sir," returned Joe, rising in his stirrups to get a better view. "Lights in the large room, and a fire glimmering in the best bedchamber? Why, what company can this be for, I wonder!"

"Some benighted horseman wending towards London, and deterred from going on to-night by the marvellous tales of my friend the highwayman, I suppose," said Edward.

"He must be a horseman of good quality to have such accommodations. Your bed too, sir—!"

"No matter, Joe. Any other room will do for me. But come—there's nine striking. We may push on."

They cantered forward at as brisk a pace as Joe's charger could attain, and presently stopped in the little copse where he had left her in the morning. Edward dismounted, gave his bridle to his companion, and walked with a light step towards the house.

A female servant was waiting at a side gate in the garden-wall, and admitted him without delay. He hurried along the terrace-walk, and darted up a flight of broad steps leading into an old and gloomy hall, whose walls were ornamented with rusty suits of armour, antlers, weapons of the chase, and suchlike garniture. Here he paused, but

not long; for as he looked round, as if expecting the attendant to have followed, and wondering she had not done so, a lovely girl appeared, whose dark hair next moment rested on his breast. Almost at the same instant a heavy hand was laid upon her arm, Edward felt himself thrust away, and Mr. Haredale stood between them.

He regarded the young man sternly without removing his hat; with one hand clasped his niece, and with the other, in which he held his riding-whip, motioned him towards the door. The young man drew himself up, and returned his gaze.

"This is well done of you, sir, to corrupt my servants, and enter my house unbidden and in secret, like a thief!" said Mr. Haredale. "Leave it, sir, and return no more."

"Miss Haredale's presence," returned the young man, "and your relationship to her, give you a license which, if you are a brave man, you will not abuse. You have compelled me to this course, and the fault is yours—not mine."

"It is neither generous, nor honourable, nor the act of a true man, sir," retorted the other, "to tamper with the affections of a weak, trusting girl, while you shrink, in your unworthiness, from her guardian and protector, and dare not meet the light of day. More than this I will not say to you, save that I forbid you this house, and require you to be gone."

"It is neither generous, nor honourable, nor the act of a true man to play the spy," said Edward. "Your words imply dishonour, and I reject them with the scorn they merit."

"You will find," said Mr. Haredale, calmly, "your trusty go-between in waiting at the gate by which you entered. I have played no spy's part, sir. I chanced to see you pass the gate, and followed. You might have heard me knocking for admission, had you been less swift of foot, or lingered in the garden. Please to withdraw. Your presence here is offensive to me and distressful to my niece." As he said these words, he passed his arm about the waist of the terrified and weeping girl, and drew her closer to him; and though the habitual severity of his manner was scarcely changed, there was yet apparent in the action an air of kindness and sympathy for her distress.

"Mr. Haredale," said Edward, "your arm encircles her on whom I have set my every hope and thought, and to purchase one minute's happiness for whom I would gladly lay down my life; this house is the casket that holds the precious jewel of my existence. Your niece has plighted her faith to me, and I have plighted mine to her. What have I done that you should hold me in this light esteem, and give me these discourteous words?"

"You have done that, sir," answered Mr. Haredale, "which must be undone. You have tied a lover's-knot here which must be cut asunder. Take good heed of what I say. Must I cancel the bond between ye. I reject you, and all of your kith and kin—all the false, hollow, heartless stock."

"High words, sir," said Edward scornfully.

"Words of purpose and meaning, as you will find," replied the other. "Lay them to heart."

"Lay you then, these," said Edward. "Your cold and sullen temper, which chills every breast about you, which turns affection into fear, and changes duty into dread, has forced us on this secret course, repugnant to our nature and our wish, and far more foreign, sir, to us than you. I am not a false, a hollow, or a heartless man; the character is yours, who poorly venture on these injurious terms, against the truth, and under the shelter whereof I reminded you just now. You shall not cancel the bond between us. I will not abandon this pursuit. I rely upon your niece's truth and honour, and set your influence at nought. I leave her with a confidence in her pure faith, which you will never weaken, and with no concern but that I do not leave her in some gentler care."

With that, he pressed her cold hand to his lips, and once more encountering and returning Mr. Haredale's steady look, withdrew.

A few words to Joe as he mounted his horse sufficiently explained what had passed, and renewed all that young gentleman's despondency with tenfold aggravation. They rode back to the Maypole without exchanging a syllable, and arrived at the door with heavy hearts.

Old John, who had peeped from behind the red curtain as they rode up shouting for Hugh, was out directly, and said with great importance as he held the young man's stirrup,

"He's comfortable in bed—the best bed. A thorough gentleman; the smilingest, affablest gentleman I ever had to do with."

"Who, Willet?" said Edward carelessly, as he dismounted.

"Your worthy father, sir," replied John. "Your honourable, venerable father."

"What does he mean?" said Edward, looking with a mixture of alarm and doubt at Joe.

"What *do* you mean?" said Joe. "Don't you see Mr. Edward doesn't understand, father?"

"Why, didn't you know of it, sir?" said John, opening his eyes wide. "How very singular! Bless you, he's been here ever since noon to-day, and Mr. Haredale has been having a long talk with him, and hasn't been gone an hour."

"My father, Willet!"

"Yes, sir, he told me so—a handsome, slim, upright gentleman, in green-and-gold. In your old room up yonder, sir. No doubt you can go in, sir," said John, walking backwards into the road and looking up at the window. "He hasn't put out his candles yet, I see."

Edward glanced at the window also, and hastily murmuring that he had changed his mind—forgotten something—and must return to London, mounted his horse again and rode away; leaving the Willets, father and son, looking at each other in mute astonishment.

## CHAPTER THE FIFTEENTH.

AT noon next day, John Willet's guest sat lingering over his breakfast in his own home, surrounded by a variety of comforts, which left the Maypole's highest flight and utmost stretch of accommodation at an infinite distance behind, and suggested comparisons very much to the disadvantage and disfavour of that venerable tavern.

In the broad old-fashioned window-seat—as capacious as many modern sofas, and cushioned to serve the purpose of a luxurious set-tee—in the broad old-fashioned window-seat of a roomy chamber, Mr. Chester lounged, very much at his ease, over a well-furnished breakfast-table. He had exchanged his riding-coat for a handsome morning-gown, his boots for slippers; had been at great pains to atone for the having been obliged to make his toilet when he rose without the aid of dressing-case and tiring equipage; and, having gradually forgotten through these means the discomforts of an indifferent night and an early ride, was in a state of perfect complacency, indolence, and satisfaction.

The situation in which he found himself, indeed, was particularly favourable to the growth of these feelings; for, not to mention the lazy influence of a late and lonely breakfast, with the additional sedative of a newspaper, there was an air of repose about his place of residence peculiar to itself, and which hangs about it, even in these times, when it is more bustling and busy than it was in days of yore.

There are, still, worse places than the Temple, on a sultry day, for basking in the sun, or resting idly in the shade. There is yet a drowsiness in its courts, and a dreamy dulness in its trees and gardens; those who pace its lanes and squares may yet hear the echoes of their footsteps on the sounding stones, and read upon its gates, in passing from the tumult of the Strand or Fleet Street, 'Who enters here leaves noise behind.' There is still the plash of falling water in fair Fountain Court, and there are yet nooks and corners where dun-haunted* students may look down from their dusty garrets, on a vagrant ray of sunlight patching the shade of the tall houses, and seldom troubled to reflect a passing stranger's form. There is yet, in the Temple, something of a clerkly monkish atmosphere, which public offices of law have not disturbed, and even legal firms have failed to scare away. In summer time, its pumps suggest to thirsty idlers, springs cooler, and more sparkling, and deeper than other wells; and as they trace the spillings of full pitchers on the heated ground, they snuff the freshness, and, sighing, cast sad looks towards the Thames, and think of baths and boats, and saunter on, despondent.

It was in a room in Paper Buildings—a row of goodly tenements, shaded in front by ancient trees, and looking, at the back, upon the Temple Gardens*—that this, our idler, lounged; now taking up again the paper he had laid down a hundred times; now trifling with the fragments of his meal; now pulling forth his golden toothpick, and glancing leisurely about the room, or out at window into the trim garden walks, where a few early loiterers were already pacing to and fro. Here a pair of lovers met to quarrel and make up; there a dark-eyed nursery-maid had better eyes for Templars than her charge; on this hand an ancient spinster, with her lapdog in a string, regarded both enormities with scornful sidelong looks; on that a weazen old gentleman, ogling the nursery-maid, looked with like scorn upon the spinster, and wondered she didn't know she was no longer young. Apart from all these, on the river's margin, two or three couple of business-talkers walked slowly up and down in earnest conversation; and one young man sat thoughtfully on a bench, alone.

"Ned is amazingly patient!" said Mr. Chester, glancing at this last-named person as he set down his teacup and plied the golden tooth-pick, "immensely patient! He was sitting yonder when I began to dress, and has scarcely changed his posture since. A most eccentric dog!"

As he spoke, the figure rose, and came towards him with a rapid pace.

"Really, as if he had heard me," said the father, resuming his newspaper with a yawn. "Dear Ned!"

Presently the room-door opened, and the young man entered; to whom his father gently waved his hand, and smiled.

"Are you at leisure for a little conversation, sir?" said Edward.

"Surely, Ned. I am always at leisure. You know my constitution.—Have you breakfasted?"

"Three hours ago."

"What a very early dog!" cried his father, contemplating him from behind the toothpick, with a languid smile.

"The truth is," said Edward, bringing a chair forward, and seating himself near the table, "that I slept but ill last night, and was glad to rise. The cause of my uneasiness cannot but be known to you, sir; and it is upon that, I wish to speak."

"My dear boy," returned his father, "confide in me, I beg. But you know my constitution—don't be prosy, Ned."

"I will be plain, and brief," said Edward.

"Don't say you will, my good fellow," returned his father, crossing his legs, "or you certainly will not. You are going to tell me—"

"Plainly this, then," said the son, with an air of great concern, "that I know where you were last night—from being on the spot, indeed—and whom you saw, and what your purpose was."

"You don't say so!" cried his father. "I am delighted to hear it. It saves us the worry, and terrible wear and tear of a long explanation, and is a great relief for both. At the very house! Why didn't you come up? I should have been charmed to see you."

"I knew that what I had to say would be better said after a night's reflection, when both of us were cool," returned the son.

"'Fore Gad, Ned," rejoined the father, "I was cool enough last night. That detestable Maypole! By some infernal contrivance of the builder, it holds the wind, and keeps it fresh. You remember the sharp east wind that blew so hard five weeks ago? I give you my honour it was rampant in that old house last night, though out of doors there was a dead calm. But you were saying—"

"I was about to say, Heaven knows how seriously and earnestly, that you have made me wretched, sir. Will you hear me gravely for a moment?"

"My dear Ned," said his father, "I will hear you with the patience of an anchorite. Oblige me with the milk."

"I saw Miss Haredale last night," Edward resumed, when he had complied with this request; "her uncle, in her presence, immediately after your interview, and, as of course I know, in consequence of it, forbade me the house, and, with circumstances of indignity which are of your creation I am sure, commanded me to leave it on the instant."

"For his manner of doing so, I give you my honour, Ned, I am not accountable," said his father. "That you must excuse. He is a mere boor, a log, a brute, with no address in life.—Positively a fly in the jug. The first I have seen this year."

Edward rose, and paced the room. His imperturbable parent sipped his tea.

"Father," said the young man, stopping at length before him, "we must not trifle in this matter. We must not deceive each other, or ourselves. Let me pursue the manly open part I wish to take, and do not repel me by this unkind indifference."

"Whether I am indifferent or no," returned the other, "I leave you, my dear boy, to judge. A ride of twenty-five or thirty miles, through miry roads—a Maypole dinner—a tête-à-tête with Haredale, which, vanity apart, was quite a Valentine and Orson* business—a Maypole bed—a Maypole landlord, and a Maypole retinue of idiots and centaurs;*—whether the voluntary endurance of these things looks like indifference, dear Ned, or like the excessive anxiety, and devotion, and all that sort of thing, of a parent, you shall determine for yourself."

"I wish you to consider, sir," said Edward, "in what a cruel situation I am placed. Loving Miss Haredale as I do—"

"My dear fellow," interrupted his father with a compassionate smile, "you do nothing of the kind. You don't know anything about it. There's no such thing, I assure you. Now, do take my word for it. You have good sense, Ned,—great good sense. I wonder you should be guilty of such amazing absurdities. You really surprise me."

"I repeat," said his son firmly, "that I love her. You have interposed to part us, and have, to the extent I have just now told you of, succeeded. May I induce you, sir, in time, to think more favourably of our attachment, or is it your intention and your fixed design to hold us asunder if you can?"

"My dear Ned," returned his father, taking a pinch of snuff and pushing his box towards him, "that *is* my purpose most undoubtedly."

"The time that has elapsed," rejoined his son, "since I began to know her worth, has flown in such a dream that until now I have hardly once paused to reflect upon my true position. What is it? From my childhood I have been accustomed to luxury and idleness, and have been bred as though my fortune were large, and my expectations almost without a limit. The idea of wealth has been familiarised to me from my cradle. I have been taught to look upon those means, by which men raise themselves to riches and distinction, as being beyond my heeding, and beneath my care. I have been, as the phrase is, liberally educated, and am fit for nothing. I find myself at last wholly dependent upon you, with no resource but in your favour.

In this momentous question of my life we do not, and it would seem we never can, agree. I have shrunk instinctively alike from those to whom you have urged me to pay court, and from the motives of interest and gain which have rendered them in your eyes eligible objects for my suit. If there never has been thus much plain-speaking between us before, sir, the fault has not been mine, indeed. If I seem to speak too plainly now, it is, believe me father, in the hope that there may be a franker spirit, a worthier reliance, and a kinder confidence between us in time to come."

"My good fellow," said his smiling father, "you quite affect me. Go on, my dear Edward, I beg. But remember your promise. There is great earnestness, vast candour, a manifest sincerity in all you say, but I fear I observe the faintest indications of a tendency to prose."

"I am very sorry, sir."

"I am very sorry too, Ned, but you know that I cannot fix my mind for any long period upon one subject. If you'll come to the point at once, I'll imagine all that ought to go before, and conclude it said. Oblige me with the milk again. Listening, invariably makes me feverish."

"What I would say then, tends to this," said Edward. "I cannot bear this absolute dependence, sir, even upon you. Time has been lost and opportunity thrown away, but I am yet a young man, and may retrieve it. Will you give me the means of devoting such abilities and energies as I possess, to some worthy pursuit? Will you let me try to make for myself an honourable path in life? For any term you please to name—say for five years if you will—I will pledge myself to move no further in the matter of our difference without your full concurrence. During that period, I will endeavour earnestly and patiently, if ever man did, to open some prospect for myself, and free you from the burden you fear I should become if I married one whose worth and beauty are her chief endowments. Will you do this, sir? At the expiration of the term we agree upon, let us discuss this subject again. Till then, unless it is revived by you, let it never be renewed between us."

"My dear Ned," returned his father, laying down the newspaper at which he had been glancing carelessly, and throwing himself back in the window-seat, "I believe you know how very much I dislike what are called family affairs, which are only fit for plebeian Christmas days, and have no manner of business with people of our condition. But as you are proceeding upon a mistake, Ned— altogether upon a mistake—I will conquer my repugnance to entering on such matters, and give you a perfectly plain and candid answer, if you will do me the favour to shut the door."

Edward having obeyed him, he took an elegant little knife from his pocket, and paring his nails, continued:

"You have to thank me, Ned, for being of good family; for your mother, charming person as she was, and almost broken-hearted, and so forth, as she left me, when she was prematurely compelled to become immortal—had nothing to boast of in that respect."

"Her father was at least an eminent lawyer, sir," said Edward.

"Quite right, Ned; perfectly so. He stood high at the bar, had a great name and great wealth, but having risen from nothing—I have always closed my eyes to the circumstance and steadily resisted its contemplation, but I fear his father dealt in pork, and that his business did once involve cow-heel and sausages—he wished to marry his daughter into a good family. He had his heart's desire, Ned. I was a younger son's younger son, and I married her. We each had our object, and gained it. She stepped at once into the politest and best circles, and I stepped into a fortune which I assure you was very necessary to my comfort—quite indispensable. Now, my good fellow, that fortune is among the things that have been. It is gone, Ned, and has been gone—how old are you? I always forget."

"Seven-and-twenty, sir."

"Are you indeed?" cried his father, raising his eyelids in a languishing surprise. "So much! Then I should say, Ned, that as nearly as I remember, its skirts vanished from human knowledge, about eighteen or nineteen years ago. It was about that time when I came to live in these chambers (once your grandfather's, and bequeathed by that extremely respectable person to me), and commenced to live upon an inconsiderable annuity and my past reputation."

"You are jesting with me, sir," said Edward.

"Not in the slightest degree, I assure you," returned his father with great composure. "These family topics are so extremely dry, that I am sorry to say they don't admit of any such relief. It is for that reason, and because they have an appearance of business, that I dislike them so very much. Well! You know the rest. A son, Ned, unless he is old enough to be a companion—that is to say, unless he is some two or three and twenty—is not the kind of thing to have about one. He is a restraint upon his father, his father is a restraint upon him, and they make each other mutually uncomfortable. Therefore, until within the last four years or so—I have a poor memory for dates, and if I mistake, you will correct me in your own mind—you pursued your studies at a distance, and picked up a great variety of accomplishments. Occasionally we passed a week or two together here, and disconcerted each other as only such near relations can. At last you came home. I candidly tell you, my dear boy, that if you had been awkward and overgrown, I should have exported you to some distant part of the world."

"I wish with all my soul you had, sir," said Edward.

"No you don't, Ned," rejoined his father coolly; "you are mistaken, I assure you. I found you a handsome, prepossessing, elegant fellow, and I threw you into the society I can still command. Having done that, my dear fellow, I consider that I have provided for you in life, and rely on your doing something to provide for me in return."

"I do not understand your meaning, sir."

"My meaning, Ned, is obvious—I observe another fly in the cream-jug, but have the goodness not to take it out as you did the first, for their walk when their legs are milky, is extremely ungraceful and disagreeable—my meaning is, that you must do as I did; that you must marry well and make the most of yourself."

"A mere fortune-hunter!" cried the son, indignantly.

"What in the devil's name, Ned, would you be!" returned the father. "All men are fortune-hunters, are they not? The law, the church, the court, the camp—see how they are all crowded with fortune-hunters, jostling each other in the pursuit. The Stock-exchange, the pulpit, the counting-house, the royal drawing-room, the senate,—what but fortune-hunters are they filled with? A fortune-hunter! Yes. You *are* one; and you would be nothing else, my dear Ned, if you were the greatest courtier, lawyer, legislator, prelate, or merchant, in existence. If you are squeamish and moral, Ned, console yourself with the reflection that at the worst your fortune-hunting can make but one person miserable or unhappy. How many people do you suppose these other kinds of huntsmen crush in following their sport—hundreds at a step? Or thousands?"

The young man leant his head upon his hand, and made no answer.

"I am quite charmed," said the father rising, and walking slowly to and fro—stopping now and then to glance at himself in a mirror, or survey a picture through his glass, with the air of a connoisseur, "that we have had this conversation, Ned, unpromising as it was. It establishes a confidence between us which is quite delightful, and was certainly necessary, though how you can ever have mistaken our position and designs, I confess I cannot understand. I conceived, until I found your fancy for this girl, that all these points were tacitly agreed upon between us."

"I knew you were embarrassed, sir," returned the son, raising his head for a moment, and then falling into his former attitude, "but I had no idea we were the beggared wretches you describe. How could I suppose it, bred as I have been; witnessing the life you have always led; and the appearance you have always made?"

"My dear child," said the father—"for you really talk so like a child that I must call you one—you were bred upon a careful principle; the very manner of your education, I assure you, maintained my credit surprisingly. As to the life I lead, I must lead it, Ned. I must have these little refinements about me. I have always been used to them, and I cannot exist without them. They must surround me, you observe, and therefore they are here. With regard to our circumstances, Ned, you may set your mind at rest upon that score. They are desperate. Your own appearance is by no means despicable, and our joint pocket-money alone devours our income. That's the truth."

"Why have I never known this before? Why have you encouraged me, sir, to an expenditure and mode of life to which we have no right or title?"

"My good fellow," returned his father more compassionately than ever, "if you made no appearance how could you possibly succeed in the pursuit for which I destined you? As to our mode of life, every man has a right to live in the best way he can; and to make himself as comfortable as he can, or he is an unnatural scoundrel. Our debts, I grant, are very great, and therefore it the more behoves you, as a young man of principle and honour, to pay them off as speedily as possible."

"The villain's part," muttered Edward, "that I have unconsciously played! I to win the heart of Emma Haredale! I would, for her sake, I had died first!"

"I am glad you see, Ned," returned his father, "how perfectly self-evident it is, that nothing can be done in that quarter. But apart from this, and the necessity of your speedily bestowing yourself in another (as you know you could to-morrow, if you chose), I wish you'd look upon it pleasantly. In a religious point of view alone, how could you ever think of uniting yourself to a catholic, unless she was amazingly rich? You who ought to be so very Protestant, coming of such a Protestant family as you do. Let us be moral, Ned, or we are nothing. Even if one could set that objection aside, which is impossible, we come to another which is quite conclusive. The very idea of marrying a girl whose father was killed, like meat! Good God, Ned, how disagreeable! Consider the impossibility of having any respect for your father-in-law under such unpleasant circumstances—think of his having been 'viewed' by jurors, and 'sat upon' by coroners, and of his very doubtful position in the family ever afterwards. It seems to me such an indelicate sort of thing that I really think the girl ought to have been put to death by the state to prevent its happening. But I tease you perhaps. You would rather be alone? My dear Ned, most willingly. God bless you. I shall be going out presently, but we shall meet to-night, or if not to-night, certainly to-morrow. Take care of yourself in the mean time, for both our sakes. You are a person of great consequence to me, Ned—of vast consequence indeed. God bless you!"

With these words, the father, who had been arranging his cravat in the glass, while he uttered them in a disconnected careless manner, withdrew, humming a tune as he went. The son, who had appeared so lost in thought as not to hear or understand them, remained quite still and silent. After the lapse of half an hour or so, the elder Chester, gaily dressed, went out. The younger still sat with his head resting on his hands, in what appeared to be a kind of stupor.

## CHAPTER THE SIXTEENTH.

A SERIES of pictures representing the streets of London in the night, even at the comparatively recent date of this tale, would present to the eye something so very different in character from the reality which is witnessed in these times, that it would be difficult for the beholder to recognise his most familiar walks in the altered aspect of little more than half a century ago.

They were, one and all, from the broadest and best to the narrowest and least frequented, very dark. The oil and cotton lamps, though regularly trimmed twice or thrice in the long winter nights, burnt feebly at the best; and at a late hour, when they were unassisted by the lamps and candles in the shops, cast but a narrow track of doubtful light upon the footway, leaving the projecting doors and housefronts in the deepest gloom. Many of the courts and lanes were left in total darkness; those of the meaner sort, where one glimmering light twinkled for a score of houses, being favoured in no slight degree. Even in these places, the inhabitants had often good reason for extinguishing their lamp as soon as it was lighted; and the watch being utterly inefficient and powerless to prevent them, they did so at their pleasure. Thus, in the lightest thoroughfares, there was at every turn some obscure and dangerous spot whither a thief might fly for shelter, and few would care to follow; and the city being belted round by fields, green lanes, waste grounds, and lonely roads, dividing it at that time from the suburbs that have joined it since, escape, even where the pursuit was hot, was rendered easy.

It is no wonder that with these favouring circumstances in full and constant operation, street robberies, often accompanied by cruel wounds, and not unfrequently by loss of life, should have been of nightly occurrence in the very heart of London, or that quiet folks should have had great dread of traversing its streets after the shops were closed. It was not unusual for those who wended home alone at midnight, to keep the middle of the road, the better to guard against surprise from lurking footpads; few would venture to repair at a late hour to Kentish Town or Hampstead, or even to Kensington or Chelsea, unarmed and unattended; while he who had been loudest and most valiant at the supper-table or the tavern, and had but a mile or so to go, was glad to fee a link-boy* to escort him home.

There were many other characteristics—not quite so disagreeable—about the thoroughfares of London then, with which they had been long familiar. Some of the shops, especially those to the eastward of Temple Bar, still adhered to the old practice of hanging out a sign; and the creaking and swinging of these boards in their iron frames on windy nights, formed a strange and mournful concert for the ears of those who lay awake in bed or hurried through the streets. Long stands of hackney-chairs and groups of chairmen, compared with whom the coachmen of our day are gentle and polite, obstructed the way and filled the air with clamour; night-cellars, indicated by a little stream of light crossing the pavement, and stretching out half way into the road, and by the stifled roar of voices from below, yawned for the reception and entertainment of the most abandoned of both sexes; under every shed and bulk small groups of link-boys gamed away the earnings of the day; or one more weary than the rest, gave way to sleep, and let the fragment of his torch fall hissing on the puddled ground.

Then there was the watch with staff and lanthorn crying the hour, and the kind of weather; and those who woke up at his voice and turned them round in bed, were glad to hear it rained, or snowed, or blew, or froze, for very comfort's sake. The solitary passenger was startled by the chairmen's cry of "By your leave there!" as two came trotting past him with their empty vehicle—carried backwards to show its being disengaged—and hurried to the nearest stand. Many a private chair too, inclosing some fine lady, monstrously hooped and furbeloved,* and preceded by running-footmen bearing flambeaux—for which extinguishers are yet suspended before the doors of a few houses of the better sort—made the way gay and light as it danced along, and darker and more dismal when it had passed. It was not unusual for these running gentry, who carried it with a very high hand, to quarrel in the servants' hall while waiting for their masters and mistresses; and, falling to blows either there or in the street without, to strew the place of skirmish with hair-powder, fragments of bag-wigs, and scattered nosegays. Gaming, the vice which ran so high among all classes (the fashion being of course set by the upper), was generally the cause of these disputes; for cards and dice were as openly used, and worked as much mischief, and yielded as much excitement below stairs, as above. While incidents like these, arising out of drums* and masquerades and parties at quadrille,* were passing at the west end of the town, heavy stage-coaches and scarce heavier waggons were lumbering slowly towards the city, the coachmen, guard, and passengers, armed to the teeth, and the coach—a day or so, perhaps, behind its time, but that was nothing—despoiled by highwaymen; who made no scruple to attack, alone and single-handed, a whole caravan of goods and men, and sometimes shot a passenger or two and were sometimes shot themselves, just as the case might be. On the morrow, rumours of this new act of daring on the road yielded matter for a few hours' conversation through the town, and a Public Progress of some fine gentleman (half drunk) to Tyburn,* dressed in the newest fashion and damning the ordinary* with unspeakable gallantry and grace, furnished to the populace, at once a pleasant excitement and a wholesome and profound example.

Among all the dangerous characters who, in such a state of society, prowled and skulked in the metropolis at night, there was one man, from whom many as uncouth and fierce as he, shrunk with an involuntary dread. Who he was, or whence he came, was a question often asked, but which none could answer. His name was unknown, he had never been seen until within eight days or thereabouts, and was equally a stranger to the old ruffians, upon whose haunts he ventured fearlessly, as to the young. He could be no spy, for he never removed his slouched hat to look about him, entered into conversation with no man, heeded nothing that passed, listened to no discourse, regarded nobody that came or went. But so surely as the dead of night set in, so surely this man was in the midst of the loose concourse in the night-cellar where outcasts of every grade resorted; and there he sat till morning.

He was not only a spectre at their licentious feasts; a something in the midst of their revelry and riot that chilled and haunted them; but out of doors he was the same. Directly it was dark, he was abroad— never in company with any one, but always alone; never lingering or loitering, but always walking swiftly; and looking (so they said who had seen him) over his shoulder from time to time, and as he did so quickening his pace. In the fields, the lanes, the roads, in all quarters of the town—east, west, north, and south—that man was seen gliding on, like a shadow. He was always hurrying away. Those who encountered him, saw him steal past, caught sight of the backward glance, and so lost him in the darkness.

This constant restlessness and flitting to and fro, gave rise to strange stories. He was seen in such distant and remote places, at times so nearly tallying with each other, that some doubted whether there were not two of them, or more—some, whether he had not unearthly means of travelling from spot to spot. The footpad hiding in a ditch had marked him passing like a ghost along its brink; the vagrant had met him on the dark high-road; the beggar had seen him pause upon the bridge to look down at the water, and then sweep on again; they who dealt in bodies with the surgeons* could swear he slept in churchyards, and that they had beheld him glide away among the tombs, on their approach. And as they told these stories to each other, one who had looked about him would pull his neighbour by the sleeve, and there he would be among them.

At last, one man—he was of those whose commerce lay among the graves—resolved to question this strange companion. Next night, when he had eat his poor meal voraciously (he was accustomed to do that, they had observed, as though he had no other in the day), this fellow sat down at his elbow.

"A black night, master!"

"It is a black night."

"Blacker than last, though that was pitchy too. Didn't I pass you near the turnpike in the Oxford-road?"

"It's like you may. I don't know."

"Come, come, master," cried the fellow, urged on by the looks of his comrades, and slapping him on the shoulder; "be more companionable and communicative. Be more the gentleman in this good company. There are tales among us that you have sold yourself to the devil, and I know not what."

"We all have, have we not?" returned the stranger, looking up. "If we were fewer in number, perhaps he would give better wages."

"It goes rather hard with you, indeed," said the fellow, as the stranger disclosed his haggard unwashed face, and torn clothes. "What of that? Be merry, master. A stave of a roaring song now—"

"Sing you, if you desire to hear one," replied the other, shaking him roughly off; "and don't touch me, if you're a prudent man; I carry arms which go off easily—they have done so, before now—and make it dangerous for strangers who don't know the trick of them, to lay hands upon me."

"Do you threaten?" said the fellow.

"Yes," returned the other, rising and turning upon him, and looking fiercely round as if in apprehension of a general attack.

His voice, and look, and bearing—all expressive of the wildest recklessness and desperation—daunted while they repelled the bystanders. Although in a very different sphere of action now, they were not without much of the effect they had wrought at the Maypole Inn.

"I am what you all are, and live as you all do," said the man sternly, after a short silence. "I am in hiding here like the rest, and if we were surprised would perhaps do my part with the best of ye. If it's my humour to be left to myself, let me have it. Otherwise,"—and here he swore a tremendous oath—"there'll be mischief done in this place, though there *are* odds of a score against me."

A low murmur, having its origin perhaps in a dread of the man and the mystery that surrounded him, or perhaps in a sincere opinion on the part of some of those present, that it would be an inconvenient precedent to meddle too curiously with a gentleman's private affairs if he saw reason to conceal them, warned the fellow who had occasioned this discussion that he had best pursue it no further. After a short time, the strange man lay down upon a bench to sleep, and when they thought of him again, they found that he was gone.

Next night, as soon as it was dark, he was abroad again and traversing the streets; he was before the locksmith's house more than once, but the family were out, and it was close shut. This night he crossed London bridge and passed into Southwark. As he glided down a bye street, a woman with a little basket on her arm, turned into it at the other end. Directly he observed her, he sought the shelter of an archway, and stood aside until she had passed. Then he emerged cautiously from his hiding-place, and followed.

She went into several shops to purchase various kinds of household necessaries, and round every place at which she stopped he hovered like her evil spirit; following her when she reappeared. It was nigh eleven o'clock, and the passengers in the streets were thinning fast, when she turned, doubtless to go home. The phantom still followed her.

She turned into the same bye street in which he had seen her first, which, being free from shops, and narrow, was extremely dark. She quickened her pace here, as though distrustful of being stopped, and robbed of such trifling property as she carried with her. He crept along on the other side of the road. Had she been gifted with the speed of wind, it seemed as if his terrible shadow would have tracked her down.

At length the widow—for she it was—reached her own door, and, panting for breath, paused to take the key from her basket. In a flush and glow, with the haste she had made, and the pleasure of being safe at home, she stooped to draw it out, when, raising her head, she saw him standing silently beside her; the apparition of a dream.

His hand was on her mouth, but that was needless, for her tongue clove to its roof, and her power of utterance was gone. "I have been looking for you many nights. Is the house empty? Answer me. Is any one inside?"

She could only answer by a rattle in her throat.

"Make me a sign."

She seemed to indicate that there was no one there. He took the key, unlocked the door, carried her in, and secured it carefully behind them.

## CHAPTER THE SEVENTEENTH.

IT was a chilly night, and the fire in the widow's parlour had burnt low. Her strange companion placed her in a chair, and stooping down before the half-extinguished ashes, raked them together and fanned them with his hat. From time to time he glanced at her over his shoulder, as though to assure himself of her remaining quiet and making no effort to depart; and that done, busied himself about the fire again.

It was not without reason that he took these pains, for his dress was dank and drenched with wet, his jaws rattled with cold, and he shivered from head to foot. It had rained hard during the previous night and for some hours in the morning, but since noon it had been fine. Wheresoever he had passed the hours of darkness, his condition sufficiently betokened that many of them had been spent beneath the open sky. Besmeared with mire; his saturated clothes clinging with a damp embrace about his limbs; his beard unshaven, his face unwashed, his meagre cheeks worn into deep hollows,—a more miserable wretch could hardly be, than this man who now cowered down upon the widow's hearth, and watched the struggling flame with bloodshot eyes.

She had covered her face with her hands, fearing, as it seemed, to look towards him. So they remained for some short time in silence. Glancing round again, he asked at length:

"Is this your house?"

"It is. Why, in the name of Heaven, do you darken it?"

"Give me meat and drink," he answered sullenly, "or I dare do more than that. The very marrow in my bones is cold, with wet and hunger. I must have warmth and food, and I will have them here."

"You were the robber on the Chigwell road."

"I was."

"And nearly a murderer then."

"The will was not wanting. There was one came upon me and raised the hue-and-cry, that it would have gone hard with, but for his nimbleness. I made a thrust at him."

"You thrust your sword at *him!*" cried the widow, looking upwards. "You hear this man! you hear and saw!"

He looked at her, as, with her head thrown back, and her hands tight clenched together, she uttered these words in an agony of appeal. Then, starting to his feet as she had done, he advanced towards her.

"Beware!" she cried in a suppressed voice, whose firmness stopped him midway. "Do not so much as touch me with a finger, or you are lost; body and soul, you are lost."

"Hear me," he replied, menacing her with his hand. "I, that in the form of a man live the life of a hunted beast; that in the body am a spirit, a ghost upon the earth, a thing from which all creatures shrink, save those curst beings of another world, who will not leave me;—I am, in my desperation of this night, past all fear but that of the hell in which I exist from day to day. Give the alarm, cry out, refuse to shelter me. I will not hurt you. But I will not be taken alive; and so surely as you threaten me above your breath, I fall a dead man on this floor. The blood with which I sprinkle it, be on you and yours, in the name of the Evil Spirit that tempts men to their ruin!"

As he spoke, he took a pistol from his breast, and firmly clutched it in his hand.

"Remove this man from me, good Heaven!" cried the widow. "In thy grace and mercy, give him one minute's penitence, and strike him dead!"

"It has no such purpose," he said, confronting her. "It is deaf. Give me to eat and drink, lest I do that, it cannot help my doing, and will not do for you."

"Will you leave me, if I do thus much? Will you leave me and return no more?"

"I will promise nothing," he rejoined, seating himself at the table, "nothing but this—I will execute my threat if you betray me."

She rose at length, and going to a closet or pantry in the room, brought out some fragments of cold meat and bread and put them on the table. He asked for brandy, and for water. These she produced likewise; and he ate and drank with the voracity of a famished hound. All the time he was so engaged she kept at the uttermost distance of the chamber, and sat there shuddering, but with her face towards him. She never turned her back upon him once; and although when she passed him (as she was obliged to do in going to and from the cupboard) she gathered the skirts of her garment about her, as if even its touching his by chance were horrible to think of, still, in the midst of all this dread and terror, she kept her face directed to his own, and watched his every movement.

His repast ended—if that can be called one, which was a mere ravenous satisfying of the calls of hunger—he moved his chair towards the fire again, and warming himself before the blaze which had now sprung brightly up, accosted her once more.

"I am an outcast, to whom a roof above his head is often an

uncommon luxury, and the food a beggar would reject is delicate fare. You live here at your ease. Do you live alone?"

"I do not," she made answer with an effort.

"Who dwells here besides?"

"One—it is no matter who. You had best begone, or he may find you here. Why do you linger?"

"For warmth," he replied, spreading out his hands before the fire. "For warmth. You are rich, perhaps?"

"Very," she said faintly. "Very rich. No doubt I am very rich."

"At least you are not penniless. You have some money. You were making purchases to-night."

"I have a little left. It is but a few shillings."

"Give me your purse. You had it in your hand at the door. Give it to me."

She stepped to the table and laid it down. He reached across, took it up, and told the contents into his hand. As he was counting them, she listened for a moment, and sprung towards him.

"Take what there is, take all, take more if more were there, but go before it is too late. I have heard a wayward step without, I know full well. It will return directly. Begone."

"What do you mean?"

"Do not stop to ask. I will not answer. Much as I dread to touch you, I would drag you to the door if I possessed the strength, rather than you should lose an instant. Miserable wretch! fly from this place."

"If there are spies without, I am safer here," replied the man, standing aghast. "I will remain here, and will not fly till the danger is past."

"It is too late!" cried the widow, who had listened for the step, and not to him. "Hark to that foot upon the ground. Do you tremble to hear it! It is my son, my idiot son!"

As she said this wildly, there came a heavy knocking at the door. He looked at her, and she at him.

"Let him come in," said the man, hoarsely. "I fear him less than the dark, houseless night. He knocks again. Let him come in!"

"The dread of this hour," returned the widow, "has been upon me all my life, and I will not. Evil will fall upon him, if you stand eye to eye. My blighted boy! Oh! all good angels—ye who know the truth—hear a poor mother's prayer, and spare my boy from knowledge of this man!"

"He rattles at the shutters!" cried the man. "He calls you. That voice and cry! It was he who grappled with me in the road. Was it he?"

She had sunk upon her knees, and so knelt down, moving her lips, but uttering no sound. As he gazed upon her, uncertain what to do or where to turn, the shutters flew open. He had barely time to catch a knife from the table, sheathe it in the loose sleeve of his coat, hide in the closet, and do all with the lightning's speed, when Barnaby tapped at the bare glass, and raised the sash exultingly.

"Why, who can keep out Grip and me!" he cried, thrusting in his head, and staring round the room. "Are you there, mother? How long you keep us from the fire and light."

She stammered some excuse and tendered him her hand. But Barnaby sprung lightly in without assistance, and putting his arms about her neck, kissed her a hundred times.

"We have been afield, mother—leaping ditches, scrambling through hedges, running down steep banks, up and away, and hurrying on. The wind has been blowing, and the rushes and young plants bowing and bending to it, lest it should do them harm, the cowards—and Grip—ha ha ha!—brave Grip, who cares for nothing, and when the wind rolls him over in the dust, turns manfully to bite it—Grip, bold Grip, has quarrelled with every little bowing twig—thinking, he told me, that it mocked him—and has worried it like a bull-dog. Ha ha ha!"

The raven, in his little basket at his master's back, hearing this frequent mention of his name in a tone of exultation, expressed his sympathy by crowing like a cock, and afterwards running over his various phrases of speech with such rapidity, and in so many varieties of hoarseness, that they sounded like the murmurs of a crowd of people.

"He takes such care of me besides!" said Barnaby. "Such care, mother! He watches all the time I sleep, and when I shut my eyes, and make-believe to slumber, he practises new learning softly; but he keeps his eye on me the while, and if he sees me laugh, though never so little, stops directly. He won't surprise me till he's perfect."

The raven crowed again in a rapturous manner which plainly said, "Those are certainly some of my characteristics, and I glory in them." In the meantime, Barnaby closed the window and secured it, and coming to the fire-place, prepared to sit down with his face to the closet. But his mother prevented this, by hastily taking that side herself, and motioning him towards the other.

"How pale you are to-night!" said Barnaby, leaning on his stick. "We have been cruel, Grip, and made her anxious!"

Anxious in good truth, and sick at heart! The listener held the door of his hiding-place open with his hand, and closely watched her son. Grip—alive to everything his master was unconscious of—had his head out of the basket, and in return was watching him intently with his glistening eye.

"He flaps his wings," said Barnaby, turning almost quickly enough to catch the retreating form and closing door, "as if there were strangers here; but Grip is wiser than to fancy that. Jump then!"

Accepting this invitation with a dignity peculiar to himself, the bird hopped up on his master's shoulder, from that to his extended hand, and so to the ground. Barnaby unstrapping the basket and putting it down in a corner with the lid open, Grip's first care was to shut it down with all possible despatch, and then to stand upon it. Believing, no doubt, that he had now rendered it utterly impossible, and beyond the power of mortal man, to shut him up in it any more, he drew a great many corks in triumph, and uttered a corresponding number of hurrahs.

"Mother!" said Barnaby, laying aside his hat and stick, and returning to the chair from which he had risen, "I'll tell you where we have been to-day, and what we have been doing,—shall I?"

She took his hand in hers, and holding it, nodded the word she could not speak.

"You mustn't tell," said Barnaby, holding up his finger, "for it's a secret, mind, and only known to me, and Grip, and Hugh. We had the dog with us, but he's not like Grip, clever as he is, and doesn't guess it yet, I'll wager.—Why do you look behind me so?"

"Did I!" she answered faintly. "I didn't know I did. Come nearer me."

"You are frightened!" said Barnaby, changing colour. "Mother—you don't see—"

"See what?"

"There's—there's none of this about, is there?" he answered in a whisper, drawing closer to her and clasping the mark upon his wrist. "I am afraid there is, somewhere. You make my hair stand on end, and my flesh creep. Why do you look like that? Is it in the room as I have seen it in my dreams, dashing the ceiling and the walls with red? Tell me. Is it?"

He fell into a shivering fit as he put the question, and shutting out the light with his hands, sat shaking in every limb until it had passed away. After a time, he raised his head and looked about him.

"Is it gone?"

"There has been nothing here," rejoined his mother, soothing him. "Nothing indeed, dear Barnaby. Look! You see there are but you and me."

He gazed at her vacantly, and, becoming reassured by degrees, burst into a wild laugh.

"But let us see," he said, thoughtfully. "Were we talking? Was it you and me? Where have we been?"

"Nowhere but here."

"Aye, but Hugh, and I," said Barnaby, "—that's it. Maypole Hugh, and I, you know, and Grip—we have been lying in the forest, and among the trees by the road side, with a dark-lanthorn after night came on, and the dog in a noose ready to slip him when the man came by."

"What man?"

"The robber; him that the stars winked at. We have waited for him after dark these many nights, and we shall have him. I'd know him in a thousand. Mother, see here! This is the man. Look!"

He twisted his handkerchief round his head, pulled his hat upon his brow, wrapped his coat about him, and stood up before her: so like the original he counterfeited, that the dark figure peering out behind him might have passed for his own shadow.

"Ha ha ha! We shall have him," he cried, ridding himself of the semblance as hastily as he had assumed it. "You shall see him, mother, bound hand and foot, and brought to London at a saddle-girth; and you shall hear of him at Tyburn Tree if we have luck. So Hugh says. You're pale again, and trembling. And why *do* you look behind me so?"

"It is nothing," she answered. "I am not quite well. Go you to bed, dear, and leave me here."

"To bed!" he answered. "I don't like bed. I like to lie before the fire, watching the prospects in the burning coals—the rivers, hills, and dells, in the deep, red sunset, and the wild faces. I am hungry too, and Grip has eaten nothing since broad noon. Let us to supper. Grip! To supper, lad!"

The raven flapped his wings, and, croaking his satisfaction, hopped to the feet of his master, and there held his bill open, ready for snapping up such lumps of meat as he should throw him. Of these he received about a score in rapid succession, without the smallest discomposure.

"That's all," said Barnaby.

"More!" cried Grip. "More!"

But it appearing for a certainty that no more was to be had, he retreated with his store; and disgorging the morsels one by one from his pouch, hid them in various corners—taking particular care, however, to avoid the closet, as being doubtful of the hidden man's propensities and power of resisting temptation. When he had concluded these arrangements, he took a turn or two across the room with an elaborate assumption of having nothing on his mind (but with one eye hard upon his treasure all the time), and then, and not till then, began to drag it out, piece by piece, and eat it with the utmost relish.

Barnaby, for his part, having pressed his mother to eat, in vain, made a hearty supper too. Once, during the progress of his meal, he wanted more bread from the closet and rose to get it. She hurriedly interposed to prevent him, and, summoning her utmost fortitude, passed into the recess, and brought it out herself.

"Mother," said Barnaby, looking at her stedfastly as she sat down beside him after doing so; "is to-day my birthday?"

"To-day!" she answered. "Don't you recollect it was but a week or so ago, and that summer, autumn, and winter have to pass before it comes again?"

"I remember that it has been so till now," said Barnaby. "But I think to-day must be my birthday too, for all that."

She asked him why? "I'll tell you why," he said. "I have always seen you—I didn't let you know it, but I have—on the evening of that day grow very sad. I have seen you cry when Grip and I were most glad; and look frightened with no reason; and I have touched your hand, and felt that it was cold—as it is now. Once, mother (on a birthday that was, also) Grip and I thought of this after we went up stairs to bed, and when it was midnight, striking one o'clock, we came down to your door to see if you were well. You were on your knees. I forget what it was you said. Grip, what was it we heard her say that night?"

"I'm a devil!" rejoined the raven promptly.

"No, no," said Barnaby. "But you said something in a prayer; and when you rose and walked about, you looked (as you have done ever since, mother, towards night on my birthday) just as you do now. I have found that out, you see, though I am silly. So I say you're wrong; and this must be my birthday—my birthday, Grip!"

The bird received this information with a crow of such duration as a cock, gifted with intelligence beyond all others of his kind, might usher in the longest day with. Then, as if he had well considered the sentiment, and regarded it as apposite to birthdays, he cried, "Never say die!" a great many times, and flapped his wings for emphasis.

The widow tried to make light of Barnaby's remark, and endeavoured to divert his attention to some new subject; too easy a task at all times, as she knew. His supper done, Barnaby, regardless of her entreaties, stretched himself on the mat before the fire; Grip perched upon his leg, and divided his time between dozing in the grateful warmth, and endeavouring (as it presently appeared) to recal a new accomplishment he had been studying all day.

A long and profound silence ensued, broken only by some change of position on the part of Barnaby, whose eyes were still wide open and intently fixed upon the fire; or by an effort of recollection on the part of Grip, who would cry in a low voice from time to time, "Polly put the ket—" and there stop short, forgetting the remainder, and go off in a doze again.

After a long interval, Barnaby's breathing grew more deep and regular, and his eyes were closed. But even then the unquiet spirit of the raven interposed. "Polly put the ket—" cried Grip, and his master was broad awake again.

At length Barnaby slept soundly; and the bird with his bill sunk upon his breast, his breast itself puffed out into a comfortable alderman-like form, and his bright eye growing smaller and smaller, really seemed to be subsiding into a state of repose. Now and then he muttered in a sepulchral voice, "Polly put the ket—" but very drowsily, and more like a drunken man than a reflecting raven.

The widow, scarcely venturing to breathe, rose from her seat. The man glided from the closet, and extinguished the candle.

"—tle on," cried Grip, suddenly struck with an idea and very much excited. "—tle on. Hurrah! Polly put the ket-tle on, we'll all have tea; Polly put the ket-tle on, we'll all have tea. Hurrah, hurrah, hurrah! I'm a devil I'm a devil, I'm a ket-tle on, Keep up your spirits, Never say die, Bow wow wow, I'm a devil, I'm a ket-tle, I'm a—Polly put the ket-tle on we'll all have tea."

They stood rooted to the ground, as though it had been a voice from the grave.

But even this failed to awaken the sleeper. He turned over towards the fire, his arm fell to the ground, and his head drooped heavily upon it. The widow and her unwelcome visitor gazed at him and at each other for a moment, and then she motioned him towards the door.

"Stay," he whispered. "You teach your son well."

"I have taught him nothing that you heard to-night. Depart instantly, or I will rouse him."

"You are free to do so. Shall *I* rouse him?"

"You dare not do that."

"I dare do anything, I have told you. He knows me well, it seems. At least I will know him."

"Would you kill him in his sleep?" cried the widow, throwing herself between them.

"Woman," he returned between his teeth, as he motioned her aside, "I would see him nearer, and I will. If you want one of us to kill the other, wake him."

With that he advanced, and bending down over the prostrate form, softly turned back the head and looked into the face. The light of the fire was upon it, and its every lineament was revealed distinctly. He contemplated it for a brief space, and hastily uprose.

"Observe," he whispered in the widow's ear: "In him, of whose existence I was ignorant until to-night, I have you in my power. Be careful how you use me. Be careful how you use me. I am destitute and starving, and a wanderer upon the earth. I may take a sure and slow revenge."

"There is some dreadful meaning in your words. I do not fathom it."

"There is a meaning in them, and I see you fathom it to its very depth. You have anticipated it for years; you have told me as much. I leave you to digest it. Do not forget my warning."

He pointed, as he left her, to the slumbering form, and stealthily withdrawing, made his way into the street. She fell on her knees beside the sleeper, and remained like one stricken into stone, until the tears which fear had frozen so long, came tenderly to her relief.

"Oh Thou," she cried, "who hast taught me such deep love for this one remnant of the promise of a happy life, out of whose affliction, even, perhaps the comfort springs that he is ever a relying, loving child to me—never growing old or cold at heart, but needing my care and duty in his manly strength as in his cradle-time—help him, in his darkened walk through this sad world, or he is doomed, and my poor heart is broken!"

## CHAPTER THE EIGHTEENTH.

GLIDING along the silent streets, and holding his course where they were darkest and most gloomy, the man who had left the widow's house crossed London Bridge, and arriving in the City, plunged into the back ways, lanes, and courts, between Cornhill and Smithfield; with no more fixedness of purpose than to lose himself among their windings, and baffle pursuit, if any one were dogging his steps.

It was the dead time of the night, and all was quiet. Now and then a drowsy watchman's footsteps sounded on the pavement, or the lamp-lighter on his rounds went flashing past, leaving behind a little track of smoke mingled with glowing morsels of his hot red link. He hid himself even from these partakers of his lonely walk, and, shrinking in some arch or doorway while they passed, issued forth again when they were gone and so pursued his solitary way.

To be shelterless and alone in the open country, hearing the wind moan and watching for day through the whole long weary night; to listen to the falling rain, and crouch for warmth beneath the lee of some old barn or rick, or in the hollow of a tree; are dismal things— but not so dismal as the wandering up and down where shelter is, and beds and sleepers are by thousands; a houseless rejected creature. To pace the echoing stones from hour to hour, counting the dull chimes of the clocks; to watch the lights twinkling in chamber windows, to think what happy forgetfulness each house shuts in; that here are children coiled together in their beds, here youth, here age, here poverty, here wealth, all equal in their sleep, and all at rest; to have nothing in common with the slumbering world around, not even sleep, Heaven's gift to all its creatures, and be akin to nothing but despair; to feel, by the wretched contrast with everything on every hand, more utterly alone and cast away than in a trackless desert;— this is a kind of suffering, on which the rivers of great cities close full many a time, and which the solitude in crowds alone awakens.

The miserable man paced up and down the streets—so long, so wearisome, so like each other—and often cast a wistful look towards the east, hoping to see the first faint streaks of day. But obdurate night had yet possession of the sky, and his disturbed and restless walk found no relief.

One house in a back street was bright with the cheerful glare of lights; there was the sound of music in it too, and the tread of dancers, and there were cheerful voices, and many a burst of laugh-ter. To this place—to be near something that was awake and glad— he returned again and again; and more than one of those who left it when the merriment was at its height, felt it a check upon their mirthful mood to see him flitting to and fro like an uneasy ghost. At last the guests departed, one and all; and then the house was close shut up, and became as dull and silent as the rest.

His wanderings brought him at one time to the city jail. Instead of hastening from it as a place of ill omen, and one he had cause to shun, he sat down on some steps hard by, and, resting his chin upon his hand, gazed upon its rough and frowning walls as though even they became a refuge in his jaded eyes. He paced it round and round, came back to the same spot, and sat down again. He did this often, and once, with a hasty movement, crossed to where some men were watching in the prison lodge, and had his foot upon the steps as though determined to accost them. But looking round, he saw that the day began to break, and failing in his purpose, turned and fled.

He was soon in the quarter he had lately traversed, and pacing to and fro again as he had done before. He was passing down a mean street, when from an alley close at hand some shouts of revelry arose, and there came straggling forth a dozen madcaps, whooping and calling to each other, who, parting noisily, took different ways and dispersed in smaller groups.

Hoping that some low place of entertainment which would afford him a safe refuge might be near at hand, he turned into this court when they were all gone, and looked about for a half-opened door, or lighted window, or other indication of the place whence they had come. It was so profoundly dark, however, and so ill-favoured, that he concluded they had but turned up there, missing their way, and were pouring out again when he observed them. With this impression, and finding there was no outlet but that by which he had entered, he was about to turn, when from a grating near his feet a sudden stream of light appeared, and the sound of talking came. He retreated into a doorway to see who these talkers were, and to listen to them.

The light came to the level of the pavement as he did this, and a man ascended, bearing in his hand a torch. This figure unlocked and held open the grating as for the passage of another, who presently appeared, in the form of a young man of small stature and uncommon self-importance, dressed in an obsolete and very gaudy fashion.

"Good night, noble captain," said he with the torch. "Farewell, commander. Good luck, illustrious general!"

In return to these compliments, the other bade him hold his

tongue, and keep his noise to himself; and laid upon him many similar injunctions, with great fluency of speech and sternness of manner.

"Commend me, captain, to the stricken Miggs," returned the torch-bearer in a lower voice. "My captain flies at higher game than Miggses. Ha, ha, ha! My captain is an eagle, both as respects his eye and soaring wings. My captain breaketh hearts as other bachelors break eggs at breakfast."

"What a fool you are, Stagg!" said Mr. Tappertit, stepping on the pavement of the court, and brushing from his legs the dust he had contracted in his passage upward.

"His precious limbs!" cried Stagg, clasping one of his ancles. "Shall a Miggs aspire to these proportions! No, no, my captain. We will inveigle ladies fair, and wed them in our secret cavern. We will unite ourselves with blooming beauties, captain."

"I'll tell you what, my buck," said Mr. Tappertit, releasing his leg, "I'll trouble you not to take liberties, and not to broach certain questions unless certain questions are broached to you. Speak when you're spoke to on particular subjects, and not otherways. Hold the torch up till I've got to the end of the court, and then kennel yourself, do you hear?"

"I hear you, noble captain."

"Obey then," said Mr. Tappertit haughtily. "Gentlemen, lead on!" With which word of command (addressed to an imaginary staff or retinue) he folded his arms, and walked with surpassing dignity down the court.

His obsequious follower stood holding the torch above his head, and then the observer saw for the first time, from his place of concealment, that he was blind. Some involuntary motion on his part caught the quick ear of the blind man, before he was conscious of having moved an inch towards him, for he turned suddenly and cried, "Who's there?"

"A man," said the other, advancing. "A friend."

"A stranger!" rejoined the blind man. "Strangers are not my friends. What do you do there?"

"I saw your company come out, and waited here till they were gone. I want a lodging."

"A lodging at this time!" returned Stagg, pointing towards the dawn as though he saw it. "Do you know the day is breaking?"

"I know it," rejoined the other, "to my cost. I have been traversing this iron-hearted town all night."

"You had better traverse it again," said the blind man, preparing to descend, "till you find some lodgings suitable to your taste. I don't let any."

"Stay!" cried the other, holding him by the arm.

"I'll beat this light about that hangdog face of yours (for hangdog it is, if it answers to your voice), and rouse the neighbourhood besides, if you detain me," said the blind man. "Let me go. Do you hear?"

"Do *you* hear!" returned the other, chinking a few shillings together, and hurriedly pressing them into his hand. "I beg nothing of you. I will pay for the shelter you give me. Death! Is it much to ask of such as you! I have come from the country, and desire to rest where there are none to question me. I am faint, exhausted, worn out, almost dead. Let me lie down, like a dog, before your fire. I ask no more than that. If you would be rid of me, I will depart to-morrow."

"If a gentleman has been unfortunate on the road," muttered Stagg, yielding to the other, who, pressing on him, had already gained a footing on the steps—"and can pay for his accommodation—"

"I will pay you with all I have. I am just now past the want of food, God knows, and wish but to purchase shelter. What companion have you below?"

"None."

"Then fasten your grate there, and show me the way. Quick!"

The blind man complied after a moment's hesitation, and they descended together. The dialogue had passed as hurriedly as the words could be spoken, and they stood in his wretched room before he had had time to recover from his first surprise.

"May I see where that door leads to, and what is beyond?" said the man, glancing keenly round. "You will not mind that?"

"I will show you myself. Follow me, or go before. Take your choice."

He bade him lead the way, and, by the light of the torch which his conductor held up for the purpose, inspected all three cellars, narrowly. Assured that the blind man had spoken truth, and that he lived there alone, the visitor returned with him to the first, in which a fire was burning, and flung himself with a deep groan upon the ground before it.

His host pursued his usual occupation without seeming to heed him any further. But directly he fell asleep—and he noted his falling into a slumber, as readily as the keenest-sighted man could have done—he knelt down beside him, and passed his hand lightly but carefully over his face and person.

His sleep was checkered with starts and moans, and sometimes with a muttered word or two. His hands were clenched, his brow bent, and his mouth firmly set. All this, the blind man accurately marked; and as if his curiosity were strongly awakened, and he had already some inkling of his mystery, he sat watching him, if the expression may be used, and listening, until it was broad day.

## CHAPTER THE NINETEENTH.

DOLLY VARDEN'S pretty little head was yet bewildered by various recollections of the party, and her bright eyes were yet dazzled by a crowd of images, dancing before them like motes in the sunbeams, among which the effigy of one partner in particular did especially figure, the same being a young coachmaker (a master in his own right) who had given her to understand, when he handed her into the chair at parting, that it was his fixed resolve to neglect his business from that time, and die slowly for the love of her—Dolly's head, and eyes, and thoughts, and seven senses, were all in a state of flutter and confusion for which the party was accountable, although it was now three days old, when, as she was sitting listlessly at breakfast, reading all manner of fortunes (that is to say, of married and flourishing fortunes) in the grounds of her teacup, a step was heard in the workshop, and Mr. Edward Chester was descried through the glass door, standing among the rusty locks and keys, like love among the roses*—for which apt comparison the historian may by no means take any credit to himself, the same being the invention, in a sentimental mood, of the chaste and modest Miggs, who, beholding him from the doorsteps she was then cleaning, did, in her maiden meditation, give utterance to the simile.

The locksmith, who happened at the moment to have his eyes thrown upward and his head backward, in an intense communing with Toby, did not see his visitor, until Mrs. Varden, more watchful than the rest, had desired Sim Tappertit to open the glass door and give him admission—from which untoward circumstance the good lady argued (for she could deduce a precious moral from the most trifling event) that to take a draught of small ale in the morning was to observe a pernicious, irreligious, and Pagan custom, the relish whereof should be left to swine, and Satan, or at least to Popish persons, and should be shunned by the righteous as a work of sin and evil. She would no doubt have pursued her admonition much further, and would have founded on it a long list of precious precepts of inestimable value, but that the young gentleman standing by in a somewhat uncomfortable and discomfited manner while she read her spouse this lecture, occasioned her to bring it to a premature conclusion.

"I'm sure you'll excuse me sir," said Mrs. Varden, rising and curtseying. "Varden is so very thoughtless, and needs so much reminding—Sim, bring a chair here."

Mr. Tappertit obeyed, with a flourish implying that he did so, under protest.

"And you can go, Sim" said the locksmith.

Mr. Tappertit obeyed again, still under protest; and betaking himself to the workshop, began seriously to fear that he might find it necessary to poison his master, before his time was out.

In the meantime, Edward returned suitable replies to Mrs. Varden's courtesies, and that lady brightened up very much; so that when he accepted a dish of tea from the fair hands of Dolly, she was perfectly agreeable.

"I am sure if there's anything we can do,—Varden, or I, or Dolly either,—to serve you, sir, at any time, you have only to say it, and it shall be done," said Mrs. V.

"I am much obliged to you, I am sure" returned Edward. "You encourage me to say that I have come here now, to beg your good offices."

Mrs. Varden was delighted beyond measure.

"It occurred to me that probably your fair daughter might be going to the Warren, either to-day or to-morrow" said Edward, glancing at Dolly; "and if so, and you will allow her to take charge of this letter, Ma'am, you will oblige me more than I can tell you. The truth is, that while I am very anxious it should reach its destination, I have particular reasons for not trusting it to any other conveyance; so that without your help, I am wholly at a loss."

"She was not going that way sir, either to-day, or to-morrow, nor indeed all next week," the lady graciously rejoined, "but we shall be very glad to put ourselves out of the way on your account, and if you wish it, you may depend upon its going to-day. You might suppose" said Mrs. Varden, frowning at her husband, "from Varden's sitting there so glum and silent, that he objected to this arrangement; but you must not mind that, sir, if you please. It's his way at home. Out of doors, he can be cheerful and talkative enough."

Now, the fact was, that the unfortunate locksmith, blessing his stars to find his helpmate in such good humour, had been sitting with a beaming face, hearing this discourse with a joy past all expression. Wherefore this sudden attack quite took him by surprise.

"My dear Martha—" he said.

"Oh yes, I dare say" interrupted Mrs. Varden, with a smile of mingled scorn and pleasantry. "Very dear! We all know that."

"No, but my good soul" said Gabriel, "you are quite mistaken. You are indeed. I was delighted to find you so kind and ready. I waited, my dear, anxiously, I assure you, to hear what you would say."

"You waited anxiously," repeated Mrs. V. "Yes! Thank you, Varden. You waited, as you always do, that I might bear the blame, if any came of it. But I am used to it," said the lady with a kind of solemn titter, "and that's my comfort!"

"I give you my word, Martha—" said Gabriel.

"Let me give you *my* word, my dear," interposed his wife with a christian smile, "that such discussions as these between married people, are much better left alone. Therefore, if you please Varden, we'll drop the subject. I have no wish to pursue it. I could. I might say a great deal. But I would rather not. Pray don't say any more."

"I don't want to say any more," rejoined the goaded locksmith.

"Well then, don't," said Mrs. Varden.

"Nor did I begin it Martha," added the locksmith, good humouredly, "I must say that."

"You did not begin it, Varden!" exclaimed his wife, opening her eyes very wide and looking round upon the company, as though she would say, You hear this man! "You did not begin it, Varden! But you shall not say I was out of temper. No, you did not begin it, oh dear no, not you, my dear!"

"Well, well," said the locksmith. "That's settled then."

"Oh yes," rejoined his wife, "quite. If you like to say Dolly began it, my dear, I shall not contradict you. I know my duty. I need know it, I am sure. I am often obliged to bear it in mind, when my inclination perhaps would be for the moment to forget it. Thank you, Varden." And so, with a mighty show of humility and forgiveness, she folded her hands, and looked round again, with a smile which plainly said "If you desire to see the first and foremost among female martyrs, here she is, on view!"

This little incident, illustrative though it was of Mrs. Varden's extraordinary sweetness and amiability, had so strong a tendency to check the conversation and to disconcert all parties but that excellent lady, that only a few monosyllables were uttered until Edward withdrew; which he presently did, thanking the lady of the house a great many times for her condescension, and whispering in Dolly's ear that he would call on the morrow, in case there should happen to be an answer to the note—which, indeed, she knew without his telling, as Barnaby and his friend Grip had dropped in on the previous night to prepare her for the visit which was then terminating.

Gabriel, who had attended Edward to the door, came back with his hands in his pockets; and, after fidgeting about the room in a very uneasy manner, and casting a great many sidelong looks at Mrs. Varden (who with the calmest countenance in the world was five fathoms deep in the Protestant Manual), inquired of Dolly how she meant to go. Dolly supposed by the stage-coach, and looked at her lady mother, who finding herself silently appealed to, dived down at least another fathom into the Manual, and became unconscious of all earthly things.

"Martha—" said the locksmith.

"I hear you, Varden," said his wife, without rising to the surface.

"I am sorry, my dear, you have such an objection to the Maypole and old John, for otherways as it's a very fine morning, and Saturday's not a busy day with us, we might have all three gone to Chigwell in the chaise, and had quite a happy day of it."

Mrs. Varden immediately closed the Manual, and bursting into tears, requested to be led up-stairs.

"What is the matter now Martha?" inquired the locksmith.

To which Martha rejoined "Oh! don't speak to me," and protested in agony that if anybody had told her so, she wouldn't have believed it.

"But Martha" said Gabriel, putting himself in the way as she was moving off with the aid of Dolly's shoulder, "wouldn't have believed what? Tell me what's wrong now. Do tell me. Upon my soul I don't know. Do *you* know child? Damme!" cried the locksmith, plucking at his wig in a kind of frenzy, "nobody does know, I verily believe, but Miggs!"

"Miggs," said Mrs. Varden faintly, and with symptoms of approaching incoherence, "is attached to me, and that is sufficient to draw down hatred upon her in this house. She is a comfort to me, whatever she may be to others."

"She's no comfort to me," cried Gabriel, made bold by despair. "She's the misery of my life. She's all the plagues of Egypt in one."

"She's considered so, I have no doubt," said Mrs. Varden. "I was prepared for that; it's natural; it's of a piece with the rest. When you taunt me as you do to my face, how can I wonder that you taunt her behind her back!" And here the incoherence coming on very strong, Mrs. Varden wept, and laughed, and sobbed, and shivered, and hic-coughed, and choaked; and said she knew it was very foolish but she couldn't help it; and that when she was dead and gone, perhaps they would be sorry for it—which really under the circumstances did not appear quite so probable as she seemed to think—with a great deal more to the same effect. In a word, she passed with great decency through all the ceremonies incidental to such occasions; and being supported up-stairs, was deposited in a highly spasmodic state on her own bed, where Miss Miggs shortly afterwards flung herself upon the body.

The philosophy of all this was, that Mrs. Varden wanted to go to Chigwell; that she did not want to make any concession or explan-ation; that she would only go on being implored and entreated so to do; and that she would accept no other terms. Accordingly, after a vast amount of moaning and crying up-stairs, and much damping of foreheads, and vinegaring of temples, and hartshorning* of noses, and so forth; and after most pathetic adjurations from Miggs, assisted by warm brandy-and-water not over-weak, and divers other cordials, also of a stimulating quality, administered at first in teaspoonsful and afterwards in increasing doses, and of which Miss Miggs herself partook as a preventive measure (for fainting is infectious); after all these remedies, and many more too numerous to mention, but not to take, had been applied; and many verbal consolations, moral, religious, and miscellaneous, had been superadded thereto; the locksmith humbled himself, and the end was gained.

"If it's only for the sake of peace and quietness, father," said Dolly, urging him to go up-stairs.

"Oh, Doll, Doll," said her good-natured father. "If you ever have a husband of your own—"

Dolly glanced at the glass.

"—Well, *when* you have," said the locksmith, "never faint, my darling. More domestic unhappiness has come of easy fainting, Doll, than from all the greater passions put together. Remember that, my dear, if you would be really happy, which you never can be, if your husband isn't. And a word in your ear, my precious. Never have a Miggs about you!"

With this advice he kissed his blooming daughter on the cheek, and slowly repaired to Mrs. Varden's room; where that lady, lying all pale and languid on her couch, was refreshing herself with a sight of her last new bonnet, which Miggs, as a means of calming her scattered spirits, displayed to the best advantage at her bedside.

"Here's master, mim," said Miggs. "Oh, what a happiness it is when man and wife come round again! Oh gracious, to think that him and her should ever have a word together!" In the energy of these sentiments, which were uttered as an apostrophe to the Heavens in general, Miss Miggs perched the bonnet on the top of her own head, and folding her hands, turned on her tears.

"I can't help it," cried Miggs. "I couldn't, if I was to be drownded in 'em. She has such a forgiving spirit! She'll forget all that has passed, and go along with you, sir—Oh, if it was to the world's end, she'd go along with you."

Mrs. Varden with a faint smile gently reproved her attendant for this enthusiasm, and reminded her at the same time that she was far too unwell to venture out that day.

"Oh no, you're not, mim, indeed you're not," said Miggs; "I repeal to master; master knows you're not, mim. The hair, and motion of the shay, will do you good, mim, and you must not give way, you must not raly. She must keep up mustn't she, sir, for all our sakes? I was a telling her that, just now. She must remember us, even if she forgets herself. Master will persuade you, mim, I'm sure. There's Miss Dolly's a going you know, and master, and you, and all so happy and so comfortable. Oh!" cried Miggs, turning on the tears again, previous to quitting the room in great emotion, "I never see such a blessed one as she is for the forgiveness of her spirit, I never, never, never did. Nor more did master neither; no, nor no one—never!"

For five minutes or thereabouts, Mrs. Varden remained mildly opposed to all her husband's prayers that she would oblige him by taking a day's pleasure, but relenting at length, she suffered herself to be persuaded, and granting him her free forgiveness (the merit whereof, she meekly said, rested with the Manual and not with her), desired that Miggs might come and help her dress. The handmaid attended promptly, and it is but justice to their joint exertions to record that, when the good lady came down-stairs in course of time, completely decked out for the journey, she really looked as if nothing had happened, and appeared in the very best health imaginable.

As to Dolly, there she was again, the very pink and pattern of good looks, in a smart little cherry-coloured mantle, with a hood of the same drawn over her head, and upon the top of that hood, a little straw hat trimmed with cherry-coloured ribbons, and worn the merest trifle on one side—just enough in short to make it the wickedest and most provoking head-dress that ever malicious milliner devised. And not to speak of the manner in which these cherry-coloured decorations brightened her eyes, or vied with her lips, or shed a new bloom on her face, she wore such a cruel little muff, and such a heart-rending pair of shoes, and was so surrounded and hemmed in, as it were, by aggravations of all kinds, that when Mr. Tappertit, holding the horse's head, saw her come out of the house alone, such impulses came over him to decoy her into the chaise and drive off like mad, that he would unquestionably have done it, but for certain uneasy doubts besetting him as to the shortest way to Gretna Green;* whether it was up the street or down, or up the right-hand turning or the left; and whether, supposing all the turnpikes to be carried by storm, the blacksmith in the end would marry them on credit; which by reason of his clerical office appeared, even to his excited imagination, so unlikely, that he hesitated. And while he stood hesitating, and looking post-chaises-and-six at Dolly, out came his master and his mistress, and the constant Miggs, and the opportunity was gone for ever. For now the chaise creaked upon its springs, and Mrs. Varden was inside; and now it creaked again, and more than ever, and the locksmith was inside; and now it bounded once, as if its heart beat lightly, and Dolly was inside; and now it was gone and its place was empty, and he and that dreary Miggs were standing in the street together.

The hearty locksmith was in as good a humour as if nothing had occurred for the last twelve months to put him out of his way, Dolly was all smiles and graces, and Mrs. Varden was agreeable beyond all precedent. As they jogged through the streets talking of this thing and of that, who should be descried upon the pavement but that very coachmaker, looking so genteel that nobody would have believed he had ever had anything to do with a coach but riding in it, and bowing like any nobleman. To be sure Dolly was confused when she bowed again, and to be sure the cherry-coloured ribbons trembled a little when she met his mournful eye, which seemed to say, 'I have kept my word, I have begun, the business is going to the devil, and you're the cause of it.' There he stood, rooted to the ground: as Dolly said, like a statue; and as Mrs. Varden said, like a pump; till they turned the corner: and when her father thought it was like his impudence, and her mother wondered what he meant by it, Dolly blushed again till her very hood was pale.

But on they went, not the less merrily for this, and there was the locksmith in the incautious fulness of his heart "pulling-up" at all manner of places, and evincing a most intimate acquaintance with all the taverns on the road, and all the landlords and all the landladies, with whom, indeed, the little horse was on equally friendly terms, for he kept on stopping of his own accord. Never were people so glad to see other people as these landlords and landladies were to behold Mr. Varden and Mrs. Varden and Miss Varden; and wouldn't they get out, said one; and they really must walk up-stairs, said another; and she would take it ill and be quite certain they were proud if they wouldn't have a little taste of something, said a third; and so on, that it really was quite a Progress rather than a ride, and one continued scene of hospitality from beginning to end. It was pleasant enough to be held in such esteem, not to mention the refreshments; so Mrs. Varden said nothing at the time, and was all affability and delight—but such a body of evidence as she collected against the unfortunate locksmith that day, to be used thereafter as occasion might require, never was got together for matrimonial purposes.

In course of time—and in course of a pretty long time too, for these agreeable interruptions delayed them not a little,—they arrived upon the skirts of the Forest, and riding pleasantly on among the trees, came at last to the Maypole, where the locksmith's cheerful "Yoho!" speedily brought to the porch old John, and after him young Joe, both of whom were so transfixed at sight of the ladies, that for a moment they were perfectly unable to give them any welcome, and could do nothing but stare.

It was only for a moment, however, that Joe forgot himself, for speedily reviving he thrust his drowsy father aside—to Mr. Willet's mighty and inexpressible indignation—and darting out, stood ready to help them to alight. It was necessary for Dolly to get out first. Joe had her in his arms;—yes, though for a space of time no longer than you could count one in, Joe had her in his arms. Here was a glimpse of happiness!

It would be difficult to describe what a flat and common-place affair the helping Mrs. Varden out afterwards was, but Joe did it, and did it too with the best grace in the world. Then old John, who, entertaining a dull and foggy sort of idea that Mrs. Varden wasn't fond of him, had been in some doubt whether she might not have come for purposes of assault and battery, took courage, hoped she was well, and offered to conduct her into the house. This tender being amicably received, they marched in together; Joe and Dolly followed, arm-in-arm, (happiness again!) and Varden brought up the rear.

Old John would have it that they must sit in the bar, and nobody objecting, into the bar they went. All bars are snug places, but the Maypole's was the very snuggest, cosiest, and completest bar, that ever the wit of man devised. Such amazing bottles in old oaken pigeon-holes; such gleaming tankards dangling from pegs at about the same inclination as thirsty men would hold them to their lips; such sturdy little Dutch kegs ranged in rows on shelves; so many lemons hanging in separate nets, and forming the fragrant grove already mentioned in this chronicle, suggestive, with goodly cans and snowy sugar stowed away hard by, of punch, idealised beyond all mortal knowledge; such closets, such presses, such drawers full of pipes, such places for putting things away in hollow window-seats, all crammed to the throat with eatables, drinkables, or savoury con-diments; lastly, and to crown all, as typical of the immense resources of the establishment, and its defiances to all visitors to cut and come again, such a stupendous cheese!

It is a poor heart that never rejoices—it must have been the poor-est, weakest, and most watery heart that ever beat, which would not have warmed towards the Maypole bar. Mrs. Varden's did directly. She could no more have reproached John Willet among those house-hold gods, the kegs and bottles, lemons, pipes, and cheese, than she could have stabbed him with his own bright carving-knife. The order for dinner too—it might have soothed a savage. "A bit of fish," said John to the cook, "and some lamb chops (breaded, with plenty of ketchup), and a good salad, and a roast spring chicken, with a dish of sausages and mashed potatoes, or something of that sort." Some-thing of that sort! The resources of these inns! To talk carelessly about dishes, which in themselves were a first-rate holiday kind of dinner, suitable to one's wedding day, as something of that sort: meaning, if you can't get a spring chicken, any other trifle in the way of poultry will do—such as a Peacock, perhaps! The kitchen too, with its great broad cavernous chimney; the kitchen, where nothing in the way of cookery seemed impossible; where you could believe in anything to eat, they chose to tell you of. Mrs. Varden returned from the contemplation of these wonders to the bar again, with a head quite dizzy and bewildered. Her housekeeping capacity was not large enough to comprehend them. She was obliged to go to sleep. Waking was pain, in the midst of such immensity.

Dolly in the meanwhile, whose gay heart and head ran upon other matters, passed out at the garden door, and glancing back now and then (but of course not wondering whether Joe saw her), tripped away by a path across the fields with which she was well acquainted, to discharge her mission at the Warren; and this deponent hath been informed and verily believes, that you might have seen many less pleasant objects than the cherry-coloured mantle and ribbons, as they went fluttering along the green meadows in the bright light of the day, like giddy things as they were.

## CHAPTER THE TWENTIETH.

THE proud consciousness of her trust, and the great importance she derived from it, might have advertised it to all the house if she had had to run the gauntlet of its inhabitants; but as Dolly had played in every dull room and passage many and many a time, when a child, and had ever since been the humble friend of Miss Haredale, whose foster-sister she was,* she was as free of the building as the young lady herself. So, using no greater precaution than holding her breath and walking on tiptoe as she passed the library door, she went straight to Emma's room as a privileged visitor.

It was the liveliest room in the building. The chamber was sombre like the rest for the matter of that, but the presence of youth and beauty would make a prison cheerful (saving alas! that confinement withers them), and lend some charms of their own to the gloomiest scene. Birds, flowers, books, drawing, music, and a hundred such graceful tokens of feminine loves and cares, filled it with more of life and human sympathy than the whole house besides seemed made to hold. There was heart in the room; and who that has a heart, ever fails to recognize the silent presence of another!

Dolly had one undoubtedly, and it was not a tough one either, though there was a little mist of coquettishness about it, such as sometimes surrounds that sun of life in its morning, and slightly dims its lustre. Thus, when Emma rose to greet her, and kissing her affectionately on the cheek, told her, in her quiet way, that she had been very unhappy, the tears stood in Dolly's eyes, and she felt more sorry than she could tell; but next moment she happened to raise them to the glass, and really there was something there so exceedingly agreeable, that as she sighed, she smiled, and felt surprisingly consoled.

"I have heard about it Miss," said Dolly, "and it's very sad indeed, but when things are at the worst they are sure to mend."

"But are you sure they are at the worst?" asked Emma with a smile.

"Why, I don't see how they can very well be more unpromising than they are; I really don't," said Dolly. "And I bring something to begin with."

"Not from Edward?"

Dolly nodded and smiled, and feeling in her pockets (there were pockets in those days) with an affectation of not being able to find what she wanted, which greatly enhanced her importance, at length produced the letter. As Emma hastily broke the seal and became absorbed in its contents, Dolly's eyes, by one of those strange accidents for which there is no accounting, wandered to the glass again. She could not help wondering whether the coachmaker suffered very much, and quite pitied the poor man.

It was a long letter—a very long letter, written close on all four sides of the sheet of paper, and crossed afterwards;* but it was not a consolatory letter, for as Emma read it she stopped from time to time to put her handkerchief to her eyes. To be sure Dolly marvelled greatly to see her in so much distress, for to her thinking a love affair ought to be one of the best jokes, and the slyest, merriest kind of thing in life. But she set it down in her own mind that all this came from Miss Haredale's being so constant, and that if she would only take on with some other young gentleman—just in the most innocent way possible, to keep her first lover up to the mark—she would find herself inexpressibly comforted.

"I am sure that's what I should do if it was me," thought Dolly. "To make one's sweethearts miserable is well enough and quite right, but to be made miserable one's self is a little too much!"

However it wouldn't do to say so, and therefore she sat looking on in silence. She needed a pretty considerable stretch of patience, for when the long letter had been read once all through it was read again, and when it had been read twice all through it was read again. During this tedious process, Dolly beguiled the time in the most improving manner that occurred to her, by curling her hair on her fingers, with the aid of the looking-glass before mentioned, and giving it some killing twists.

Everything has an end. Even young ladies in love cannot read their letters for ever. In course of time the packet was folded up, and it only remained to write the answer.

But as this promised to be a work of time likewise, Emma said she would put it off until after dinner, and that Dolly must dine with her. As Dolly had made up her mind to do so beforehand, she required very little pressing; and when they had settled this point, they went to walk in the garden.

They strolled up and down the terrace walks, talking incessantly—at least, Dolly never left off once—and making that quarter of the sad and mournful house quite gay. Not that they talked loudly or laughed much, but they were both so very handsome, and it was such a breezy day, and their light dresses and dark curls appeared so free and joyous in their abandonment, and Emma was so fair, and Dolly so rosy, and Emma so delicately shaped, and Dolly so plump, and—in short, there are no flowers for any garden like such flowers, let horticulturists say what they may, and both house and garden seemed to know it, and to brighten up sensibly.

After this, came the dinner and the letter writing, and some more talking, in the course of which Miss Haredale took occasion to charge upon Dolly certain flirtish and inconstant propensities, which accusations Dolly seemed to think very complimentary indeed, and to be mightily amused with. Finding her quite incorrigible in this respect, Emma suffered her to depart; but not before she had confided to her that important and never-sufficiently-to-be-taken-care-of answer, and endowed her moreover with a pretty little bracelet as a keepsake. Having clasped it on her arm, and again advised her half in jest and half in earnest to amend her roguish ways, for she knew she was fond of Joe at heart (which Dolly stoutly denied, with a great many haughty protestations that she hoped she could do better than that indeed! and so forth), she bade her farewell; and after calling her back to give her more supplementary messages for Edward, than anybody with tenfold the gravity of Dolly Varden could be reasonably expected to remember, at length dismissed her.

Dolly bade her good bye, and tripping lightly down the stairs arrived at the dreaded library door, and was about to pass it again on tiptoe, when it opened, and behold! there stood Mr. Haredale. Now, Dolly had from her childhood associated with this gentleman the idea of something grim and ghostly, and being at the moment conscience-stricken besides, the sight of him threw her into such a flurry that she could neither acknowledge his presence nor run away, so she gave a great start, and then with downcast eyes stood still and trembled.

"Come here, girl" said Mr. Haredale, taking her by the hand. "I want to speak to you."

"If you please sir, I'm in a hurry," faltered Dolly, "and—and you have frightened me by coming so suddenly upon me sir—I would rather go sir, if you'll be so good as to let me."

"Immediately," said Mr. Haredale, who had by this time led her into the room and closed the door. "You shall go directly. You have just left Emma?"

"Yes sir, just this minute.—Father's waiting for me sir, if you'll please to have the goodness—"

"I know. I know," said Mr. Haredale. "Answer me a question. What did you bring here to-day?"

"Bring here, sir?" faltered Dolly.

"You will tell me the truth, I am sure. Yes."

Dolly hesitated for a little while, and somewhat emboldened by his manner, said at last, "Well then sir. It was a letter."

"From Mr. Edward Chester, of course. And you are the bearer of the answer?"

Dolly hesitated again, and not being able to decide upon any other course of action, burst into tears.

"You alarm yourself without cause," said Mr. Haredale. "Why are you so foolish? Surely you can answer me. You know that I have but to put the question to Emma and learn the truth directly. Have you the answer with you?"

Dolly had what is popularly called a spirit of her own, and being now fairly at bay, made the best of it.

"Yes sir," she rejoined, trembling and frightened as she was. "Yes sir, I have. You may kill me if you please sir, but I won't give it up. I'm very sorry,—but I won't. There sir."

"I commend your firmness, and your plain-speaking," said Mr. Haredale. "Rest assured that I have as little desire to take your letter as your life. You are a very discreet messenger and a good girl."

Not feeling quite certain, as she afterwards said, whether he might not be "coming over her" with these compliments, Dolly kept as far from him as she could, cried again, and resolved to defend her pocket (for the letter was there) to the last extremity.

"I have some design" said Mr. Haredale after a short silence, during which a smile, as he regarded her, had struggled through the gloom and melancholy that was natural to his face, "of providing a companion for my niece; for her life is a very lonely one. Would you like the office? You are the oldest friend she has, and the best entitled to it."

"I don't know sir," answered Dolly, not sure but he was bantering her; "I can't say. I don't know what they might wish at home. I couldn't give an opinion sir."

"If your friends had no objection, would you have any?" said Mr. Haredale. "Come. There's a plain question; and easy to answer."

"None at all that I know of sir," replied Dolly. "I should be very glad to be near Miss Emma of course, and always am."

"That's well" said Mr. Haredale. "That is all I had to say. You are anxious to go. Don't let me detain you."

Dolly didn't let him, nor did she wait for him to try, for the words had no sooner passed his lips than she was out of the room, out of the house, and in the fields again.

The first thing to be done, of course, when she came to herself and considered what a flurry she had been in, was to cry afresh; and the next thing, when she reflected how well she had got over it, was to laugh heartily. The tears once banished gave place to the smiles, and at last Dolly laughed so much that she was fain to lean against a tree, and give vent to her exultation. When she could laugh no longer, and was quite tired, she put her head-dress to rights, dried her eyes, looked back very merrily and triumphantly at the Warren chimneys, which were just visible, and resumed her walk.

The twilight had come on, and it was quickly growing dusk, but the path was so familiar to her from frequent traversing that she hardly thought of this, and certainly felt no uneasiness at being alone. Moreover, there was the bracelet to admire; and when she had given it a good rub, and held it out at arm's length, it sparkled and glittered so beautifully on her wrist, that to look at it in every point of view and with every possible turn of the arm, was quite an absorbing business. There was the letter, too, and it looked so mysterious and knowing, when she took it out of her pocket, and it held, as she knew, so much inside, that to turn it over and over, and think about it, and wonder how it began, and how it ended, and what it said all through, was another matter of constant occupation. Between the bracelet and the letter, there was quite enough to do without thinking of anything else; and admiring each by turns, Dolly went on gaily.

As she passed through a wicket gate to where the path was narrow, and lay between two hedges garnished here and there with trees, she heard a rustling close at hand, which brought her to a sudden stop. She listened. All was very quiet, and she went on again—not absolutely frightened, but a little quicker than before perhaps, and possibly not quite so much at her ease, for a check of that kind is startling.

She had no sooner moved on again, than she was conscious of the same sound, which was like that of a person tramping stealthily among bushes and brushwood. Looking towards the spot whence it appeared to come, she almost fancied she could make out a crouching figure. She stopped again. All was quiet as before. On she went once more—decidedly faster now—and tried to sing softly to herself. It must be the wind.

But how came the wind to blow only when she walked, and cease when she stood still? She stopped involuntarily as she made the reflection, and the rustling noise stopped likewise. She was really frightened now, and was yet hesitating what to do, when the bushes crackled and snapped, and a man came plunging through them, close before her.

## CHAPTER THE TWENTY-FIRST.

IT was for the moment an inexpressible relief to Dolly, to recognize in the person who forced himself into the path so abruptly, and now stood directly in her way, Hugh of the Maypole, whose name she uttered in a tone of delighted surprise that came from her heart.

"Was it you?" she said, "how glad I am to see you! and how could you terrify me so!"

In answer to which, he said nothing at all, but stood quite still, looking at her.

"Did you come to meet me?" asked Dolly.

Hugh nodded, and muttered something to the effect that he had been waiting for her, and had expected her sooner.

"I thought it likely they would send," said Dolly, greatly re-assured by this.

"Nobody sent me," was his sullen answer. "I came of my own accord."

The rough bearing of this fellow, and his wild, uncouth appearance, had often filled the girl with a vague apprehension even when other people were by, and had occasioned her to shrink from him involuntarily. The having him for an unbidden companion in so

solitary a place, with the darkness fast gathering about them, renewed and even increased the alarm she had felt at first.

If his manner had been merely dogged and passively fierce, as usual, she would have had no greater dislike to his company than she always felt—perhaps, indeed, would have been rather glad to have had him at hand. But there was something of coarse bold admiration in his look, which terrified her very much. She glanced timidly towards him, uncertain whether to go forward or retreat, and he stood gazing at her like a handsome satyr; and so they remained for some short time without stirring or breaking silence. At length Dolly took courage, shot past him, and hurried on.

"Why do you spend so much breath in avoiding me?" said Hugh, accommodating his pace to hers, and keeping close at her side.

"I wish to get back as quickly as I can, and you walk too near me," answered Dolly.

"Too near!" said Hugh, stooping over her so that she could feel his breath upon her forehead. "Why too near? You're always proud to *me*, mistress."

"I am proud to no one. You mistake me," answered Dolly. "Fall back, if you please, or go on."

"Nay, mistress," he rejoined, endeavouring to draw her arm through his. "I'll walk with you."

She released herself, and clenching her little hand, struck him with right good will. At this, Maypole Hugh burst into a roar of laughter, and passing his arm about her waist, held her in his strong grasp as easily as if she had been a bird.

"Ha ha ha! Well done mistress! Strike again. You shall beat my face, and tear my hair, and pluck my beard up by the roots, and welcome, for the sake of your bright eyes. Strike again mistress. Do. Ha ha ha! I like it."

"Let me go," she cried, endeavouring with both her hands to push him off. "Let me go this moment."

"You had as good be kinder to me, Sweetlips," said Hugh. "You had, indeed. Come. Tell me now. Why are you always so proud? I don't quarrel with you for it. I love you when you're proud. Ha ha ha! You can't hide your beauty from a poor fellow; that's a comfort!"

She gave him no answer, but as he had not yet checked her progress, continued to press forward as rapidly as she could. At length, between the hurry she had made, her terror, and the tightness of his embrace, her strength failed her, and she could go no further.

"Hugh," cried the panting girl, "good Hugh; if you will leave me I will give you anything—everything I have—and never tell one word of this to any living creature."

"You had best not," he answered. "Harkye, little dove, you had best not. All about here know me, and what I dare do if I have a mind. If ever you are going to tell, stop when the words are on your lips, and think of the mischief you'll bring, if you do, upon some innocent heads that you wouldn't wish to hurt a hair of. Bring trouble on me, and I'll bring trouble and something more on them in return. I care no more for them than for so many dogs; not so much—why should I? I'd sooner kill a man than a dog any day. I've never been sorry for a man's death in all my life, and I have for a dog's."

There was something so thoroughly savage in the manner of these expressions, and the looks and gestures by which they were accompanied, that her great fear of him gave her new strength, and enabled her by a sudden effort to extricate herself and run fleetly from him. But Hugh was as nimble, strong, and swift of foot, as any man in broad England, and it was but a fruitless expenditure of energy, for he had her in his encircling arms again before she had gone a hundred yards.

"Softly, darling—gently—would you fly from rough Hugh, that loves you as well as any drawing-room gallant?"

"I would," she answered, struggling to free herself again. "I will. Help!"

"A fine for crying out," said Hugh. "Ha ha ha! A fine, pretty one, from your lips. I pay myself! Ha ha ha!"

"Help! Help! Help!" As she shrieked with the utmost violence she could exert, a shout was heard in answer, and another, and another.

"Thank Heaven!" cried the girl in an ecstacy. "Joe, dear Joe, this way. Help!"

Her assailant paused, and stood irresolute for a moment, but the shouts drawing nearer and coming quick upon them, forced him to a speedy decision. He released her, whispered with a menacing look, "Tell *him;* and see what follows!" and leaping the hedge, was gone in an instant. Dolly darted off, and fairly ran into Joe Willet's open arms.

"What is the matter? are you hurt? what was it? who was it? where is he? what was he like?" with a great many encouraging expressions and assurances of safety, were the first words Joe poured forth. But poor little Dolly was so breathless and terrified, that for some time she was quite unable to answer him, and hung upon his shoulder, sobbing and crying as if her heart would break.

Joe had not the smallest objection to have her hanging on his shoulder; no, not the least, though it crushed the cherry-coloured ribbons sadly, and put the smart little hat out of all shape. But he couldn't bear to see her cry; it went to his very heart. He tried to console her, bent over her, whispered to her—some say kissed her, but that's a fable. At any rate he said all the kind and tender things he could think of, and Dolly let him go on and didn't interrupt him once, and it was a good ten minutes before she was able to raise her head and thank him.

"What was it that frightened you?" said Joe.

A man whose person was unknown to her had followed her, she answered; he began by begging, and went on to threats of robbery, which he was on the point of carrying into execution, and would have executed, but for Joe's timely aid. The hesitation and confusion with which she said this, Joe attributed to the fright she had sustained, and no suspicion of the truth occurred to him for a moment.

"Stop when the words are on your lips." A hundred times that night, and very often afterwards, when the disclosure was rising to her tongue, Dolly thought of that, and repressed it. A deeply rooted dread of the man; the conviction that his ferocious nature, once roused, would stop at nothing; and the strong assurance that if she impeached him, the full measure of his wrath and vengeance would be wreaked on Joe, who had preserved her; these were considerations she had not the courage to overcome, and inducements to secrecy too powerful for her to surmount.

Joe, for his part, was a great deal too happy to inquire very curiously into the matter; and Dolly being yet too tremulous to walk without assistance, they went forward very slowly, and in his mind very pleasantly, until the Maypole lights were near at hand, twinkling their cheerful welcome, when Dolly stopped suddenly and with a half scream exclaimed,

"The letter!"

"What letter?" cried Joe.

"That I was carrrying—I had it in my hand. My bracelet too," she said, clasping her wrist. "I have lost them both."

"Do you mean just now?" said Joe.

"Either I dropped them then, or they were taken from me," answered Dolly, vainly searching her pocket and rustling her dress. "They are gone, both gone. What an unhappy girl I am!" With these words poor Dolly, who to do her justice was quite as sorry for the loss of the letter as for her bracelet, fell a crying again, and bemoaned her fate most movingly.

Joe tried to comfort her with the assurance that directly he had housed her safely in the Maypole, he would return to the spot with a lantern (for it was now quite dark) and make strict search for the missing articles, which there was great probability of his finding, as it was not likely that anybody had passed that way since, and she was not conscious of their having been forcibly taken from her. Dolly thanked him very heartily for this offer, though with no great hope of his quest being successful; and so, with many lamentations on her side, and many hopeful words on his, and much weakness on the part of Dolly and much tender supporting on the part of Joe, they reached the Maypole bar at last, where the locksmith and his wife and old John were yet keeping high festival.

Mr. Willet received the intelligence of Dolly's trouble with that surprising presence of mind and readiness of speech for which he was so eminently distinguished above all other men. Mrs. Varden expressed her sympathy for her daughter's distress by scolding her roundly for being so late; and the honest locksmith divided himself between condoling with and kissing Dolly, and shaking hands heartily with Joe, whom he could not sufficiently praise or thank.

In reference to this latter point, old John was far from agreeing with his friend; for besides that he by no means approved of an adventurous spirit in the abstract, it occurred to him that if his son and heir had been seriously damaged in a scuffle, the consequences would assuredly have been expensive and inconvenient, and might perhaps have proved detrimental to the Maypole business. Wherefore, and because he looked with no favourable eye upon young girls, but rather considered that they and the whole female sex were a kind of nonsensical mistake on the part of Nature, he took occasion to retire and shake his head in private at the boiler; inspired by which silent oracle, he was moved to give Joe various stealthy nudges with his elbow, as a parental reproof and gentle admonition to mind his own business and not make a fool of himself.

Joe, however, took down the lantern and lighted it; and arming himself with a stout stick, asked whether Hugh was in the stable.

"He's lying asleep before the kitchen fire, sir," said Mr. Willet. "What do you want with him?"

"I want him to come with me to look after this bracelet and letter," answered Joe. "Halloa there! Hugh!"

Dolly turned pale as death, and felt as if she must faint forthwith. After a few moments, Hugh came staggering in, stretching himself and yawning according to custom, and presenting every appearance of having been roused from a sound nap.

"Here, sleepy-head," said Joe, giving him the lantern. "Carry this, and bring the dog, and that small cudgel of yours. And woe betide the fellow if we come upon him."

"What fellow?" growled Hugh, rubbing his eyes and shaking himself.

"What fellow!" returned Joe, who was in a state of great valour and bustle; "a fellow you ought to know of, and be more alive about. It's well for the like of you, lazy giant that you are, to be snoring your time away in chimney-corners, when honest men's daughters can't cross even our quiet meadows at nightfall without being set upon by footpads, and frightened out of their precious lives."

"They never rob me" cried Hugh with a laugh. "I have got nothing to lose. But I'd as lief knock them at head as any other men. How many are there?"

"Only one" said Dolly faintly, for everybody looked at her.

"And what was he like, mistress?" said Hugh with a glance at young Willet, so slight and momentary that the scowl it conveyed was lost on all but her. "About my height?"

"Not—not so tall," Dolly replied, scarce knowing what she said.

"His dress" said Hugh, looking at her keenly, "like—like any of ours now? I know all the people hereabouts, and maybe could give a guess at the man, if I had anything to guide me."

Dolly faltered and turned paler yet; then answered that he was wrapped in a loose coat and had his face hidden by a handkerchief, and that she could give no other description of him.

"You wouldn't know him if you saw him then, belike?" said Hugh with a malicious grin.

"I should not" answered Dolly, bursting into tears again. "I don't wish to see him. I can't bear to think of him. I can't talk about him any more. Don't go to look for these things, Mr. Joe, pray don't. I entreat you not to go with that man."

"Not to go with me!" cried Hugh. "I'm too rough for them all. They're all afraid of me. Why, bless you mistress, I've the tenderest heart alive. I love all the ladies ma'am" said Hugh, turning to the locksmith's wife.

Mrs. Varden opined that if he did, he ought to be ashamed of himself; such sentiments being more consistent (so she argued) with a benighted Mussulman* or wild Islander* than with a stanch Protestant. Arguing from this imperfect state of his morals, Mrs. Varden further opined that he had never studied the Manual. Hugh admitting that he never had, and moreover that he couldn't read, Mrs. Varden declared with much severity, that he ought to be even more ashamed of himself than before, and strongly recommended him to save up his pocket-money for the purchase of one, and further to teach himself the contents with all convenient diligence. She was still pursuing this train of discourse, when Hugh, somewhat unceremoniously and irreverently, followed his young master out, and left her to edify the rest of the company. This she proceeded to do, and finding that Mr. Willet's eyes were fixed upon her with an appearance of deep attention, gradually addressed the whole of her discourse to him, whom she entertained with a moral and theological lecture of considerable length, in the conviction that great workings were taking place in his spirit. The simple truth was, however, that Mr. Willet, although his eyes were wide open and he saw a woman before him whose head by long and steady looking at seemed to grow bigger and bigger until it filled the whole bar, was to all other intents and purposes fast asleep; and so sat leaning back in his chair with his hands in his pockets until his son's return caused him to wake up with a deep sigh, and a faint impression that he had been dreaming about pickled pork and greens—a vision of his slumbers which was no doubt referable to the circumstance of Mrs. Varden's having frequently pronounced the word "Grace" with much emphasis; which word, entering the portals of Mr. Willet's brain as they stood ajar, and coupling itself with the words "before meat," which were there ranging about, did in time suggest a particular kind of meat together with that description of vegetable which is usually its companion.

The search was wholly unsuccessful. Joe had groped along the path a dozen times, and among the grass, and in the dry ditch, and in the hedge, but all in vain. Dolly, who was quite inconsolable for her loss, wrote a note to Miss Haredale giving her the same account of it that she had given at the Maypole, which Joe undertook to deliver as soon as the family were stirring next day. That done, they sat down to tea in the bar, where there was an uncommon display of buttered toast, and—in order that they might not grow faint for want of sustenance, and might have a decent halting-place or half-way house between dinner and supper—a few savoury trifles in the shape of great rashers of broiled ham, which being well cured, done to a turn, and smoking hot, sent forth a tempting and delicious fragrance.

Mrs. Varden was seldom very Protestant at meals, unless it

happened that they were under-done, or over-done, or indeed that anything occurred to put her out of humour. Her spirits rose considerably on beholding these goodly preparations, and from the nothingness of good works, she passed to the somethingness of ham and toast with great cheerfulness. Nay, under the influence of these wholesome stimulants, she sharply reproved her daughter for being low and despondent (which she considered an unacceptable frame of mind) and remarked, as she held her own plate for a fresh supply, that it would be well for Dolly who pined over the loss of a toy and a sheet of paper, if she would reflect upon the voluntary sacrifices of the missionaries in foreign parts* who lived chiefly on salads.

The proceedings of such a day occasion various fluctuations in the human thermometer, and especially in instruments so sensitively and delicately constructed as Mrs. Varden. Thus, at dinner Mrs V. stood at summer heat; genial, smiling, and delightful. After dinner, in the sunshine of the wine, she went up at least half-a-dozen degrees, and was perfectly enchanting. As its effect subsided, she fell rapidly, went to sleep for an hour or so at temperate, and woke at something below freezing. Now she was at summer heat again, in the shade; and when tea was over, and old John, producing a bottle of cordial from one of the oaken cases, insisted on her sipping two glasses thereof in slow succession, she stood steadily at ninety for one hour and a quarter. Profiting by experience, the locksmith took advantage of this genial weather to smoke his pipe in the porch, and in consequence of this prudent management, he was fully prepared, when the glass went down again, to start homewards directly.

The horse was accordingly put in, and the chaise brought round to the door. Joe, who would on no account be dissuaded from escorting them until they had passed the most dreary and solitary part of the road, led out the grey mare at the same time; and having helped Dolly into her seat (more happiness!) sprung gaily into the saddle. Then, after many good nights, and admonitions to wrap up, and glancing of lights, and handing in of cloaks and shawls, the chaise rolled away, and Joe trotted beside it—on Dolly's side, no doubt, and pretty close to the wheel too.

## CHAPTER THE TWENTY-SECOND.

IT was a fine bright night, and for all her lowness of spirits Dolly
kept looking up at the stars in a manner so bewitching (and *she* knew
it!) that Joe was clean out of his senses, and plainly showed that if
ever a man were—not to say over head and ears, but over the
Monument and the top of Saint Paul's in love,* that man was himself.
The road was a very good one; not at all a jolting road, or an uneven
one; and yet Dolly held the side of the chaise with one little hand, all
the way. If there had been an executioner behind him with an
uplifted axe ready to chop off his head if he touched that hand, Joe
couldn't have helped doing it. From putting his own hand upon it as
if by chance, and taking it away again after a minute or so, he got to
riding along without taking it off at all; as if he, the escort, were
bound to do that as an important part of his duty, and had come out
for the purpose. The most curious circumstance about this little
incident was, that Dolly didn't seem to know of it. She looked so
innocent and unconscious when she turned her eyes on Joe, that it
was quite provoking.

She talked though; talked about her fright, and about Joe's coming
up to rescue her, and about her gratitude, and about her fear that she
might not have thanked him enough, and about their always being
friends from that time forth—and about all that sort of thing. And
when Joe said, not friends he hoped, Dolly was quite surprised, and
said not enemies she hoped; and when Joe said, couldn't they be
something much better than either, Dolly all of a sudden found out a
star which was brighter than all the other stars, and begged to call his
attention to the same, and was ten thousand times more innocent and
unconscious than ever.

In this manner they travelled along, talking very little above a
whisper, and wishing the road could be stretched out to some dozen
times its natural length—at least that was Joe's desire—when, as
they were getting clear of the forest and emerging on the more
frequented road, they heard behind them the sound of a horse's feet
at a round trot, which growing rapidly louder as it drew nearer,
elicited a scream from Mrs. Varden, and the cry "a friend!" from the
rider, who now came panting up, and checked his horse beside them.

"This man again!" cried Dolly, shuddering.

"Hugh!" said Joe. "What errand are you upon?"

"I come to ride back with you," he answered, glancing covertly at the locksmith's daughter. "*He* sent me."

"My father!" said poor Joe; adding under his breath, with a very unfilial apostrophe, "Will he never think me man enough to take care of myself!"

"Ay!" returned Hugh to the first part of the inquiry. "The roads are not safe just now he says, and you'd better have a companion."

"Ride on then," said Joe. "I'm not going to turn yet."

Hugh complied, and they went on again. It was his whim or humour to ride immediately before the chaise, and from this position he constantly turned his head, and looked back. Dolly felt that he looked at her, but she averted her eyes and feared to raise them once, so great was the dread with which he had inspired her.

This interruption, and the consequent wakefulness of Mrs. Varden, who had been nodding in her sleep up to this point, except for a minute or two at a time, when she roused herself to scold the locksmith for audaciously taking hold of her to prevent her nodding herself out of the chaise, put a restraint upon the whispered conversation, and made it difficult of resumption. Indeed, before they had gone another mile, Gabriel stopped at his wife's desire, and that good lady protested she would not hear of Joe's going a step further on any account whatever. It was in vain for Joe to protest on the other hand that he was by no means tired, and would turn back presently, and would see them safely past such and such a point, and so forth. Mrs. Varden was obdurate, and being so was not to be overcome by mortal agency.

"Good night—if I must say it," said Joe, sorrowfully.

"Good night," said Dolly. She would have added, "Take care of that man, and pray don't trust him," but he had turned his horse's head, and was standing close to them. She had therefore nothing for it but to suffer Joe to give her hand a gentle squeeze, and when the chaise had gone on for some distance, to look back and wave it, as he still lingered on the spot where they had parted, with the tall dark figure of Hugh beside him.

What she thought about, going home; and whether the coach-maker held as favourable a place in her meditations as he had occupied in the morning, is unknown. They reached home at last—at last, for it was a long way, made none the shorter by Mrs. Varden's grumbling. Miggs hearing the sound of wheels was at the door immediately.

"Here they are, Simmun! Here they are!" cried Miggs, clapping her hands, and issuing forth to help her mistress to alight. "Bring a chair, Simmun. Now, an't you the better for it, mim? Don't you feel more yourself than you would have done if you'd have stopped at home? Oh, gracious! how cold you are! Goodness me, sir, she's a perfect heap of ice."

"I can't help it, my good girl. You had better take her in to the fire," said the locksmith.

"Master sounds unfeeling, mim," said Miggs, in a tone of commiseration, "but such is not his intentions, I'm sure. After what he has seen of you this day, I never will believe but that he has a deal more affection in his heart than to speak unkind. Come in and sit yourself down by the fire; there's a good dear—do."

Mrs. Varden complied. The locksmith followed with his hands in his pockets, and Mr. Tappertit trundled off with the chaise to a neighbouring stable.

"Martha, my dear," said the locksmith, when they reached the parlour, "if you'll look to Dolly yourself, or let somebody else do it, perhaps it will be only kind and reasonable. She has been frightened, you know, and is not at all well to-night."

In fact, Dolly had thrown herself upon the sofa, quite regardless of all the little finery of which she had been so proud in the morning, and with her face buried in her hands was crying very much.

At first sight of this phenomenon (for Dolly was by no means accustomed to displays of this sort, rather learning from her mother's example to avoid them as much as possible) Mrs. Varden expressed her belief that never was any woman so beset as she; that her life was a continued scene of trial; that whenever she was disposed to be well and cheerful, so sure were the people around her to throw, by some means or other, a damp upon her spirits; and that, as she had enjoyed herself that day, and Heaven knew it was very seldom she did enjoy herself, so she was now to pay the penalty. To all such propositions Miggs assented freely. Poor Dolly, however, grew none the better for these restoratives, but rather worse, indeed; and seeing that she was really ill, both Mrs. Varden and Miggs were moved to compassion, and tended her in earnest.

But even then, their very kindness shaped itself into their usual course of policy, and though Dolly was in a swoon, it was rendered clear to the meanest capacity, that Mrs. Varden was the sufferer. Thus when Dolly began to get a little better, and passed into that stage in which matrons hold that remonstrance and argument may be successfully applied, her mother represented to her, with tears in her eyes, that if she had been flurried and worried that day, she must remember it was the common lot of humanity, and in especial of womankind, who through the whole of their existence must expect no less, and were bound to make up their minds to meek endurance and patient resignation. Mrs. Varden entreated her to remember that one of these days she would, in all probability, have to do violence to her feelings so far as to be married; and that marriage, as she might see every day of her life (and truly she did) was a state requiring great fortitude and forbearance. She represented to her in lively colours, that if she (Mrs. V.) had not, in steering her course through this vale of tears, been supported by a strong principle of duty which alone upheld and prevented her from drooping, she must have been in her grave many years ago; in which case she desired to know what would have become of that errant spirit (meaning the locksmith), of whose eye she was the very apple, and in whose path she was, as it were, a shining light and guiding star?

Miss Miggs also put in her word to the same effect. She said that indeed and indeed Miss Dolly might take pattern by her blessed mother, who, she always had said, and always would say, though she were to be hanged, drawn, and quartered for it next minute, was the mildest, amiablest, forgivingest-spirited, longest-sufferingest female as ever she could have believed; the mere narration of whose excellencies had worked such a wholesome change in the mind of her own sister-in-law, that, whereas, before, she and her husband lived like cat and dog, and were in the habit of exchanging brass candlesticks, pot-lids, flat-irons, and other such strong resentments, they were now the happiest and affectionatest couple upon earth; as could be proved any day on application at Golden Lion Court, number twenty-sivin, second bell-handle on the right-hand post. After glancing at herself as a comparatively worthless vessel, but still as one of some desert, she besought her to bear in mind that her aforesaid dear and only mother was of a weakly constitution and excitable temperament, who had constantly to sustain afflictions in domestic life, compared with which thieves and robbers were as nothing, and yet never sunk down or gave way to despair or wrath, but, in prize-fighting phraseology, always came up to time with a cheerful countenance, and went in to win as if nothing had happened. When Miggs had finished her solo, her mistress struck in again, and the two together performed a duet to the same purpose; the burden being, that Mrs. Varden was persecuted perfection, and Mr. Varden, as the representative of mankind in that apartment, a creature of vicious and brutal habits, utterly insensible to the blessings he enjoyed. Of so refined a character, indeed, was their talent of assault under the mask of sympathy, that when Dolly, recovering, embraced her father tenderly, as in vindication of his goodness, Mrs. Varden expressed her solemn hope that this would be a lesson to him for the remainder of his life, and that he would do some little justice to a woman's nature ever afterwards—in which aspiration Miss Miggs, by divers sniffs and coughs, more significant than the longest oration, expressed her entire concurrence.

But the great joy of Miggs's heart was, that she not only picked up a full account of what had happened, but had the exquisite delight of conveying it to Mr. Tappertit for his jealousy and torture. For that gentleman, on account of Dolly's indisposition, had been requested to take his supper in the workshop, and it was conveyed thither by Miss Miggs's own fair hands.

"Oh, Simmun!" said the young lady, "such goings on to-day! Oh, gracious me, Simmun!"

Mr. Tappertit, who was not in the best of humours, and who disliked Miss Miggs more when she laid her hand on her heart and panted for breath than at any other time, as her deficiency of outline was most apparent under such circumstances, eyed her over in his loftiest style, and deigned to express no curiosity whatever.

"I never heard the like, nor nobody else," pursued Miggs. "The idea of interfering with *her*. What people can see in her to make it worth their while to do so, that's the joke—he, he, he!"

Finding there was a lady in the case, Mr. Tappertit haughtily requested his fair friend to be more explicit, and demanded to know what she meant by "her."

"Why, that Dolly," said Miggs, with an extremely sharp emphasis on the name. "But, oh upon my word and honour, young Joseph Willet is a brave one; and he do deserve her, that he do."

"Woman!" said Mr. Tappertit, jumping off the counter on which he was seated; "beware!"

"My stars, Simmun!" cried Miggs, in affected astonishment. "You frighten me to death! What's the matter?"

"There are strings," said Mr. Tappertit, flourishing his bread-and-cheese knife in the air, "in the human heart that had better not be wibrated. That's what's the matter."

"Oh, very well—if you're in a huff," cried Miggs, turning away.

"Huff or no huff," said Mr. Tappertit, detaining her by the wrist. "What do you mean, Jezebel? What were you going to say? Answer me!"

Notwithstanding this uncivil exhortation, Miggs gladly did as she was required; and told him how that their young mistress, being alone in the meadows after dark, had been attacked by three or four tall men, who would have certainly borne her away and perhaps murdered her, but for the timely arrival of Joseph Willet, who with his own single hand put them all to flight, and rescued her; to the

lasting admiration of his fellow-creatures generally, and to the eternal love and gratitude of Dolly Varden.

"Very good," said Mr. Tappertit, fetching a long breath when the tale was told, and rubbing his hair up till it stood stiff and straight on end all over his head. "His days are numbered."

"Oh, Simmun!"

"I tell you," said the 'prentice, "his days are numbered. Leave me. Get along with you."

Miggs departed at his bidding, but less because of his bidding than because she desired to chuckle in secret. When she had given vent to her satisfaction, she returned to the parlour; where the locksmith, stimulated by quietness and Toby, had become talkative, and was disposed to take a cheerful review of the occurrences of the day. But Mrs. Varden, whose practical religion (as is not uncommon) was usually of the retrospective order, cut him short by declaiming on the sinfulness of such junkettings, and holding that it was high time to go to bed. To bed therefore she withdrew, with an aspect as grim and gloomy as that of the Maypole's own state couch; and to bed the rest of the establishment soon afterwards repaired.

### CHAPTER THE TWENTY-THIRD.

WILIGHT had given place to night some hours, and it was high noon in those quarters of the town in which "the world" condescended to dwell—the world being then, as now, of very limited dimensions and easily lodged—when Mr. Chester reclined upon a sofa in his dressing-room in the Temple, entertaining himself with a book.

He was dressing, as it seemed, by easy stages, and having performed half the journey was taking a long rest. Completely attired as to his legs and feet in the trimmest fashion of the day, he had yet the remainder of his toilet to perform. The coat was stretched, like a refined scarecrow, on its separate horse; the waistcoat was displayed to the best advantage; the various ornamental articles of dress were severally set out in most alluring order; and yet he lay dangling his legs between the sofa and the ground, as intent upon his book as if there were nothing but bed before him.

"Upon my honour," he said, at length raising his eyes to the ceiling with the air of a man who was reflecting seriously on what he had read; "upon my honour, the most masterly composition, the most delicate thoughts, the finest code of morality, and the most gentlemanly sentiments in the universe! Ah Ned, Ned, if you would but form your mind by such precepts, we should have but one common feeling on every subject that could possibly arise between us!"

This apostrophe was addressed, like the rest of his remarks, to empty air: for Edward was not present, and the father was quite alone.

"My Lord Chesterfield,"* he said, pressing his hand tenderly upon the book as he laid it down, "if I could but have profited by your genius soon enough to have formed my son on the model you have left to all wise fathers, both he and I would have been rich men. Shakspeare was undoubtedly very fine in his way; Milton good, though prosy; Lord Bacon deep, and decidedly knowing; but the writer who should be his country's pride, is my Lord Chesterfield."

He became thoughtful again, and the toothpick was in requisition.

"I thought I was tolerably accomplished as a man of the world," he continued, "I flattered myself that I was pretty well versed in all those little arts and graces which distinguish men of the world from boors and peasants, and separate their character from those intensely vulgar sentiments which are called the national character. Apart from any natural prepossession in my own favour, I believed I was. Still, in every page of this enlightened writer, I find some captivating hypocrisy which has never occurred to me before, or some superlative piece of selfishness to which I was utterly a stranger. I should quite blush for myself before this stupendous creature, if, remembering his precepts, one might blush at anything. An amazing man! a nobleman indeed! any King or Queen may make a Lord, but only the Devil himself—and the Graces—can make a Chesterfield."

Men who are thoroughly false and hollow, seldom try to hide those vices from themselves; and yet in the very act of avowing them, they lay claim to the virtues they feign most to despise. "For," say they, "this is honesty, this is truth. All mankind are like us, but they have not the candour to avow it." The more they affect to deny the existence of any sincerity in the world, the more they would be thought to possess it in its boldest shape; and this is an unconscious compliment to Truth on the part of these philosophers, which will turn the laugh against them to the Day of Judgment.

Mr. Chester, having extolled his favourite author as above recited, took up the book again in the excess of his admiration and was composing himself for a further perusal of its sublime morality, when he was disturbed by a noise at the outer door; occasioned as it seemed by the endeavours of his servant to obstruct the entrance of some unwelcome visitor.

"A late hour for an importunate creditor," he said, raising his eyebrows with as indolent an expression of wonder as if the noise were in the street, and one with which he had not the smallest personal concern. "Much after their accustomed time. The usual pretence I suppose. No doubt a heavy payment to make up to-morrow. Poor fellow, he loses time, and time is money as the good proverb says—I never found it out though. Well. What now? You know I am not at home."

"A man, Sir," replied the servant, who was to the full as cool and negligent in his way as his master, "has brought home the riding-whip you lost the other day. I told him you were out, but he said he was to wait while I brought it in, and wouldn't go till I did."

"He was quite right," returned his master, "and you're a block-head, possessing no judgment or discretion whatever. Tell him to come in, and see that he rubs his shoes for exactly five minutes first."

The man laid the whip on a chair, and withdrew. The master, who had only heard his foot upon the ground and had not taken the trouble to turn round and look at him, shut his book, and pursued the train of ideas his entrance had disturbed.

"If time were money," he said, handling his snuff-box, "I would compound with my creditors, and give them—let me see—how much a day? There's my nap after dinner—an hour—they're extremely welcome to that, and to make the most of it. In the morning, between my breakfast and the paper, I could spare them another hour; in the evening before dinner, say another. Three hours a day. They might pay themselves in calls, with interest, in twelve months. I think I shall propose it to them. Ah, my centaur, are you there?"

"Here I am," replied Hugh, striding in, followed by a dog, as rough and sullen as himself; "and trouble enough I've had to get here. What do you ask me to come for, and keep me out when I *do* come?"

"My good fellow," returned the other, raising his head a little from the cushion and carelessly surveying him from top to toe, "I am delighted to see you, and to have, in your being here, the very best proof that you are not kept out. How are you?"

"I'm well enough," said Hugh impatiently.

"You look a perfect marvel of health. Sit down."

"I'd rather stand," said Hugh.

"Please yourself, my good fellow," returned Mr. Chester rising, slowly pulling off the loose robe he wore, and sitting down before the dressing-glass. "Please yourself by all means."

Having said this in the politest and blandest tone possible, he went on dressing, and took no further notice of his guest, who stood in the same spot as uncertain what to do next, eyeing him sulkily from time to time.

"Are you going to speak to me, master?" he said, after a long silence.

"My worthy creature," returned Mr. Chester, "you are a little ruffled and out of humour. I'll wait till you're quite yourself again. I am in no hurry."

This behaviour had its intended effect. It humbled and abashed the man, and made him still more irresolute and uncertain. Hard words he could have returned, violence he would have repaid with interest; but this cool, complacent, contemptuous, self-possessed reception, caused him to feel his inferiority more completely than the most elaborate arguments. Everything contributed to this effect. His own rough speech, contrasted with the soft persuasive accents of the other; his rude bearing, and Mr. Chester's polished manner; the disorder and negligence of his ragged dress, and the elegant attire he saw before him; with all the unaccustomed luxuries and comforts of the room, and the silence that gave him leisure to observe these things, and feel how ill at ease they made him; all these influences, which have too often some effect on tutored minds and become of almost resistless power when brought to bear on such a mind as his, quelled Hugh completely. He moved by little and little nearer to Mr. Chester's chair, and glancing over his shoulder at the reflection of his face in the glass, as if seeking for some encouragement in its expression, said at length, with a rough attempt at conciliation,

"*Are* you going to speak to me, master, or am I to go away?"

"Speak you," said Mr. Chester, "speak you, good fellow. I have spoken, have I not? I am waiting for you."

"Why, look'ee sir," returned Hugh with increased embarrassment, "am I the man that you privately left your whip with before you rode away from the Maypole, and told to bring it back whenever he might want to see you on a certain subject?"

"No doubt the same, or you have a twin brother," said Mr. Chester, glancing at the reflection of his anxious face; "which is not probable, I should say."

"Then I have come sir," said Hugh, "and I have brought it back, and something else along with it. A letter sir, it is, that I took from the person who had charge of it." As he spoke, he laid upon the dressing-table, Dolly's lost epistle. The very letter that had cost her so much trouble.

"Did you obtain this by force, my good fellow?" said Mr. Chester, casting his eye upon it without the least perceptible surprise or pleasure.

"Not quite," said Hugh. "Partly."

"Who was the messenger from whom you took it?"

"A woman. One Varden's daughter."

"Oh indeed!" said Mr. Chester, gaily. "What else did you take from her?"

"What else?"

"Yes," said the other, in a drawling manner, for he was fixing a very small patch of sticking-plaster on a very small pimple near the corner of his mouth. "What else?"

"Well—a kiss," replied Hugh, after some hesitation.

"And what else?"

"Nothing."

"I think," said Mr. Chester, in the same easy tone, and smiling twice or thrice to try if the patch adhered—"I think there was something else. I have heard a trifle of jewellery spoken of—a mere trifle—a thing of such little value, indeed, that you may have forgotten it. Do you remember anything of the kind—such as a bracelet now, for instance?"

Hugh with a muttered oath thrust his hand into his breast, and drawing the bracelet forth, wrapped in a scrap of hay, was about to lay it on the table likewise, when his patron stopped his hand and bade him put it up again.

"You took that for yourself, my excellent friend," he said, "and may keep it. I am neither a thief, nor a receiver. Don't show it to me.

You had better hide it again, and lose no time. Don't let me see where you put it either," he added, turning away his head.

"You're not a receiver!" said Hugh bluntly, despite the increasing awe in which he held him. "What do you call *that*, master?" striking the letter with his heavy hand.

"I call that quite another thing," said Mr. Chester coolly. "I shall prove it presently, as you will see. You are thirsty, I suppose?"

Hugh drew his sleeve across his lips, and gruffly answered yes.

"Step to that closet, and bring me a bottle you will see there, and a glass."

He obeyed. His patron followed him with his eyes, and when his back was turned, smiled as he had never done when he stood beside the mirror. On his return he filled the glass, and bade him drink. That dram despatched, he poured him out another, and another.

"How many can you bear?" he said, filling the glass again.

"As many as you like to give me. Pour on. Fill high. A bumper with a bead in the middle! Give me enough of this," he added, as he tossed it down his hairy throat, "and I'll do murder if you ask me!"

"As I don't mean to ask you, and you might possibly do it without being invited if you went on much further," said Mr. Chester with great composure, "we will stop, if agreeable to you my good friend, at the next glass.—You were drinking before you came here."

"I always am when I can get it," cried Hugh boisterously, waving the empty glass above his head, and throwing himself into a rude dancing attitude. "I always am. Why not? Ha ha ha! What's so good to me as this? What ever has been? What else has kept away the cold on bitter nights, and driven hunger off in starving times? What else has given me the strength and courage of a man, when men would have left me to die, a puny child? I should never have had a man's heart but for this. I should have died in a ditch. Where's he who when I was a weak and sickly wretch, with trembling legs and fading sight, bade me cheer up, as this did? I never knew him; not I. I drink to the drink, master. Ha ha ha!"

"You are an exceedingly cheerful young man," said Mr. Chester, putting on his cravat with great deliberation, and slightly moving his head from side to side to settle his chin in its proper place. "Quite a boon companion."

"Do you see this hand, master," said Hugh, "and this arm?" baring the brawny limb to the elbow. "It was once mere skin and bone, and would have been dust in some poor church-yard by this time, but for the drink."

"You may cover it," said Mr. Chester, "it's sufficiently real in your sleeve."

"I should never have been spirited up to take a kiss from the proud little beauty, master, but for the drink," cried Hugh. "Ha ha ha! It was a good one. As sweet as honey-suckle I warrant you. I thank the drink for it. I'll drink to the drink again, master. Fill me one more. Come. One more!"

"You are such a promising fellow," said his patron, putting on his waistcoat with great nicety, and taking no heed of this request, "that I must caution you against having too many impulses from the drink, and getting hung before your time. What's your age?"

"I don't know."

"At any rate," said Mr. Chester, "you are young enough to escape what I may call a natural death for some years to come. How can you trust yourself in my hands on so short an acquaintance, with a halter round your neck. What a confiding nature yours must be!"

Hugh fell back a pace or two and surveyed him with a look of mingled terror, indignation, and surprise. Regarding himself in the glass with the same complacency as before, and speaking as smoothly as if he were discussing some pleasant chit-chat of the town, his patron went on:

"Robbery on the king's highway, my young friend, is a very dangerous and ticklish occupation. It is pleasant, I have no doubt, while it lasts; but like many other pleasures in this transitory world, it seldom lasts long. And really if, in the ingenuousness of youth, you open your heart so readily on the subject, I am afraid your career will be an extremely short one."

"How's this?" said Hugh, "What do you talk of, master? Who was it set me on?"

"Who?" said Mr. Chester, wheeling sharply round, and looking full at him for the first time. "I didn't hear you. Who was it?"

Hugh faltered, and muttered something which was not audible.

"Who was it? I am curious to know," said Mr. Chester, with surpassing affability. "Some rustic beauty perhaps? But be cautious, my good friend. They are not always to be trusted. Do take my advice now, and be careful of yourself." With these words he turned to the glass again, and went on with his toilet.

Hugh would have answered him that he, the questioner himself, had set him on, but the words stuck in his throat. The consummate art with which his patron had led him to this point, and managed the whole conversation, perfectly baffled him. He did not doubt that if he had made the retort which was on his lips when Mr. Chester turned round and questioned him so keenly, he would straightway have given him into custody and had him dragged before a justice with the stolen property upon him; in which case it was as certain he would have been hung as it was that he had been born. The ascendency which it was the purpose of the man of the world to establish over this savage instrument, was gained from that time. Hugh's submission was complete. He dreaded him beyond description; and felt that accident and artifice had spun a web about him, which at a touch from such a master-hand as his, would bind him to the gallows.

With these thoughts passing through his mind, and yet wondering at the very same time how he who came there rioting in the confidence of this man (as he thought), should be so soon and so thoroughly subdued, Hugh stood cowering before him, regarding him uneasily from time to time, while he finished dressing. When he had done so, he took up the letter, broke the seal, and throwing himself back in his chair, read it leisurely through.

"Very neatly worded upon my life! Quite a woman's letter, full of what people call tenderness, and disinterestedness, and heart, and all that sort of thing!"

As he spoke, he twisted it up, and glancing lazily round at Hugh as though he would say "You see this?" held it in the flame of the candle. When it was in a full blaze, he tossed it into the grate, and there it smouldered away.

"It was directed to my son," he said, turning to Hugh, "and you did quite right to bring it here. I opened it on my own responsibility, and you see what I have done with it. Take this, for your trouble."

Hugh stepped forward to receive the piece of money he held out to him. As he put it in his hand, he added:

"If you should happen to find anything else of this sort, or to pick up any kind of information you may think I would like to have, bring it here will you, my good fellow?"

This was said with a smile which implied—or Hugh thought it did—"fail to do so at your peril!" He answered that he would.

"And don't," said his patron, with an air of the very kindest patronage, "don't be at all downcast or uneasy respecting that little rashness we have been speaking of. Your neck is as safe in my hands, my good fellow, as though a baby's fingers clasped it, I assure you.— Take another glass. You are quieter now."

Hugh accepted it from his hand, and looking stealthily at his smiling face, drank the contents in silence.

"Don't you,—ha ha!—don't you drink to the drink any more?" said Mr. Chester, in his most winning manner.

"To you, sir," was the sullen answer, with something approaching to a bow. "I drink to you."

"Thank you. God bless you. By the bye, what is your name, my good soul? You are called Hugh, I know, of course—your other name?"

"I have no other name."

"A very strange fellow! Do you mean that you never knew one, or that you don't choose to tell it? Which?"

"I'd tell it if I could," said Hugh, quickly. "I can't. I have been always called Hugh; nothing more. I never knew, nor saw, nor thought about a father; and I was a boy of six—that's not very old—when they hung my mother up at Tyburn for a couple of thousand men to stare at. They might have let her live. She was poor enough."

"How very sad!" exclaimed his patron, with a condescending smile. "I have no doubt she was an exceedingly fine woman."

"You see that dog of mine?" said Hugh, abruptly.

"Faithful, I dare say?" rejoined his patron, looking at him through his glass; "and immensely clever? Virtuous and gifted animals, whether man or beast, always are so very hideous."

"Such a dog as that, and one of the same breed, was the only living thing except me that howled that day," said Hugh. "Out of the two thousand odd—there was a larger crowd for its being a woman—the dog and I alone had any pity. If he'd have been a man, he'd have been glad to be quit of her, for she had been forced to keep him lean and half-starved; but being a dog, and not having a man's sense, he was sorry."

"It was dull of the brute, certainly," said Mr. Chester, "and very like a brute."

Hugh made no rejoinder, but whistling to his dog, who sprung up

at the sound and came jumping and sporting about him, bade his
sympathising friend good night.

"Good night," he returned. "Remember; you're safe with me—
quite safe. So long as you deserve it, my good fellow, as I hope you
always will, you have a friend in me, on whose silence you may rely.
Now do be careful of yourself, pray do, and consider what jeopardy
you might have stood in. Good night! bless you!"

Hugh truckled before the hidden meaning of these words as much
as such a being could, and crept out of the door so submissively and
subserviently—with an air, in short, so different from that with
which he had entered—that his patron on being left alone, smiled
more than ever.

"And yet," he said, as he took a pinch of snuff, "I do not like their
having hanged his mother. The fellow has a fine eye, and I am sure
she was handsome. But very probably she was coarse—red-nosed
perhaps, and had clumsy feet. Aye. It was all for the best, no doubt."

With this comforting reflection, he put on his coat, took a farewell
glance at the glass, and summoned his man, who promptly attended,
followed by a chair and its two bearers.

"Foh!" said Mr. Chester. "The very atmosphere that centaur has

breathed, seems tainted with the cart and ladder. Here, Peak. Bring some scent and sprinkle the floor; and take away the chair he sat upon, and air it; and dash a little of that mixture upon me. I am stifled!"

The man obeyed; and the room and its master being both purified, nothing remained for Mr. Chester but to demand his hat, to fold it jauntily under his arm, to take his seat in the chair and be carried off; humming a fashionable tune.

## CHAPTER THE TWENTY-FOURTH.

How the accomplished gentleman spent the evening in the midst of a dazzling and brilliant circle; how he enchanted all those with whom he mingled by the grace of his deportment, the politeness of his manner, the vivacity of his conversation, and the sweetness of his voice; how it was observed in every corner, that Chester was a man of that happy disposition that nothing ruffled him, that he was one on whom the world's cares and errors sat lightly as his dress, and in whose smiling face a calm and tranquil mind was constantly reflected; how honest men, who by instinct knew him better, bowed down before him nevertheless, deferred to his every word, and courted his favourable notice; how people, who really had good in them, went with the stream, and fawned and flattered, and approved, and despised themselves while they did so, and yet had not the courage to resist; how, in short, he was one of those who are received and cherished in society (as the phrase is) by scores who individually would shrink from and be repelled by the object of their lavish regard; are things of course, which will suggest themselves. Matter so common-place needs but a passing glance, and there an end.

The despisers of mankind—apart from the mere fools and mimics, of that creed—are of two sorts. They who believe their merit neglected and unappreciated, make up one class; they who receive adulation and flattery, knowing their own worthlessness, compose the other. Be sure that the coldest-hearted misanthropes are ever of this last order.

Mr. Chester sat up in bed next morning, sipping his coffee, and remembering with a kind of contemptuous satisfaction how he had shone last night, and how he had been caressed and courted, when his servant brought in a very small scrap of dirty paper, tightly sealed in two places, on the inside whereof was inscribed in pretty large text these words. "A friend. Desiring of a conference. Immediate. Private. Burn it when you've read it."

"Where in the name of the Gunpowder Plot* did you pick up this?" said his master.

It was given him by a person then waiting at the door, the man replied.

"With a cloak and dagger?" said Mr. Chester.

With nothing more threatening about him, it appeared, than a leather apron and a dirty face. "Let him come in." In he came—Mr. Tappertit; with his hair still on end, and a great lock in his hand, which he put down on the floor in the middle of the chamber as if he were about to go through some performances in which it was a necessary agent.

"Sir," said Mr. Tappertit with a low bow, "I thank you for this condescension, and am glad to see you. Pardon the menial office in which I am engaged sir, and extend your sympathies to one, who, humble as his appearance is, has inn'ard workings far above his station."

Mr. Chester held the bed-curtain farther back, and looked at him with a vague impression that he was some maniac, who had not only broken open the door of his place of confinement, but had brought away the lock. Mr. Tappertit bowed again, and displayed his legs to the best advantage.

"You have heard sir," said Mr. Tappertit, laying his hand upon his breast, "of G. Varden Locksmith and bell-hanger and repairs neatly executed in town and country, Clerkenwell, London?"

"What then?" asked Mr. Chester.

"I am his 'prentice, sir."

"What *then*?"

"Ahem!" said Mr. Tappertit. "Would you permit me to shut the door sir, and will you further, sir, give me your honour bright, that what passes between us is in the strictest confidence?"

Mr. Chester laid himself calmly down in bed again, and turning a perfectly undisturbed face towards the strange apparition, which had by this time closed the door, begged him to speak out, and to be as rational as he could, without putting himself to any very great personal inconvenience.

"In the first place sir," said Mr. Tappertit, producing a small pocket-handkerchief, and shaking it out of the folds, "as I have not a card about me (for the envy of masters debases us below that level) allow me to offer the best substitute that circumstances will admit of. If you will take that in your own hand, sir, and cast your eye on the right-hand corner," said Mr. Tappertit, offering it with a graceful air, "you will meet with my credentials."

"Thank you," answered Mr. Chester, politely accepting it, and turning to some blood-red characters at one end. "'Four. Simon Tappertit. One.' Is that the—"

"Without the numbers, sir, that is my name," replied the 'prentice. "They are merely intended as directions to the washerwoman, and have no connection with myself or family. *Your* name, sir," said Mr. Tappertit, looking very hard at his nightcap, "is Chester, I suppose? You needn't pull it off, sir, thank you. I observe E. C.* from here. We will take the rest for granted."

"Pray, Mr. Tappertit," said Mr. Chester, "has that complicated piece of ironmongery which you have done me the favour to bring with you, any immediate connexion with the business we are to discuss?"

"It has not, sir," rejoined the 'prentice. "It's going to be fitted on a ware'us door in Thames Street."

"Perhaps, as that is the case," said Mr. Chester, "and as it has a stronger flavour of oil than I usually refresh my bedroom with, you will oblige me so far as to put it outside the door?"

"By all means, sir," said Mr. Tappertit, suiting the action to the word.

"You'll excuse my mentioning it, I hope?"

"Don't apologise, sir, I beg. And now, if you please, to business."

During the whole of this dialogue, Mr. Chester had suffered nothing but his smile of unvarying serenity and politeness to appear upon his face. Sim Tappertit, who had far too good an opinion of himself to suspect that anybody could be playing upon him, thought within himself that this was something like the respect to which he was entitled, and drew a comparison from this courteous demeanour of a stranger, by no means favourable to the worthy locksmith.

"From what passes in our house," said Mr. Tappertit, "I am aware, sir, that your son keeps company with a young lady against your inclinations. Sir, your son has not used me well."

"Mr. Tappertit," said the other, "you grieve me beyond description."

"Thank you, sir," replied the 'prentice. "I'm glad to hear you say so. He's very proud, sir, is your son; very haughty."

"I am afraid he *is* haughty," said Mr. Chester. "Do you know I was really afraid of that before; and you confirm me?"

"To recount the menial offices I've had to do for your son, sir," said Mr. Tappertit; "the chairs I've had to hand him, the coaches I've had to call for him, the numerous degrading duties, wholly unconnected with my indenters, that I've had to do for him, would fill a family Bible. Besides which, sir, he is but a young man himself, and I do not consider 'thank'ee Sim,' a proper form of address on those occasions."

"Mr. Tappertit, your wisdom is beyond your years. Pray go on."

"I thank you for your good opinion, sir," said Sim, much gratified, "and will endeavour so to do. Now sir, on this account (and perhaps for another reason or two which I needn't go into) I am on your side. And what I tell you is this—that as long as our people go backwards and forwards, to and fro, up and down, to that there jolly old Maypole, lettering, and messaging, and fetching and carrying, you couldn't help your son keeping company with that young lady by deputy,—not if he was minded night and day by all the Horse Guards, and every man of 'em in the very fullest uniform."

Mr. Tappertit stopped to take breath after this, and then started fresh again.

"Now, sir, I am a coming to the point. You will inquire of me, 'how is this to be prevented?' I'll tell you how. If an honest, civil, smiling gentleman like you—"

"Mr. Tappertit—really—"

"No, no, I'm serious," rejoined the 'prentice, "I am, upon my soul. If an honest, civil, smiling gentleman like you, was to talk but ten minutes to our old woman—that's Mrs. Varden—and flatter her up a bit, you'd gain her over for ever. Then there's this point got—that her daughter Dolly,"—here a flush came over Mr. Tappertit's face—"wouldn't be allowed to be a go-between from that time forward; and till that point's got, there's nothing ever will prevent her. Mind that."

"Mr. Tappertit, your knowledge of human nature—"

"Wait a minute," said Sim, folding his arms with a dreadful

calmness. "Now I come to THE point. Sir, there is a villain at that Maypole, a monster in human shape, a vagabond of the deepest dye, that unless you get rid of, and have kidnapped and carried off at the very least—nothing less will do—will marry your son to that young woman, as certainly and surely as if he was the Archbishop of Canterbury himself. He will, sir, for the hatred and malice that he bears to you; let alone the pleasure of doing a bad action, which to him is its own reward. If you knew how this chap, this Joseph Willet— that's his name—comes backwards and forwards to our house, libelling, and denouncing, and threatening you, and how I shudder when I hear him, you'd hate him worse than I do,—worse than I do sir," said Mr. Tappertit wildly, putting his hair up straighter, and making a crunching noise with his teeth; "if sich a thing is possible."

"A little private vengeance in this, Mr. Tappertit?"

"Private vengeance, sir, or public sentiment, or both combined— destroy him," said Mr. Tappertit. "Miggs says so too. Miggs and me both say so. We can't bear the plotting and undermining that takes place. Our souls recoil from it. Barnaby Rudge and Mrs. Rudge are in it likewise; but the villain, Joseph Willet, is the ringleader. Their plottings and schemes are known to me and Miggs. If you want information of 'em, apply to us. Put Joseph Willet down, sir. Destroy him. Crush him. And be happy."

With these words, Mr. Tappertit, who seemed to expect no reply, and to hold it as a necessary consequence of his eloquence that his hearer should be utterly stunned, dumb-foundered, and over-whelmed, folded his arms so that the palm of each hand rested on the opposite shoulder, and disappeared after the manner of those mysterious warners of whom he had read in cheap story-books.

"That fellow," said Mr. Chester, relaxing his face when he was fairly gone, "is good practice. I *have* some command of my features, beyond all doubt. He fully confirms what I suspected, though; and blunt tools are sometimes found of use, where sharper instruments would fail. I fear I may be obliged to make great havoc among these worthy people. A troublesome necessity! I quite feel for them."

With that he fell into a quiet slumber:—subsided into such a gentle, pleasant sleep, that it was quite infantine.

## CHAPTER THE TWENTY-FIFTH.

LEAVING the favoured, and well-received, and flattered of the world; him of the world most worldly, who never compromised himself by an ungentlemanly action and was never guilty of a manly one; to lie smilingly asleep—for even sleep, working but little change in his dissembling face, became with him a piece of cold, conventional hypocrisy—we follow in the steps of two slow travellers on foot, making towards Chigwell.

Barnaby and his mother. Grip in their company, of course.

The widow, to whom each painful mile seemed longer than the last, toiled wearily along; while Barnaby, yielding to every inconstant impulse, fluttered here and there, now leaving her far behind, now lingering far behind himself, now darting into some by-lane or path and leaving her to pursue her way alone, until he stealthily emerged again and came upon her with a wild shout of merriment, as his wayward and capricious nature prompted. Now he would call to her from the topmost branch of some high tree by the roadside; now, using his tall staff as a leaping-pole, come flying over ditch or hedge or five-barred gate; now run with surprising swiftness for a mile or more on the straight road, and halting, sport upon a patch of grass with Grip till she came up. These were his delights; and when his patient mother heard his merry voice, or looked into his flushed and healthy face, she would not have abated them by one sad word or murmur, though each had been to her a source of suffering in the same degree as it was to him of pleasure.

It is something to look upon enjoyment, so that it be free and wild and in the face of nature, though it is but the enjoyment of an idiot. It is something to know that Heaven has left the capacity of gladness in such a creature's breast; it is something to be assured that, however lightly men may crush that faculty in their fellows, the Great Creator of mankind imparts it even to his despised and slighted work. Who would not rather see a poor idiot happy in the sunlight, than a wise man pining in a darkened jail!

Ye men of gloom and austerity, who paint the face of Infinite Benevolence with an eternal frown; read in the Everlasting Book, wide open to your view, the lesson it would teach. Its pictures are not in black and sombre hues, but bright and glowing tints; its music—

save when ye drown it—is not in sighs and groans, but songs and cheerful sounds. Listen to the million voices in the summer air, and find one dismal as your own. Remember, if ye can, the sense of hope and pleasure which every glad return of day awakens in the breast of all your kind who have not changed their nature; and learn some wisdom even from the witless, when their hearts are lifted up they know not why, by all the mirth and happiness it brings.

The widow's breast was full of care, was laden heavily with secret dread and sorrow; but her boy's gaiety of heart gladdened her, and beguiled the long journey. Sometimes he would bid her lean upon his arm, and would keep beside her steadily for a short distance; but it was more his nature to be rambling to and fro, and she better liked to see him free and happy, even than to have him near her, because she loved him better than herself.

She had quitted the place to which they were travelling, directly after the event which had changed her whole existence; and for two-and-twenty years had never had courage to revisit it. It was her native village. How many recollections crowded on her mind when it appeared in sight!

Two-and-twenty years. Her boy's whole life and history. The last time she looked back upon those roofs among the trees, she carried him in her arms, an infant. How often since that time had she sat beside him night and day, watching for the dawn of mind that never came; how had she feared, and doubted, and yet hoped, long after conviction forced itself upon her! The little stratagems she had devised to try him, the little tokens he had given in his childish way—not of dullness but of something infinitely worse, so ghastly and unchild-like in its cunning—came back as vividly as if but yesterday had intervened. The room in which they used to be; the spot in which his cradle stood; he, old and elfin-like in face, but ever dear to her, gazing at her with a wild and vacant eye, and crooning some uncouth song as she sat by and rocked him; every circumstance of his infancy came thronging back, and the most trivial, perhaps, the most distinctly.

His older childhood, too; the strange imaginings he had; his terror of certain senseless things—familiar objects he endowed with life; the slow and gradual breaking out of that one horror, in which, before his birth, his darkened intellect began; how, in the midst of all, she had found some hope and comfort in his being unlike another child, and had gone on almost believing in the slow development of his mind until he grew a man, and then his childhood was complete and lasting; one after another, all these old thoughts sprung up within her, strong after their long slumber and bitterer than ever.

She took his arm and they hurried through the village street. It was the same as it was wont to be in old times, yet different too, and wore another air. The change was in herself, not it; but she never thought of that, and wondered at its alteration, and where it lay, and what it was.

The people all knew Barnaby, and the children of the place came flocking round him—as she remembered to have done with their fathers and mothers round some silly beggarman, when a child herself. None of them knew her; they passed each well-remembered house, and yard, and homestead; and striking into the fields, were soon alone again.

The Warren was the end of their journey. Mr. Haredale was walking in the garden, and seeing them as they passed the iron-gate, unlocked it, and bade them enter that way.

"At length you have mustered heart to visit the old place," he said to the widow. "I am glad you have."

"For the first time, and the last, sir," she replied.

"The first for many years, but not the last?"

"The very last."

"You mean," said Mr. Haredale, regarding her with some surprise, "that having made this effort, you are resolved not to persevere and are determined to relapse? This is unworthy of you. I have often told you, you should return here. You would be happier here than elsewhere, I know. As to Barnaby, it's quite his home."

"And Grip's," said Barnaby, holding the basket open. The raven hopped gravely out, and perching on his shoulder and addressing himself to Mr. Haredale, cried—as a hint, perhaps, that some temperate refreshment would be acceptable—"Polly put the ket-tle on, we'll all have tea!"

"Hear me, Mary," said Mr. Haredale kindly, as he motioned her to walk with him towards the house. "Your life has been an example of patience and fortitude, except in this one particular which has often given me great pain. It is enough to know that you were cruelly involved in the calamity which deprived me of an only brother, and Emma of her father, without being obliged to suppose (as I sometimes am) that you associate us with the author of our joint misfortunes."

"Associate *you* with him, sir!" she cried.

"Indeed," said Mr. Haredale, "I think you do. I almost believe that because your husband was bound by so many ties to our relation, and died in his service and defence, you have come in some sort to connect us with his murder."

"Alas!" she answered. "You little know my heart, sir. You little know the truth!"

"It is natural you should do so; it is very probable you may, without being conscious of it," said Mr. Haredale, speaking more to himself than her. "We are a fallen house. Money, dispensed with the most lavish hand, would be a poor recompense for sufferings like yours; and thinly scattered by hands so pinched and tied as ours, it becomes a miserable mockery. I feel it so, God knows," he added, hastily. "Why should I wonder if she does!"

"You do me wrong, dear sir, indeed," she rejoined with great earnestness; "and yet when you come to hear what I desire your leave to say—"

"I shall find my doubts confirmed?" he said, observing that she faltered and became confused. "Well!"

He quickened his pace for a few steps, but fell back again to her side, and said:

"And have you come all this way at last, solely to speak to me?"

She answered, "Yes."

"A curse," he muttered, "upon the wretched state of us proud beggars, from whom the poor and rich are equally at a distance; the one being forced to treat us with a show of cold respect; the other condescending to us in their every deed and word, and keeping more aloof, the nearer they approach us.—Why, if it were pain to you (as it must have been) to break for this slight purpose the chain of habit forged through two-and-twenty years, could you not let me know your wish, and beg me to come to you?"

"There was not time, sir," she rejoined. "I took my resolution but last night, and taking it, felt that I must not lose a day—a day! an hour—in having speech with you."

They had by this time reached the house. Mr. Haredale paused for a moment, and looked at her as if surprised by the energy of her manner. Observing, however, that she took no heed of him, but glanced up, shuddering, at the old walls with which such horrors were connected in her mind, he led her by a private stair into his library, where Emma was seated in a window, reading.

The young lady, seeing who approached, hastily rose and laid aside her book, and with many kind words, and not without tears, gave her a warm and earnest welcome. But the widow shrunk from her embrace as though she feared her, and sunk down trembling on a chair.

"It is the return to this place after so long an absence," said Emma, gently. "Pray ring, dear uncle—or stay—Barnaby will run himself and ask for wine—"

"Not for the world," she cried. "It would have another taste—I could not touch it. I want but a minute's rest. Nothing but that."

Miss Haredale stood beside her chair, regarding her with silent pity. She remained for a little time quite still; then rose and turned to Mr. Haredale, who had sat down in his easy chair, and was contemplating her with fixed attention.

The tale connected with the mansion borne in mind, it seemed, as has been already said, the chosen theatre for such a deed as it had known. The room in which this group were now assembled—hard by the very chamber where the act was done—dull, dark, and sombre; heavy with worm-eaten books; deadened and shut in by faded hangings, muffling every sound; shadowed mournfully by trees whose rustling boughs gave ever and anon a spectral knocking at the glass; wore, beyond all others in the house, a ghostly, gloomy air. Nor were the group assembled there, unfitting tenants of the spot. The widow, with her marked and startling face and downcast eyes; Mr. Haredale stern and despondent ever; his niece beside him, like, yet most unlike, the picture of her father, which gazed reproachfully down upon them from the blackened wall; Barnaby, with his vacant look and restless eye; were all in keeping with the place, and actors in the legend. Nay, the very raven, who had hopped upon the table and with the air of some old necromancer appeared to be profoundly studying a great folio volume that lay open on a desk, was strictly in unison with the rest, and looked like the embodied spirit of evil biding his time of mischief.

"I scarcely know," said the widow, breaking silence, "how to begin. You will think my mind disordered."

"The whole tenor of your quiet and reproachless life since you

were last here," returned Mr. Haredale, mildly, "shall bear witness
for you. Why do you fear to awaken such a suspicion? You do not
speak to strangers. You have not to claim our interest or consideration for the first time. Be more yourself. Take heart. Any advice or
assistance that I can give you, you know is yours of right, and freely
yours."

"What if I came, sir," she rejoined, "I, who have but one other
friend on earth, to reject your aid from this moment, and to say that
henceforth I launch myself upon the world, alone and unassisted, to
sink or swim as Heaven may decree!"

"You would have, if you came to me for such a purpose," said Mr.
Haredale calmly, "some reason to assign for conduct so extraordinary, which—if one may entertain the possibility of anything so wild
and strange—would have its weight, of course."

"That, sir," she answered, "is the misery of my distress. I can give
no reason whatever. My own bare word is all that I can offer. It is my
duty, my imperative and bounden duty. If I did not discharge it, I
should be a base and guilty wretch. Having said that, my lips are
sealed, and I can say no more."

As though she felt relieved at having said so much, and had nerved herself to the remainder of her task, she spoke from this time with a firmer voice and heightened courage.

"Heaven is my witness, as my own heart is—and yours, dear young lady, will speak for me, I know—that I have lived, since that time we all have bitter reason to remember, in unchanging devotion, and gratitude to this family. Heaven is my witness that go where I may, I shall preserve those feelings unimpaired. And it is my witness, too, that they alone impel me to the course I must take, and from which nothing now shall turn me, as I hope for mercy."

"These are strange riddles," said Mr. Haredale.

"In this world, sir," she replied, "they may, perhaps, never be explained. In another, the Truth will be discovered in its own good time. And may that time," she added in a low voice, "be far distant!"

"Let me be sure," said Mr. Haredale, "that I understand you, for I am doubtful of my own senses. Do you mean that you are resolved voluntarily to deprive yourself of those means of support you have received from us so long—that you are determined to resign the annuity we settled on you twenty years ago—to leave house, and home, and goods, and begin life anew—and this, for some secret reason or monstrous fancy which is incapable of explanation, which only now exists, and has been dormant all this time? In the name of God, under what delusion are you labouring?"

"As I am deeply thankful," she made answer, "for the kindness of those, alive and dead, who have owned this house; and as I would not have its roof fall down and crush me, or its very walls drip blood, my name being spoken in their hearing; I never will again subsist upon their bounty, or let it help me to subsistence. You do not know," she added, suddenly, "to what uses it may be applied; into what hands it may pass. I do, and I renounce it."

"Surely," said Mr. Haredale, "its uses rest with you."

"They did. They rest with me no longer. It may be—it *is*—devoted to purposes that mock the dead in their graves. It never can prosper with me. It will bring some other heavy judgment on the head of my dear son, whose innocence will suffer for his mother's guilt."

"What words are these!" cried Mr. Haredale, regarding her with wonder. "Among what associates have you fallen? Into what guilt have you ever been betrayed?"

"I am guilty, and yet innocent; wrong, yet right; good in intention, though constrained to shield and aid the bad. Ask me no more questions, sir; but believe that I am rather to be pitied than condemned. I must leave my house to-morrow, for while I stay there, it is haunted. My future dwelling, if I am to live in peace, must be a secret. If my poor boy should ever stray this way, do not tempt him to disclose it or have him watched when he returns; for if we are hunted, we must fly again. And now this load is off my mind, I beseech you—and you, dear Miss Haredale, too—to trust me if you can, and think of me kindly as you have been used to do. If I die and cannot tell my secret even then (for that may come to pass), it will sit the lighter on my breast in that hour for this day's work; and on that day, and every day until it comes, I will pray for and thank you both, and trouble you no more."

With that, she would have left them, but they detained her, and with many soothing words and kind entreaties besought her to consider what she did, and above all to repose more freely upon them, and say what weighed so sorely on her mind. Finding her deaf to their persuasions, Mr. Haredale suggested, as a last resource, that she should confide in Emma, of whom, as a young person and one of her own sex, she might stand in less dread than of himself. From this proposal, however, she recoiled with the same indescribable repugnance she had manifested when they met. The utmost that could be wrung from her was, a promise that she would receive Mr. Haredale at her own house next evening, and in the mean time re-consider her determination and their dissuasions—though any change on her part, as she told them, was quite hopeless. This condition made at last, they reluctantly suffered her to depart, since she would neither eat nor drink within the house; and she, and Barnaby, and Grip, accordingly went out as they had come, by the private stair and garden gate; seeing and being seen of no one by the way.

It was remarkable in the raven that during the whole interview he had kept his eye on his book with exactly the air of a very sly human rascal, who, under the mask of pretending to read hard, was listening to everything. He still appeared to have the conversation very strongly in his mind, for although, when they were alone again, he issued orders for the instant preparation of innumerable kettles for purposes of tea, he was thoughtful, and rather seemed to do so from an abstract sense of duty, than with any regard to making himself agreeable, or being what is commonly called good company.